THE SEDUCER

A Novel

Claudia Moscovici

Hamilton Books
A member of
The Rowman & Littlefield Publishing Group
Lanham · Boulder · New York · Toronto · Plymouth, UK

Copyright © 2012 by
Hamilton Books
4501 Forbes Boulevard
Suite 200
Lanham, Maryland 20706
Hamilton Books Acquisitions Department (301) 459-3366

Estover Road
Plymouth PL6 7PY
United Kingdom

Library of Congress Control Number: 2011943256
ISBN: 978-0-7618-5807-2 (paperback : alk. paper)
eISBN: 978-0-7618-5808-9

Cover image: *Timeless* by Edson Campos.

This book is a work of fiction. Names, characters, places, and incidents
are either products of the author's imagination or are used fictitiously.
Any resemblance to actual events or locales or persons, living or dead,
is entirely coincidental.

Advance Praise for Claudia Moscovici's *The Seducer*

Like the best, most delicious novels, Claudia Moscovici's psychological thriller, *The Seducer*, grips you in its opening pages and holds you in its addictive clutches straight through to its dramatic, remarkable conclusion. This is a fascinating novel, on every page of which Moscovici's intimate understanding of the psychology of psychopaths and their victims gleams with a laser's concentrated brilliance. The result is a narrative that builds with a patient, yet propulsive, force; a narrative whose intensity and suspense, in tandem, leave the reader eager to know, at every step of the way, what happens next? I encourage the reader to start this novel with a full set of nails, because it's a nail biter in the most literal sense.

Steve Becker, MSW, LCSW LoveFraud.com feature columnist, Expert/Consultant on Narcissism and Psychopathy

The Seducer offers a thrilling look at the most dangerous men out there, that every woman is warned about and many encounter: the psychopathic predator. We've seen these men featured in the news for their gruesome crimes. But few would expect them to be the charming, debonair, romantic seducers that love stories are made of. When the heroine of the novel, Ana, met Michael, she was in for the roller-coaster ride of her life. In her exciting second novel, *The Seducer*, Claudia Moscovici depicts with talent and psychological accuracy the spellbinding power of these charming yet dangerous Don Juan's.

D. R. Popa, author of *Lady V and Other Stories* (Spuyten Duyvil, 2007)

What is love in this seductive new novel? Hypnotic attraction or deadly trap? A dream come true or a world filled with obsessions in the absence of genuine feelings? *The Seducer* probes the chilling depths of alienation and selfishness as the heroine, Ana, is caught in the spider's web of her narcissistic lover, Michael. No magic, just cruelty. Claudia Moscovici wrote a powerful novel about an unfortunate reality many women face: the unraveling of their romantic dreams as love turns into a cold and calculated game of chess.

Carmen Firan, author of *Words and Flesh*

Claudia Moscovici's new psychological thriller, *The Seducer*, reminds us of classics like *Anna Karenina* and *Madame Bovary*, but with a contemporary twist. The new seducer is a psychopath, a dangerous predator without genuine emotion. And yet, we remain fascinated as he charms two women: one of them utterly dependent, the other seduced but autonomous. The reader's outrage toward the reprehensible Michael may feel neutralized by the author's meticulous studies of the psychopath in action and by what I call "ethical irony," an often hidden moral perspective. Moscovici's epic of betrayal and self-deception draws the reader into the convoluted mind of sexual predators and their victims. The narrative is bold, vivid and lucid.

Edward K. Kaplan, Kaiserman Professor in the Humanities and Chair of the Program in Religious Studies, Brandeis University *to Jewel, my muse, and to "Dr. Emmert," an inspiration*

Part I

Chapter 1

All happy families are alike; each unhappy family is unhappy in its own way — Leo Tolstoy, Anna Karenina

What if Tolstoy was wrong when he said that all happy families are alike while each unhappy family is unhappy in its own way? Michael mused. Turn that statement on its head and it rings even more true. If there was any way he'd manage to screw up his marriage plans with Karen it would be, let's just say, in the usual manner, he speculated. Oh well, *c'est la vie!* he shrugged. After all, there were plenty of other fish in the sea. Better not focus on negative things on such an awesome, sunny day, he reminded himself. He noticed through the translucent curtains the conic outlines of the two majestic pine trees growing right outside his bedroom window. They shielded him from the prying eyes of neighbors, making him feel like the king of his castle. Michael stretched out his arms above his head and wiggled his body. He enjoyed the cool smoothness of the sheets against his warm back. Every morning he rose with a sense of wellbeing peppered by a restless excitement. He thought to himself, "Ladies, fasten your seatbelts because IT'S SHOW TIME!" in bold capital letters of a flashing neon sign, like at his favorite strip club, *Foxy Lady.* Beep, beep! A loud noise suddenly jolted him. He hit the alarm clock with the flat of his hand.

"Michael, you'll miss your class!" he heard Karen's singsong voice echoing from the bathroom, intermingled with the sound of running water.

"I'm already up," he announced, but apparently not convincingly enough, since his fiancée emerged out of the bathroom, toothbrush in hand. She wanted to make sure that Michael was telling the truth. "Well it's your class, your job," she mumbled. Her mouth was still partially filled with a pasty mix of water and toothpaste. Karen often assumed a maternal manner with him, projecting the attitude that she had enough common sense for the both of them. In her heart of hearts, she hoped that no matter what temptations Michael might face with other women, as far as the deeper matters of human existence were concerned, she was indispensable to him.

From time to time, Michael slipped away on vacation or to scholarly conferences without her. Before he left, Karen felt very apprehensive. She'd give him a fidelity lecture, to make him feel that the idea of hooking up with or, worse yet, falling in love with another woman would be sheer frivolity compared to the depth of commitment she had to offer. Sometimes Michael couldn't help but smile. Karen genuinely believed that there was an inverse proportion between libido and depth. Which is perhaps why, for her, daily communication over dinner and in the evenings was obligatory. In her estimation, good communication consisted, first and foremost, of a detailed account of their daily activities. For him, these entailed teaching, taking graduate seminars, eating, screwing around with other women (however, this particular detail he understandably omitted) and returning home. For her, it entailed going over the minutia of her job as administrative manager in a physician's office.

Moreover, about once a month, Karen initiated "us conversations," or thorough debriefings about the state of their relationship. These conversations usually culminated in Karen melting into a heap of self-doubt that took Michael hours of effort to comfort. He recalled how often he'd seen his fiancée's scrunched up face, the sides of her nose rosy from crying. Karen would wipe her tears away with two quick butterfly wing movements. They started from the inner eye, along the curve of her nose, then brushed her cheeks and vanished into the air, she hoped, unnoticed. But Michael did notice, of course. Most of the time, however, he pretended not to and craftily changed the subject to something more pleasant. His evasive behavior led his fiancée to suspect that something was lacking in their relationship. That something, she hoped, could be compensated by his constant verbal reassurances.

"You don't talk enough about your feelings," Karen would periodically complain to him. Granted, Michael manifested all the outward signs of romantic sensibility. He bought her flowers on special occasions. He took her to fancy restaurants. He said "I love you" with commendable frequency. He patiently listened to her concerns. Yet there was something flat and mechanical about his emotional reactions. It's as if Michael were rehearsing a role or just going through the motions. Sometimes he'd greet her anxiety with a plastic smile. At others, he'd brush it aside with an inappropriate joke. One minute he'd be gazing lovingly into her eyes, his attention fully absorbed by her. The next minute he'd be whistling, completely distracted, ending their conversation abruptly with a non sequitur.

He's so immature, Karen would tell herself. Although he was twenty-seven, Michael looked and acted younger than his age. His abrupt movements and brief attention span reminded Karen of the children who came in with their parents to the doctor's office: particularly those diagnosed with attention deficit disorder. They wouldn't sit still in their chairs for more than a few seconds. They quickly flipped through the books and magazines on the table, moved around, sat back down, doing everything they could to relieve a perpetual state of restlessness.

Was that what led Michael to moon his parents at the end of their visit last Thanksgiving? Karen wondered. After saying their goodbyes in a more or less civil manner, Michael had suddenly turned around, pulled off his pants and bent over like a drunken frat boy. He peered over his shoulder and burst into laughter at his parents' and fiancée's visibly perplexed reactions. Karen couldn't comprehend such outbursts of puerile behavior coming from a grown man. Yet, at other times, this very same Michael would appear wise beyond his years. He'd listen to her attentively, gazing at her with a reptilian tranquility that she had never encountered in anyone else. He'd tell her calmly his reasoned opinion, in a voice as smooth and soothing as silk. Her insecurities would temporarily melt away in the fusion of her gratitude and his affection, only to resurface later, when the insensitive boyfriend suddenly returned. Through the perplexing oscillations of his mercurial temperament, Michael held his fiancée fascinated and captive, under his spell.

"What do you want me to say?" he'd object when put on the defensive about his apparent lack of interest in their conversation.

"If I have to tell you what to say, that defeats the whole purpose of talking in the first place. I might as well deliver a monologue," Karen retorted. And often, she did. As far as communication was concerned, she presented herself as a role model since, in point of fact, she did open up to him—and only to him. To everyone else, Karen presented a cool, unflappable exterior. Even her own parents viewed her as a pillar of strength. Only Michael knew that this pillar had deep emotional fissures, like a ruin. "The reason I go on these eating binges is because I feel so insecure about my self-image," Karen had commented earlier that week, when they were having lunch together at *Panera*. She had looked up at him from her oriental salad, scooting with some regret the unopened package of peppercorn dressing towards his side of the table. "Here. You can have it."

To spare her the extra calories, Michael gallantly poured the dressing over his own salad. After saturating each leaf, he looked up at his fiancée and thought of a defense strategy, before the conversation headed towards another meltdown. At worst, she's about fifteen pounds overweight, he estimated. But they hang pretty well on her tall frame. "You look mighty fine to me," he observed, thinking that massaging her ego would pacify her.

This prediction, however, proved a bit too optimistic. "I don't understand how other women stay so thin," Karen responded with a sigh, looking around at her competition in the restaurant. "After all, I watch what I eat and I'm as tall as a skyscraper. It must be my mother's genes." She blamed her slow metabolism on her mother, a two hundred pound diabetes patient. That weighed less on her conscience than acknowledging the periodic binges on gallons of ice cream, atoned by brief semi-starvation periods, when she survived solely on herbal tea and salad. And that was part of their underlying problem. Karen recalled how often people would look at her and her fiancé with a gaze that measured them up and determined that they were a mismatched couple. Michael was shorter, only 5'9" compared to her towering 5'11." But what struck the eye most was not the slight difference in their heights but the big discrepancy in their physical appearance.

"Your son's so cute," a little girl once said to Karen during a shopping trip at *Filenes's Basement*. Michael had emerged out of the changing room in a brand new gray suit he intended to purchase for future job interviews. He looked striking, standing proud, his jet-black hair set off by the paleness of the gray suit. His bright brown eyes, mischievous yet angelic, beamed with an inflated awareness of his own good looks. "So is yours," Michael replied, looking at the stuffed animal that the little girl held in her hand. Ostensibly, he tried to diffuse the tension, being painfully aware of his fiancée's insecurity about her appearance. Tall, plain, with long legs and stringy brown hair, Karen thought that her best feature was her deep brown eyes. But even in that domain, she couldn't compare to him.

Michael's eyes had an amazing ability to fix your gaze, seize your attention, then glide all over you slowly, covering you in a visual syrup. After being anointed with such sweetness, you felt blessed that this angel looked in your direction and you were instantly his. The problem was, however, that Michael's wondering eyes glazed every pretty woman they encountered, lingering over her features with a feral hunger that simultaneously intimidated and flattered. Karen feared that she'd never be able to fulfill her fiancée's constant need for sexual stimulation. This thought deeply concerned her, no matter how hard she tried to dismiss physical attraction as merely superficial. If you can't fix a big problem all at once, start by taking smaller steps, she had read something to this effect in an advice column. And that was precisely what she decided to do by focusing most of her energies on losing the extra weight.

Given that Karen had avoided putting any dressing on her salad, Michael took this opportunity to expound upon his own, more liberal, theory of dieting. "Being on a diet is the wrong way of going about losing weight. In France, people eat whatever the hell they please. But they do it in moderation. Plus they walk a lot. That's how most Europeans stay so thin," he proposed the only strategy he thought worked. It was modeled after his favorite culture, which he happened to teach as a graduate student in the Department of French and Italian at Michigan University. For as long as the magnifying glass wasn't placed directly on him, Michael's ostensible emotional generosity expanded. He did his best to coach his fiancée into improving her self-image, which only fueled her dependency on him.

"Yeah, well, maybe that works for those skeletal French waifs. But I come from peasant Irish stock," Karen shot his argument clear out of the water.

"What you have to remember is that image isn't just about how you look," Michael altered his approach.

"That only goes to show how little you know about women," she countered.

As a matter of fact, Michael had done more empirical research on the subject than he cared to admit. Since that argument wouldn't have impressed his fiancée, however, he contented himself with nuancing his point. "Well, I realize that looks are important to women, since they're often judged by their physical appearance. But it's the inside that counts." That's the kind of crap women like to hear, he thought.

"Oh, yeah?" Karen challenged him. "Then why is it that when we're at the mall you start drooling over those bimbos in miniskirts? I have yet to see your tongue hanging out over their intelligence!"

"That's only because I don't know any of them. Our contact's strictly visual. But once you get to know a person, the inside matters far more," Michael countered philosophically. I wriggled my way pretty good out of that hole, he observed, pleased with the double entendre.

Indeed, those proved to be the magic words. They confirmed Karen's innermost conviction that she had depth while other women—particularly the sexy ones—were just plain surface. Which is why Michael worked hard to veer the "us conversations" away from sexual matters towards the higher spheres of human existence where his fiancée preferred to dwell.

"Well, how much do you tell me about yourself?" Michael had turned the tables on her during one of their infamous "us conversations."

"What do you mean?" Karen acted surprised. "I told you about how Mary's leaving the office. And about how Maxine got a bonus of one and a half pay even though she only works for us part-time. And about how I suspect that she's having an affair with Dr. Tolbe. I tell you everything that's going on in my life."

"Yeah, but that only tells me about what other people *do*. It doesn't say anything about who you *are*," Michael objected, with a meaningful arch of the eyebrow.

Karen looked perplexed. "We've been together for over two years. You know me."

"Do you even know yourself?" Michael, a self-proclaimed hedonist, suddenly turned Socratic.

"You sound like a fortune cookie," Karen observed, becoming skeptical of this line of inquiry.

"Not at all. Fortune cookies predict your future in a generic fashion. I'm asking you to tell me who you are as an *individual*," he emphasized. "Like, for instance, what do you like to do in life?"

Karen shifted nervously in her seat. "You already know what I do. I go to work. I help others. I give to charity."

"But you don't really like doing any of those things. You do them mostly out of duty," Michael pointed out.

"That's not fair. I enjoy helping others," she retorted. After all, every Christmas she donated ten percent of her annual income to *Amnesty International* and *Doctors without borders*.

"Fair enough," Michael conceded, taking note of his fiancée's agitation. "But it takes you a few minutes to write those checks. What do you enjoy doing the rest of the time? I mean, when you're not working?"

"Now that's a silly question!" Karen's face lit up. "I like to be with you."

Michael rapped the table with impatience with the tip of his fingers. "Sure, but aside from that? Who are you as a person? What makes you tick?" he insisted on keeping the ball in her court. The only sound he heard in answer to this question was the ticking of the mechanical watch his maternal grandfather had given him on his sixteenth birthday.

After considering the matter for a few moments, Karen replied: "Well, for instance, this week I read an interesting book. It was about this woman whose dream had always been to live in Japan," she picked up momentum. "Then she had kids really young, so she got stuck in the States and became really depressed. Her therapist explained to her that when you have small kids, accomplishing your goals could be done gradually, by taking baby steps."

"No pun intended," Michael interrupted, glad to have spotted a *jeux-de-mots* in what he considered to be an otherwise uninspiring narrative.

"Yeah," Karen ignored the joke. "And then she started taking Japanese language classes. The next summer, she took a short vacation to Japan with her family. So in the end she felt happier. At least she partially accomplished her goal."

"So she sold out?" Michael drew his own conclusion.

"What? No. That's not what I meant to suggest at all."

He shook his head. "I don't see how taking a vacation with one's family in Japan constitutes moving there. Nor what any of this has to do with my original question."

"Which was?"

"What do you want to do with your life? Once you figure that out, we'll see about taking baby steps or having babies or whatever."

Karen stared at him as if the answer were transparently obvious. "I want to be your wife," she replied with disarming honesty. "But I don't want any kids," she added. Which was another point of contention between them.

Her answer doubly discouraged Michael. First of all because, someday, he wanted to have children. And not just the imaginary kids they made up, by way of compensation. On their first Valentine's Day, Michael had given Karen a stuffed stingray. They named it "Ray," for short. They concocted stories about it, as if Ray were their real adopted child. Henceforth, whenever they ran out of things to say, they slipped into the momentary complicity of make-believe. Gradually, they expanded their imaginary menagerie. Next came a horse named Stallion, which Michael gave Karen on her birthday. On the anniversary of their first date, they adopted Peanut, an elephant. Each stuffed animal had its own personality. The stallion was wild and stubborn. Peanut was large and clumsy, with dependency issues. Ray was sweet but spoiled, since, after all, he was their first child.

More importantly, even before seriously contemplating starting a family together, Michael wished that his fiancée would get a life. Granted, in the beginning, he had fostered Karen's dependency. He had enjoyed the thrill of seduction. He had basked in the sense of being needed by a woman to the point of becoming her whole existence. But Karen's complete focus on him, though flattering, soon got in the way of his numerous other conquests. It also placed the burden of her happiness upon his shoulders. Michael preferred not to carry that weight by himself. Perhaps others could help. He kindly encouraged Karen to meet more frequently with her acquaintances from work. Unfortunately, this request only aroused her suspicions: "You want me to see Susan? Why? Did you make plans with anyone else?" she'd ask, narrowing her oblique eyes.

The very insecurities that made Karen appear too possessive and cramped his style, however, also made her seem appealing in Michael's eyes. Unlike most of the other women he had been with, his fiancée could be trusted one hundred percent. Karen had no sexual desire worth mentioning, so Michael felt quite confident that she'd never cheat on him. She was hardworking, putting in overtime at work to compensate for his modest graduate student scholarship. She had no interests to speak of, except perhaps for the growing obsession with her vacillating weight and self-esteem. If he ever needed her support, he knew Karen would be there for him. She listened to him almost to a fault, so much so that he felt compelled to fabricate facts to satisfy her appetite for meaningful communication. She managed their money responsibly and was almost as averse to spending it as he was. They shopped together for groceries, armed with a handful of coupons. They bought most of their clothes at *Goodwill*, despite their decent joint income. In short, Karen was dependable, devoted, virtuous, frugal and hardworking. Weren't those the qualities of a model wife? What more could a man want? After all, Michael thought, for pleasure and entertainment, he would always have flings, affairs and one-night stands. Following this logic, after nearly one year of dating, he decided to propose to her. After pretending to consider the matter for a few days, to appear hard to get, Karen gladly accepted.

Now, a year into their engagement, Michael went over his fiancée's qualities, to remind himself that the reasons for marrying her remained valid. He examined Karen's towering frame as she stepped out of the bathroom. She stood two inches taller than him, covered almost from head to toe by loose-fitting flannel pajamas. He peered into her eyes, in which he hopelessly sought a come-hither look. His gaze then fixed upon her square jaw, which reflected the locally strong will of a desperately dependent woman. Her thin mouth was still caked with a white pasty liquid, which he would have preferred to furnish himself. Unfortunately, she rarely gave him that opportunity. Still, Michael thought, feeling his midsection harden at the possibility of a quickie, it never hurts to try.

Karen saw his hand slip underneath the covers. His familiar "I'm up to no good" grin made her feel viscerally uncomfortable. Michael's prospects were grim. Unfortunately for him, earlier that morning, Karen had weighed herself. She had made the tragic discovery that instead of losing weight, she had gained two pounds. No more sex until I lose it, she had resolved. "Don't even think about it!" Karen preempted his move. She then pointed sternly to the alarm clock as her alibi: "It's 8:30 and you teach at 9:00. It takes you twenty minutes to get ready. You do the math..."

Michael's dark eyes shifted languorously from underneath their long lashes towards the alarm clock. "8:31 a.m." it announced in bright red neon, reinforcing his fiancée's message. "Okay," he relented. He swung his lean, muscular legs out of bed, to gather enough momentum for a quick shower. But then he changed his mind, noticing that Karen had removed her pajamas and was sliding on a pair of underwear. He swiftly grabbed her from behind.

Her spine straightened defensively. "Geesh! You startled me. Aren't you going to shower already?"

"I prefer to spot wash like Chairman Mao." He had read a recent biography that claimed that the Chinese dictator only "washed" himself in women: a practice that may have been somewhat unhygienic, but that had other health benefits. "You're so sexy in those granny panties. Grrrr, you turn me on, Baby," Michael growled, simultaneously making light of his own desire and of his fiancée's need to de-eroticize her body.

Stung, Karen clamed up. "Well, if you don't find me attractive, then go take a cold shower!" This time her pride was at stake. But even then, only momentarily. Whenever she felt that Michael eluded her grasp, she became sweet and clingy again. Sometimes he hoped that his fiancée would stay mad at him a bit longer. At least that would give him a few extra hours of fun with other chicks. But no such luck… Oh well, you can't win them all, he sighed, regretting that he couldn't even flirt with his own fiancée. In the beginning, Karen's seriousness had made him feel like she was more mature than him. But at deflating times like these, he thought that she should loosen up a bit.

The thought of looseness reminded him of Lisa, his student in first period French 102. Lisa was everything that Karen was not and then some. Michael released his fiancée without too much regret. In fact, he was suddenly in a hurry to get to class on time. He looked forward to explaining the distinction between the *imparfait* and the *passé composé* while scoping out Lisa's double D boobs. The way she emphasized her chest in low-cut blouses—those protruding mounds of flesh that lengthened like ripe bananas whenever she leaned down to pick up a pen that she had deliberately dropped on the floor—made him tingle with the desire to scale those natural twin peaks with his hands, tongue and lips.

Karen had had a few moments to recover from his jab. She started to have second thoughts, feeling uncomfortable about letting Michael out of the house in such a dangerous condition. "You don't give up, do you?" she smiled sheepishly at him. "Maybe we have time for a little quickie," she relented. On the one hand, she'd starve herself the rest of the day to lose those stubborn extra pounds. And, on the other, no matter what Catholic reservations she may have had about premarital sex, Karen considered it her womanly duty to satisfy her man.

But Michael could sense that, in her heart of hearts, she still felt guilty about it. Her pangs of conscience generally coincided with the times she spent with her family and Sunday mornings at church. She even stopped going to confession once she actually had something to confess. But Michael's needs usually swayed her, playing upon her preemptive jealousy. Karen noticed the way other women looked at her fiancé. Why give another woman the opportunity to take care of a problem that she could, when hard-pressed, efficiently handle herself? Karen emboldened herself and firmly grasped his member. Despite his hurry, Michael wasn't one to miss an opportunity. In a race against the clock, he hastily propped Karen up against the sink. He wrapped her legs around his waist, then glided in between her lips, which, despite their intimidating dryness, quickly pushed him to the brink. Michael knew that he could rest easy on that score since, fortunately for him though somewhat less fortunately for her, Karen had been on the pill since the age of twelve to alleviate the symptoms of endometriosis. He then kissed his fiancée quickly on the cheek, said "I love you" and wiped himself clean with a piece of toilet tissue.

"I love you too," she replied. But the sense of postcoital guilt was already imprinted upon her features. "You're thirty years old. You can decide for yourself and do whatever the hell you want! You don't need a goddamn preacher to tell you what to do," he'd exclaim whenever she made him lose his temper over what he perceived as her outdated prudishness.

"Please leave my priest out of it. He's got nothing to do it with it."

Bullshit! Michael thought whenever he became fed up with frustration. "Don't you think it's a bit strange that you still live with your parents at your age?"

Although Karen fell head over heals in love with Michael practically from the moment that she laid eyes on him, she didn't want to rush into a serious relationship. She'd been burned by men before. This time she wanted to play it safe. Yet no matter how much she tried to protect herself, as far as Michael was concerned, Karen's heart led the way far ahead of her head. The only thing she could control was when she actually moved in with him. On this issue alone she put her foot down. Like a good Catholic girl, she told him they'd live together only after they got married. "It would kill my folks," Karen tried to explain the situation to Michael more diplomatically. She wanted him to understand the disappointment her parents would feel if she openly lived with a man, as opposed to doing what she was doing now: which is to say, sneak into his apartment in the mornings and afternoons and return home in the evenings, feeling ashamed and impure.

But Michael refused to be alone. Though completely untouched by the suffering of others, a sense of painful emptiness overcame him late at night, when he went to sleep without holding a woman—and not just any woman, but *his* woman—in his arms. What the hell! If she won't commit to me, then I won't commit to her either. He made a conscious decision to continue his philandering ways while giving Karen the distinct impression that they were dating exclusively. "You're the woman of my life," he'd declare looking dreamingly into his fiancée's eyes, right after he had been with one or two women on that day. Which was only fair, Michael thought, savoring the duplicity. Because in his mind, Karen's choice was telling. Her parents and their antiquated morals were far more important to her than he was. In which case, he felt, rationalizing the worst of his behavior for the smallest of her infractions, he was also entitled to pursue other priorities. At the moment, he had three of them to be exact: not counting, that is, the scores of flings and one-night stands.

Chapter 2

Michael walked briskly towards the *Department of French and Italian.*
Since he was running late, he rushed into his office without stopping to banter,
as usual, with fellow graduate students. As soon as he opened the door, Mireille,
the officemate who had provided him with pleasant companionship for the past
two years, greeted him. She lunged into his arms and plastered her lips upon his.

"I'm late to class!" Michael announced as soon as he managed to regain his
breath. "Which, incidentally, starts in about 30 seconds," he added, glancing at
his watch.

At the moment, however, Mireille had a more pressing concern than his
class. "Double D dropped by earlier this morning looking for you," she said with
an ambiguous look in her eyes, half-taunting, half-reproachful. "Double D" was
their code name for Lisa, his well-endowed student from French 101. Michael
preferred to avoid, as much as possible, crossing wires among his women. But
Double D came by his office so frequently during the past few weeks that
Mireille would have to be blind not to get the picture. Not that he felt that bad
about it. After all, Mireille was no saint either. She was engaged to Jack, an all-
American blond, tall law school student, through whom she hoped to obtain U.S.
citizenship.

"Don't get me wrong, I love my fiancé," Mireille had said to Michael when
she first informed him that she was engaged. But this exchange of factual information didn't prevent either of them from taking every possible opportunity to
lock the office door and do whatever it took to make sure the desk would need
cleaning up with plenty of *Kleenex* tissues dabbed in *Evian* water afterwards.

Although Michael never erred on the side of caution in his actions, he was
usually pretty careful with his words. "That girl's so huge, she's a freak show!"
he tried to make Mireille feel more at ease with the whole situation.

Fortunately, Mireille wasn't one to hold a grudge for long. "See you at
lunch," she confirmed. *"Tu me manques,"* she added sweetly in her native
tongue.

In moments like these, Michael felt that it might be wrong to lead on the
poor girl into believing that he loved her. But what else could a man do when,
after having carnal relations with a woman on a regular basis for two years, she
whispered *je t'aime* into his ear with such genuine ardor several times a week?
Could he afford to say nothing in response? Michael was clever enough to realize that when you mess around with a chick for that long, you've got to have the
decency to tell her "I love you" once in awhile.

Besides, truth be told, he was genuinely fond of Mireille. He hated to sound
superficial, but what got in the way of a deeper commitment was the gap between her two front teeth and her excessively lanky body, which looked downright skeletal at the shoulders and hips. Which is why he preferred to view her
from behind: say, bent over a desk. If he positioned her like a master photogra-

pher and the light seeped through the blinds at just the right angle, one could plausibly claim that Mireille looked like a model, at least one of those anorexic, Twiggy types.

Once in class, Michael found it difficult to focus on explaining the difference between *l'imparfait* and *le passé compose*. As usual, Lisa made goo-goo eyes at him from the front row. She occasionally passed her tongue over her lips and snickered into her hand, amused by his frazzled reaction. Though certainly no prude, Michael was somewhat disconcerted by Lisa's behavior. He was quite sure that the other students must have noticed that she received what could be easily misconstrued as "preferential treatment" from the teacher. Of course, in class, Michael tried his best to be friendly and fair to everyone. He joked around and bantered with the boys and was as avuncular as an exceedingly horny twenty-something male could be to barely legal girls.

But Lisa violated the unspoken code by making suggestive comments to him, since part of the thrill of seduction was being acknowledged as the teacher's pet by her classmates. She got it into her head that her main academic goal that semester would be to seduce her male instructors. She selected her courses carefully on the basis of who would be most open to such extracurricular activities. As it turns out, Lisa's judgment proved impeccable: she was 3 for 0. Michael was her favorite instructor, since being with him was not just about the thrill of the chase, but also about the pleasure of the game.

Michael knew the risk he was taking. He realized that if he conveyed favoritism towards one of his students, some of her classmates, particularly the weaker ones who got, God forbid, a B- in a gut course like French, might complain to the department chair about his conduct. Then he could kiss his teaching assistantship goodbye. On the other hand, Michael thought, Lisa's tits were well worth the risk. No matter how much he tried to avoid looking at her ample chest during class, his gaze was magnetically drawn to it. Quite simply, Lisa's boobs had the capacity to hypnotize a man more than a beautiful woman's eyes. Which, when he considered the matter more coolly, right after he had taken care of business, didn't make a lot of sense, because Lisa wasn't even his type.

Aesthetically speaking, Michael preferred medium-sized implants that give the chest the perfect hemispherical look favored by men's magazines. Erotically, he preferred small boobs with tiny sensitive nipples that became instantly erect under his touch. But reason had little to do with his fascination with Lisa's chest. When she came to his office hours for the first time to allegedly complain about her low exam grade—a D+, appropriately enough—he offered to give her a make-up exam which turned out to be the best oral he'd ever had. That morning, Lisa surreptitiously slipped him a note as he walked around the classroom, checking to see if the students had done their conjugation exercises: *"See you at our usual place. I cunt wait!"* Michael read her girlish cursive with a bemused smile. Although a stay-at-home mom well into her thirties, Lisa had the sense of humor of an eighth-grader. A woman after my own taste, he thought approvingly.

Since Mireille usually waited for him in their shared office, the love nest he reserved for Lisa turned out to be even less glamorous. They made out in a handicapped bathroom with a single stall. Michael recalled the first time Lisa unhooked her bra for him. Her ample chest cascaded forward, overflowing into his open hands. He placed his perspiring palms under her breasts gently lifting them up, one at a time. "Double D's?" he estimated with closed eyes.

"How did you guess?" she marveled at his scientific accuracy.

"I'm an expert," he modestly replied. He then proceeded to prove his point by massaging, licking and sucking those mounds of flesh for the next five minutes, until someone began knocking with a sense of urgency on the bathroom door.

"It must be a deaf person," Michael whispered, zipping up his pants. He had a look of regret each time Lisa stuffed those awesome mounds of flesh back into her bra, as if putting the genie back into the magic bottle.

When Michael emerged out of the bathroom followed by Lisa, as if by sheer coincidence, Mireille crossed their path, on her way to the Xerox machine.

He noticed her look of wounded dignity. "Hey!" Michael placed his hand on her shoulder, to appease her. "Do you need help with this stuff?" he offered to help her carry the pile of papers.

"No thanks!" Mireille snapped back, in an uncharacteristically irate tone.

This time I need to finesse her, Michael told himself. He wasn't about to lose a perfectly decent long-term lover for a short-lived, albeit large-chested, fling.

"*On déjeune ensemble?*" he amiably invited his officemate to lunch. "*Au revoir Lisa! Bonne chance avec les devoirs. A demain!*" he turned to dismiss Lisa as graciously as possible. She left him with his colleague, but only after giving him an incriminating wink.

"Aren't you worried about screwing your own student? You could easily be fired for this, you know," Mireille said loudly enough to be overheard by Ms. Jones-Alter, the Senior Administrative Manager, who looked up disapprovingly from her computer.

But Michael didn't mind Mireille's indiscretion. On the contrary, he felt touched by it. After all, the poor girl was jealous and in love with him. To demonstrate his appreciation, he made love to her more tenderly than usual on that day. And when he said *je t'aime* to her, he almost meant it.

Chapter 3

"So did I choose well or did I choose well?" asked Alain Boulanger, a Frenchman whose last name sounded very seductive to American women: until, that is, they learned it meant "baker."

Though not one to be an ingrate, Jose, the future groom, who happened to be a sculptor specializing in female nudes, upheld his high standards: "Yeah, we loved the slot machines. They were almost as much fun as those at *Chucky Cheese's*!" he said with a good-natured laugh, opening the front door to usher his friends into his modest studio apartment.

Although the slot machines at the local casino may not have been the most exciting venue for a bachelor party, it would be unfair to hold it against Alain. After all, he had done his best. He was one of those men who was mostly talk and no bite. Alain bragged about his success with the ladies whenever he wasn't chaperoned by Sara, his second wife. From what Jose and the others could tell, he tried to pick up anything that moved and wore panties, with only limited success. Around his wife, however, the Frenchman assumed a lap dog demeanor. He never leered at other women when in her company, knowing full well that the more he displayed his predilection for the fair sex, the shorter his leash become. "What do you mean *Chuck E. Cheese's*?" he objected to the unflattering comparison. "That was a world class casino."

"Call me crazy, but I think I speak for everyone here," Jose gestured towards his distinguished companions, "when I say that we'd have preferred to see some of the racier shows."

Alain frowned at his friend's ingratitude. "Although I do quite well for myself and my family, *excuse moi*, but I'm not a millionaire, you know!" he attempted to justify why the only part of the bachelor party he had sponsored was the one where destitute retirees dispensed with their monthly Social Security checks.

"Yeah, well, I prefer the *slut* machines myself," Michael intervened jovially. "Speaking of which, when is she coming?"

"In which sense of the term?" Alain was quick on the draw himself.

"Hopefully both," Michael remarked frankly.

"I expressly asked for a Latin, model type," Jose reiterated, feeling that with such boorish buddies there was no room for subtlety.

"You mean you want your wife to be your stripper? If so, count me in!" Michael announced with a laugh, since Jose was about to marry Maria, a Latina mamasita who had been his model and muse for the past three years.

"No," Jose objected in all seriousness, "but I explicitly requested a stripper who looks like her."

"I have a solution! Why don't we all jack off to Maria's picture and call it a night?" Michael pushed the envelope.

Jose breathed in and out to control his anger. He didn't particularly appreciate the implication that his future wife was a slut, even if he did meet her at a gentlemen's club on the outskirts of Detroit, where he used to scout for cheap models. Cheap as in inexpensive, of course, since Maria was obviously virtuous. Otherwise he wouldn't have even contemplated marriage.

"Philippe, my man, you're being awfully quiet tonight," Michael slapped his colleague from the graduate French program on his reed-like back. One could see, even through his dated yellow *Izod* tee shirt, the relief of every knobby ridge of his spine.

"I don't like smoking or drinking. As for women, I have more sophisticated tastes than the rest of you guys," Philippe declared, telling himself that he should have stuck to his general policy of being friends only with cute and, preferably, much younger women.

"I realize that, but unfortunately the middle school is closed. I'm afraid you'll have to wait until tomorrow morning," Michael teased his buddy about his predisposition for little Lolitas.

"Laugh all you want. But everyone knows that, objectively speaking, girls are much prettier than women. The ideal age for human females is between twelve and sixteen," Philippe stated scientifically, then switched to poetic mode: "Girls are blooming rose buds whereas women are wilted flowers."

"I couldn't agree with you more, mon cher Baudelaire," Michael responded. "I mean, what man in his right mind would prefer a woman with tits and ass over a flat-chested little girl with popsicle sticks for legs?"

As usual, Philippe took the bait: "Make fun all you want, but for your information, in Thailand, where I went on vacation, the strippers were usually between ten and sixteen. By the time they're twenty-one, many of them have already died of AIDS," he added, to bolster his case.

"Now there's a humane society!" Alain commented, relishing the fact that, for once, he was not the butt of Michael's jokes.

Why do I even bother with these brutes? Philippe wondered. Fortunately, he was literally saved by the bell.

"That must be her!" Michael exclaimed. He was far more excited about the stripper's visit than the finicky groom himself, who, at any rate, had feasted his eyes upon nude models most of his adult life.

Such a waste of hard-earned money, Alain thought, glad that someone else had taken care of that unnecessary expense.

Michael rushed to open the door. He was pleasantly surprised by Anita, since that was the petite Puerto Rican's name.

"Ehh... Is this the fiesta for... Jose?" she asked, coyly looking at Michael.

What fiery, lovely eyes, he couldn't help but notice. His gaze then lowered approvingly to her compact curves. "Absolutely. Please come in," he played the role of the polite gentleman, which was somewhat difficult to maintain once Anita whispered into his ear that she was usually paid double for the extra. "Sure thing," Michael confirmed their earlier understanding. He slipped into her hand two hundred dollar bills for a little treat for the groom.

The show was sufficiently impressive to engage even Philippe, who didn't have to retire to a different room with the copy of *Barely Legal* he had brought along, just in case the stripper turned out to be too mature for his taste. "*Pas mal*," he told himself, eyeing approvingly Anita's doll-like face and thin, narrow shoulder blades that, despite the fact she was in her late twenties, had retained an air of girlish fragility.

At 5 feet 2 inches with heels on and barely 100 pounds, the curvy Anita, who happened to be an expert at nude salsa dancing, proved to be to everyone's liking. "For such a little thing, she sure has nice tits," Michael observed as he watched her quick, sensual moves. His tongue tingled for a taste of those car-melicious globes of flesh from which he couldn't unpeel his eyes.

"She looks so much like my future wife!" Jose observed. "I wonder how much she'd charge for nude modeling," was his next thought, since Maria was planning to take a break from her job as soon as they got busy creating a little Josito or Marisita together.

Alain concentrated his gaze upon the dancer's heart-shaped ass and slim, muscular legs. The legs of a dancer, he noted with satisfaction. Anita did a polite bow at the end of the show. Her dark eyes glittered naughtily towards Jose, lingering upon him for a few seconds. Then, without uttering a word, she slipped into the bathroom ostensibly to change back into her street clothes, while leaving the door slightly ajar.

Without much further ado, Michael gave Jose an encouraging nudge towards the bathroom. The future groom entered the room looking pretty nervous but, after about ten minutes during which some grunts and a few exclamations in Spanish could be overheard, he reemerged triumphant.

Since he had orchestrated the most entertaining part of the bachelor party, Michael felt entitled to walk in next. He asked Anita how much she charged for the usual, smiling very sweetly, hoping for a discount. The stripper looked at his warm brown eyes. "For you, half price, but shhhh, don't tell nobody else," she placed her index finger to her crimson lips. As soon as he slipped the hundred-dollar bill into her hand, she got down on her knees and masterfully wrapped him up into a condom. She's so adorable, Michael thought as he turned her little body around over the sink, her hands plastered like suction cups on the mirror. Focusing on the tattoo of a little butterfly on the small of her back, he lifted Anita off the floor. They pollinated each other for quite some time. When the soles of her bare feet touched the floor again, he allowed his profound gratitude to gush. The stripper seemed so pleased with the experience that she even rewarded Michael with a kiss on the cheek. As a gesture of camaraderie, she placed the hundred-dollar bill he had given her back into his hand, closing his fingers upon it one at a time.

Alain was next. But by then Anita must have already been exhausted. Or perhaps she just looked at his Inspector Clouseau disheveled hair and his little Charlie Chaplin mustache and thought that these alone required extra cash and fortitude. "It's going to be three hundred dollars," she announced in a business-like tone. "That's kind of expensive, don't you think?" Alain protested. But he was in too desperate a state to refuse her offer.

Philippe went in last. Almost as soon as he entered the bathroom, Anita stepped out with a wounded look upon her face. She mumbled that the gentleman must be "loco." Apparently, after she announced her price, Philippe expressed a preference for being alone with his copy of *Barely Legal* magazine over her expert services. Meanwhile, Alain had already found out from Michael about the wide discrepancy in the exotic dancer's extra fees. A dispute concerning unfair treatment was about to ensue had Jose not promptly intervened. He dispatched Anita with a small bonus while diverting his buddies' attention to the free booze.

Chapter 4

Michael returned home from the bachelor party around 4 a.m. As soon as he stepped into the living room, he noticed that the red light of the answering machine was blinking. He figured it was nothing important. Whatever it was could wait until the following morning. He proceeded to crash on the living room couch without changing his clothes.

At 9:23 a.m.—Michael checked his watch twice since he felt it was way too early to get up—he heard Karen fiddle with her spare key in the front lock, which had a slight imperfection. "Hold on a sec!" he called out groggily and got up to open the door for her.

It's only when Karen's eyes moved over him disapprovingly that he realized he was still wearing the previous day's outfit. "I was wasted last night," he said by way of explanation.

"You mean this morning? Did you enjoy the stripper?" Karen inquired matter-of-factly, but her lips pursed into a tense smile.

"She was alright," Michael shrugged, knowing better than to elaborate.

"Was she pretty?" In spite of her best efforts to be cool about it, Karen felt a knot of jealousy constricting her throat.

Michael's policy had always been to mix a grain of truth with the lies, so that she couldn't tell the difference. But this time he saw no harm in answering Karen's question quite honestly: "Actually, as far as strippers go, she wasn't too shabby," he replied as he stepped into the bathroom, leaving the door slightly ajar.

Karen heard a light tinkle, followed by a vigorous flush. He can't even close the door like a civilized human being! she muttered to herself. Although she realized that bachelor parties were a culturally accepted institution, she had little patience with this sleazy ritual right before a man enters into a so-called monogamous marriage. What kind of training for monogamy was that anyway? To distract herself from her mounting indignation, Karen began cleaning Michael's apartment. She collected the socks and shirts scattered on the floor and lined up his shoes neat and parallel by the front door. "We're still on the same wavelength about the justice of the peace thing, right?" she double-checked. She certainly didn't want Michael having another bachelor party with his buddies, all of whom she considered big-time losers and hard-core womanizers. If not having her fiancé fool around with strippers before their wedding day implied foregoing the fairytale wedding she had dreamed about ever since she began collecting *Bride Magazine* at the age of twelve, then so be it.

"Sure thing!" Michael called out from the bathroom. "Why? Are you having second thoughts about it?" Karen didn't reply, so he began to wonder if she had gotten it into her head to have the big wedding she originally wanted. He had worked hard to persuade his fiancée that an elaborate reception would be expensive. Worse yet, it would require spending time with each other's families, something both of them preferred to avoid. "We wouldn't have much time to plan the wedding anyway," he said, washing his hands.

When Michael stepped out of the bathroom, Karen had a strange look upon her face. She looks like a deer trapped in front of the headlights, he thought, noticing her frozen expression. "What the hell happened? Did you decide you want a huge wedding after all?" he asked with a chuckle, prepared to fight her tooth and nail.

Karen shook her head.

"Did your mother try to convince you that you're missing out? You want to have a Catholic ceremony or something?" Michael pursued. What was it with women and big weddings anyways?

"There's not going to be any wedding," Karen announced quietly, barely moving her lips.

Although evidently his fiancée wasn't too thrilled about their minimalist wedding, Michael relaxed. At least his desires had—for once—triumphed over her mother's. He approached Karen to embrace her with gratitude, perhaps even a little more, if he felt so inspired.

"Please don't come near me," she said, extending her arm out like a stop sign.

"Why are you so upset?" he asked, puzzled by her reaction.

"Who's Lisa?" she asked him dryly.

"Lisa?" he repeated, buying himself a few moments to formulate a credible answer.

"Who is she?"

"Oh, she's just a student in my introductory French class."

"Are you fucking her?" Karen asked him point-blank.

Now where the hell was this random accusation coming from? Michael wondered with indignation, as if it were false. Besides, Karen never used that kind of language. Generally speaking, vulgarity was his domain. His wheels started spinning in place. What do you say to a woman at a time like this? It didn't happen? It wasn't serious? I wasn't in love? Every answer sounded kind of lame. Besides, he had run through all of them before. Now, the second time he got caught cheating by his fiancée, Michael realized that he couldn't rely upon his usual arsenal of excuses. The absurdity of his predicament amused him. The corners of his mouth twisted into a smile: the shameless, idiotic grin of a mischievous child who's been caught with his hand in the cookie jar.

"You're laughing in my face, you... you bastard!" Karen lashed out at him. The mixture of indignation and self-pity brought tears to her eyes, which streamed soundlessly down her cheeks. I have to remain strong, she told herself. I can't let this womanizer see me fall apart.

She cries like a man, Michael observed, remaining silent.

"Why are you screwing around on me? After you promised me that you'd never do it again?" Karen demanded.

The answer was on the tip of his tongue: because I like it. But he couldn't say that since he didn't want to sound tactless. What Michael couldn't quite figure out was why Karen felt so confident in her charge. Did he forget to toss away Lisa's note? "How did you find out?" he asked her.

"Didn't I give you enough chances already?" she ignored his question. Her eyes were full of reproach. "When I found out you cheated on me with that sleazy French girl, didn't I give you a second chance? How many women would have done that?"

At this point, Michael did his best to appear genuinely contrite. He looked away, to muster a somber expression. He recalled how only a few months earlier, Karen had arrived home early from work with a splitting headache. She caught him in the midst of a heated phone conversation with Mireille, who was pressing upon him the importance of committing to her. She was ready to dump her fiancé and marry him instead. At first, Michael had tried to remain diplomatic in dissuading his overzealous colleague. He cautioned her to be prudent and not leave her fiancé, who, he reminded her, loved her and was a good man. But, as it turns out, his strategy backfired.

"What are you talking about? It's you I love. *Je suis folle amoureuse de toi*," Mireille protested.

Why couldn't side dishes remain side dishes? Why did they insist on becoming the main course? Michael wondered. He tried to persuade Mireille that, in point of fact, the most fulfilling relationship between a man and a woman entailed hooking up several times a week with no strings attached, especially for the man.

"*Non!*" Mireille vehemently disagreed. "*Merde.* This is bullshit! If you can't commit to our relationship, *c'est fini entre nous.*" At which point Michael realized that Mireille meant business, since whenever she got upset—or ecstatic, depending upon the circumstances—she slipped into French.

But rejection was not something Michael liked to hear from his women. If anybody were going to do the dumping, it would have to be him. So by the time Karen slipped quietly into the living room, he was too absorbed in the discussion with his girlfriend to hear his fiancée come in.

"*Tu me prends pour une conne?*" Mireille was shouting into the receiver loudly enough for Karen, who understood French, to overhear. Michael opted not to answer her question, which he interpreted as rhetorical anyway. "How long did you think you could pull the wool over my eyes? You said you loved me!" Mireille switched back to English.

"But you're engaged to another man," Michael weakly protested.

"*Et alors?*" Mireille challenged him. "It's not like you give a damn about fidelity!"

She had a point, or, more precisely, half of one. Because Michael cared a great deal about fidelity when it came to the women he dated. He was just willing to overlook such minor indiscretions when they arose from his side, that's all. Consequently, even if he could manage to get over her alarming thinness, Mireille could never be marriage material given that she was cheating with him on her fiancé. After all, he had his standards.

"Am I your girlfriend or just a friend with benefits?" Mireille asked with an uncharacteristic lucidity that made Michael feel somewhat uncomfortable.

"What kind of a dumb question is that? Of course you're my girlfriend!" he blurted out. But before Mireille could find out what level of commitment such an elastic concept entailed, Karen had heard enough. She slammed her purse loudly upon the glass coffee table. Michael turned around to watch with some trepidation the glass quiver upon its metal frame. What the hell does she carry in that purse anyway? Rocks? "Gotta go," he whispered hastily into the receiver, and then hung up the phone.

Karen assailed him with a plethora of questions. "Who is she?" "A fellow teaching assistant in our department," he said. "How long have you been hooking up with her?" "We started the Master's program together," "How long have you been her lover?" "Since before we met," he replied, hoping this fact would exonerate him. Apparently, it didn't, since Karen pursued, "Why didn't you break up with her once the two of us became serious?" That question proved to be somewhat trickier. Thinking quickly on his feet, Michael did his best to address it. "You're freaking' unbelievable!" Karen exploded after he had calmly informed her that he'd been trying to break up with Mireille for the past year and ten months. "The whole time we've been together you've been screwing around with another woman," she concluded. That was not entirely correct, however. Technically speaking, he had been consorting with dozens of women, if one counted Lisa plus all the one night, one day and few minutes stands. "This was my wake-up call," Michael solemnly declared. "I promise I'll break up with her. In fact, that's exactly what I was trying to do just now. You witnessed it yourself."

"Do you love her?" Karen asked, her anger subsiding and starting to turn into self-doubt.

"Not really. I'm just a little infatuated with her."

Instead of appeasing his fiancée, however, this seemingly harmless comment only infuriated her more: "I don't want to hear about your... abominable infatuations!" she exploded.

Michael felt obliged to switch tactics: "It's you I love, Baby. You're the woman of my life," he said, walking towards Karen to give her a hug. She bristled under his touch. "I promise it will never happen again," he added, hoping to soften her up. But Karen averted her eyes, with disgust. He pulled up her chin gently, obliging her to look him in the eyes. "Listen to me," he said soothingly. "I mean it. This will never happen again, all right? It's you I care about."

Karen hesitated. She felt too wounded to forgive him yet too proud to give up on their relationship. Because, for her, Michael was the only one. She didn't want any other man. The only glitch in their relationship was that he obviously wanted other women.

In all fairness, Michael tried to keep his promise to Karen. After their fight over Mireille, he went cold turkey on sex for three whole days, since, needless to say, his fiancée wasn't in the mood anymore. During this period of time, Michael recalled, he felt like a monk whose vows of chastity are mocked by the stubborn resilience of frequent erections.

At work, more of the same. Wounded to the core, Mireille made it a point of leaving the office in a huff every time he entered it. Women are so hypersensitive, Michael observed. But after three days of Cold War on both fronts, he couldn't take the tension anymore. He dropped by Mireille's apartment when he knew that her fiancé would be at work. At first, she didn't want to let him in. She carried their negotiations via the intercom, for everyone's listening pleasure. A few nosy neighbors strained their ears to hear the heated exchange between the former lovers.

"Can't we discuss this in private?" Michael pleaded over the loudspeaker.

"There's nothing to say. You're a jerk," Mireille denied his request.

"Isn't she already engaged?" one of the neighbors, a homemaker with kids asked another.

"Yes, but she's French," a more open-minded neighbor graciously undertook her defense.

"I can explain everything," Michael persisted.

"What's there to explain? That you treated me like a piece of ass?"

"I love you and came here to ask for your forgiveness," he announced to everyone's delight, including Mireille's.

Now that's more like it, the young woman thought to herself, pressing the button to let in her penitent lover. Michael observed that Mireille wore a tee shirt with no bra underneath and a pair of pink shorts.

He was about to celebrate their reconciliation, when she spoiled the mood with superfluous emotions. "Michael, I love you so much. I was so unhappy when I thought it was all over between us."

His arms folded tenderly around her. "You silly little thing. You worried yourself for nothing," he cooed reassuringly into her ear. Since it was a sunny, beautiful day, the lovers went on the balcony for some fresh air. Michael sat across from Mireille. His gaze couldn't help but wonder up the openings of her shorts to determine if she was wearing any panties. He concluded with sufficient confidence that she wasn't. To test his hypothesis, he began stroking her knees, hoping to gradually inch his way up her leg to her crotch, like a tiny, harmless spider.

Mireille, however, was still in the mood for a serious conversation concerning his level of commitment, his level of arousal having never been called into question. "If you love me, then why do you treat me so badly?" his girlfriend inquired, strangely echoing his fiancée. "Why is it that Karen's always your priority?" she pursued. "You're always like, I can't see you because Karen's dropping by soon. Why does she always have to trump me? What does she have that I don't?"

Hips, tits and ass, Michael wanted to say. "Because you're already taken, my love," he replied wistfully, allowing his roaming fingers to graze the soft folds of her skin.

With one swift gesture, Mireille removed his brazen hand. "I'm not in the mood for fooling around!" she announced, visibly upset.

Great! Nobody's in the mood anymore, Michael thought, feeling rejected by all of his women, or at least the two that counted most. "Listen," he tried to reason with his girlfriend. "When you and I got involved, you were already engaged. Since you weren't available, I began dating other women."

"I wasn't aware that you had ever stopped."

"If you wish," Michael graciously conceded that insignificant point. "But the fact remains that you were seeing someone else, so I had to find a partner of my own," he reinforced his main point. "After a few months, Karen and I became pretty serious. And just like you have to hide the fact that you're still seeing me from your fiancé, I have to hide the fact I'm seeing you from her," he revealed the perfect symmetry of their relationship.

"The only difference is that I'm prepared to leave my fiancé for you. But you don't seem even remotely willing to leave Karen for me," Mireille pulverized his otherwise elegant explanation.

"Yeah, well, I don't think that either of us are prepared to leave our partners just yet. That would be a bit rash, don't you think? Maybe some day though." Michael's general policy with women was: to keep them hopelessly attached, you always have to leave them hope.

"Like when hell freezes over?"

"I don't know. It's pretty hot in here." Michael decided it was time to cut out the useless chatter, especially since he was losing the debate. He leaned over to kiss Mireille on the mouth. There was nothing bilingual about that kiss; it was most definitely French. The couple celebrated their romantic reconciliation by making love *à plein air*, on the balcony.

Once the floodgates were opened again, Michael began to justify other indiscretions. After all, he told himself, the promise to Karen had already been broken. The women began streaming into his life at the same steady rate as before.

Now that he had been caught red-handed for the second time by his fiancée, however, Michael realized that the consequences of his actions could be more serious. "Who told you such a thing?" he repeated, prepared to deny the allegations unless the evidence was incontestable.

Karen walked to the phone and pushed "play" on the answering machine, with the same heavy-hearted sense of resolve that a president must feel when he presses the button to launch a nuclear missile.

"Hi Michael," Lisa's voice greeted him in a suggestive tone. "I miss you! My pink parts are missing you! Hope to see you this weekend, if you manage to get away from the Dragon Lady. *Bisous!*" Click. That was all the message said. It wasn't much, but even Michael was obliged to admit that it was as incriminating as it gets.

"She makes it a point of pride to screw her instructors," he innocently explained.

"Why did you let her do it with *you*?"

"She seduced me with her humongous boobs," Michael continued in the same vein.

His comment made Karen feel exceedingly inadequate. She gazed at her fiancé with sadness, the way one looks at a person one has already lost. "Why must you cheat on me?" she asked him. "If I cheated on you, how would you feel?"

"Like shit," he readily admitted, realizing that a show of remorse was expected of him at this point in the game.

"Then why do you do that to me?"

Michael contemplated her question for a moment. Quite frankly, he didn't see any compelling reason not to.

Since he didn't reply, Karen continued venting her spleen. "Even after I gave you a second chance? What have I done to deserve this?"

The self-doubt implied by her question gave him an opening. Perhaps if Michael had said nothing and acted duly contrite he might have averted disaster. But he chose instead to tempt fate. "You won't even have the guts to live with me that's what!" he shouted, a wave of self-righteous indignation washing over him. "I'm lonely. I go to sleep all by myself and wake up all alone," he said, nearly stating the truth, since he frequently consoled himself with temporary female companionship. "I asked you for almost two years to move in with me," he pursued. "But you refused to listen. After awhile, I finally got the message. Your parents' screwed-up morality is far more important to you than I am!"

Although this flash of anger dissipated as quickly as it appeared, his own vehemence took him by surprise. Michael had never realized that he was filled with so much pent-up resentment. Whenever he stepped into his empty apartment, he was overcome by a mixture of loneliness and dread. Dread of an inconsolable emptiness that he couldn't displace no matter how many women he slept with. Dread of being lost and not even knowing where to look for meaning. Dread of slipping underneath the cold sheets without a warm body lying next to him. And, all too often, he'd go back out on the prowl, hunting for pleasure, hoping that the fleeting excitement of the flesh could make him forget the emptiness within.

Karen looked at him, appalled. "You coward! So now your cheating's all my fault?" She paused for a moment, then reached a decision. "You know what? Enough's enough! I'm tired of all your lame excuses. I'm tired of the way you make me feel like crap. I'm tired of the way you make me feel like every damn floozy with big tits matters more to you than I do. You can take back your ring," she yanked the engagement ring off her finger and flung it at him. It bounced off his chest and fell soundlessly unto the carpet. Michael was too surprised by her reaction to pick it up immediately (although he did remember to retrieve it shortly afterwards, since after all, he had paid over a thousand bucks for it).

"You bitterly disappoint me," Karen added more quietly. "I can't go on like this. I don't deserve such mistreatment. One day you'll regret how you treated me. You'll be left all alone in the world with nobody but those whores who don't give a damn about you!" she punctuated her statement by slamming the door behind her.

Michael gazed coolly after her, defiant and unmoved. It's better this way, he told himself. If she can't keep up, she should get out of my way. Besides, I give her at most a week. She loves me way too much to have the strength to leave me, he calmly predicted. Either way, I can't lose. If she leaves me, then I'm free to do whatever the hell I wish. If she changes her mind, then things will pick up exactly where they left off. Except that I'll have much more leeway, since, after all, the elastic's already been stretched twice and by now it's pretty darn loose, he calculated with a smile.

Chapter 5

In the days following the blowup with Karen, Michael took a short break from his hyperactive sex life. He made a genuine effort to miss his fiancée. He remembered Karen's patience. The way she was so loyal to him. The way she stood by him even after she caught him cheating the first time. The way she clung to him. As he was going over his fiancée's qualities, the perfect metaphor occurred to him. Karen was a boa constrictor. Whenever she felt him detach from her, she'd press tighter, refusing to let go. In spite of its negative connotations, this image amused him. As an adolescent, Michael had often imagined making love to one of those busty women, curvaceous and seductive, stretched out butt naked on a shag rug with a boa constrictor wrapped around her neck. But he had never envisioned dating the actual boa!

Granted, he had given his fiancée plenty of reasons to be hypervigilant. Why beat around the bush? He was a lying, cheating bastard. That much was undeniable. The problem was, Michael absolved himself, that Karen didn't appeal to him anymore. So cheating on her wasn't really his fault. He had a glimpse of this realization a few weeks earlier. During one of the rare weekends when her parents were away visiting relatives, Karen spent Saturday night with him. Around 3:30 a.m., she woke up in a sweat. She tapped him on the shoulder to make sure that he was also awake. Then she asked him, as she did during holidays and other special occasions, to make a bullet point list of the top ten qualities he liked about her. "Number one. You let me sleep," Michael mumbled. But since that night Karen was particularly persistent, he quickly spewed off a list, hoping that she'd let him go back to sleep: "You have soft skin. You give to charity. You're a good listener. You communicate well. You love me. You're considerate to others. You're solid as a rock."

"What do you mean 'as a rock'?" she took offense.

"I mean I can always count on you. Plus you're a hard worker," he went on. "And you smell nice."

"I smell like sweat right now," she pointed out.

"So what? Maybe that turns me on. Is that ten yet?"

She counted by her fingers. "You still have one left."

Michael thought for a moment. "You're all mine."

"And you mine," she replied adding, after a few seconds, "most of the time."

Now that he thought about it, Michael felt somewhat disingenuous about saying that he loved all of Karen's qualities. Because some of them had an underside. For instance: sure, Karen was steadfast and solid. But that's also because she was so damn cold. It occurred to him that even her displays of emotion were generally manifestations of self-pity or efforts to move him, not genuine other-regarding impulses. Come to think of it, Karen never radiated any real warmth. He suspected that she gave to charity mostly to feel better about herself. Goodness was an act for her, just as fidelity was for him. All of this would have been all right with him, since after all he was no Gandhi either, if only she were more sexually available to him. What did I ever see in her? Michael wondered with the ingratitude of a man who has fallen out of love. He had a visual flashback to when they first met. Karen had been thinner, tall and leggy: the kind of woman he usually went for. She had posted a note in the *Department of French and Italian* that she needed a tutor to practice her French. As soon as he saw a female name, Michael spotted a potential opportunity for an easy score. Boy was he wrong...

Karen smiled a lot and acted friendly enough, but she remained all business during their meetings. There was something puritan yet enticingly corruptible about this woman that drew Michael to her. For two long, tantalizing months she flirted with him, even going so far as to pet and kiss. In spite of his relentless efforts, however, she refused to go all the way with him. Michael had never actually encountered such a specimen: the semi-virtuous woman. He had frequently run into loose women (his favorite kind, at least from a pragmatic perspective) and, less often, women who weren't interested in him (which he conveniently categorized as "lesbians"). He had also encountered the kind of women he wasn't interested in. Generally speaking, after a few drinks, that category became negligibly small. But nobody had tried to pull the "I don't have sex before marriage" crap on him before. Wasn't that over and done with since in the sixties? After all, what did all those chicks burn their bras for? This was the one triumph of women's lib Michael wholeheartedly supported. The rest, he thought, were sexist against men.

Used to getting his way with women, after two months of dating Michael dropped the pining lover routine. One evening when they were making out in the back seat of his car, he unzipped his pants and pulled up her skirt. Karen objected, but Michael was no longer disposed to heed her protestations. I've put more than enough time into this freaking relationship, he thought, ready to reap his rewards. He pushed Karen's shoulders down and lay on top of her, pinning down her arms with his hands and prying her legs open with his knees. She tried to discourage him but was cut short by a voice she hardly recognized, uttering something between a bark and a command. "Shut the fuck up woman!" Had she heard right? Karen blinked in disbelief. The man who stared into her eyes with a cold and fierce gaze was not the sweet boyfriend she was madly in love with, who respected and honored her wishes. Stunned by this sudden transformation, Karen closed her eyes. She lay there passively, waiting for him to finish and hoping that the real Michael would return to save her. Fortunately, she didn't have to wait long. Within a few minutes, he was done. "Oh God, how I love you! You drive me crazy," Michael whispered heatedly into her ear, like a man who had been in the throes of an irrepressible passion. "I wanted to wait until our wedding night," Karen said with a note of regret. "I know Baby, but I wanted you too much. I just couldn't wait that long," Michael replied in a raspy and melodious voice, covering her face with moist kisses. This familiar and tender lover almost instantly effaced the unsettling impression left by the double that had momentarily usurped his place.

Although Karen's virtue bent easily to Michael's will, her general air of reticence, even coolness, persisted. Which is why their dating relationship became his top challenge in life, far more interesting than the merely physical conquests he continued to have on the side. Basically, Michael wanted to get a cold fish to behave like a cat in heat. If only he could manage that biological feat, not only would he live in marital bliss, but also he might even get an award for genetic hybridization from the *National Science Foundation*. Like all good scientists, Michael experimented extensively. He treated Karen warmly and tried to kiss and caress her copiously, but that only made her nervous and withdrawn. He withdrew and complained, but usually that only scored him the rebuttal that he didn't communicate enough. He haggled, trading watching a chick flick for a little flicker of passion, but ended up getting the raw end of the deal since Karen remained lukewarm with him.

Then again, Michael had to be fair about the whole situation. He didn't screw around because Karen deprived him of sex. He screwed around because he liked chasing women and sleeping with them. I just haven't found the woman of my dreams yet, Michael told himself. What do I really want from a partner? he asked himself. The two-year stretch of dating Karen had nearly made him forget his own dreams. Let's see, he tried to recall. Basically, he wanted what most men want from their mate. A woman who was faithful and dependable yet a slut with her man. A woman who was sexy and elegant yet remained fiscally responsible, even frugal. A woman who was girlish with him yet mature and maternal with their children. A woman who was smart and accomplished, but never put her career before him. A woman who was ready to follow him around anywhere he wanted to go. And, ever since he was a sophomore in high school, he knew exactly where that place was.

After finishing his Master's degree, on which he had less than a year of studies left, Michael wanted to move to Phoenix, Arizona, a place he had scoped out with his parents during one of their trips across the country. Phoenix had it all. It was a big city yet also a vacationland lost in the mountains. It was warm and sunny all year round yet had seasonal refreshing rains that alleviated the scorching heat. Michael recalled the thrill of being caught in one of those monsoons. The revitalizing shower flowed like a warm curtain from the sky, a veritable benediction from nature. Ever since those summer vacations had whetted his appetite for sunny Arizona, his plan was to find an easy prep school job teaching French in Phoenix. Work would consist of rolling out of bed to entertain hot teenagers while incidentally also teaching them a few words of French, then come home to a horny wife waiting for him with her legs spread eagle on the appropriately named love chair.

When he shared some of these plans with his fiancée, Karen didn't seem too excited. She objected that her family lived in the Detroit area. Besides, she really liked the physician's office where she was currently employed. But agreeing upon a location wasn't the main obstacle to their future bliss. The more Michael got to know Karen, the more he realized that she could never be the kind of wife he had dreamed of. Did such a woman even exist? Or was he engaging in wishful thinking when he hoped to find a woman with the perfect mixture of seemingly opposite qualities—the faithful and devoted whore, the frugal and modest hottie—that was most men's wet dream? If he couldn't find the ideal woman, then he might as well enjoy his freedom and play the field, he concluded.

Women have it so much easier, Michael mused. They don't have to do quite as much empirical research. They pick the first fool who's foolish enough to hand them an engagement ring. Wait a minute, I was such a fool, it occurred to him. Michael released a shiver of relief. Holy shit! I barely escaped the shackles of matrimony. He sprung up from bed and poured himself a glass of cognac, his favorite cocktail. He drank it slowly, allowing each drop to glide smoothly down his throat and tickle his palate. He then climbed out of his bedroom window to the roof, as he used to do as a child in his parents' house. Michael stretched out his body on the warm shingles like a tomcat. He looked up at the expanse of blue sky. Not a single cloud in sight, he observed with a sense of inner satisfaction, perceiving the endless horizon as a symbol of his newly regained freedom.

Chapter 6

Karen drove back home, her eyes clouded by tears. She entered her parents' house and headed straight for the refrigerator. A therapeutic gallon of chocolate swirl ice cream awaited her for precisely such dire occasions. Grabbing a soupspoon, she dug into it with a vengeance. She was consumed with anger and, even more so, with disgust. Yet, somehow, the icy tingles at the back of her throat, combined with the sugary taste melting in her mouth, momentarily took her mind off her emotional distress. She was simultaneously punishing and rewarding herself. She hated herself but blamed him more. What is a binge on chocolate vanilla swirl if not the perfect blend of opposites? Immediately afterwards, Karen knew what she had to do to expiate this moment of guilty pleasure. She went into the bathroom, leaned over the toilet, stuck her index finger deep into her throat and made repeated efforts to gag. Nothing came out at first, but she was eventually rewarded for her persistence by a little cascade of sour-sweet liquid that she quickly flushed away.

She then lay down on the sofa and stared blankly at the ceiling. How I loved him! she lamented. And now it's all over. I'm stuck in an impossible situation. I can't forgive him but I can't forget him either. He's probably in her arms right now. Although she had never met Lisa, Karen had a graphic mental picture of Michael having sex with a big-breasted woman. Even if we tried to get back together, it would be impossible to trust him again, she tried to convince herself that she made the right decision. At the same time, the thought of a permanent separation was unbearably painful to her. In spite of what her fiancé had done, Karen loved Michael even more now that she had lost him for good. She needed to talk to someone about this. In the absence of any close friends, she decided to call her older sister, Maggie, who was indifferently married to a plumber with whom she had two kids plus one on the way. Generally speaking, Karen preferred to avoid discussing personal matters with family members. But this time she felt desperate.

"Hello?" Maggie answered.

"Hi, it's me... "

"Karen? Is something wrong?" her sister asked her, attempting to sound concerned about her evidently distraught tone, then addressed her eldest daughter, to the side: "Miranda, leave Adam alone!" Karen overheard the six year old voice a few squeaky protests, to which her mother replied, "That's okay. He can play with your toys. What did I tell you before? You need to share." After a pause she added, apparently in response to her daughter's further objections: "So what if you don't like his toys? The point is that if you did, he'd have to share them with you." Then, recalling that her sister was still on the phone, she repeated, "Is something wrong?"

As if on cue, Karen began crying.

"What's the matter?" Maggie asked amidst the background noise of feuding children. "Hold on a sec." She then shouted in an imperious tone: "That's it! Miranda, go to time out. And don't you dare adopt that tone with me, young lady!" the mother added after the little girl questioned the fairness of her decision, since whatever she was being blamed for was all her little brother's fault. Maggie let out a sigh. "Sorry about the interruptions. These kids drive me crazy. I hardly have a minute to myself."

Witnessing other people's problems helped soothe Karen's nerves. "I broke up with Michael," she announced more calmly.

"What? You mean the wedding's off?"

"Everything's off. We're no longer together."

"Why? What happened?"

Karen hesitated for a moment. "Promise not to tell Mom about this?"

"She's bound to find out eventually if there's no wedding anymore," Maggie pointed out.

"I know. But I want to tell her myself. If I ever find the strength." Before meeting Michael, her mother had been predicting for years that she'd end up a lonely old maid.

"So why did you guys break up?"

"He cheated on me with one of his students."

"Who?"

"Some slut with big boobs." Having gotten this bit of information off her own modestly sized chest, Karen regretted sharing her problems with her sister. The last thing she needed now, she belatedly realized, was a show of fake sympathy.

But Maggie didn't try to console her. As during a dispute between her children, she wanted to determine the facts first. "Are you sure about that?"

"One hundred percent. She left a sexually explicit message on his answering machine."

"You heard it with your own ears?" Maggie persisted, intrigued.

Karen recalled Lisa's chipper tone and suggestive language. "Yes," she confirmed. But she couldn't bring herself to give her sister any of the sordid details that the latter, waiting in silence, seemed to expect. She felt humiliated enough as it was.

"I'm sorry..." Maggie finally said. "Listen to me. I've been married for eight years. I know how men work. These little trysts don't mean nothing to them."

"They sure mean a lot to me!"

"Probably John's been no saint either," Maggie said, referring to her own husband.

"You mean he cheated on you?"

"Who knows? He's a plumber. He goes from house to house all day long. I'm not there to monitor him. Most of the time, it's the women who wait for him at home. But as long as he puts our family first, I don't give a hoot about the rest."

"How can you not care if your own husband sleeps around?" Karen asked, surprised by her sister's permissive attitude.

"Because he draws a line between me and the other women. Those floosies are disposable to him, like Kleenex tissue. When it comes right down to it, it's me and the kids he loves and supports."

Karen attempted to process this information. "Do you have a lover?" she reached the only possible conclusion that made any sense to her.

Maggie laughed out loud. "Don't I wish! I hardly have time to brush my teeth, let alone tend to other body parts. Why? Do you have somebody in mind for me?"

"How can you joke about something like this?" Karen objected. Her sister's inexplicable tolerance got on her nerves. "I don't see things the way you do. I could never forgive Michael."

"It's up to you. But mark my words: no man's a saint. The best you can hope for is someone who takes good care of you and treats you with respect."

"How does a man treat you with respect when he's cheating on you?" Karen countered.

"Bah! A little fun on the side don't mean nothing. Plus, now that you left him, he's probably learned his lesson."

Though still intolerant of her sister's first argument, Karen was open to the second. "So you think he won't cheat on me again?" she asked her sister, in need of reassurance.

Maggie obliged. "Well, if I were him, I'd think twice before messing around next time. I mean, losing a good, decent woman—my future wife no less—over some floozy!"

"Yes, but would you forgive him? This isn't the first time he's done it, you know. It's the second time I caught him."

"As they say, boys will be boys. If I were you, I'd give up all those romantic ideals floating in your head."

Softened by the moment of rare complicity with her sister, Karen felt like she had just been slapped in the face. She recalled why she generally avoided confiding in Maggie, or any other family member, for that matter. "I don't think that expecting mutual fidelity between future husband and wife constitutes immaturity."

"Maybe not," her sister conceded. "But life will teach you that nobody's perfect. If you love Michael half as much as you say you do, you should find it in your heart to forgive him."

"Give me a break! How much did he love me when he was in the arms of another woman?" Karen exploded. "Besides, I already forgave him once. And this is the thanks I got."

"Well, you could give him just one last chance," Maggie proposed a reasonable compromise. "If he screws up again, he's out. Like in baseball. Three strikes and you're out."

Karen contemplated her sister's advice. Although she rejected the truisms validating philandering, she wanted to believe that Michael was worth a final chance. After all, no matter how much he had hurt her, surely he still loved her. And maybe Maggie was right. Maybe this time Michael had finally learned his lesson. Seen that she meant business. Understood that she wouldn't put up with the kind of mistreatment that some women, including her own sister, were apparently all too willing to tolerate from their men. She had higher standards. But she also had a strong spirit of generosity and forgiveness. In fact, if she took him back this time, Michael would be so touched by her magnanimity that he couldn't bear to hurt her again. "Yes, I can forgive him," Karen declared, speaking more to herself than to her sister. "We could start over from a blank slate, as if nothing happened. Otherwise it wouldn't be real forgiveness, now would it?"

"No, of course not," Maggie concurred, preoccupied with the fact that Adam had spilled *Cheerios* on the floor. "Please pick those up!" she instructed the four year old.

"I better let you go," Karen said, overhearing the little boy's whinny pro-tests. "Thanks so much for our talk. It really helped," she added, to her own sur-prise, with some sincerity.

"No problem. You'll see. Michael will straighten out real good," Maggie predicted.

After saying goodbye to her sister and placing the phone upon the receiver, Karen walked up to the mirror. The sight of her reflection made her freeze on the spot, locked in her own evaluative gaze. Her face was pale; her eyelids swol-len from tears. Her arms were too thick, she decided, as her disapproving glance glided down to her slightly flabby stomach. Suddenly, Karen felt that she finally understood the root of the problem. It wasn't him, it was her. How could Mi-chael possibly love someone like her? When there were all these women with large boobs, slim waists, flat stomachs, curvy hips and tight bottoms prancing around in miniskirts, how could he possibly want her? Starting with this physi-cal self-examination, Karen began to sense a more fundamental imbalance in their relationship, which she had always intuited but never consciously admitted to herself. Compared to her, Michael was more educated, had more interesting interests, more charisma and humor, better looks and far more appeal to mem-bers of the opposite sex. It was this constitutional asymmetry between them, which Karen painfully sensed anytime another woman flirted with her boy-friend, which made her feel so profoundly insecure in their relationship. If she had less to offer as a woman, then she had to hold on that much tighter to her man, she deduced.

Karen longed to start from a clean slate. To prove herself to Michael and regain his respect. She wanted to show him that she was worthy of his faithful devotion. She'd exercise enough to acquire a toned, slim body, like the kind of women who attracted him. She'd become less inhibited sexually and more affec-tionate, just like he wanted. She'd read interesting books, to expand the scope of her interests and knowledge. She'd be light-hearted and fun. All of the assump-tions he had made about her during the past two years, well, she'd work on her personal growth to prove them wrong. Except for the qualities he claimed to like in her, like her loyalty, fidelity, generosity and soft skin. Those she would keep, of course. Everything else would undergo a radical transformation. Then Mi-chael would fall in love with her all over again, only this time more deeply than ever.

Karen entered the kitchen and opened the refrigerator. She removed the gal-lon of therapeutic ice cream and tossed it straight into the trashcan. The *Dove* ice cream bars smothered in chocolate were the next to go. The blueberry waffles were also purged. The bacon, egg salad and white bread disappeared next. Fi-nally, all the bags of candy stashed away as stress relievers throughout the house were condemned to the garbage as well. Her parents would also have to go on a diet, she belatedly realized, since most of the food she had disposed of was theirs.

Karen then sat down at the kitchen table, armed with a piece of paper and pencil in hand. She proceeded to write down the following list:

1.　　eat ONLY healthy food (no cheating allowed)
2.　　exercise four times a day (yoga in the morning for flexibility and relaxation; followed by a 45 minute walk up and down the hill; after lunch go to the gym for some cardio; and in the evening, swim)
3.　　lose the glasses and get contacts
4.　　wear make-up and buy new sexy outfits and shoes
5.　　read some of that erotic literature that turns guys on and, last but not least...
6.　　GET BACK MY MAN!!!

Chapter 7

Michael returned home exhausted. He plopped down on the couch, propping his feet up on the coffee table. He turned on the T.V. and flipped channels. Not finding anything of interest, he turned it off. Truth be told, he missed having a woman he could count on in his life. Not necessarily Karen, but a woman he could call his own nonetheless. Since they had broken up, he'd been going out on the prowl, bar hopping every night. At first, he enjoyed being free to do whatever the hell he pleased, hooking up with whoever caught his eye. But after awhile, even absolute freedom began to bore him. There was nobody to fool, nobody to cheat on, nobody to manipulate. It was kind of like pushing hard against something that offered no resistance.

That evening had been particularly unproductive. After a mind-blowingly tedious conversation with a stuck-up blond, Michael returned home empty-handed. That's how he'd been rewarded for his patience! He had listened to Janet, Janice or whatever the hell her name was talk about her divorced parents. She also told him that she focused all her energies on her studies and had no time for commitment. Which would have been fine with him had she stopped the conversation right then and there. But she went on and on. Michael listened to her drivel, hating to quit, hoping to score. He didn't even roll his eyes when she bragged about her near-genius IQ, which wasn't in evidence that evening. He graciously indulged her in a dialogue about her business major. He even nodded approvingly when she told him that she wanted to follow in her father's footsteps and go "like, into advertising," minus the late hours, working on weekends and extramarital affairs. For Michael, the most challenging part of the conversation was focusing on her face as opposed to the low cut, V-neck sweater, which exposed a fine pair of boobs. He had trouble coping with his impatient erection, which seemed to be humming the Elvis song which called for "a little less conversation, a little more action please." To move things along, he inquired with strategic vagueness: "Wanna go somewhere else?"

"Sure." Her response led him to believe that he'd finally be rewarded for his patience! As they headed towards the parking lot, Michael took it a step further by inquiring where she had left her car, to narrow the field of possible "somewheres" from everywhere to his place, her place or her car. She pointed towards a red BMW convertible parked a few feet away. They proceeded to squeeze into it. Everything seemed to go as planned, except for the irksome fact that every time Michael attempted to make a bolder move and see if he could entice the girl into a quickie, Jennie launched into a plaintive monologue about her life which couldn't be interrupted by the trivial exigencies of his bodily needs.

After about an hour of what he perceived as a free one-way therapy session rather than a mutually satisfactory score, Michael randomly let out, as one might emit an unexpected burp, one of his least judicious pick-up lines at a most inopportune moment. Just when Jennie was complaining about how her parents' screwed up relationship had traumatized for her life, he inquired: "If your left leg was Thanksgiving and your right leg was Christmas, how about we meet between the holidays?" Michael thought the worst he'd have to endure for this irreverent remark was a response to the effect, "No thanks, I'm Jewish," in which case he'd be more than happy to substitute Christmas with Hanukah. The sharp slap landing on his left cheek took him by surprise. Before he could react to it, Jenny leaned over and threw open the car door, so he could let himself out. Clearly, Michael thought, I have to find a different venue for my needs. Although it had some obvious advantages, prostitution was out of the question, since it cost more than the bars, where he usually went Dutch.

As he was contemplating this sad state of affairs, Michael had an illuminating flashback. He recalled that in one of his French graduate seminars he had met a woman who complained about being a sex addict. She had mentioned something about participating in an organization called *Sexoholics Anonymous*, but it seemed to Michael that she was far from cured. As a matter of fact, she had thoroughly enjoyed stripping in the middle of a quiet spot of a nearby park and getting nailed from behind against the grills of the gate. That sizzling experience alone must have set her back at least four sessions of group therapy.

He hopped on the computer to look up this potential pot of gold. Narrowing down the search, Michael typed in "Detroit" and "Sexoholics Anonymous." He couldn't believe his good fortune when he discovered that they were convening that very evening at 9:30 p.m. in a nearby Detroit church. There's no time like the present, he thought. It occurred to him that he might be obliged to introduce himself and justify his presence at the meeting. Perhaps giving the real reason, which was to pick up desperate and depraved women, might seem a little suspect. It would help if he knew a little more about this organization. He looked it up on the internet and discovered some interesting factoids.

"Many of us felt inadequate, unworthy, alone and afraid," the website stated. Good, Michael approved. That means the women who show up there are likely to have their guard down. *"Early on, we came to feel disconnected—from peers, from parents, from ourselves,"* the website went on. Whatever that means, Michael murmured to himself. *We tuned out with fantasy and masturbation.* I have to agree, that's a bit boring, he conceded. *"We lusted and wanted to be lusted after,"* the narrative went on. What the hell's wrong with that? his lips curled disapprovingly into an inverted smile. Whoever came up with these tenets

is more prudish than the nuns at my old Catholic school, he noted. No matter, Michael dismissed his misgivings, since the participants were likely to have irrepressible urges. Speaking of that, *"We became true addicts: sex, promiscuity, adultery, and more fantasy."* Ah...now we're talking! At least I'll find partners who enjoy the same activities that I do, Michael told himself. He had grown tired of the bar scene, where he had to fake deeper interest and, worse yet, engage in tiresome conversations in order to score. At least at this *Sexoholics Anonymous* group, he'd be more likely to run into the kind of woman where no effort whatsoever was necessary. Even foreplay would be superfluous, he cheerfully predicted.

Encouraged by these findings, he read on. *"Our sex addiction made true intimacy impossible. It made us incapable of love."* So what? Who cares about love? As he liked to say, love I hate, but the sex is great. He moved on to the next point. *"The first step in our recovery is admitting our sickness, our sexual addiction. Forgiving those who injured us, asking forgiveness from those we have hurt."* Although this injunction sounded rather ominous, Michael found an escape clause. I can't possibly do this since I didn't keep the phone numbers of any of my one-night stands and don't even recall their names, he relieved himself of that unpleasant function. The next step, which posited believing that *"a Power greater than ourselves could return us to sanity"* also troubled him, since he hadn't been aware that he was insane.

Steps four and five weren't much more comforting either. They required the penitents to make *"a moral inventory of ourselves"* (why look for trouble? Michael asked himself) and admit *"to God, to ourselves, and to another human being the exact nature of our wrongs."* Aside from the aforementioned problem that he'd have to hire a damn good private investigator to track down his army of ex-lovers, Michael generally preferred to avoid admitting he was wrong even in the context of more lasting relationships. In his modest experience with faking remorse, women nagged him even more whenever he apologized to them.

He read steps six and seven with a sense of stupefaction: *"We're entirely ready to have God remove all these defects of character* and *humbly ask him to remove our shortcomings."* Had this list been formulated by one of his students? the French instructor wondered. First of all, if that student was female and even remotely attractive, he'd try to nail her, and second, afterwards he'd point out the egregious error that the list was repetitious, since points 5 and 6 expressed pretty much the same message. And if that rhetorical problem weren't serious enough, Michael felt uncomfortable with the whole objective of the program: namely, that of eliminating human imperfections, or at least some of his favorite ones. Becoming a saint had never been his top priority. Therefore, Michael logically concluded, the goal of this program could be dismissed in its entirety since its premises were all wrong and the conclusions even worse.

Next Michael examined the list described by the flyer as the "Twelve Traditions," which, mercifully, moved away from the elaboration of lofty spiritual goals to explain the protocol of the meetings. He approved of point two in particular, which announced, *"Our leaders are but trusted servants; they do not*

govern." Good, then this wasn't going to be like one of those counseling sessions, with someone bossing him around by telling him what to do, think, feel or
talk about. In fact, he'd say nothing at all and just scope out the women, if he
felt so inclined. Point three, however, was somewhat more problematic. "*The
only requirement for membership is a desire to stop lusting and become sexually
sober.*" Yeah right! Like that's ever going to happen before I hit the age of
ninety... And even then, there's always hope with *Viagra*, Michael dismissed
that ridiculous idea. On the other hand, he skipped ahead, point twelve didn't
sound too shabby: "*Anonymity is the spiritual foundation of all our tradition.*"
Now that's a good policy, he approved. That way he could issue a surgically
precise strike, moving in and out of some desperate woman, without anybody
being the wiser, especially not him.

   Having finished browsing through the website, Michael glanced at his
watch. It was already 9:00 pm. He estimated that it would take him approximately half an hour to get to the *Our Lady of the Immaculate Conception Catholic Church* near the *RenCen*, in downtown Detroit, where the meeting in question was being held. He managed to arrive at the church around 9:40 p.m.

   "Should I just go in?" he asked a young man seated at a counter in the
church foyer, indicating with his hand the majestic room filled with long
benches and a high-vaulted, spiritually inspiring ceiling.

   "Nope, our meeting's in the basement," the young man replied flatly, barely
looking up from a particularly absorbing issue of *Penthouse* magazine. "It's
where they hold Sunday school for the kids," he mumbled.

   "How appropriate!" Michael commented. He climbed down a set of stairs to
an empty classroom with tiny plastic chairs arranged in a circle, like in kinder-
garten or foreign language classes. As soon as he entered the room, Michael felt
relieved that he had arrived a little late, after everyone else was already seated.
That way he could choose a spot next to whoever caught his eye. There were
only three women and five men in the room, not counting himself. Michael was
struck by the contrast between the men and the women. The guys looked completely average: two nerdy dudes with glasses; one overweight schlep; a man in
a gray suit who resembled an accountant, plus a young man with a beard dressed
in a long-sleeved tee-shirt and jeans that was probably a student. A nondescript
lineup, he observed. None of these men seemed even remotely sleazy, much less
depraved.

   The women, on the other hand, were a whole different story. First of all,
Michael noted with a tinge of disappointment, there was not a single knockout in
the bunch. Granted, with only three females to choose from, the pickings were
rather slim. The three women had clustered together on adjacent chairs for solidarity, as it were. On the left sat a butch looking girl with short brown hair. She
probably swings the other way, Michael surmised. Next to her sat an average
looking woman who reminded him of his former high school nurse: wavy black
hair, hazel eyes, red painted lips, bland clothes and an average looking figure, a
little on the chubby side, but not altogether unappealing. She'll have to be my
pick for the evening, Michael decided. He wasn't particularly thrilled by the

prospect of hooking up with her, but then again, beggars can't be choosers. A tall, thin woman with blond hair and dark-rimmed glasses occupied the seat next to hers. Michael selected a chair across from the only acceptable potential partner in the bunch. Her name was Maria, he discovered a few minutes later when they went around the circle to introduce themselves. Michael couldn't help but notice that these women had a hungry look in their eyes. Curiously, nothing gave them away—neither their clothes nor their physical appearance—except for that predatory gaze.

"Why don't we go around again and tell everyone why we're here? No pressure, of course. Those of us who prefer to just sit back and listen feel free to do so," the skinny woman who was the group leader for that session initiated the discussion.

Maria, his half-hearted pick for the evening, began. "Hi. like I said, I'm Maria," she repeated with a slight Spanish accent. "I'm here because... How to splain it? I like sex too much," she confessed with an embarrassed, girlish giggle into her hand. "I go with different man every night. Sometimes more. It's hard to stop."

"Why do you feel the need to do so, Maria?" the young man with the beard asked her almost tenderly, with a sparkle in his pale blue eyes.

Damn, this guy's after her too, Michael identified his rival.

"Eh... It's because... Men make me feel very pretty, you know, sexy, when they make love," she said very quickly, to hide her embarrassment.

"Do you need to have sex with men to feel beautiful?" the group leader interjected in a high-pitched tone.

"No, but it helps," Maria replied with an embarrassed smile. Two of the men laughed out loud. "It shows how much they desire me. And that makes me feel good inside." Her voice sounds like honey, Michael began to feel some genuine attraction, more to the sensual inflections in Maria's voice than to her physical appearance. I'll make her feel damn beautiful tonight, he resolved.

After the session concluded, Michael approached Maria as they were exiting the room. "How long have you been coming here?" he asked her.

"Three months," she replied.

"Does it help?"

Maria shrugged. "A little. It helps me understand why I do the things I do," she mimicked the Motown song.

"But did it change your behavior?"

"Not very much," she admitted sheepishly.

"Would you like some help with that?" Michael asked gently, moving a few steps closer to her.

"It doesn't hurt to try." Her tone was overtly suggestive. Without much further ado, Michael grabbed her hand and pulled her into the Men's Room. Years of experience had taught him that guys tended to be much more tolerant of such shenanigans than women. He pinned her hands up to the wall of the spacious handicapped stall with one hand and liberated himself with the other. In the meantime, Maria aided him by pulling down her thong and lifting up her skirt. They found mutual relief within minutes.

"See you at the next session?" Maria asked him after they had readjusted their clothes and stepped out of the restroom.

She had a beseeching look in her eyes that made Michael feel somewhat uncomfortable. "Maybe."

Noting his hesitation, Maria took matters into her own hands. She dug into her purse and took out a pen and a tiny notepad. She tore out a piece of paper and hurriedly scribbled something on it. "Here's my name and number," she extended him the note.

"Thanks," he slipped it into his coat pocket, fully intending to dispose of it later, as was his habit following such encounters.

Instead of saying goodbye, however, Maria looked expectantly into his eyes.

What the hell more does she want from me? Michael wondered, annoyed by her persistence.

"May I have your number also?" Before he could reply, she ripped another piece of paper from her notepad and offered it to him along with a pen.

Michael wrote his first name along with his phone number, inverting the last two digits.

"See you soon!" Maria slipped the note into her purse.

"Sure thing," he replied, looking through her, not at her as before.

Although he had maintained a modicum of civility, Maria could see in his empty glance that Michael was no longer interested in her. His post-coital change of demeanor reminded her of those salespeople who are exceedingly friendly when they think you're going to buy something, then switch abruptly to cold indifference as soon as you tell them that you're only window shopping.

Michael sensed her disappointment but didn't care. What's the point of masticating on a piece of chewing gum after the flavor is gone? he asked himself. You spit it out and pop a fresh one into your mouth. But he hadn't gotten as much flavor out of Maria as he had hoped. Unfortunately, the women at *Sexaholics Anonymous* didn't present enough of a challenge. There was no suspense, no resistance whatsoever, which kind of removed the whole thrill of the chase in the first place.

A rather unpleasant thought occurred to him. Am I like those poor wretches at *Sexaholics Anonymous*? he wondered, but quickly dismissed the idea. Absolutely not, he decided. How could sex possibly be an addiction if it gives me so much pleasure and makes me happy? He noticed that the other participants appeared troubled by their behavior. But not him! Michael always remained cool as a cucumber. When he managed to pull it off successfully, he enjoyed the whole process of seduction, from beginning to end: the chase, the capture and the sex itself, of course. He even relished the final goodbye, when he looked a woman straight in the eyes and deliberately gave her the wrong phone number with a friendly smile. As they say, all is fair in love and war. Besides, I could stop this behavior anytime I wanted to, Michael told himself, the protective shell of his impenetrable ego blocking out even the tiniest ray of self-doubt.

Chapter 8

Michael gazed outside and, despite the religious setting, cursed under his breath when he saw that it was pouring buckets. In just nine months, I'll leave this wretched Midwest to bask in the sunshine of Arizona, he consoled himself. As he was about to brace himself for the downpour and dash out of the church, his glance was caught by a young woman who stood before a lit candle. Her lips moved slightly, in a quiet murmur that sounded like an incantation in a foreign tongue. He examined her profile. Her wavy black hair reached down to the small of her back and thick bangs covered her forehead. She was dressed in a brown skirt cut just above the knees and a modest white blouse with an old-fashioned rounded collar. Feeling the intensity of his gaze upon her, she turned, her dark eyes quizzing him.

Uncharacteristically, Michael didn't utter a word. He just stood there, enthralled. The sight of the young woman made his heart skip a few beats. His throat constricted, making it difficult to breathe. Apnea, a physician might have called it. But as he attempted to regulate his breathing and strike up a conversation, Michael recognized a *coup de foudre* when he felt it. He was drawn to her not because of her modest attire and feminine grace, but because there was something so tender and expressive in her features. He was struck by the straight, thick line of her bangs, by the paleness of her cheeks against the background of those waves of dark hair and by the rigidity with which she stood holding the candle in her hand, contradicted by the uncontainable drama of her eyes. She reminds me of a Georges De La Tour painting, he thought, captivated by the angelic innocence of her face, illuminated from below by the soft candlelight. It occurred to him to say, "I've never seen you in this church before," but that sounded too much like one of his cheesy pick-up lines. It would be practically a sacrilege to use it in church, Michael thought, momentarily forgetting that he had engaged in far more sinful behavior in that very context only a few moments earlier.

"Are you looking for someone?" the young woman asked him with a slight foreign accent.

Under ordinary circumstances, Michael would have volleyed back a clever reply to the effect of, "I sure am. I've been looking for you all of my life, Babe." Yet this time he responded, quite honestly, "No. It's just that the way your face was lit up by that candle reminded me of a painting by Georges de La Tour I once saw."

The young woman felt flattered yet also disconcerted by his powerful gaze, which was so piercing and intense that it made her wonder if anyone had ever really looked at her before. "You're very kind. I'm relieved you didn't compare me to a ghost. That might have been more accurate, but far less flattering." Seeing that his face reflected a mixture of amusement and puzzlement at her reply, she added: "Are you an art lover?"

Michael was surprised that he didn't even feel tempted to shoot out his usual response to such an easy overture, "No, but I've been told that I'm a pretty good lover." He said instead, "Not really. I dabble in everything. Art, poetry, literature. I guess you could say I admire all forms of beauty, which makes me a dilettante."

"That's what I am too, I suppose," she quietly replied.

"You suppose?"

"I imagine that one has to love art to create it."

"You're an artist?"

"Or trying to be."

"What do you mean, trying?"

"Just because you call yourself an artist doesn't mean that people actually buy your paintings," she replied with an amused smile.

"What do you like to paint?" Michael pursued.

"Scenes that are filled with sadness."

"Why sadness?"

She carefully placed the candle on the table and put her hand upon her heart with a gesture that, despite its theatricality, seemed completely sincere: "Because there's still so much sorrow in my heart."

"Why so?" Michael asked, approaching her slowly. He became once again attuned to the trace of an accent in her voice, which he couldn't quite place. "Where are you from, originally?" Then it occurred to him that he might look like he was prying into her personal life, which he most certainly was, but there was no point in doing it clumsily. "If you don't mind my asking," he added.

"We all carry with us the weight of our past," the young woman replied somewhat enigmatically to his first inquiry. "I'm originally from Romania," she answered directly the easier question.

"I thought I detected a Slavic accent," Michael observed.

"That's strange, given that Romanian is a Romance language. It's similar to Italian and Spanish."

Ana had corrected him politely. But Michael wanted to make sure she understood that he was a man of the world: "Sure. But, as far as I know, it has some Slavic vocabulary and inflections."

The young woman seemed amused by his reply. "*Da? Si cine te-a facut expert, domnule?*" she challenged him.

"Pardon?"

"I said, oh yeah? And who made you an expert, mister?" she translated.

"I'm no expert in Romanian, but I like to dabble in the Romance languages. I'm fluent in Spanish, Italian and French," he boasted modestly.

"Hmmm... You seem to dabble in a lot of things."

Normally, Michael would have replied "Especially beautiful women." But clearly, these weren't ordinary circumstances. The Romanian intrigued him. "I used to. When I was younger, I wanted to become a Renaissance man. But now I just content myself with teaching French," he shrugged with the air of resignation of a man who has abandoned his own dreams.

"I see."

Silences can be awkward when two people seem to have run out of things to say, after the initial burst of conversation in becoming acquainted. But as the young woman and Michael peered into each other's eyes, the silence that settled between them was peaceful and pleasant.

"Where are my manners? My name is Ana," she said after a few seconds, extending her hand to him.

Michael took it between his hands, pressing it lightly rather than shaking it. Ana's hand felt soft and fragile. "Nice to meet you. I'm Michael."

"Do you belong to this church? I've never seen you here before," she commented.

"I only come here occasionally," Michael replied vaguely, not wishing to delve into details about the meeting he had just attended, which, he surmised, was not likely to impress his new acquaintance.

"Me too," Ana replied. "I only come here to pray for my parents. They were both Catholic."

"*Were?*"

Ana looked pensively into the flickering flame. "They passed away a long time ago. During the revolution of '89."

"In Bucharest?" Michael asked, to show that he knew a thing or two about Eastern European history.

Ana shook her head. "No, in Timisoara. The spark that started the Romanian revolution. My mother's of Hungarian origin," she said elliptically, as if Michael could understand why that fact was of particular importance. "Few people know this, but it's the ethnic Hungarians who revolted against the Ceausescu regime first," she elaborated. "You know how it goes. The most oppressed tend to be the most courageous. Maybe because they also have the least to lose."

"It doesn't seem like it was so little for you," he commented, responding to the sadness in her voice.

"I was ten, still only a child when I lost my parents. They were my whole world."

Michael looked away, feeling slightly awkward under the pressure of this sudden intimacy. "Do you go back to visit Romania?" he shifted the conversation from emotions to events.

She shook her head. "Returning there would bring back too many painful memories."

"Do you still have family there?"

"Yes, but not close relatives. My real family lives here, in Michigan." When she said this, her tone seemed lighter.

"What do you mean your *real family*?"

"My husband and two kids," Ana clarified.

Michael took a step back, as if he had not expected this response. It had never occurred to him that Ana, who looked so young, might be a married woman with kids. "Oh, I see…"

Ana noticed his disappointment. She thought that she might have unwittingly given him the wrong impression. "Anyways, I should go now. It's getting late. It was very nice to meet you, Michael," she politely concluded their conversation.

But he didn't want to let her go on such a final note. "Before you leave, there's something I meant to ask you. You've made me kind of curious about your art. May I take a look at your paintings sometime?" Michael congratulated himself for this burst of inspiration, only to wonder, a moment later, whether he was being too forward. He felt strange about caring about his overtures. Brazenness, along with corny pick-up lines, had never bothered him in his interactions with women before. Failure and success are basically one and the same when the stakes are so low, he thought, retrospectively. But in meeting Ana, Michael became reacquainted with his own timidity, which had been buried so deeply in the cynicism of years of libertine encounters that he had almost forgotten how wonderful it felt to get to know a woman. Few human experiences could compete with that mixture of uncertainty and hope that, when you least expect it, sneaks up on you and takes your breath away. The thought that he might never see Ana again released dozens of butterflies in his stomach. Would she politely excuse herself from seeing him again, the way he, himself, had proceeded with so many women before?

"Sure," she replied, without any trace of subterfuge. "Here's my card," she handed him a business card, with the address of her art studio and a telephone number.

Looking at it, Michael noticed that Ana's last name, Popescu, sounded Romanian: "Your husband's also Romanian?"

"No, he's American. I kept my last name," she said, then added, by way of explanation, "In memory of my parents."

Michael placed the card carefully into his wallet. "Would you like my number also? Just in case you wish to let me know when it would be convenient to drop by your studio?"

"Yes, of course."

Michael wrote down his name and number on the other side of the scrap of paper Maria had given him earlier. "Sorry, I don't have a business card yet," he extended her the note.

"Thanks," she slipped it into her coat pocket.

This is a bad sign, he nervously followed her movements. That's where I usually put the numbers I want to get rid of…

"But I must warn you in advance that my art's not to everyone's taste. My paintings aren't exactly pretty."

"Since when does art have to be beautiful?" Michael hoped to show through this rhetorical question that he was automatically on her side and, more importantly, that he intuitively understood her.

"Oh, but there's such tragic beauty in human suffering," Ana replied with a barely detectable tremor in her voice. It was her tone more so than her words, wavering on the permeable boundary between abandon and restraint, which stayed with him for the rest of the evening. It haunted him with the promise of pleasures more subtle, richer and more intense than he had ever tasted in his life before.

Chapter 9

Driving home after his encounter with Ana, Michael felt elated. Not so much because he thought that he had made an indelible impression upon the young woman, but because she, herself, had moved him. At the moment of his deepest doubt in his ability to fall in love, Ana had reawakened his faith in his own capacity for human emotion.

"Whoa! Let's not put the cart ahead of the horse," he reminded himself. Once he arrived at his apartment, he flung the keys on the kitchen counter. By association, he fell back upon a play on words, "Let's not put the heart ahead of the whore," to take the edge off his euphoria. No point in taking a little crush too seriously, he made a second attempt to bring himself back down to earth.

Yet the ruse of cynicism proved ineffective. That night, he couldn't fall asleep. He lay with his head propped up upon two pillows, contemplating his recent encounter with Ana. He went over their conversation, her glances, each gesture she made, his own overtures and reactions. He recalled how when he looked into her eyes, he felt like for the first time he saw a woman in Technicolor, as it were. Everything else he had experienced, every other woman he had met before, now seemed like a faded black and white photograph compared to the kaleidoscope of emotions that had burst within him the instant he saw her.

She's the one, Michael told himself. Then, once again, he tried to find a joke or at the very least a pun in his own observation, embarrassed by his premature sense of conviction. This time, however, the joke was on him. There was a freshness and fire about this woman that disarmed him of the artillery of hackneyed phrases he usually deployed in his encounters with women. A vision of Ana appeared before his eyes. He imagined caressing the curves of her breasts over her modestly buttoned-up blouse, incapable of resisting their soft invitation. She had told him about the death of her parents, about her difficult childhood as an orphan. But was she happy now, with her own family? Was her husband good to her? Above all, he wondered, has this woman ever tasted the pleasure of falling madly in love?

In his hubris, Michael felt quite certain that she hadn't. His heart skipped a beat when he sensed that he could be the first to give Ana that experience. What about her husband? it occurred to him, but then he quickly dismissed the idea. In his own mind, the real litmus test would be Ana's response. If she welcomed his advances, then they'd have a real chance. The children, however, were a differ-

---

ent story. In some respects, Michael calculated, they could be viewed as a bonus. For nearly two years he had longed to be with a more affectionate woman than Karen. He dreamt of becoming a father one day. Granted, he had envisioned achieving that goal in the traditional, biological manner rather than robbing another man's nest. But, then again, there would be time for that as well. After all, Ana seemed to be in her early twenties. Surely, if they fell in love and married, she wouldn't deny him their own child together.

A sobering thought then occurred to him. *Have I gone bonkers? Why the hell am I thinking about marriage? For Christ's sake, I just met the woman, who, incidentally, happens to already have a husband and kids. I must be in dire need of some heavy-duty therapy, or at the very least a decent blowjob. Better take it easy, get some apparently much-needed sleep and allow myself to calm down,* he advised himself. *This woman's trouble,* Michael concluded. *If I pursue her and she goes along, shit! It risks becoming serious. And what would be the point of that?* he debated with his own self. *Nothing, that's what,* he answered his own rhetorical question. *After all, I've just gotten out of a serious relationship. Which, technically speaking, means I'm on the rebound. Better give myself some time to heal,* he decided, but without any real conviction. *Obviously, something's wrong with my head, otherwise I wouldn't have fallen for Ana so easily,* he concluded. And yet, another part of him rebutted, *it's so exciting to finally feel so excited!*

Michael glanced at the alarm clock. *Holy crap!* It was past 3:00 a.m. and he had to teach in the morning. As he removed one of the pillows and changed position in bed to make himself more comfortable, he heard a hesitant rap on the door. He listened carefully. Hearing nothing more, he thought that he must have imagined the noise. It was confirmed, however, only a few seconds later by an even louder knock. *Could it be Ana?* Michael wondered with the irrationality of a man woken up from a dream that he couldn't yet distinguish from reality. Feeling rather than seeing his way down the hallway, he turned on the light and opened the front door.

"Karen?" She was the last person Michael expected to see.

"Sorry to come by so late," she excused herself. Even in the dim hallway light, Michael noticed that Karen looked different. For one thing, she wasn't wearing glasses. She also seemed to have lost some weight. Uncharacteristically, she was wearing a skirt that fell well above the knees, practically a miniskirt. He stared at her, trying to adjust her new image to his former recollections. "Where are your glasses?" was all he could think of saying.

Karen smiled with a visible sense of satisfaction. "I got contacts," she replied, hoping that he'd also notice that she had lost seven pounds, her biggest achievement during their separation.

"Where are my manners? Please come in," he invited her with an air of formality that he generally reserved for older acquaintances.

Karen walked in with a deliberate sway of her hips. *Has she been taking walking lessons?* Michael wondered, following her movements. In the past, he had teased her that she walked in a flatfooted swaggering manner, like a man.

His attention was diverted by the colorful package Karen was carrying in her right hand. "Gone Christmas shopping in September?"

"Not exactly," she turned to him and handed him the bag. "It's my birthday present for you."

"But my birthday's not 'till December."

"It's an early gift."

Michael peered inside, then looked up at her blankly: "A cactus?"

"It's for our new apartment," Karen clarified. This response left him even more baffled.

"What apartment?"

"The one we'll move into this summer in Phoenix," she said with a complicit smile that dissolved into slight quivers of emotion at the corners of her mouth. He tried to focus upon the meaning of her words. *What in the world is she trying to tell me?*

Michael must have looked as puzzled as he felt, since Karen felt compelled to add, "I've been doing a lot of soul-searching lately and have found the strength to forgive you," she delivered the line that she had been rehearsing in her own mind during the past few weeks.

He didn't react.

"To prove to you my commitment to making our relationship work, I quit my job. I'm ready to move with you to Phoenix, like you asked me earlier," she elaborated.

"You quit your job? Just like that?"

Karen nodded. "I gave them three weeks' notice. Starting this Monday will be my last week."

Michael felt unprepared for this news. "What about your family? Did you tell them you want to move to Arizona?"

"Not yet. I thought you might want to be informed first," Karen replied with a smile.

"And you still want to marry me? After everything I did to you?" Michael looked incredulous.

By way of response, Karen reached over to kiss him on the mouth: little pecks with puckered closed lips that, it occurred to him, she mistook for sensual abandon, punctuated by tearful, ecstatic affirmations: "Yes... yes... yes!" Then, fearing that Michael might not be as enthusiastic as she had hoped, she pulled back to examine his reaction. His perplexed look didn't say enough. "Don't you want to marry me?" she asked him, suddenly overcome by self-doubt.

"I'm just a little surprised, that's all," Michael struggled to regain his composure. This ambiguous reply sufficed to reassure Karen. He was obviously as moved as she was by her generosity, willingness to improve herself and self-sacrifice for the sake of their relationship. Whatever was left of her emotional barriers crumbled. "If you only knew how much I missed you. These past few weeks without you have been such," Karen wanted to say "hell," but thought it might sound too dramatic and, at any rate, she preferred to avoid using sacrilegious language, "so difficult," she said instead, wrapping her arms around her fiancé. Michael reciprocated her embrace, crossing his arms around her back, still slightly dazed by the impact of her unexpected visit.

Chapter 10

Ana rushed to her car in the pouring rain, placing her purse above her head in lieu of an umbrella. She braced herself for the traffic she'd have to face on her way back to Ann Arbor. As she ran to the parking lot, she had the strange feeling that she was running away from something rather than towards it. She kept seeing Michael's warm brown eyes gazing at her furtively, with shyness. She recalled noticing that, at some point during their conversation, the lower lobes of his ears had turned crimson and he looked away. That small gesture of disavowed attraction had sent a shiver of desire up and down her spine. "Thank God I'm going back to my kids and my nice quiet life," Ana told herself as she fished for the car keys in her coat pocket. Her fingers grazed a slip of paper. It was the one upon which Michael had jotted down his name and number with rounded, almost calligraphic letters. By reflex, an image of her kids flashed before her eyes. Michelle was delicate and high-strung. Though only nine, in some ways she was as mature and independent as a teenager. By way of contrast, Allen, who was a year younger than his sister, constantly sought the warmth and protection of his mother's love.

Ana pressed the button to unlock her car. On impulse, she crumpled up the note Michael had given her and tossed it into the trash bin. Traffic was slow, but her mind raced. Lulled by the regular, back-and-forth movements of the windshield wipers, Ana thought of her husband. She could anticipate Rob's every move. He would arrive home from work at about 7:30 p.m., feeling stressed and tired. By that time, she and the kids would have already eaten dinner. He'd remove his suit jacket. Then, without saying a word to her, he'd warm up his supper. At some point, Michelle would greet her father. She'd deluge him with reports about her day. Sometimes, in a honey-sweet voice that she reserved especially for such occasions, she'd ask her father's permission for future play dates or sleepovers with her friends. Out of expediency and affection, he'd grant her wishes without even thinking twice about it. Then they'd retreat to different rooms, in a symmetrical division of labor. Rob would help Michelle with her homework while Ana would help Allen with his. After the kids went to bed, Rob would lock himself up in his office. He'd read political blogs to unwind, while Ana would take out a sketchpad to map out some of her paintings. Hardly a word, other than matters related to their children, would be exchanged between husband and wife.

The night didn't bring them any closer. Ever since Allen was born, the couple got used to sleeping in separate bedrooms. With one notable exception, Ana recalled. About twice a week, when the kids were asleep or otherwise occupied, Rob would rap lightly on Ana's bedroom door and peep in with an ingratiating smile. Ana knew what that meant. Since she hardly ever refused, her biweekly wifely duty would be wordlessly concluded within a matter of minutes. She'd be left feeling sad and empty as Rob, more satiated than satisfied, closed the door behind him. Aside from their children, whom they both loved, Ana felt like they had little left to bind them together anymore.

When did our marriage turn into such a sham? she wondered. It wasn't like this from the start. In the beginning, Ana recalled, Rob also looked at her with admiration and desire, the way Michael had. When they met back in college at Michigan University, she was studying at the School of Art and Design and Rob was enrolled in the Carter School of Business. Their interests were worlds apart, yet they still managed to find common ground. They engaged in heated conversations about everything under the sun: art, religion, philosophy, and politics, even quantum physics. When they walked together, Ana recalled, Rob used to hold her hand. Now, she thought with regret, whenever they went out, her husband walked hurriedly a few steps ahead of her and the kids, like the head of a pack rather than of a family. Before, when they drove, Ana remembered, she used to place her hand upon his so affectionately that he got used to driving with only one hand. Now they hardly held hands anymore. Before, when they used to make love, she'd wrap her arms and her legs around him, grateful for the gift of his desire. Now she'd close her eyes and wait for the whole ordeal to be over. Piece by piece, so gradually that they barely noticed it, they had shed like so much dead skin each protective layer of their love.

Ana arrived at the kids' school in rather low spirits. But she was quickly jolted out of her bad mood by Michelle, who ran to the door to greet her. "Mama, guess what?" she asked, her delicate face radiating excitement. "You know that drawing I made, of the two spiders?"

Ana tried to recall which drawing her daughter was referring to, since Michelle was even more prolific than herself when it came to artistic production. "You mean the one of the two spiders in love?" she asked her, alluding to a drawing where the spiders in question were lying practically on top of each other.

The girl's pale blue eyes seemed to shoot daggers at her mother: "They weren't in love, Mama!" Michelle objected to all matters related to love or, worse yet, boys, whom she considered immature and dorky. "They were just building a web together."

Ana nodded, thinking to herself, kind of like your father and I. "Sorry, I didn't mean to insinuate anything."

"What's *insinuate?*"

"It means to suggest."

Michelle's level of enthusiasm rose again: "Well, anyways. My art teacher, Mrs. Posner, entered that drawing in the state art fair! Isn't it great? I'm the only one she chose out of the whole class!"

Ana beamed with pride at her daughter's accomplishment. "Congratulations! I'm so proud of you. Didn't I tell you that you have real talent? Who knows? Maybe one day you'll become an artist."

"Mama, you know how hard it is to make money from art. I only want to do it for fun."

Ana couldn't help but feel a little stung by her daughter's comment. It sounded too close for comfort to something her pragmatic husband would say. When the art sales went well a couple of years ago and she was able to bring in roughly 50,000 dollars annual income from her paintings, their marriage felt more balanced, if not actually warmer. Ana had more say in the way they spent their money, in their vacation plans and even in decisions regarding the children. But once the recession took a turn for the worse, art was the first luxury people dispensed with and Ana could only bring a half of her usual salary. Along with the diminished income, she sensed the power balance shift in their family. "Why don't you get a real job? One that actually makes money rather than wasting it on art supplies," her husband had suggested in the middle of a dispute over finances. "Because I want to devote my time to art. I never misled you about that," Ana had replied. "Well, I'd love to devote my life to napping, but unfortunately I don't have that luxury," Rob rebutted. "Art isn't exactly the same thing as sleep," she objected. "The point is that I do things I hate so that I can make a living and support our family. Meanwhile, you sit around in your studio all day doing whatever you please!" he had snapped back. The fact that Ana enjoyed painting while Rob, a manager at Ford Motor Company, disliked his job was another source of contention between them. She's been indoctrinated by her father, Ana concluded, still contemplating her daughter's remark. "That's a good idea," she responded to Michelle's comment attempting to sound unfazed. "But there's plenty of time to think about what you want to do with your life. The important thing is that you like it."

"It's not all about doing what you like, Mama," Michelle rebutted. "It's about survival," she repeated word-by-word one of her father's statements.

Ana winced at the comment. "Let's pick up your brother," she placed her hand upon Michelle's shoulder, directing her towards Allen's classroom.

Even within the boundaries of his familiar surroundings, little Allen looked confused. Ana's eyes lit up as soon as she saw him. "Did you have a nice day at school today?" she asked him, planting a kiss upon the velvety softness of his cheek.

"I guess."

"What did you do?"

The boy shrugged. "I don't know. Nothing special."

"You don't know? Weren't you there, in class?" his sister interjected.

Allen's buttons were easily pushed. "Stop it!" he objected in a whinny tone, already brought to the edge of tears by her comment. "We didn't do any stuff today!"

"That's all right. On some days, they review," Ana intervened in her son's defense. She had already retrieved his lunch box, coat and backpack, since, when left to his own devices, Allen let them find shelter on the lost and found table outside the classroom.

"You always take his side," Michelle looked reproachfully at her mother as they made their way through the busy parking lot.

"Only when you poke it," Ana unlocked the car doors. "Make sure you put on your seatbelts."

"I know, Mama, I'm not stupid," the girl protested. Then her tone changed, as she remembered something. "Know what? Our Social Studies teacher told us that the Renaissance Festival is coming to Ann Arbor this weekend. Can we go there please?"

"It's fine with me. But we'll have to ask your father."

That evening, after Rob had already eaten dinner and retreated into his office, Ana knocked lightly on his door to consult with him about their weekend plans. She overheard him talking on the phone but entered nonetheless. She was greeted by his aggressive gaze. His left hand fluttered rapidly in the air to shoo her away. Ordinarily, Ana didn't let Rob's dismissive behavior get to her. But on that evening, for some reason, it did. She went into the bedroom. To calm down her nerves, she turned on the radio to her favorite jazz station. The lulling, sultry sounds of a singer bemoaning lost love fit her melancholy mood. As she became lost in the chords of resonant emotions, Rob poked his head through the door. His features were distorted by a familiar smile. Ana looked at him with undisguised contempt and fluttered her hand, exactly as he had done to her. "Not now, please. I'm relaxing," she said. Rob retreated, troubled by the lingering intuition that they had little left to hope for in their marriage.

Chapter 11

Ana stepped into the gallery which exhibited her artwork. She secretly hoped that an important art critic would drop by, see her work and whip up a sensational article on her paintings, which would instantly catapult her to celebrity. Not that she painted to become famous. She painted to express herself, as any artist does. But with fame came money, which, Ana felt, would shift the balance of power in her family. If she were more successful, Rob might treat her with more respect, like he used to back in college, when she was winning all those prizes and he saw in her so much artistic promise. In turn, Michelle would see that pursuing your dreams isn't necessarily a waste of time. As for Allen, Ana was obliged to admit that her son's attitude wouldn't change much. He was the least judgmental member of the family.

Surveying the gallery, Ana noticed a woman with asymmetrical salt-and-pepper hair. She was examining her work down the sharp incline of her pointy nose, an impressive feat given that the paintings were hung above eye-level. She looks snooty, Ana assessed her. She then spotted a more promising prospect. A gentleman in a dark suit was contemplating her latest painting. It featured two naked lovers locked in an embrace: but not a happy one, God forbid! The figures' tortuous positioning, the angular shapes of their bodies, the grayish tint of their sickly skin and the anguish reflected upon their pasty features, all suggested an attitude of suffering and despair. Well, I had to put a sexier painting in this show since Tracy asked me to, Ana justified to herself this concession to what she considered to be popular taste. Tracy, the gallery owner, had recently speculated that perhaps the reason why Ana's paintings weren't selling so well was because they were too somber: "When the economy's bad, people want to look at something bright and cheerful," she had suggested.

"But my paintings are meaningful and expressive," Ana had modestly retorted. "They're more likely to touch art critics who actually care about the human condition," she defended her aesthetic standards over trivial market considerations.

"Too bad those critics haven't set foot in my gallery yet," Tracy had responded. Although she was as sensitive as a businesswoman could be without going bankrupt, Tracy nonetheless indicated that perhaps the expression of anguish, which was obviously Ana's forte, could be combined with motifs that were more popular, such as nudity and sex.

"So you want me to depict rape scenes?" Ana put two and two together.

"What? No, of course not! I was only making a suggestion. If I were you, I'd paint pretty landscapes, flowers or vases. Something neutral that people might actually want to display in their homes and offices," Tracy advanced a novel idea.

But Ana dismissed such a crude vulgarization of her artistic talent. "I don't paint to sell. I paint to express," she said. Tracy, however, politely reminded her that if she wanted to continue expressing in her gallery, she'd need to become more adaptable to the taste of their customers. As she was focusing upon such sobering recollections, Ana spotted a young man with glossy hair and dark eyes. For some reason, he looked familiar to her. Within a few seconds, she recognized him. It's Michael, that nice, adorably shy Catholic young man she recently met in church! Without making direct eye contact with Ana, Michael went straight to her new painting of the two lovers. He appeared to be examining it closely.

"Hi. Thanks for coming to my exhibit," Ana approached him.

"I said I would, didn't I?" Michael turned to her with a friendly smile.

Gosh, he's even better looking than I remembered, she observed. Don't look at her tits, Michael told himself, attempting to focus on Ana's eyes instead. But he couldn't help but notice in passing that her outfit was less modest than the one she had worn in church. This time the young woman wore a short brown dress that hugged her curves.

"I really like this painting," he said, assuming a contemplative demeanor. "I especially love the set of contrasts you establish here."

"Which ones?" In her mind, the painting expressed a unified theme: the suffering that results from a dying love.

"Well, the angularity of the lovers' position versus the soft curves of their bodies, for instance," Michael remarked, gesturing towards relevant parts of the painting. "Plus the antithesis between the tenderness with which they hold each other and the anguish of their facial expressions," he pursued. "Not to mention the complementary color palette you use," he added, risking overkill.

As she listened to Michael's comments, Ana wondered, does he even notice that this painting shows two naked people having sex? She was surprised that Michael seemed to mention every other element of her work, omitting only the most obvious. "You know, this painting's mainly about sex and love," she helpfully explained.

"Really? I hadn't noticed," Michael replied with a bemused smile.

"My gallery owner asked me to do a painting about something that sells," Ana shrugged with an air of resignation.

"And you thought that two people looking like they're both in excruciating pain while making love would do the trick?" Michael followed the lead of her conversational directness. Will she take offense? he wondered.

To his relief, Ana laughed good-naturedly. "That's what I call a compromise. Usually, I paint only serious themes," she made a sweeping movement with her hand to indicate her other paintings, which featured popular themes, such as death, disease, massacre, hunger and despair. "I depicted the scene just to please Tracy."

Michael nodded in agreement. "I get it. Enough anguish to please critics and enough nudity to please customers."

"That was precisely my theory," the quirky artist concurred.

"Just out of curiosity, has anybody expressed interest in buying this particular painting yet?"

"Let's just say that my hypothesis has not yet been confirmed."

"Good. Because I'd like to buy it," Michael offered, surprised by his own atypical impulse of generosity.

Ana directed him an incredulous look. "Did you take a peek at the price tag yet?"

"Why? Do I look that poor to you?"

"I didn't mean to suggest that…"

Michael glanced at the title of the painting. "*Goodbye forever*? What's that all about?" Then he noticed the price, "Three thousand bucks? Holy shit!"

"You are aware of the fact this is a posh art gallery, not a flea market, right?" Ana double-checked.

"Yes and I stand by my offer," he confirmed.

"You really don't need to, honestly. I'm sufficiently impressed by your noble intentions," she assured him.

"No, I mean what I say. I want to buy it," Michael insisted.

"Are you sure?" When he nodded, Ana's face lit up with childlike joy. "Thank you so much!" She stepped forward and hugged him so tightly that he could feel the softness of her breasts pressed up against his chest. As she whispered a few more words of gratitude, currents of tingles ran from his ear to his neck, through his torso, all the way down to his toes.

"I really do like your art, Ana," Michael said. "You have a way of expressing the sadder emotions. You give them nuance and range. Personally, I haven't

seen many contemporary painters who are able to do that as well as you do." As
he uttered the word range, he made a sweeping gesture with his hand, which
accidentally brushed up against Ana's hip. Michael's whole body quivered, electrified by this unexpected touch. "Sorry," he apologized.

"Don't worry about it," she placed her hand briefly upon his shoulder. "I'm
Romanian. We Latin women are used to a lot worse."

He looked at her with a sense of relief. She's absolutely radiant, he thought.
And that wasn't just his impression. In point of fact, Ana beamed with delight.
Many people had complimented her paintings and some had bought them. But
hardly anyone grasped their essence as well as Michael. "I really appreciate your
gesture. It's so nice of you," she repeated.

"Well, don't thank me yet. I still have to seal the deal with the gallery
owner," Michael reminded her. The young woman promptly ushered him into
Tracy's office.

After they parted on that Friday afternoon, Ana left the gallery in a daze.
She looked up at the sunny September sky. The clouds were so clearly defined
that they almost looked painted upon a pale blue background. I must be floating
on air, she told herself, uplifted by a sense of peaceful elation. Each time she
recalled Michael's fluid gaze gliding over her body and pausing to look admir-
ingly into her eyes, she fell into a trance, like a schoolgirl experiencing her first
infatuation.

Under the spell of these fresh impressions, Ana crossed the street to take the
People Mover to the RenCen, where she had parked her car. When she arrived
downtown, there seemed to be a big commotion around the subway station.

"What happened?" an elderly woman asked.

"A man fell under the train," replied a middle-aged woman wearing clogs.

"Did someone push him?" a young man wanted to know.

"No. I heard this guy who was a friend of his say that he threw himself under the train," a young woman commented.

"But why?" the first woman inquired.

The young woman shrugged. "Who knows? Poor guy... His friend was saying that has a wife and three kids. Can you imagine what those poor souls will
feel when they find out about what happened to their dad?"

These snippets of conversation sobered Ana, taking her mind off her recent
encounter with Michael. On the drive back home, she kept thinking about that
misfortunate man's suicide. What could have driven him to such a desperate
act? she wondered. Was it alcohol? Debt? Drugs? An illness? Losing his job?
Heartache from a failed love affair? Ana went through a few possible reasons.
None of them seemed compelling, however. Nothing could be bad enough to
abandon your children, she told herself. When she picked up Michelle and Allen
from school that afternoon, she embraced them warmly, as one does when reuniting with loved ones after a long separation.

"Mama, stop it! I'm not a baby anymore," her daughter protested.

But Ana disagreed. No matter how old they are, they'll always be my babies, she told herself.

Chapter 12

Although Ana had closed the bedroom door, she could still hear the children's voices shouting and laughing. On that Friday evening, they were hosting a double slumber party. In the spirit of equality and fairness, Rob had allowed both Michelle and Allen to invite their friends over for pizza and a sleepover. It was already past ten. Ana hoped that the kids' energy level would go down, but no such luck. They were charged up like batteries, while she and Rob felt exhausted. To relax, Ana went online to check her email. She found five spams and three messages. Four of them advertised enlarging various body parts while the last one, by way of contrast, suggested liposuction. The three real messages came from people she didn't know.

Let's see, Ana opened the first, with only mild curiosity. It was from an artist who wanted to know if she had an art agent. No I don't, she replied. The second was from a man who claimed to have seen her painting of the two lovers. He wondered if she would be willing to do an idealized representation of him and his wife. Ana responded that she didn't do portraits. The last note was from an artist who wanted her to recommend his work to her gallery owner. Ana replied that she'd be happy to, but she'd have to take a look at his art first. As she was about to log off, she became aware that the house was unusually quiet. Back in the old days, when the kids were calm without adult supervision for more than a few minutes, it often meant they were up to no good. Once she even caught them making mud pies in the living room with the leftover fudge.

She found the boys in Allen's bedroom, playing Nintendo. Ana headed next for Michelle's room. It was empty. She checked the playroom and her studio, down in the basement. Nobody was there either. She proceeded to search in the front and back yards. Still no sign of the girls. "Rob?" she called out. "Where are the girls?"

Her husband was on the phone with a childhood friend. He winced at the interruption. "Don't worry about it. They're having *fun*."

"But I looked everywhere and couldn't find them," his wife insisted.

"They're probably playing outside."

"At 10:30 p.m.? In the dark? By themselves?"

Ana's anxious tone set off his trigger. "Listen, I'll have to call you back. My wife's freaking out about something," he informed his friend, then turned to his wife: "Why must you ruin everybody else's pleasure? Let the kids enjoy their childhood!" he exclaimed. Ever since Michelle and Allen had become old enough to have some independence, Rob resented his wife's over-protective attitude. She's just being neurotic, was his default explanation for most of her maternal anxiety.

"I'm just more responsible than you," Ana rebutted. "I don't let young girls run around unsupervised at night."

"If you truly cared, you wouldn't be answering emails or tinkering with your drawings instead of looking after the kids," Rob objected.

"Excuse me, but I'm only human. I may need to take a break in the evening just as you do," Ana replied, surprised by the shrillness of her own voice.

"A break from what?"

She could see disdain flaring in her husband's eyes. A feeling of resentment welled up in her throat. At that moment, Michelle and her friend Marsha stepped in. Ana's pent-up anger was instantly released: "Michelle, where have you been?"

"Outside. By the little stream."

"What were you doing walking around in the dark without adult supervision?" her mother pursued.

"Daddy gave me permission," Michelle fell back upon her usual defense.

Ana turned to her husband again. "She's only ten. What if she gets kidnapped? There wouldn't even be any witnesses around this late at night."

"Mama, don't be such a scaredy cat!"

"I'm just trying to protect you from harm," Ana replied more calmly.

"No, you're not," Rob countered. "You're just being neurotic, worrying about nothing."

"I may be neurotic, but at least I'm not irresponsible."

At this point, Michelle intervened. She was growing weary of witnessing conflagrations between her parents. "Stop it. Both of you. Can't you see? You're both right," she attempted to mediate. She first turned to her father. "Daddy, you're right to let me do more things. I'm getting older, so I should have more freedom." Then she addressed her mother. "And Mom, you're also right to tell me that I shouldn't go wondering around the neighborhood at night."

Ana's anger evaporated. She felt sorry for the girl, obliged by the mounting tension between her parents to mature beyond her years. She recalled several heated discussions with Rob that had been stopped by Michelle's tearful pleas, "Don't fight, because if you do, you'll end up like Natalie's parents. And I'll kill myself if you get a divorce!" their daughter had threatened. Those words, and especially the desperation and intensity with which her daughter clung to an image of loving, unified parents, daunted her mother. For years, Ana believed that such an image was only a mirage, if it had ever existed at all. Yet she was afraid to shatter her daughter's dreams of a happy family. "You're right, Michelle. You may be only nine, but you're wiser than both of us put together," Ana remarked, looking straight into her husband's eyes. Rob couldn't understand the dangers out there, she told herself. The unforgiving harshness of the world. But she did. Because, unlike him, she had experienced real trauma rather than watching it on television as a form of entertainment.

When she went to bed that night, Ana could tell that she'd be overtaken by the spell again. The nausea rose from the pit of her stomach all the way up to her throat. She heard herself break into tears, in spite of herself, outside the realm of conscious control. *Sanglots de desespoir*, a French poet might have written with his elegant *Monblanc* fountain pen. *Neuralgic hysteria*, an old-fashioned psychiatrist might have diagnosed, prescribing some barbiturates to calm her down.

As for Ana, she just called it unhappiness. A deep, visceral sadness periodically filled her with a negative energy without any identifiable source or solace. To help soothe her nerves, she went into the bathroom and removed the package of sleeping pills from the right-hand drawer. She gathered four little elongated white capsules into the cup of her hand, popped them into her mouth and washed them down with a glass of water. She then went to bed and slipped under the covers.

Her eyes wide open and her mind wondering far away, Ana had a flashback to a day in the park that, in retrospect, she viewed as the last day of her childhood. Ana recalled a Sunday afternoon when she was allowed to wear white again, since nearly a year had passed since her parents' death in the Timisoara massacre. She was eleven going on twelve. The anti-communist revolution was already behind them and life began to change beyond recognition in Romania. Within the space of one year, the country suddenly transformed. It became filled with shops, markets, bars, strip clubs and a growing black market, as people, especially the seedier elements, thrived by consuming the corpse of the decaying communist society.

On that warm June afternoon, however, Ana was focusing on life's simple pleasures. She was licking a chocolate ice cream cone, glad that food was finally readily available. Feeling sympathy for the eleven year old girl who had lost her parents, Grandma Anca spent her precious savings on taking her granddaughter to an amusement park so that Ana could feel like a child again.

As the girl was enjoying her ice cream cone standing next to the carousel, Nicu, the neighbor's eighteen year old son, who already drank too much and was what Grandma Anca referred to as a "derbedeu," yelled out loud, among his group of friends, "Nice pink panties, Ana! Can we take them off?"

Perhaps that was only a harmless joke. But Ana blushed, not even daring to look down to check if her panties could be seen through her white summer dress.

"Don't pay any attention to that hooligan," her grandmother whisked the girl away from the group of rowdy young men.

But Ana couldn't conquer her embarrassment. "I should have worn the white ones instead," she mumbled.

"It doesn't matter," Grandma Anca said. "What matters is that you know how to respect yourself," she peered meaningfully at her granddaughter through her large, pink-rimmed glasses.

"Okay." Ana replied, eager to forget about the whole unpleasant episode.

But Grandma Anca squeezed her hand emphatically: "If you don't treat yourself with respect, no man ever will," she repeated. "They'll only spit on you their dirty seed."

"That sounds pretty gross," the girl decided, throwing away the remains of the soggy ice cream cone.

As far as she could recall, that was the only birds and bees conversation Ana ever had with her grandmother. Yet she relived that moment in her dreams disturbingly often, down to the dusty, heavy feel of the hot air on that June afternoon; the derisory sexual comment whose sharp jab she had never felt before; the sense of shame towards her budding sexuality and her grandmother's resolve to inculcate in her a sense of dignity that, the elderly lady sensed, would be her strength against the onslaught of predatory young men in a nascent capitalist society filled with a disconcerting mixture of opportunity and corruption.

Then, in another flashback, Ana saw Nicu again. He was bent over her, with his tender brown eyes, aquiline nose and an abandoned smile upon his lips. One moment he was gazing sweetly into her eyes, the next she felt the heat of his breath flowing in a string of incoherent words. She sensed him delving into her body, despite her repeated cries for him to stop. As so often before when she recalled her first so-called lover, Ana felt her skin become saturated with cold beads of perspiration. At first he had been sugary sweet, that Nicu. He reminded her of the honey drop candies her grandmother used to buy for her as a special treat, with their hard shell exterior and soft, nectar-like interior, which, once she bit into them with a crunch, spilled a gooey liquid into the cavern of her mouth, inundating her with an overpowering sweetness that bordered on nausea.

After that incident, Ana thought, her grandmother's words of advice about preserving her feminine virtue became more or less meaningless, the way injunctions about propriety and honesty are rendered derisory by the reality of murder, famine and war. Live through what I've lived through at the hands of your fellow human beings, of your own friend and neighbor no less, she addressed her husband in her own mind, and only then you'll have the right to lecture me about spoiling the children's fun! He'll never understand me, Ana concluded, feeling misunderstood and alone in her new country, in her own house. But I am not alone, she reminded herself. I have Allen and Michelle. Dear God, please let him not turn my own children against me, was Ana's last coherent thought before finally drifting off to sleep.

Chapter 13

Michael felt himself sinking into the giving softness of the pillow. A warm, tingling sensation enveloped his midsection. He didn't dare open his eyes, fearing that it might break his concentration. In the dark, he intuited her presence. Her long dark hair covered him like a silky blanket. Her mouth wrapped around him, determining the pulse of his desire. When he was about to lose control, he pulled her up towards him. Strangely, however, he felt more resistance than anticipated. Something isn't right about this, it occurred to him. She didn't glide up his body with sufficient ease; her curves didn't envelop him with the fragile softness he expected. As Michael opened his eyes, the fantasy of Ana vanished. "Karen?" he asked incredulously. Once fully awake, he realized that his life was back to normal. "What a pleasant morning surprise," he attempted to mask his disappointment.

"Good morning, sweetie!" Karen cooed in a melodious tone that rang false to his well-trained ears.

Why does her behavior strike me as fake? he wondered. Well, maybe not fake, he reconsidered. Because, in all fairness, she's trying her damnedest to please me. But it still seems... forced. Like she's trying to be something she's not. He recalled the last time they had attempted this particular activity, nearly two years ago, when Karen had lunged into the bathroom afterwards, to rinse her mouth out with *Listerine*. "You don't have to do this."

"But I want to, honey," she assured him.

There goes that word again. "Honey." It sounds so strange coming from her mouth. What in the world does she want from me? Michael wondered. In the past, whenever Karen did him any sexual favors, afterwards, she'd either ask him to do something for her in return (such as spend the weekend with her sister or her parents) or, worse yet, kindly inform him that she had already made plans for them. "I don't want to have brunch with either your parents or your sister's family today," he preempted in one breath two possible requests.

Karen's lips quivered into a smile that she maintained for a few seconds. "But I wasn't asking you to do that, sweetie."

I can't recall the last time she called me "sweetie," Michael reflected. Karen's saccharine behavior gave him the strange sensation of swimming against the current in a sea of molasses.

"What would you like to do today?" she asked him, her mouth pressed to his ear.

With a sudden motion, Michael slipped out from underneath her and threw his legs unto the floor, ready to shower. "I read in the paper that the Renaissance festival's in town this weekend. Any interest?" he asked her.

"Fine by me," she readily accepted.

As he was lathering up, Michael contemplated this new turn of events. For the past few days, Karen had moved in with him. Strangely enough, not once did she complain about how her parents would be devastated by her immoral behavior. If they had protested at all, Michael couldn't tell, so obliging and chipper was his fiancée. Speaking of which, that was another confusing matter. Were they still engaged? So far, they had carefully skirted the whole marriage issue. He was afraid to broach the subject for fear that it might land him into more commitment than he wanted. Karen, too, avoided the topic, afraid of losing ground and getting less than what she had before. The situation was ambiguous enough that Michael hesitated on a course of action. When Karen proposed to move in with him, he agreed to what he considered to be a provisional arrangement. But Karen's sweetness troubled him as well, giving him another sort of headache. She's swimming to shore as fast as possible, while I'm trying to tread water. How the hell am I going to keep marriage at bay? he wondered.

"I made your favorite breakfast. Chocolate chip pancakes," Karen announced peeking through the bedroom door. Michael was slipping on a plain burgundy tee shirt. He caught a look of envy on her face. Gosh, he looks so good in everything, Karen couldn't help but notice. Even that simple shirt brought out the deep brown of his eyes. She advanced towards him, working on a naughty smile.

She's really scaring me now, Michael thought.

With a sense of unshakable determination, Karen firmly placed her hand upon his member. She planted a host of kisses all over his cheek. Michael leaned back, with the same recoil reaction he experienced whenever a friendly dog tried to lick his face. Karen withdrew, stung by the rejection.

"Thanks so much for making me pancakes. That's so sweet of you," he tried to recover.

But it was too late. "Why am I so repulsive to you, Michael?" she asked him, her tone more sad than angry.

"You're not." He avoided her gaze.

"Then why don't you want to kiss me anymore?"

"I do. You just caught me off guard. I wasn't in the mood."

"The problem is, you're never in the mood anymore." Her words rang true, yet at the same time sounded strange, given that's exactly what he used to reproach her. Still harboring some residual resentment, he couldn't resist pointing out the justice of it all: "Hey, what goes around comes around. You used to be that way with me, remember?"

"So this is payback?" Karen narrowed her eyes to a slit, her voice chilly, back to normal.

Finding himself on familiar territory, Michael relaxed. "No, not really. But remember, you're the one who dumped me. You can't expect me to hop back in the saddle as if nothing happened. It takes some time to heal." He watched her reaction. Is she buying it or not?

Karen nodded in sympathy. "I understand. But remember, I didn't break up with you over nothing. You cheated on me twice, as I recall."

Michael felt relieved that, at least for the moment, his strategy proved effective. He had bought himself the luxury of time to figure out what he wanted. "Alright," he conceded. "But let's not start playing the blaming game," he chivalrously proposed, feeling at a slight disadvantage as far as ethics were concerned.

"I'm all for that," Karen agreed, with artificial optimism. "Let's get our relationship back on track." She then paused, holding her breath for a moment, hesitating before taking the next step. "Which, by the way, means what?"

Now that Karen had openly broached the touchy subject of marriage, Michael felt like a cornered animal. "I don't know yet. Let's just play it by ear, okay?" That catch phrase had saved him in many a difficult situation before.

Karen nodded in agreement, but her face showed disappointment.

When they made love that morning, both had the impression that they were relenting to what the other expected of them. So this is what conjugal sex must feel like, Michael observed, after it was all over. He recalled that his relations with Karen had been "conjugal" from the very start. Without fire, without passion. When he was particularly perseverant, Karen would relent. He'd make love to her thinking of the latest one nightstand that was still fresh enough on his mind that he could conjure up her image. Meanwhile, Karen would wrap her arms around him and assume the attitude of a woman submitting, out of an admirable sense of duty, to a form of mild torture. "Are you done yet?" she'd ask whenever he took longer than anticipated to release his demons. However hard she tries, this is what we'd revert to for the rest of our lives, he concluded. I'm so over this, he thought, removing his condom and tossing it into the trash bin. The only question is, where the hell am I heading? Michael asked himself, as a comical image of a cartoon character throwing himself off a cliff and remaining suspended in midair only for as long as it takes him to realize that he's about to fall randomly popped into his head.

Chapter 14

"Today's the day! I'm taking out the trash," Ana announced on Saturday morning. Being a neatness freak, she celebrated the day of the week when the garbage got collected.

"*Vayas con Dios, mi amor*," Rob hummed a farewell song to the garbage, amused by his wife's enthusiasm for the mundane.

Meanwhile, the kids were busy wolfing down the remains of that morning's batch of pancakes.

"Let's finish up so we can have a full day at the Renaissance Fair," Rob urged them, keeping in mind the fact that no matter how late you got there, you still had to pay full price for the tickets.

"Stop staring at me!" Michelle snapped at her brother.

Allen was looking innocently past her at the T.V., which happened to feature an exciting episode of *Sponge Bob Square Pants*. "I'm not!" the falsely accused protested.

"Instead of picking on your brother, why don't you go put on your costume?" Rob suggested.

"But Daddy, I can't be a fairy anymore!" Michelle objected.

"Why not? We paid a hundred bucks for that costume last year."

"Because. Last year I was still a little girl."

"And what are you now? An old lady?"

"No, but I'm too old for that girly stuff. I can't dress as a fairy anymore. It's *embarrassing*."

Great! Another hundred bucks thrown out the window, Rob concluded. Meanwhile, his wife was deciding which outfit in her wardrobe looked appropriately medieval for the festival. According to Michelle, everything her mother wore pretty much qualified. Nevertheless, Ana was faced with a tough decision. Should she wear ordinary clothes and act like she's going to the fair just to please the kids? Or should she be a good sport and wear her Romanian folk costume with the golden brocade? Since she felt in pretty good spirits that morning, she opted for the Romanian costume.

"Why are you dressed like a clown?" Michelle politely inquired, watching her mother step down the stairs. Ana was wearing a white blouse puffed at the sleeves and covered with bright red and gold roses around the neck along with a black skirt filled, Michelle could swear, with the very same flowers she saw at her great-grandmother's funeral last October.

"Hey! Show some respect for your cultural heritage. For your information, this is a Ro-ma-ni-an fol-klo-ric cos-tume," Ana enunciated.

"No wonder you wanted to escape from that country," Michelle commented.

"What are you going to wear?" Ana turned the focus away from herself.

"Daddy's buying me something at the fair."

"What happened to your fairy costume?"

"She says she outgrew it," Rob replied.

Ana's gaze shifted towards the brave little Robin Hood emerging from the bathroom, wooden sword in one hand, the other pulling up his zipper.

"Too old for it? Nonsense. Look at your brother. He's worn the same costume for three years and still hasn't outgrown it," Ana offered her son as a role model.

"That's because he's lame and has no style," Michelle offered two possible explanations.

"No I'm not. You are!" Allen returned the compliment.

As soon as they got into the car, another aesthetic debate ensued: this time on the controversial subject of music.

"Put on Hannah," Michelle suggested a singer who was popular among the tween community.

"I hate that girly stuff," Allen vetoed the proposal. "Put on AC/DC. I only like loud music."

"When I listen to that awful noise, I'll get a pounding headache," Ana chimed in. "Why don't you play some nice and soothing classical music?"

"I have a better idea. Let's play the game of silence," Rob suggested.

That game lasted almost thirty seconds. Ana's eyes shifted anxiously out the window. The beautiful pastures, colorful trees garnished by fall foliage and sleepy cows couldn't distract her from a pressing matter: "Rob, can we please stop at the next Rest Area?"

"Already? We just left the house. How come you didn't go before we got in the car?"

"I did. It just so happens that I have to go again," Ana replied in a whisper, embarrassed that her personal needs were becoming a subject of public debate.

"Then why did you have ten cups of coffee before we left?" Rob asked.

"I only had two."

"Why did you need two when you know very well that you make ten pit stops for just one?"

"Because I took a few sleeping pills last night, thanks to our pleasant conversation," Ana said, hoping that would put an end to the discussion.

"It's not my fault you freak out over nothing," Rob said, turning sharply into the nearest gas station.

Ana looked at her husband before getting out of the car. She couldn't help but feel repelled by the furrowed lines on his brow. His bad disposition has distorted his features, she observed, slamming the door behind her.

Fortunately, the atmosphere lightened once they entered the fair. They were quickly surrounded by warm greetings from lasses and lads dressed up in authentic medieval and Renaissance costumes, most of which were New Age, imported from California.

"Do you want to see the jousting match first?" Rob asked the children. If his memory served him right, in previous years that had been the highlight of their visit.

"Not yet," Michelle replied. "First I want to find a nice outfit." To her parents' chagrin, she proceeded to peruse every shop with overpriced costumes on the premises.

Michael and Karen had also made it to the Renaissance Festival that morning, half an hour earlier. Although the jousting was entertaining and the beer tasty, Michael's main source of diversion was examining closely the outfits of the better-looking lasses. They're fine on top, but leave much to be desired on the bottom, he observed. The costumes tended to have a satisfactory décolleté but obscenely long skirts that went all the way down to the ankles. Those skirts should be banned, he decided.

I wonder if he'd be more attracted to me if I had a big chest, Karen wondered, following her fiancé's gaze. Maybe I should invest in some implants, she answered her own question.

As they were meandering about, Michael spotted a show called "Saucy Lasses." A group of three women in temptingly low-cut outfits sang suggestive limericks that might have turned on an inebriated English professor specializing in Shakespeare. "Do you want to see the jousting match? It's about to begin in fifteen minutes," Karen tugged at his sleeve, to divert his attention away from the lasses.

"I want to listen these excellent singers first," Michael expressed a preference for high culture.

"I can't understand half the things they bellow," Karen objected.

"Who the hell cares about what they sing?" Michael retorted with a laugh.

Apparently, he was the only one amused. "Let's go see the jousting," Karen repeated more firmly.

She means business, Michael realized with some regret, since dirty limericks were right up his alley, not to mention the saucy lasses. "Alright," he relented.

At one of the four entrances to the jousting match, Michael's attention was caught by a woman dressed in a colorful outfit that stood out, like a harlequin's costume, even in the midst of the carnival. The young woman struck him as Eastern European, perhaps Polish or Russian. She wore her hair in two long braids on either side, which made her resemble a Matrushka doll. "Ana?" he said out loud, recognizing her.

"You know her?" Karen whispered into his ear. Every time Michael recognized a woman in public and greeted her warmly, she suspected the worst and was usually right.

"She's an artist from Ann Arbor," he informed Karen as they approached Ana and her family. "Small world, isn't it?" he said to Ana.

"The kids used to like the Renaissance Fair," she replied. "This is our third year coming here."

"Used to?" Michael addressed the little girl standing next to Ana.

"I'm never coming back here again," Michelle declared.

"Why not?" Michael asked her.

"Because a stupid maid outfit costs three hundred dollars!" the girl explained.

"But why do you have to wear a costume? Aren't you happy with your regular clothes? They look nice to me," Michael commented.

Michelle rolled her eyes at him. "Duh... Because that's the whole point of the festival. If you don't dress up, why bother coming here?"

"Please don't say 'duh.' It's rude. It implies the person you're talking to is an idiot," her mother tactfully pointed out.

"She said it, not me," Michelle retorted with a shrug addressing Michael, whom she instinctively disliked.

Who is this guy? And why is he so chummy with my wife? Rob wondered. Standing across from him, Karen was contemplating a similar set of questions. So this is what Michael wants so desperately? A little spoiled brat to mouth off at him? Maybe we could adopt, she relented, seeing Michael's eyes light up with amusement at Michelle's brashness. That way I won't have to ruin my figure, she thought, looking Ana up and down. How do some women stay thin? They must starve themselves, Karen decided, not seeing any other logical explanation. Meanwhile, Michael had examined Rob enough to conclude that Ana's husband couldn't possibly be a threat to him. For one thing, he's shorter and less muscular than me, he assessed his competition, as if they were rival knights engaged in a quest for the damsel in distress. Or the colorful matruska doll, Michael qualified, turning his gaze to Ana again. "Nice costume," he observed.

"I warned her not to wear it," Michelle conveniently mistook his compliment for sarcasm.

But Ana thanked him with a smile. With a belated sense of politeness, they introduced their significant others. After exchanging a few pleasantries, both Rob and Karen showed signs of impatience. Michael decided to seize the moment. If she gives me a sign, it was meant to be and if not, it wasn't, he told himself. As the two couples were about to go their separate ways, Michael looked at Ana straight in the eyes. On impulse, he blew her a kiss, right then and there, in front of everyone. Ana looked around, embarrassed, trying to ascertain if anyone else had seen his impetuous gesture. Then she looked back at him and smiled, with awkwardness. Michael's heart fluttered with delight. This was the signal he had been awaiting.

Chapter 15

Ana looked over her new painting again. Somehow, everything felt wrong about it: the sinuous forms of the woman; the brightness of her red dress; the smile upon her lips; the sunny, flowing background surrounding her. There was absolutely no darkness or anguish anywhere in sight. What's come over me? she wondered. The doorbell rang, but Ana didn't rush to open the door. It was usually people soliciting money for various causes she didn't support. This time, however, the solicitor must have been really desperate, since they rang the doorbell several times in a row. With an annoyed sigh, Ana lay down her brush and went upstairs to check who it was.

"Michael?" she asked with surprise. How does he know where I live? she wondered. She tried to recall if she had invited him to her house, or perhaps alluded to an invitation. But she couldn't recall any such exchange between them.

"Am I disturbing you?" he asked with a coy smile.

"No, actually, I was just finishing a new painting."

"May I see it?" he spotted an easy overture.

Ana hesitated. It crossed her mind that she didn't know Michael all that well. How much interaction had they had so far? A brief meeting in church, a short exchange at her gallery and a few seconds of conversation at the Renaissance festival, she recalled. Even her close friends called in advance before showing up at her door. "How did you get my address?" she asked him.

"The gallery owner gave it to me. I stopped by there first." That was smooth, Michael thought, always quick to praise his own glib evasions.

Ana recognized this as a lie, since Tracy never gave out her address to strangers. Ordinarily, this deception would have triggered immediate alarms. Yet, strangely, for reasons she couldn't quite fathom, she found herself charmed, even flattered, by the young man's deception, which had an almost charming, naïve transparency.

"Well? May I check out your painting?" Michael asked her.

"Yes, but I have one more question for you. What if my husband would have answered the door instead of me? What would you have said to him?" She asked this question as if by reflex, from an automatic sense of duty, not because the answer mattered all that much to her. Although she realized, of course, that the answer should have mattered, should have mattered *very much*, in fact. Yet, she was aware, even disconcerted, that it meant very little to her at the moment.

"I'd have asked him if you were home."

"And if he asked you why you're here?"

"Geez," he said, good-naturedly. "I wasn't prepared for this interrogation, although I probably should have been."

"Well?"

Boy, she's even sassier than I had her pegged, he thought. "I suppose I'd have told him the truth. That I already purchased one of your paintings and dropped by to see more of your artwork."

In her caution-suppressed state, Ana found this an adequate enough response, for the time being. But she wasn't nearly as impressed with it as Michael was. After all, he could have seen the painting when it was finished, at her gallery, as he had done before.

I'm good, really good, Michael thought. There seems to be no curve ball I can't handle. "So? Can I see it?" he pressed. "Or do you prefer to continue your interrogation?"

Thinking that he didn't lack a sense of humor, Ana relented. "Sure. But it's not done yet. I still have to add a few more touches here and there," she hastened to add, not one to share unfinished work with others. She led her guest to the basement, part of which doubled as her studio. A few easels, several containers of paint and dozens of large sheets of charcoal sketches were strewn all over the floor, turning the area into a veritable obstacle course. "Pardon the mess," she apologized, noticing that Michael was watching his footing.

"I don't mind. It looks more authentic like this," he graciously replied. The part of his brain in charge of seduction, which also happened to be the most developed, went into calculation mode. The messiness of the studio presented him with a great opportunity to find a spot close to Ana and ascertain if she might be receptive to his favorite kind of aesthetic exploration.

"Well, this is it," she pointed to the painting in question.

Michael contemplated the work in silence.

"I've never painted in this style before. I don't know what's come over me lately," she said, almost apologetically.

Michael took a seat in the middle of a sofa, deliberately not leaving her much space. "This painting's much more cheerful than any of the others I've seen by you. It's a refreshing change," he replied, taking note of Ana's slight hesitation before she took a seat next to him. Her knees pressed closely together; her body language expressed nervousness. Better inch towards her slowly. Timing is key, Michael reminded himself.

"Yeah, but this one's lighter in mood and less expressive," Ana implicitly defended her earlier work, in the spirit of a mother who wishes to be fair to all her kids.

"Not necessarily. Happy emotions can be just as important and worthwhile as sad ones." Michael shifted his position, practically eliminating the space between them.

Ana felt somewhat uncomfortable with his proximity, like when people invaded her personal space on a crowded bus. "I'm not so sure about that," she countered, although, as usual, she was quite confident she was right. "That's like saying that comedy is as serious and dramatic as tragedy. Which simply isn't true. Most of the time, comedy's just for entertainment."

"And why is that such a bad thing again?" Michael asked her with a bemused smile. The flirtatiousness in his tone bought him the opportunity to gently stroke Ana's knee, as if verbal intimacy necessarily went along with physical contact.

"Because it's all about having fun," Ana replied, distracted by his touch. She looked down at his hand with some curiosity, struck by his boldness yet hesitant to react. It's just my knee, for goodness' sake, she rationalized. I'm an artist not a prude, she emboldened herself. Yet she remained somewhat ill at ease with Michael's forwardness. Perhaps he was one of those people who believed the stereotype that artists had loose morals. She wanted to make sure that he wouldn't place her in that category. "One shouldn't create art just for fun," she said to him, trying to hint that the same logic applied to romantic encounters. "I think that art should be important, engaging and emotional."

"Can't you do both at once?" Michael asked. "I mean, have your cake and eat it too?"

"You mean combine the light and the serious?" she reformulated his statement.

"If you wish," he conceded. "Or, put differently, have fun while also being serious?" As he said this, his hand moved higher up her leg.

"What's this?" she said, now removing his hand, recovering her composure. "Is it my art or my legs that interest you, Michael?" She noted the playfulness in her tone. Why do I find it so difficult to resist him? she wondered.

"Can't I be interested in both?" he asked with a smile. "Are the two mutually exclusive?" She didn't smile in response. "I'm sorry, Ana. I must have lost my head a little bit."

Ana watched him. She noted an almost chastened expression on his face, which endeared him to her even more. "You made me lose my train of thought. What were we talking about?" She paused for a moment. "Ah yes, I recall. I was saying that in good art and literature the emotion and meaning are more important than the entertainment value."

"I wish you would have informed Shakespeare, Dickens and Balzac about that requirement. Had they known, those poor sops might have achieved something in their lives," Michael taunted her.

"Now that you mention it," she replied in the same bantering manner, "I had a discussion about it with Flaubert and Picasso and saved them from failure just in the nick of time."

Michael's face lit up when he noticed that Ana's demeanor remained flirtatious. "Oh, I see. Then you must perform telekinesis with souls as well. You're a woman of many talents." He leaned forward and brushed her left cheek with the tip of his index finger, "A little paint got on your face," he whispered.

The heat of his breath made her ears tingle, while a pleasant torpor spread all over her body. It would look really bad if Rob came in now from work, it occurred to her. "My husband might come home any minute," she said by way of warning.

Instead of withdrawing, Michael became even more excited by the prospect of rivalry and risk. "We can hear him come in." He shifted towards her and placed his hand behind her head to draw her gently towards him.

Alarmed by his aggressive behavior, Ana removed his hand and promptly stood up. "Please stop. We can't do this."

Michael realized that he had to make a bold conciliatory gesture, otherwise his plans were shot. "Going back to the subject of immortal art, I came by to see if I might purchase another one of your paintings. In fact, just to prove my earlier point, it's the cheerful one I want."

Ana felt reassured by his retreat, which inspired her trust. "You don't have to buy it. I'll give it to you for free," she offered.

"No, I want to buy it," Michael insisted.

"Why?"

"Because giving one's art as a gift, unless you're making a donation to some important museum, tends to lessen its value. And I find nothing cheap about your art," Michael replied, looking at Ana so reverently that she felt he was telling her that he found nothing cheap about her.

"You're definitely right about that!" she confirmed both hypotheses. "Okay, have it your way. You owe me another three thousand bucks." He had managed to put her at ease again, but she wasn't willing to take any more chances. "Would you like to sit out on the deck? It's nice and sunny outside and so dark and gloomy in here."

"I thought you preferred darkness and gloom," Michael remarked.

"Only in my paintings. I try to avoid it whenever possible in real life," Ana replied with a smile. "How about a cup of tea? Or coffee?" she attempted to play the role of the conventional hostess, which, Michael thought, didn't quite suit her.

"No thanks. I'm alright."

When they stepped out, Michael identified one of the few things he liked about Ana's modest, cookie-cutter house. The back yard was surrounded by a little forest, behind which he could see, hidden among the shrubbery and foliage, a delicate little stream. He appreciated this sliver of nature in the midst of the architectural conformity. "I like your yard," he commented, taking a seat on a wicker chair.

"Me too," Ana concurred. "It's actually wetlands. We're not allowed to change it in any way. Not even put a swing in the back yard for the kids. But I prefer it like this." She sat across from him, at a safe distance. "Do you have children?"

"No."

"Are you married?" She recalled that at the Renaissance fair he had introduced Karen by name, without specifying the nature of their relationship.

Michael hesitated before answering her question. For a brief moment, he considered concealing from her the fact that he was sort of engaged to Karen. But, he thought, not telling Ana the truth could backfire. I might appear more threatening to her as a single man. "Not yet. But I'm engaged. To Karen, the woman you met the other day at the Renaissance Festival."

"Congratulations," Ana attempted to sound sincere. From his behavior, she had assumed that Michael was single. Do I want him to be single? she wondered, without carrying the idea to its logical conclusion.

"We may want to have kids some day," Michael said in response to her earlier question. "But for now, we prefer to live more selfishly. You know, without taking on too many extra responsibilities."

"It's a good idea to take a few years to enjoy each other's company."

"Did you and your husband do that?"

"No, we had kids pretty young. Michelle was born a year after we got married, which happened while we were still both in college."

"You decided to have kids young so that you'd have more energy for them, right?"

"Maybe. I'm not sure we thought about it at the time."

"Do you regret it now?"

Ana didn't know how to reply to such a personal question. "There's nothing to regret," she said tensely.

He sensed a note of finality in her tone, like she was putting up her guard against him. Take it nice and slow; don't push your luck, he advised himself. Shortly thereafter, Michael took his leave, not wishing to overstay his welcome.

"Thanks so much for dropping by. It was a pleasure talking to you," Ana adopted a formal manner at the front door, as if the invisible neighbors could be potential witnesses to the young man's unexpected visit. As she closed the door behind him, she didn't know if her heart was pounding from excitement or trepidation.

Chapter 16

When Michael showed up at Ana's house on the following Wednesday, he made sure that 1) he brought his checkbook to purchase her painting, 2) he arrived around lunchtime, and 3) he dressed sharply yet casually, in khaki slacks and a white shirt, looking as clean-cut and non-threatening as possible. When she opened the door, Ana was impressed by how handsome and proper he looked in such a simple outfit. The pale colors and clean lines of his clothes brought out his athletic form. In turn, Michael noticed approvingly that Ana wore a skirt that conveniently flared right above the knees and a button-down with a rounded collar similar to the one he had seen her wear in church on the day they met.

"I seem to have perfect timing. Am I interrupting your work again?"

"No, I was just having lunch," she said, without inviting him in.

He stood there, waiting calmly.

"You have a habit of just dropping by unannounced at people's houses, don't you?" she asked him. Once again, she sensed her own ambivalent reaction to his brazenness, feeling simultaneously flattered and repelled by it.

"As a matter of fact, I don't usually do that. But... I hope you don't take this the wrong way... for some reason I feel so at ease with you, Ana. I see no point in being formal with each other," he said warmly.

Neither do I, Ana thought, appeased. "Would you like to join me for lunch?" she invited him in. She led her guest into a modest dining room, furnished with a simple wooden table and chairs. Michael surveyed the meal already set on the table: fresh plum tomatoes, French baguette and baba ghanoush, a Greek eggplant dish.

"For some strange reason, I still prefer the foods I had as a child in Romania. My grandmother used to make this amazing eggplant dish. It's called *salata de vinete.*"

"That's some kind of salad, right?"

"Eggplant salad," she confirmed. "Would you like to try it?"

"Sure, I'd love to."

Ana went into the kitchen to get him an extra plate, glass and set of silverware.

"Actually, I've had this before with pita bread," Michael said as soon as he saw the dish. As Ana busied herself placing some of the eggplant salad upon his plate, the young man scooted his chair closer to her. "Do you miss Romania?" he asked her, meticulously spreading some of the eggplant salad on a slice of bread.

"I'm kind of ambivalent about it. I've had some good experiences there and some very bad ones as well." She sliced a tomato on his plate.

"You mean because of the Ceausescu regime?"

Ana put the knife down on the table. "That plus the revolution, which led to my parents' death. But even afterwards, I went through a difficult time."

He saw she looked uncomfortable. "I didn't mean to pry."

To change the subject, Ana suggested a different way of eating the dish. "You can also try putting some of the eggplant on a slice of tomato. Or, better yet, dip the tomato into the eggplant. That's how peasants used to eat it in my country."

Michael followed her lead. "Mmm, it's pretty good like this." He covered another slice with eggplant dip and offered it to Ana. She closed her eyes to better savor the flavor. Then it was his turn again. Ana slipped a slice of tomato into his mouth. She had almost forgotten how such simple acts could bring so much delight.

"What about the baba ghanoush?" he reminded her.

"Oops, I forgot!" But the next time she didn't. To show him just how attentive she was, she even wiped a few tomato seeds from his chin with a paper napkin. He noticed that she was examining his face with curiosity. "Why are you looking at me like that? Do I still have food on my chin?"

"No, I was just wondering..." she began, but didn't finish her sentence. Everything about Michael—his forwardness, his sensuality, his gestures, even his good looks—struck her as, somehow, too slick and smooth, which simultaneously repelled and attracted her. *In both high school and college, Ana thought with a hint of pride, I managed to avoid men like him.*

"About what?" Michael prodded her.

"I'm not sure it's polite to ask."

"You can ask me anything you like."

"Are you a seducer?" Ana asked him point-blank. *Polite or not, it's better to let him know that I've got him figured out, she told herself.*

Michael couldn't help but laugh at the bluntness of her question. "What makes you say that?"

"I don't know. The way you look. The way you act. The way you look at me. You strike me as the seducer type."

Michael shifted in his seat, deciding how much information to disclose. "I was before, but I'm not anymore," he replied, his tone ambiguously suspended between the repentance Karen expected of him and the boasting manner he assumed with his buddies.

"When was that? Yesterday?" Ana quipped, coming much closer to the truth than she realized.

Michael acted wounded by her comment. "I went through a period when I had something to prove," he explained, assuming an introspective demeanor.

"To whom?" she leaned slightly forward, intrigued by his apparent honesty.

"Mostly to myself." He noticed a blend of sympathy and curiosity in her expression.

"You wanted to prove your virility?"

The way Ana had pronounced the word "virility," slightly rolling the r, triggered his desire. "I suppose. But mostly, I just wanted to prove to myself that I could get over someone."

"Who? Your fiancée?"

"No. This girl I dated back in college. Her name is Amy. She was my first love, I guess."

"You guess? You mean you don't know?"

Michael looked away, then back at Ana, as if about to reveal something still painful to him. "She left me for another guy." After a brief pause, he added, "She's the one who cheated on me yet she called me a snake. It took me months to get over her. But once I did, I kind of went overboard and started dating dozens of women."

"Dozens?" Ana repeated with alarm. *Then she recalled how many of her acquaintances in college played the field, as people tend to say. If you don't date a lot during college, when can you enjoy your youth and have some fun? And how are you supposed to know that you found the right person, without comparing?* she asked herself, becoming aware once again of her growing dissatisfaction with her marriage. *I've only dated seriously one man and we got married young. Maybe that was a mistake, she now speculated. But what in the world* motivated Michael to go to the opposite extreme? "Was that the only way you could get over the rejection?" She was intrigued by the tension between the young man's sensitive demeanor and the cavalier behavior he had just described.

"Maybe so. Some people drown out their sorrow with drink. I drowned out mine with women."

Ana considered for a moment the comparison. "This sounds like some kind of addiction," she observed. Do people ever overcome those? she wondered, recalling the popular saying that once an alcoholic, always an alcoholic. "When did you stop doing that?" She hoped he'd reply years ago.

"When I met you," Michael said instead, thinking that she'd feel flattered.

Ana, however, focused on a different angle. "So you've been cheating on your fiancée all along?" she leaned back in her seat, repelled by his confession.

"I had a lot of pent-up anger inside," he tried to explain.

"You mean because of what your first girlfriend did to you?" she asked, puzzled.

"At first, I cheated partly out of vengeance. And maybe also to overcome the rejection. But then I started having fun with it," he replied, knowing from experience that sporadic admissions of misbehavior were often confused with total honesty.

"But why couldn't you be faithful to Karen? After all, she wasn't the one who cheated on you. Or was she?" Ana pursued, feeling that Michael's behavior didn't speak well of his character yet also hoping that his explanation would resolve all the apparent contradictions in his story.

"No, she wasn't."

"Then why did you do it?"

"I don't know. I mean, clearly I'm to blame. I've been a jerk to her," Michael sounded genuinely contrite. "The truth of the matter is that Karen was never the right woman for me," he added, gazing steadily into Ana's eyes, as if to hint that she, herself, might be the one he had been looking for all along. "It's tough to explain," he went on. "Karen's nice, don't get me wrong. But she's very cold in temperament. I tried for almost two years to get her to warm up to me. I did everything I could to make her be affectionate. Unfortunately, it was a thankless task. For the longest time, she didn't even want to live with me, even though we were already engaged. She decided to live with her parents."

Ana didn't say anything, but looked unsympathetic. So what? she asked herself. Some people prefer to move in with their partners after getting married. That doesn't warrant cheating on them. It occurred to her that Michael was offering intimate details about his relationship with Karen to impress her and awaken her sympathy. I sure wouldn't want to be in his fiancée's shoes! she said to herself. What woman would appreciate being used as a pick-up line for another woman?

Reading disapproval in her expression, Michael continued his narrative. "Plus Karen's often in a bad mood. Come to think of it, I've rarely seen that woman happy. Her own nephew prefers me to her," he boasted with an obvious sense of satisfaction. "Whenever I show up at her sister's house, he lights up.

Even though I tend to play rough with him. You know, to make him into a more manly man. I toss him up into the air and catch him, then throw him over my shoulder. We like to horse around, the way dads do with their sons," he added with a faraway look in his eyes, to hint that he was secretly yearning for a family of his own.

In spite of her reservations, Ana had a quick mental image of Michael tossing her own son into the air, playfully, just as he had described. Then she came back to Earth again. "But then, why didn't you break up with Karen? I mean, once you figured out that the two of you aren't compatible?"

"I guess because I always hoped, and maybe still do, that by being nice and warm and loving to her, I can get her to reciprocate."

"One of the first things we're told as adolescents is that you shouldn't go into a relationship hoping to change the person you love. It's a futile task," Ana pointed out.

Michael peered into her eyes: "Did you remember that advice when you married your husband?"

Ana felt his gaze drill straight through her, exposing her insecurities and dissatisfactions. "I suppose not," she conceded.

"What makes you say that?" he probed further.

"Rob's very busy with his work," she replied, wanting to open up to him without getting too personal. "It doesn't leave him much free time for our family."

"Don't I wish I had that problem!" Michael exclaimed. "Karen's just the opposite. Always on my back. Very clingy. Without me, she's a lost soul."

"Maybe that's because you cheated on her, so she doesn't trust you anymore," Ana speculated.

"No doubt that's got something to do with it," he sheepishly agreed. "Although she doesn't even know the full extent of it. She's only caught me twice." He tried to repress a mischievous grin, but it twitched at the corners of his mouth.

I knew he was a player! Ana told herself. Yet she remained intrigued by the titillating possibility of a life of pleasure, with no responsibilities and moral boundaries; the very opposite of the life she led. "Just how many other women have there been?" she asked him.

"Too many," Michael replied with deliberate vagueness. "But I assure you that if Karen had been warm and loving to me, there would have been *zero*," he emphasized. "I did my best to improve our relationship. As they say, a tiger doesn't change its stripes."

What about your stripes? Ana thought looking at him. Could you ever be faithful if you fell in love? But she couldn't really ask him such a question, since he might interpret it as an overture. "How come none of your efforts to improve your relationship helped the situation?" she inquired instead.

Michael shrugged. "How do you reinvest value in a relationship that has pretty much lost its value?"

"By working on it," Ana fell back upon common wisdom.

"Yeah, but you need to have something to work with."

"And you didn't?"

Michael shook his head. "I guess not enough. If there's anything I've learned from this whole experience with Karen is that if a relationship requires work, it's not worth saving."

Thinking of her own marriage, Ana identified with Michael's sentiment. But then another explanation occurred to her. "Are you afraid of being alone?"

"What do you mean?"

"Without a girlfriend."

"I can have any woman I want!" he boasted defensively. "I haven't been single since the age of fifteen."

"Which kind of confirms what I said," Ana insisted, looking into his eyes with gentleness. "Solitude must frighten you."

"It's hard to tell," Michael decided to go with the flow of her sympathetic explanation. "Because, like I said, I've never been alone. I've had so many women that I lost count," he said in a neutral tone, this time not bragging, just making a factual observation.

"But you still seem to want to hold on to Karen," Ana emphasized, thinking to herself, why would a man need a steady girlfriend, if all he wants to do is cheat on her? The answer to this question seemed obvious to her. "Which means that you need a level of intimacy in your life that isn't possible with one night stands. Otherwise, casual relationships would suffice, wouldn't they? You wouldn't need to work so hard on your relationship with Karen."

Michael saw her observation as a perfect opening. "To tell you the truth, Ana, for so many years I've been waiting for the real deal. I want the whole package. Love, lust and friendship, all rolled up into one."

"Then how come you didn't get attached to any of the other women you dated?"

He smiled at her naiveté. "It's just like a woman to ask such a question. For men, sexual intimacy doesn't imply emotional attachment."

"I know that, of course," Ana agreed, embarrassed to show her inexperience. "But still, what I find a bit unusual, is that out of so many women you were dating, none of them attracted you in particular. I mean as human beings, not just physically."

"It's not what I wanted at the time. I wasn't looking for love. For that, I already had Karen."

Ana contemplated his answer in silence, attempting to grasp his curious mix of detachment and attachment to his fiancée.

"What women don't realize," Michael pursued, moving away from the domain of ethics and emotion, which made him viscerally uncomfortable, to that of erotic pleasure, with which he was completely at ease, "is that for men, each woman's body is different. They all have the same basic parts, or at least one hopes they do. But each woman has a unique shape and feel and ways of touching and kissing and all that's very exciting." Ana stared fixedly at him, entranced. "I mean, this may seem trivial because it's so obviously true, but in a way it's not, because it's part of why men fool around. You see," Michael continued in a confidential manner, "each woman has different kinds of breasts, some pear shaped, some round, some very small like little peaches, others elongated and ripe like bananas," he said, making light of his own hedonistic sensuality. "The same thing applies to other parts of the body. The hips, the legs," he suggestively lowered his gaze to her knees, since Ana's legs were covered by her skirt.

Realizing that their conversation was becoming too intimate, Ana shifted away from him, as if his glance had physically touched her. "I don't see the appeal of having sex with lots of people," she said.

"How do you know if you like it or not? Have you ever tried it?"

"No, because I never wanted to. You don't have to bang your head against the wall to know it hurts."

"So you've only been with your husband?"

"Basically, so far, I've only had two boyfriends. Well, the first one wasn't really my boyfriend. And then, once I came to America, I met Rob. In my country, we used to take virginity seriously," Ana said with a sense of national pride that made Michael smile.

"Why do you use the past tense?"

"Because after the fall of communism, everything changed in Romania. Now people are just as dissolute there as they are here," she replied wistfully.

"I'm glad you don't believe in cultural stereotypes."

"I just tell it like it is."

There was something about Ana's earlier statement, however, that aroused Michael's curiosity. "What did you mean when you said that your first boyfriend wasn't one?"

She fluttered her hand, to wave off the unpleasant memory. "I had a pretty bad experience."

"How so?"

"A neighbor did something to me against my will."

Michael's eyes flickered, but his tone remained calm. "He raped you?"

"When I was twelve," Ana said quietly, averting her gaze. When she turned towards Michael again, he saw tears glimmering in her eyes. "If you don't mind, I prefer not to talk about this. If I could take a magic pill to forget that part of my past forever, I'd do it in an instant," she declared heatedly.

"I understand."

"Would you like strawberries for desert?" Ana once again relied on food to change the subject. "We also have apples and blueberries."

"I'd love some strawberries, thanks."

"I could never be seduced," she announced seemingly out of the blue, returning to the table with a bowl of fruit. It struck her that her statement must have sounded absurd, given that she must have seemed pretty receptive to his overtures. But that was precisely why she felt the need to articulate some clear boundaries.

"Oh yeah?" he responded to her comment as if it were a dare.

"I don't put myself in those situations. For one thing, I don't like promiscuity. I never go out to bars."

"Not all seduction takes place in bars. And not all of it leads to sleeping around," Michael objected. "Sometimes you focus on just one person," he fixed her with his glance, which was warm and reassuring.

"Even so, I don't fall for men's fake pickup lines," Ana held her ground.

"But seduction isn't always fake," Michael countered.

"Yeah, well, seducers tend to be transparent in their purposes," she maintained.

"And what are those, might I ask?" he asked with a bemused smile, finding her frankness girlish and cute.

"To get as many women as possible into their beds." Now he'll back off, since I've called him on his moves, Ana thought with satisfaction.

She obviously didn't lie about not having much experience with men, Michael observed with satisfaction. She doesn't even realize that it's rarely in their beds. More often than not, it's in the back alley behind the bar or restaurant; in the backseat of a car; at the movie theater; in a train; in the Men's Room, even in a freaking' church, he recalled just a few of his favorite venues. We'll see if she's as immune to seduction as she claims, he told himself. "It doesn't have to be about scoring. Sometimes it's about something much more special and magical. Like falling in love," he said out loud.

"Perhaps, but that's entirely out of anyone's hands. You can't command love," she expressed this truism with an air of wisdom.

"I can't argue with that," he concurred.

Ana realized that she had opened up to Michael about aspects of her life that she hadn't even shared with some of her closest friends. I can't explain why I'm so at ease with this man, she searched for an explanation. In the past, I've avoided such "cool dudes" like the plague. But something's different about him, she told herself, without being able to identify the reasons behind her inexplicable attraction. "You know, I'm pretty surprised by how easily I can communicate with you," she avowed. "Usually, I don't open up that easily to people I don't know well."

"I feel exactly the same way about you," Michael reciprocated, taking her words of encouragement as his cue to take the next step. He leaned over to offer her a strawberry, placing it close to her mouth. Once her lips wrapped around the red fruit, he felt a wave of warmth ripple through him.

Are you going to run away from pleasure all your life? A voice inside of Ana's head urged her to stop watching on the sidelines and finally taste life again. With a trembling hand, she returned the favor, slipping a strawberry into his mouth.

Michael was so distracted by other agreeable sensations that he could barely taste its tart sweetness. "It tastes even better when you close your eyes. That way you can focus all your attention on just one sense," he suggested.

Ana hesitated.

"Come on!" he urged her. "Consider this an experiment. I promise it will taste better."

This time the young woman obediently closed her eyes and parted her lips as Michael gently placed the tip of the strawberry into the oval of her mouth. She consumed it gradually, in little bites, then reopened her eyes.

"Don't cheat! Keep your eyes closed," he whispered playfully into her ear, pressing the lower lobe between his lips, to warm her up with the heat of his breath. She quivered slightly. Encouraged, he gently caressed her waist and hip with his free hand, then fed her the strawberry with the other. He placed his lips upon hers and instead of a strawberry, he fed her the softness of his tongue, which she devoured with the same eagerness with which she had consumed the delicious fruit. As they were kissing, his fingers grazed the slightly humid fabric of her underwear, stroking it gently, until the wetness of her mouth became one with the moistness of her desire. Just as he was about to probe the situation further, however, Ana shifted away, obliging him to change focus. He brushed her long hair aside as his lips traveled down to explore the delicate curve of her neck, which made her twitch and protest that she was ticklish. Heeding her objection, Michael skillfully unbuttoned the young woman's shirt to reveal the voluptuous softness of her breasts, which he cupped into both hands. He began kissing them, taking each nipple into his mouth to taste it until it hardened to perfection.

I can't believe I'm doing this, Ana thought, feeling like she had become two different people through this sensual experience. It's as if part of her remained a prudent woman, a mother and wife, and another part, which she had struggled to repress for so long, completely overtook her senses and imagination. Only an external intervention could resolve this inner conflict. "Michael, please! We can't be doing this. My husband could come in any minute. He sometimes eats lunch at home," Ana pushed his head away, her face flushed with a mixture of arousal and alarm.

"We'll hear the front door if anybody comes in."

"We can't be doing this," she repeated more firmly.

"Okay," Michael gave in to her wishes, as before. His gaze passed with a territorial pride over her warm brown eyes, the soft lips he had just tasted, the pale breasts that seemed made for the hollow of his hands. In Ana's presence, Michael felt like he had just awakened from a long period of sedation. In one fell swoop, she had managed to reignite his senses as if, somehow, he hadn't fully tasted food, or felt pleasure or truly loved a woman before they met.

Chapter 17

Karen's fingers ran rapidly over the computer keyboard. "Michael Rogers," she typed in her fiancé's name into the search engine. She found about half a million entries ascribed to that name, 99.9 percent of which, she surmised, weren't about him. Having neither the time nor the patience to look over all of them, Karen narrowed down the search to "Michael Rogers," "Detroit, MI." She quickly located nearly a hundred entries on her fiancé. She read each and every one of them carefully, sifting through for some personal information that could function as a hook to liven up their conversations. For the past few weeks—in fact, ever since they got back together—Michael struck her as exceedingly absentminded. Although he still asked her about how her day went, often she had to repeat the same information several times and call out, "Earth to Michael, Earth to Michael!" before he actually paid any attention. Which left Karen completely baffled, since she was telling him things that, in her estimation, he should have been happy to hear.

She was taken aback, on the previous evening, when her announcement that she had lost the extra weight was greeted by an empty stare and a flatly delivered "Great." That's it? Karen asked herself, upset by Michael's obvious lack of interest. She had to remind herself to calm down before she said, in her best impersonation of a suggestive voice, "If I lose five more pounds, I'll be fitting into that sexy black lace teddy you gave me on Valentine's Day."

A vision of Ana in the black negligee crossed Michael's mind. "I'm impressed by how consistent you've been with your exercise program this time around," he remarked.

"Yeah. I've been doing four hours of exercise a day. I divide it up between cardio, yoga and weight lifting, so that it doesn't get too monotonous," she replied, encouraged by his sign of approval.

"How are your knees? Do they still hurt?" He listlessly shifted the food upon his plate.

"No. I'm giving them a break by swimming instead of walking this week, remember?" Karen couldn't believe her eyes. Here he was swishing around the meal that had taken her over two hours to prepare. Earlier that afternoon, she had made him fresh yellow fin grilled tuna with seared potatoes, green beans, tomatoes, black olives, anchovies and garlic, covered in a fancy Dijon vinaigrette. Now all that was left of her culinary masterpiece was the dark yellow sauce mixed with the colorful vegetables making a chaotic abstract expressionist painting upon the whiteness of the plate. "Don't you like the fish? It's very fresh," she assured him.

"It's delicious," Michael said, demonstratively taking a bite. "But I'm not that hungry. I had a big lunch."

"Where did you go?"

"I went to this Greek restaurant on campus where I had some baba ghanoush," he conveniently incorporated the actual meal he had with Ana.

"You like eggplant? Then I'll make you an eggplant dish for tomorrow!" Karen offered, glad to have found an easy way to please him. As luck would have it, she had just learned a new recipe for Mediterranean vegetable casserole. In fact, following her mother's motto that the way to a man's heart was through his stomach, ever since they had gotten back together, Karen had thrown herself headlong into cooking, using most of her free time to prepare his favorite meals.

She had learned how to make veal scallops; sautéed beef tenderloin with black pepper; sautéed chicken, along with all sorts of pasta dishes filled with fresh herbs and vegetables, healthy and delicious, just the way he liked it.

"I won't love you any less if you don't spend hours a day cooking for me," he commented, adding to himself, nor any more.

"I know, but I like cooking. And, more importantly, you like eating," she replied with an ingratiating smile.

"That's nice of you," Michael replied, having abandoned the effort to change her. You either love a person as she is or you don't, he recalled the conversation he had with Ana. Ever since they began living together, he was struck by Karen's dry, methodical manner, which he couldn't help but contrast with Ana's freshness and spontaneity. Whenever Karen set her mind to any goal, she threw herself into it with a determination that he had never encountered in anyone else. Out of all of the American women he had met through the French program at the university, Karen was the only one who spoke French like a native. "Did you have a hot French boyfriend?" he had asked her when they first began dating. "No," she replied. "I watched T.V. a lot and posted vocabulary words all over the apartment, to make sure that I absorbed the language and its correct pronunciation." In retrospect, Michael found this approach typical of Karen. Only she would go to France, the country of romance, and instead of finding herself a nice native boyfriend, or at least a couple of friends, she spent the year decorating her apartment with vocabulary words. Everything she does, he observed in retrospect, has method but no madness. Michael couldn't help but smile when he recalled her innuendo about the black lace teddy. Had he shown any enthusiasm for it, he was willing to bet that Karen would buy a dozen different items of lingerie. Her pliability to his will flattered him. But none of her compulsive behavior, he thought, could make up for the quality she lacked, which he had in excess: an insatiable appetite for pleasure, which could be best summarized as *joie de vivre.*

"Why are you grinning at me like that?" Karen asked, noticing his smirk.

"I was just thinking about how when you put your mind to something, you really do it. Like the way you learned French."

"That much is true," Karen replied, pleased that Michael seemed to appreciate her drive. He'll never find someone like me, she told herself. Nobody will love him like I do or put as much effort into our relationship. The problem was, it occurred to her, that what should have been smooth and easy now took so much energy. The effort to please him left her feeling drained and insecure at the end of the day. And yet, she couldn't imagine any desirable alternatives. The break-up with Michael had made her realize that she didn't want to spend her life without him. It's not even that I'm scared of being alone, Karen gazed wistfully at Michael. It's just that I want him and nobody else. She had seen what other men were like. Her own father was an alcoholic who neglected his wife. His sister's husband behaved like an overgrown frat. boy, who preferred leering at women, beer and sports to spending time with his wife. That's what most men become after a few years of marriage, Karen extrapolated. Michael was different. It's true that he enjoyed leering at women and drinking beer as much as the next guy. But at the same time, he also had manners, could be as sensitive as a woman and liked to engage in meaningful conversation. This train of thought led Karen to attempt to probe, once again, those deeper layers of their psyches. Which is why she decided the following morning to do a little research on her fiancé and find out more about his past activities. That way, she hoped, Michael would be more interested in their communication. Besides, she thought somewhat cynically, how could I possibly go wrong with this strategy? Everybody likes to talk about themselves.

Earlier that day, when she looked over the entries on Michael, she discovered that he did cross country and track in both high school and college. But she already knew that. Besides, what can one say about it? Since nothing particularly interesting occurred to her, she moved on to the entries that linked to a few articles Michael had published during grad. school. She found one essay on Flaubert, one on Marivaux and one on Rousseau, all in scholarly journals that focused on French literature and culture. Unfortunately, that field was so antiquated and impractical that, quite frankly, it didn't capture her imagination. Rousseau put her to sleep, Flaubert sounded cheesy and she hadn't even read Marivaux. As Karen was about to turn off the computer feeling disappointed that she hadn't come up with a single intriguing subject of conversation for that evening, she had an epiphany. Why don't I ask him about why he doesn't want to get a doctorate and become a French professor rather than a high school teacher? That way we'll keep the conversation focused on him, to help him figure out what he wants to do with his life, which he'll no doubt appreciate.

Just to make sure that everything went according to plan, Karen slipped on a little black dress and put on the high heels that Michael had given her for her birthday. She then set the table for the meal she had prepared earlier that morning, which was so French that it would make Michael feel like he was being transported straight to Paris. For an appetizer, she planned, they'd have escargots in a puff pastry shell with shallots, garlic, white wine, chives, butter with a hint of pernod; followed by a salade nicoise that combined fresh vegetables, tuna, tomatoes, a hard-boiled egg, anchovies and olives. The main course, her tour de force, consisted of the eggplant dish she had promised him on the previous evening, made with fresh eggplant, roasted peppers, onions and garlic, slices of zucchini and tomato and fresh herbs topped with Parmesan cheese. Initially, her strategy worked.

"Wow, you've become quite a chef lately!" Michael praised her as soon as they sat down at the table.

Karen smiled with satisfaction and poured him a glass of *Merlot*. She decided that the moment was right to broach the subject of conversation she had prepared in advance. "You know, I looked up your name on the internet today," she informed him.

Oh, oh, I wonder what dirt she dug up, Michael thought, becoming slightly apprehensive.

"I was struck by the fact that I found no entries on you since a year ago. Before, you were publishing articles regularly," Karen observed.

Michael breathed a sigh of relief. So I'm not in trouble, he concluded. "That's because I published those essays when I was taking grad. seminars and had to write papers for them," he explained. "Since the work was already done for the classes, I figured I might as well send the essays off to journals and get a few articles under my belt."

"But why did you stop writing all of a sudden?"

Michael looked at her with an air of incredulity: "Didn't you notice that I'm teaching now?"

"Any interest in pursuing a Ph.D. in French?" Karen assumed the patient tone of a career counselor.

"Nope," Michael said, taking a bite of his salad. "None whatsoever," he said with his mouth full.

"Why not? You'd make a wonderful college professor."

Michael looked at his fiancée, her head slightly cocked, a patronizing look imprinted upon her features. How many times had he explained to her that what he loved about his job was the teaching part, the human contact—preferably of the female persuasion—rather than contributing to some irrelevant scholarly dispute about how many angels can fit on the pin of a needle? She listens without really hearing me. "Like I said before, I want to be a teacher," he repeated. "I like the people contact too much to waste my time like a geek in some dusty library doing useless research to write articles nobody cares to read."

Seeing his dismissive reaction to her constructive suggestion, Karen's patience began to wear thin. She focused on the only part of his reply that was relevant to her: "People contact? Is that what you call it?" She looked down at her plate and realized she lost her appetite.

During the rest of the evening, Karen refused to speak to Michael. She retreated into the guest room, to punish him for the curt manner he had assumed with her during supper. Why do I put up with this? she asked herself, her heart overflowing with self-pity. Yet when her fiancé knocked on the door to apologize, Karen's anger quickly dissipated. Perhaps I'm overreacting, she told herself. After all, Michael knows what he wants and what he doesn't want from life. Who am I to tell him what to do? "I was only making a suggestion, trying to be helpful," she said, in her own defense.

"I know, Baby. I shouldn't have jumped on you like that." Even this minimal show of contrition touched her. As often before, following moments of tension, Karen went over Michael's attributes to persuade herself that continuing to work on their relationship was well worth the effort. After all, she reminded herself, he's a good man. He listens to me. He's handsome and desirable. He's charming and fun. He can be so sweet when he wants to be. And I'm doing my best to be interesting and attractive too. Yet, the fundamental problem remained: none of that seemed to make that much of a difference in their relationship.

That night, in bed, the couple slept back to back, a pattern initiated by Karen to avoid stimulating Michael's frequent nocturnal arousal. But lately she'd have given just about anything to be able to turn him on as easily as before. I've lost weight, she kept repeating to herself, dumbfounded by the fact that finally being in shape didn't spin their world around. Does he still love me? she wondered. She really wanted to believe that he did. Yet, at the same time, Karen felt apprehensive, as if trapped in an endless labyrinth. For some incomprehensible reason, every path she pursued in their relationship eventually turned into a dead-end. No matter how I dress; how I look; how much I exercise; how pleasant I am; how much I care about him; what I cook; what I read; what I do for him, in the end, none of it matters. She began to feel like a lab rat caught in a twisted experiment, where she had to run faster, spin the wheel harder, only to get rewarded less and less frequently with a tiny pellet of Michael's affection, the emotional fuel that was keeping her alive.

Despite her self-doubt, Karen threw herself headlong into the frenetic fervor of a desperate optimism. Sometimes she felt like a novel heroine struggling to reverse the direction of the river of indifference that was engulfing their lopsided relationship. When each and every effort failed, in the moments of deepest despair when she was drowning in waves of self-pity, Karen found the sole consolation that gave her the patience to reclaim the affection of the man she loved. I must have hurt him so badly when I broke up with him, she turned the blame upon herself. Paradoxically, whenever she could see herself as the main source of their problems, Karen felt empowered, as if the solution also lay in her hands. Maybe I should discuss our earlier breakup and apologize to him, so that we can finally put that whole nightmare behind us, she resolved that night. She turned towards Michael and tapped him on the shoulder.

Although awake and struggling with his own demons, Michael remained perfectly still curled up in a fetal position, hoping that Karen would think he was sound asleep. He was troubled by Ana's reticence, which he had encountered in dozens of women and which, quite frankly, had never daunted him before. In this case, however, he hesitated. On the one hand, being aware of Ana's difficult past, he didn't want to force his way into her life in a manner that might sabotage their budding relationship. On the other hand, he feared jeopardizing the progress they had made. As Woody Allen once said, a relationship's like a shark. It either moves forward or dies. Which is why, Michael sensed, they couldn't afford to flounder too long in ambiguity, neither lovers nor friends. He had been in that situation before and knew exactly how the story would end. Friendship would displace the attraction, the forward momentum would be lost and indifference would efface the incomparable excitement of falling in love.

Chapter 18

During the past few days, Ana couldn't work. No matter how much she tried to focus on painting, she was distracted by thoughts of Michael. She recalled his long eyelashes shading the mischievous glimmer of his dark eyes. The curve of his jaw, well defined and masculine, still invited her to trace it with the tip of her fingers. His full lips still tasted like the strawberries they had shared for lunch. The smell of his hair when he drew close to kiss her, with its fresh scent of soap free of any overpowering fragrance, still made her feel weak at the knees. And his voice—low, quiet and hypnotic—still echoed in her ears. She closed her eyes, hoping to draw the curtain on this fugue of memories. In the tranquility of darkness, however, they became more vivid, making her heart race with thoughts of him. Even the love songs on the radio, no matter how corny and trite, triggered in her a dreamy mood that dissipated her concentration like smoke.

Ana didn't know what attitude to adopt towards her own emotions. On the one hand, she hoped that, magically, their relationship would become one of those platonic romances of the heart and soul that famous poets wrote about during the nineteenth-century. On the other hand, every time the phone rang she jumped to answer it, hoping it was he. She'd have liked their friendship to deepen without gaining momentum, returning to a level of ambiguity that would excite them without troubling her conscience or unsettling her life.

When the phone rang, Ana hastened to pick it up after only one ring. "Hello?" she answered breathlessly.

"Have you been out jogging?" she heard Michael's friendly voice.

"No, I just ran to the phone hoping it was you," she confessed.

For a second, Michael was caught off balance by her frankness. "You might be disappointed. I didn't call to buy another painting," he quickly recovered.

"Oh, I don't care about that."

"Good," he approved. "Because I was calling to see if you might be interested in meeting me somewhere for lunch tomorrow." *A little ambiguity of location never hurts. Who knows? She might even agree to come by my place,* he speculated.

"I'd love to. I know this really good restaurant on State Street. It's called *Zanzibar*. Have you heard of it?"

All right, I guess it will have to be somewhere else, Michael conceded. *But there's no reason why a little action couldn't follow lunch.* "Sure. I've eaten there a couple of times. How does noonish sound? We could meet in front of the restaurant."

"Sounds good." After she hung up the phone, Ana's emotions oscillated between anticipation and apprehension. She was glad that she'd get to see Michael again. But she feared that the dangerous course their relationship had taken could not be easily reversed. *I can stop this now,* she nevertheless told herself. *I could call him back and tell him that I can't make it to our lunch date. Or I could go out to lunch with him and act friendly, without crossing any boundaries. I've done this so many times with men before. Why am I behaving so differently with him? Am I ready for more?* Ana wondered, not really sure yet what "more" meant, yet not able to calm the restlessness within.

Her thoughts turned to her husband, in search of an external restraint once again. Rob was loyal, hardworking, responsible and faithful. More importantly, he was a great father to their kids. What more could I want from a man? Ana asked herself, surprised by her own lack of fulfillment. When did our love dissipate? she tried to recall. No point of origin came to mind, but she had a distinct impression of how long it had been absent. For years now, when Rob asked her about her day, he didn't even look into her eyes. It's as if, to him, "How are you?" were a routine greeting between strangers, not a genuine question between partners. She had long given up trying to engage him. She recognized the look of a cornered animal upon his face whenever she talked to him about anything that interested her. "I'm tired of your egocentrism," Rob burst out on a number of occasions when she tried to talk to him about her dreams and struggles as an artist.

Only once she had given up hope in their love did Rob finally notice its absence. He proposed getting a babysitter and establishing a date night once a week, to reinvigorate their marriage. During those supposedly romantic dinners, they struggled to find subjects of conversation. The recent elections. Universal healthcare. The war in the Middle East. Yet none of that seemed to matter. Real conversation is like a pebble thrown into a sea of ideas, Ana mused. It doesn't matter which topic you choose, nothing makes any waves if it doesn't begin from a center—a fascination with one another—which expands like a wave into a concentric pattern of interest in other aspects of the world. Their conversations, she recalled, landed nowhere. It was as if the pebbles were thrown randomly on a beach and sank into the warm sand without making a sound. Each one came and went unnoticed, forgettable and forgotten.

Even the guilty feelings she tried to summon by thinking of her husband only left her with the impression of a void bridged, but never quite filled, by the common love for their kids. Which is what counts most, Ana reminded herself. Yet at the same time, she felt that just about any man who was currently in love with her would be better than a man who used to be in love with her. She couldn't help but wonder if all romantic relationships begin with the heat of mutual interest and dissolve into the coolness of detachment, which becomes noticeable only once it's much too late to revive a dying love.

Chapter 19

Michael parked his car in the lot closest to *Zanzibar*, the restaurant where he and Ana had agreed to meet for lunch. Although usually fearless, he felt strangely nervous, as if this single encounter would determine everything between them. He checked his watch. The hour of their rendezvous was approaching. He hesitated between allowing their relationship to take its natural course, whatever that turned out to be, and taking charge of the situation, which conformed better to his nature. A sense of fatalism displaced his ambivalence. I'll follow her signal, he resolved.

As he opened the car door to get out, he saw Ana walking towards him. Her face was flushed with anticipation. She doesn't look like a woman who wants to be just friends, Michael told himself. As she approached to kiss him on the cheek, he moved his mouth slightly to the left and planted a kiss on her lips. He savored the minty flavor of her tongue. She's just brushed her teeth for me, Michael noted, feeling emboldened by this little detail. Before Ana had time to pull away, his hands were already upon the straps of her tank top. He lowered them to expose her breasts, which he hungrily greeted with his mouth.

When Ana began to protest, Michael instantly moved up, his mouth once again planted upon hers. Since that act didn't put a stop to the flutter of her nervous movements and semi-coherent objections—"Michael," "married woman," "my kids," "husband," "restaurant," "in public"—with one swift motion he swirled her body around and pinned her hands upon the hood of his car. His torso held hers in place while his lips became glued to her ear. "Don't worry, nobody can see us here," "He never has to find out," "We're all alone," he enticed her. Yet all she heard, all that truly mattered to her at the moment, was his low murmur, "How I want you, Ana, my love." Then suddenly the soft caresses were replaced by quick slaps on her bare skin. She was struck by the clement brutality of that gesture. He had not used full force. All she sensed was the titillating contrast between his tenderness and roughness. "Au, why did you do that?" she cried out. Michael delivered his reply with the heat of his breath: "So you're trying to make my life more difficult?" he said tugging demonstratively at the lowered layers of protection—panties, pantyhose and skirt—that separated his body from hers.

Then Ana felt a dull pain inside as he thrust his way in with no further preamble, following his own preferred rhythm, fast in, slow out, until she felt concentric waves of desire disperse from that focal point to her legs, her knees and her chest. Even her grasping hands were trembling upon the warm hood of the car. Light is a particle yet functions a wave, Ana recalled a basic principle of physics. Now, feeling concentric circles of expanding desire, she understood much better what that meant. Each time Michael penetrated her, a particle lost in the ocean of her pleasure, she felt that focal point of desire expand with the resonant frequencies of consecutive waves. Her senses exploded with scattered, disorienting emotions that intermingled pleasure and pain, desire and regret.

When Ana turned around, Michael kissed her cheek, her forehead, her mouth, even her eyelids, with the unspeakable reverence that only a hedonist can have for the privileged object of his desire. "You're so beautiful and you're mine now," he said to her. His fingertips traced the graceful flow of her curves. He felt too moved by the experience to enjoy the sense of triumph he usually reveled in after conquering a woman. He was still under the spell of the tactile impression of her skin, of the warm moistness that had greeted him, of the ridges that he had felt each step of the way, of the doll-like perfection of her body.

Ana felt too confused to immediately readjust her clothes. Their unleashed desires had momentarily swept away her sense of feminine modesty. She looked into her lover's eyes and thought, he's right. I've crossed the line and now I'm his. As if reading her mind, Michael kissed her again, this time more lightly, barely touching her with the tip of closed lips. Then he made her a promise she'd never forget: "I'll be good to you, my sweet Ana. If anything happens to us, it won't be because of me."

As they were about to walk to the restaurant, Ana suddenly turned towards him and tugged at his sleeve. "You know what? I'm not hungry. Are you?" Her almond eyes beckoned to him. "Not for food," he said. They made love once in the car and twice at his place. Then they lay side by side on the bed, the moist skin of their hips still touching, each contemplating their experience. Now I have to detach myself from Karen and make sure that Ana's all mine, Michael resolved. For him, the act of making love was the logical conclusion of a set of premises he had established in advance. He hadn't decided which came first: breaking up with Karen or becoming more entangled in Ana's life and removing the rival he saw in her husband.

Ana, in turn, recalled a debate about the nature of love she had had with some of her friends back in college. The women said that what attracts them most is a man's personality. The men countered that without the looks, the personality meant nothing. Back then, she had taken the women's side of the debate. But after so many years of marriage, she realized that both arguments were equally trivial and, at root, one and the same. Now that she was embarking on a new relationship, Ana felt that what truly counted in love was not how it got started, but how it kept on going. One could be attracted to countless others, both physically and emotionally. In the end, the forces of attraction tended towards entropy. It happened in her own marriage; it happens to millions of couples. The body ages and expands; the personality becomes familiar and dull. It takes extraordinary energy and creativity, Ana sensed, to take the point of departure of any relationship, however exceptional, and bring it to fruition as beautiful and exciting as it began.

Part II

Chapter 1

"Baby, meet me at my place at one o'clock, okay? We'll have the whole afternoon to ourselves. Karen's putting in some overtime at work," Michael whispered excitedly into the phone as soon as he heard his girlfriend's voice.

Ana glanced at her watch. It was twelve thirty already. She quickly slipped on a pleated skirt, her white shirt with the rounded collar and a pair of Mary Jane shoes. Without even thinking about it, she had chosen the schoolgirl outfit that her lover preferred. She dabbed on some perfume behind her ears, even though Michael didn't like it. He feared its scent might arouse not only his desire, but also Karen's suspicions. She put on some lip-gloss, then changed her mind and removed it with a tissue. It would be pointless given all their kissing. Her heart raced. And how could it not? Breathless excitement each and every time they met. Hours of intimate conversation. Such a handsome, supportive, gentle, calm and romantic lover. Michael was exactly what she had longed for all along, only better. She hadn't even fathomed someone so thrilling, something that felt so right.

Michael slipped on his periwinkle tee shirt, since several women had commented on how it brought out his chocolate eyes. No deodorant or cologne were necessary. He opted for the minimalist approach: the fresh scent of organic soap. He brushed his hair only with his fingers, sweeping his long bangs to the side, away from his serene forehead. As he gazed at himself in the mirror, Michael took pride in his own fuss-free good looks. Some people have to work so hard just to look average, he thought, his own fiancée coming to mind. Others are born with it, he observed, thinking of himself and his new girlfriend.

But then he qualified somewhat. Ana was attractive, he mused, recalling her doll-like features and petite frame, but not gorgeous like him. He'd be more desired by other women than she'd be desired by other men, he did a quick comparison as if he and Ana were engaged in a competition. A surge of self-confidence intoxicated him with a sense of his superiority. Women fall so easily for my boyish charm, Michael thought, his hubris somewhat tempered by the boredom of predictability. Ana, however, seemed more of a challenge to him.

He was attracted to the combination of vulnerability and strength he saw in her. Michael tabulated Ana's qualities, both the plusses and the minuses. But even the minuses seemed like plusses in his eyes, since he was keenly aware that her weaknesses could be turned to his advantage. She's childlike and naïve, yet also educated and astute. She's pretty without being too beautiful, like the kind of women most men drool over, who get a big head as a result. She's pliable without being a pushover, the image of Karen suddenly popped into his mind, then quickly disappeared. She's independent and headstrong yet also vulnerable and needy. It's as if something has long been missing from her life and, fortunately, I was there, in the right place at the right time, to fill in the void. Or maybe it was fate, who the hell knows? Michael speculated. It sure felt like it to him, in that instant. When the doorbell rang, he rushed to open the door. At first, all Ana could see was a pair of dark eyes locking her gaze, then flowing all over her. Michael put his index finger to his lips to indicate that they shouldn't dispel the magical complicity of silence. He led her by the hand into the bedroom.

For once, they weren't pressed for time. Michael cradled his girlfriend into his arms, enjoying the lightness of her body, with the eagerness of a groom carrying his new bride over the threshold on their wedding night, but also, despite his virility, with the nurturing care of a mother holding an only child. "You're my little Powderpuff," he said, deciding that would be her second pet name, since she was so fragile and small. His gentleness surprised her. As he laid her down on the bed, Ana had the impression that she was levitating above it, floating with anticipation. Without removing any clothes, Michael allowed his hands to glide over her, in a gentle massage that simultaneously soothed and titillated her senses. Her body involuntarily moved to his touch, drawn to him. But Michael showed deliberate restraint this time. Even when Ana extended her arms and pulled him to her, he didn't give in to her urges, nor to his own. He was fully in control of the situation. As usual, he knew exactly what he wanted. On that day, he decided, he'd explore his new girlfriend gradually and slowly.

"Last night I dreamt about you and actually felt your soft skin embracing my whole body. I woke up quivering all over from that tactile impression of you," he murmured. When her head approached his for a kiss, Michael moved slightly lower. His lips clasped the delicate skin of her neck. He sucked it so gently, and with such patience, that Ana couldn't even tell that he had left the imprint of his teeth upon her skin until she was ready to go home. Then she glanced at herself in the mirror and hurriedly covered the mark with face powder, afraid that it would give her away. But the traces would reappear the instant the make-up wore off, exposing her illicit lover's lingering presence.

As Michael turned her over, to caress her shoulders, her back, the moist mound still covered by panties. "You're so beautiful," he said, simultaneously moved and aroused. Ana turned again and they gazed at each other. As she lay on her back, he focused on the thick line of her bangs, which brought out the fire in her eyes. "Please always cut your hair like this," he said. "I want you to stay exactly as you were on the day we met."

Ana giggled at the adorable naïveté of his comment. "Then I'm afraid you'll have to invent a genetic cure for aging."

"You've already got the genes, Baby. All you need is the desire," he replied, adding silently in his own mind, "to be mine for life." Ana looked so youthful that he couldn't imagine her ever growing old. She, in turn, thought about the implications of his comment. Somewhere in there, Michael was hinting that their love was for the long-term, just as she, herself, had hoped. When she turned over again, he whispered into her ear, with haunting sincerity, "I want you so much, Ana. I've never wanted anyone like this before."

But they didn't make love on that warm Friday afternoon. Instead, they explored each other with their lips, fingertips and tongues; with the whole surface of their warm, desirous bodies, without consummating their love. Michael was delighted by each and every physical attribute of his girlfriend, as if he were seeing Ana for the first time. The slimness of her leg, the fluid manner in which the curve of her torso seemed to melt into the straight lines of her legs, the sharp contours of her knees, the abandon in her gaze, the heavy softness of her hair, the delicacy of her lips, even the smallness of her feet. "You should cut your toenails, you little Romanian peasant," he quipped as he lifted her foot to kiss each toe, one at a time.

Ana admired the perfect polish of his muscular form. "Do you work out a lot?" she asked him.

"A few hours a day three, maybe four times a week," Michael estimated. "If I do anything less than that, I begin to feel literally sick," he added, to imply that he exercised purely for health reasons.

"Most people work out to look good," Ana speculated, since she didn't.

"Not me. I don't really care about how I look." As he said this, Michael almost believed that false statement, forgetting how proud he was of his athletic physique. "I have a present for you," he suddenly switched the subject, as if recalling something important.

"Are you sure it's not for you?" Ana asked him playfully, since his last few gifts were all items of lingerie that he wanted her to model for him.

"Okay, it's for both of us," he compromised. He walked to his desk drawer and returned holding a little black velvet box. "Open it," he offered it to Ana.

She removed from the box a black silk cord, delicate and translucent, upon which lay suspended, like a teardrop, a pear shaped aquamarine pendant. "Michael, it's absolutely gorgeous!"

"No, you are," he replied, taking the necklace from her hands and walking behind her, to place it around her neck. "What I liked about this pendant is that it wraps closely around your neck, almost like a dog collar. Yet at the same time it's so delicate and timelessly elegant," he explained.

Ana examined herself in the mirror. "I feel like that girl in the Titanic." She turned around to kiss Michael with gratitude. "Let's just hope that our ship won't run into a huge iceberg and sink," she added as an afterthought.

"Don't worry," Michael reassured her. "I'll steer us in the right direction. I wouldn't let anything bad happen to my Baby."

A few minutes later, they were back in bed. Ana licked the crevices of his ear, small and vulnerable, crimson with heat, and breathed "I love you" into it. Michael's whole body quivered, from head to toe, in a sinuous upheaval of sensation like she had never witnessed before. "You're so sensual," she observed. She was mesmerized by the potency of his touch and even more so by his extreme erotic sensibility, which, she felt quite certain, must be a symptom of great emotional depth and sensitivity. Ana still recalled the repulsive sexual brutality of her first lover and had become quite used to her husband's indifferent touch. But she couldn't remember ever being loved like this before, explored with kisses everywhere, soothed by fluid caresses that barely grazed the surface of her skin yet somehow managed to probe to the core of her being.

Michael noticed that his girlfriend's eyes lit up like someone in a delirium. "So are you," he replied, feeling like she was the one. At that moment, he wanted Ana to be completely his, from head to toe, from morning to night, as if the present were a living fossil perpetually frozen in the transparent layers of time. He was especially drawn to the ecstatic mixture of wonder and abandon he saw in her eyes. "I will love you for as long as I see my love reflected in your eyes," he vowed. With a possessive yet understated gesture, his hand grasped the flat of her throat and rested there, immobile, as he covered her ear and cheek with a flurry of kisses.

"Why are you doing this?" She was surprised by the ominous placement of his hand upon her neck, so sharply contradicted by the lightness of his touch.

"Because I like to feel the softness of your skin upon the roughness of my palm," he replied.

Ana's skeptical laugh was more of a gurgle, flowing from her like a little stream of pleasure. "Don't give me that! You like to feel like my life's in your hands, you little vampire!"

"And isn't it?" Michael asked. With an abrupt movement, he turned her head to the side, so she could look him in the eyes. His face lay in the shadow, but his eyes glimmered like candles.

"Yes, it is," she agreed, entranced. "I can't help it. I'm so in love with you, Michael," she mirrored his feelings. At that moment, Ana thought that whatever came to pass between them—whatever mixture of agony and bliss their love affair would bring them—somehow, this passion would be tremendously important to her.

Chapter 2

Michael sensed Karen's hair tickle his shoulder. Her left foot brushed up against his leg as they lay still in bed, neither of them yet ready to acknowledge that they were wide awake. Feeling her shift her position, Michael turned over, to buy himself more time to think. The situation was untenable, that much was clear. He had been seeing Ana almost every day for well over a month while still stringing Karen along. He figured that for as long as he wasn't sure that he could persuade his girlfriend to leave her husband, his fiancée would be his safety net. Besides, as much as he wanted Ana all to himself to better enjoy their torrid affair, something inside him still craved Karen's nurturing affection. Being suspended between a loving fiancée and a passionate mistress gave him the empowering sensation of being the sole king, winning a chess match against two queens.

In a recent conversation, Karen had asked him about his career plans: "What happens if you don't find a decent job in French this spring?"

"I'll probably get into real estate or some kind of some kind of business with flexible hours," Michael had an instant reply in reserve.

"Must you always have a backup plan for everything?" Karen didn't know whether she should be impressed with or apprehensive about her fiancée's resilience.

"Hey, I was born with a backup diaper," he replied with a cocky smile.

Although not one prone to worrying, that morning Michael felt slightly on edge. Karen and he were supposed to celebrate the two-year anniversary of their first date. He knew exactly what to expect. Karen insisted upon observing certain rituals on special occasions, which also included their birthdays, Valentine's Day and New Year's Eve. She'd hide little gifts for him all over the house. He found ties, love notes and chocolates inside the kitchen cabinets, in the laundry hamper, under his pillow and in his desk drawers. Although Karen considered this gesture thoughtful and romantic, it made Michael feel like she was marking her territory. Then they'd have dinner at one of the fanciest restaurants in town, ordering only hors d'oeuvres since the entrées, which ran about fifty dollars a plate not counting drinks and dessert, were prohibitively expensive. Last but not least, they'd engage in a ritual that he later regretted having invented: writing down a list of their favorite moments together that year.

"What are you thinking about?" Karen quizzed him, lying on her side, her head propped upon her hand.

"Oh, nothing. I was just going over today's activities."

Karen's eyes lit up. "Great minds think alike! I was thinking we could take a nice little walk in the park, you know, to enjoy the foliage. Then maybe we could go shopping for some new clothes for me. I've lost so much weight lately that pretty much nothing fits me anymore. And tonight we'll go to our restaurant."

"Sounds good," Michael responded without much enthusiasm.

"Did you have something else in mind?" Karen picked up on his indifference.

"Nope." He looked at his fiancée's stringy hair, her pursed lips curled into an air of forced agreeability, her sturdy, block-like body strengthened without being feminized by the frequent workouts. She's as familiar to me as an old shoe, Michael told himself, as he gallantly opened the car door for Karen.

Driving to Huron Park, a well-manicured nature reserve where they had walked and jogged together before, Michael hesitated. Should I tell her about

Ana or shouldn't I? Wouldn't it be callous of me to tell her about it on our anniversary? But wouldn't it be even worse to continue deceiving her? At any rate, he exculpated himself, the situation I've created doesn't allow for other-regarding action. With one swift, curved motion, he parked the car close to the playground.

"Go for it!" Karen nodded approvingly towards the swings, knowing full well how much her fiancé enjoyed being a big kid.

Michael gazed at the two lonely swings. A week earlier he had been there with Ana. The image of her long dark hair blowing in the wind as they sat in adjacent swings, daring each other to pump higher and higher, flashed before his eyes. These pleasant recollections were accompanied by a vague sense of frustration, however. The woman he was pursuing was still partly out of reach. "I don't really feel like swinging today," he said to Karen, walking mechanically to a familiar spot.

"Where are you going?" she followed him to the sand box. "I knew you were a kid at heart, but let's not exaggerate. Have you regressed to being a toddler now?"

Michael stood exactly where he and Ana had laid down. His skin sensed the tactile impression of her delicate body covering his own as their mouths devoured each other. He recalled Ana's objection to their public displays of affection, "Did you see that guy parked in the truck watching us make out?" as well as his own characteristically cavalier response, "That's alright, we'll charge him for the peep show. You need the extra cash anyway."

"A penny for your thoughts!" Karen said, beginning to feel ignored.

"I was going over what I'll put on the list of my favorite moments."

"Me too. But don't tell me yet, okay? Let's save it for tonight."

"Okay," he agreed, wondering what kind of surprise he'd deliver to Karen. In his current state of indecision, he was likely to surprise his own self.

"Beautiful leaves," Karen commented after a few minutes, growing uncomfortable with the silence that was settling between them.

Michael looked up at the sunlit trees. Shades of yellow, green, burgundy and brown sparkled between the cheerful patches of blue sky and the dark outlines of trees. "We must be having an Indian summer this fall," he commented.

"Yes, but nothing beats good old sunny Phoenix," Karen reminded him. She felt increasingly uneasy about the fact that Michael no longer mentioned their upcoming move. In her own mind, Phoenix and their marriage had become practically synonymous. If only they moved to Arizona that summer, they'd begin their lives from a clean slate, settling into the peaceful domestic existence she had wanted for so long.

"Actually, I've been meaning to talk to you about that," Michael took her comment as his cue. "I'm thinking of giving the Midwest another chance."

"Why?"

Michael had rehearsed his answer in advance: "Well, I did some research. Get this! As it turns out, there are only two decent prep schools in Phoenix. Plus even those pay only about three-fourths the salary of the top prep schools in the

Detroit area. There's no way in hell I'm going let them screw me over like this. Do you know what's the highest paying prep school in the nation?"

Karen didn't know, nor did she care to find out. She struggled to come to terms with this abrupt change in the plans. "No," she replied, disheartened.

"It's Grosse Point Academy, right here in Detroit!" Michael exclaimed. "It's one of the best private schools in the country, rivaling top notch places like Exeter."

"I didn't realize that you were so pretentious," Karen replied pursing her lips, to register her disappointment.

"I'm not at all!" Michael objected. "I just want a nice, cushy job that doesn't stiff me on the salary," he said, picking up the pace.

She walked faster, to keep up with him. "But what about the disgusting Midwest weather. These endless winters?"

"When I'm ready to retire, I'll be looking into sunnier places. But for now, my top priority's finding a decent job."

Karen walked in silence by Michael's side. She didn't how to respond to his announcement. Everything he said about his employment plans sounded perfectly reasonable. But his argument struck her as disingenuous, coming from a man who had repeatedly told her that his career ambition consisted of living life as an extended vacation in a warm climate. Why the emphasis on work all of a sudden? And why in Detroit of all places? Despite her misgivings, Karen tried to control her response. If I'm too pushy, he might become even more stubborn about staying here, she reminded herself. Yet she couldn't help but see his change of heart as a bad sign. Staying in Michigan meant dwelling in an emotional limbo; a state of ambiguity that she sometimes experienced as a form of psychological torture. "Okay, if you say so. . . . I thought that moving to Phoenix was important to you."

He didn't know what to say in response. The tension between them vibrated in the crisp autumn air. "There's something I need to tell you. I'm in love with another woman," Michael would have liked to blurt out at the moment when they passed by the bench where he and Ana had made out a few days earlier. He recalled vividly how his girlfriend had straddled him while exploring the crevices of his ear with the tip of her tongue, heating him from within with her humid touch.

"We don't even hold hands anymore," Karen commented with a note of reproach. Michael took her hand into his, to prove her wrong. But this gesture seemed empty to them both as her hand lay limply in his.

That evening, during dinner, the couple made an effort to sound more upbeat.

"I'd love to go skiing with you in Colorado during winter break," Karen remarked. Making plans for the future gave her a sense of security, as if it could somehow endow their precarious relationship with a sense of continuity.

"But you don't even know how to ski," Michael objected, absentmindedly twirling the stem of his wine glass between his thumb and index finger. He had planned to stick around the Detroit area during the holidays, to see Ana whenever he pleased.

"I'll ski on my behind if I have to," Karen retorted.

"My parents might be coming here for Christmas," Michael announced, hoping to dissuade her.

"That's great," she mustered some enthusiasm. "I'd love to see them again."

"The last time you saw them you hardly said a word to them," he pointed out.

"I didn't want to intrude. It looked like you guys were having a great time together."

Michael recalled that on Thanksgiving, when his parents, whom he irreverently called "the tag team of Bob and Betsy," had visited him from Utah, the three of them behaved like overgrown kids. They laughed and competed for each other's attention, while Karen sat quietly and observed, like a schoolteacher anxiously watching over a group of rowdy children during recess. As soon as his fiancée stepped into the kitchen to bring back another dish, his mother whispered something about Karen being cold and insipid. Michael kindly shared with her this bit of information as soon as they found themselves alone. The truth of the matter was that his mother didn't target Karen in particular. She democratically criticized everyone she met. But Michael didn't want his fiancée to establish a bond with his parents, or with anyone else for that matter. In his mind, loyalty was a zero sum game. Any allegiance Karen formed with someone else would take away from her absolute loyalty to him. "Sure, but I thought you were offended by what they said about you behind your back," he reminded her, taking a bite out of the scallops, which the waitress had brought to their table.

Karen scooted around with a fork the leaves of her dry salad. She had remained faithful to her diet. "Well, it takes some time to get used to one's future in-laws," she took advantage of this opportunity to emphasize their engagement and upcoming marriage.

Michael felt a bit of scallop get stuck in the back of his throat. He washed it down quickly with a few gulps of water. "I thought we were going to see how we get along living together first, before discussing marriage plans again," he found a tactful way of introducing doubt into Karen's mind.

"What have we been doing this entire month?" she demanded, her tone betraying irritation.

"A month? What can one tell in a month? I was thinking more like a year or so before reaching a final decision," Michael tried to buy himself more time, looking over the menu at the list of desserts. "What do you say we order some chocolate mousse and raspberry sorbet? We can split them half and half."

Karen could hardly believe that Michael was in the mood for sorbet when their whole future was on the line. "What do you mean wait another year? Haven't we been waiting two already?"

"We didn't live together the whole time."

"So what? What does that have to do with anything?"

"You know me. I want to sample the goods before making a purchase," he replied with a smile.

"Sample the goods?" Karen repeated his phrase with an air of indignation. She removed the napkin from her lap and threw it on the table, announcing dryly: "I'm going to the restroom." She then quickly left the table, to hide from him the fact that she had already burst into tears. When she returned a few minutes later, Michael once again felt the urge to tell her about Ana, to put an end to their sham engagement.

But before he got a chance to utter a word, Karen opened her purse and took out a piece of paper. "Here's the list of my favorite moments this year," she forced a smile. Despite her anger and resentment, she'd be damned if she let their anniversary date go down the tubes.

Michael unfolded the sheet of paper and read:

1. The day you proposed.
2. The day we got back together.
3. The day we moved in together.
4. Last year's anniversary, when you took me to Phoenix and we looked around for houses. I could already picture us living there.
5. Last year's New Year celebration, when we went dancing and made love on the patio of that cute little restaurant.
6. The first time we went to the gym together, when you coached me on how to use the exercise machines. It changed my whole outlook on life.
7. Spending time with you and your parents last Thanksgiving and Christmas (Yes, I really mean it! By the way, does this one count as two?)
8. Worst day of my life: the day we broke up.
9. Worst time of my life: the weeks we were apart.
10. My overall comment: I know in my heart that you're the only man for me and that I'll be so happy being your wife.

Wow, this woman really loves me, Michael observed with a sense of satisfaction. Perhaps my list will give her an inkling about how I feel, he calculated. "Thanks, Baby. I'm really touched by what you wrote." He reached into his pocket for a piece of paper upon which he had quickly scribbled his own thoughts. "Here's my list," he extended it to Karen.

She began reading, her heart pounding with nervousness:

1. The day you began taking care of yourself, dieting and exercising, to improve your health and boost your self-confidence.
2. Going clothes shopping two weeks ago to buy you nice outfits that make you feel better about yourself.
3. My overall comment: work on yourself. Be the person you've always wanted to be. Independently of me, follow your dreams.

Looking over Michael's note, Karen was struck by its brevity. She recalled that the previous year they had both enumerated all ten points. Obviously, I've lost some ground because of our stupid temporary break-up, she told herself. Yet she was still left with the disconcerting impression that she was reading something written by a life coach rather than her future husband. Michael's tone seemed impersonal and instructional rather than sentimental and intimate, as she would have preferred. Her powerful defense mechanisms kicked into gear. He's focusing on me this year. He realizes how much I need his support to improve my life. Rereading Michael's list in this new light, Karen felt touched by its message.

In turn, seeing emotion reflected upon her features, Michael congratulated himself for having tactfully driven home the point that their paths in life would soon diverge.

"You're so wonderful. I feel so lucky to be marrying a man like you. Someone who cares so much about me that he's willing to help me with improving myself," Karen declared, with genuine gratitude.

"No problem," Michael replied, momentarily disheartened by the fact that when faced with the reality of his fiancée's clinginess, he lacked the balls to deliver the bad news.

Each time he tried to pull away, Karen reined him in with her unconditional love. But then he saw the upside of the picture. Michael coolly contrasted his girlfriend and his fiancée, the way an economist might conduct a comparative cost-benefit analysis. While Ana was impetuous, high maintenance and volatile, Karen was reliable, low maintenance and forgiving. His fiancée's eagerness to do everything possible to please him flattered him, nursing his voracious ego. The diet, the exercise, the new clothes, the cooking, even the pathetic attempts at steamy sex, everything this woman does, she does it for me, Michael thought complacently, viewing Karen, no matter what happened, as forever belonging to him.

Chapter 3

"Mama, can you please help me with my VIP project? It's due tomorrow," Allen said in his best whinny voice late one Sunday evening. He walked towards the kitchen counter almost entirely hidden behind a large poster board.

"How come you didn't tell me about it earlier, when I asked you if you had any homework?" Ana asked the poster board with legs that was rapidly approaching.

"Because that's not really homework. It's only for Show and Tell," the boy found a loophole.

"But isn't it mandatory and due tomorrow?" his mother didn't let him off the hook on a technicality.

"I hate doing this stupid junk. School reeks!" he declared, plopping down the poster board on the kitchen table.

"Hold on. Let's clean this up first," Ana rushed to save the pristine poster board, first wiping the table with a moist paper towel, then drying it with a dishrag. "Okay, so what do we need to do?"

"I need to paste pictures of myself on here. So I can show my class what I like to do for fun," Allen replied, his lips turning slightly downward, his staple expression before throwing a temper tantrum.

"This project sounds like fun," his mother tried to preempt the upcoming storm. "We can look over the vacation photos Daddy printed last weekend from his digital camera. Do you also need to write a report?"

"No. All I have to do is talk about the pictures."

"Well then, why don't you pick out some of your favorite pictures from this pile," Ana proposed. She brought out a shoebox filled with recent family photographs and placed it in front of Allen. "Let's glue them on the poster board and see what you remember about each one."

The boy began digging through the box with both hands. He was so absorbed in his task that his tongue stuck out from the side of his mouth. After about ten minutes, Allen showed his mother eleven pictures he had selected.

"Can you try to narrow it down to six or seven?" she proposed, going to get the glue stick and a black marker from the kitchen counter.

When Ana returned to the table, Allen was holding six pictures in his hand. "These are my favorites."

"Do you remember where these pictures were taken?" his mother peered over his shoulder at the photographs.

"Sort of," Allen replied, which Ana translated as "not really."

"I'll help jog your memory," she told him.

"But Mama, I don't like to run," Allen joked, beginning to relax.

"This one here was taken in Alabama at Grandma Jenny's," Ana pointed to a photograph of her and Allen sitting on a porch at her mother-in-law's house. Both of them squinted to block off the intense afternoon light. "We barely have our eyes open. How come you picked it?"

"Because Almond's in it," Allen placed his index finger below a little black poodle, which, for several years, had been the love of his life.

"How could I forget! What about this one?" she pointed to a picture of Allen and Michelle at the beach. "Do you remember where we took it?"

"At the beach," the boy answered brilliantly.

"Which one?"

Allen shrugged.

"Remember where we went on Memorial Day?" his mother jogged his memory.

Allen shook his head.

"To Traverse City, where we stayed at that nice, expensive inn by the beach." Ana recalled how much the kids loved playing in the waves, jumping with a mixture of shock and delight whenever the ice-cold water lapped at their bare feet.

"Oh, yeah," Allen said. "My favorite part was when we went on the motor-boat ride. Daddy let me and Michelle drive it for awhile."

Ana felt quite certain that the jet skiers they almost hit didn't forget that day either. "How about these ones? They go together," she moved on to the next set of images. The first one featured Allen riding a mechanical bull, holding on for dear life. The second displayed him falling flat on his behind. "Daddy took these photos on spring break, when we went to that bull show in Tennessee."

"Ha, ha!" Allen laughed at the recollection. "That was fun. And I wasn't scared at all. It didn't even hurt when I fell down. They put straw on the ground," he boasted.

"You're so courageous," Ana patted the little boy on his soft, closely cropped hair. It occurred to her that each of these trips had been carefully orchestrated by her husband. Rob spent hours organizing each family vacation so the kids would have fun. Ana's attention was caught by the striking contrast between the last two photographs Allen lay down on the poster board. The first one was taken during their summer vacation in New Hampshire. Rob had asked a stranger to take their picture when Ana had protested that he, being the one who took most of the family photos, was hardly in any of them. The four of them looked so happy together, all smiles and, miraculously, with their eyes open—since usually at least one of them blinked at the flash. Ana recalled how much they had enjoyed that short, easy hike. She also remembered the vicarious pleasure, even complicity, she and her husband had shared in seeing the kids skip down the trails like mountain goats. She felt a tinge of regret when she realized that, given her infidelity, she might never relive such untainted pleasure with her family again.

The second photograph confirmed this intuition. It was taken earlier that fall in their back yard, right after she had become involved with Michael. The whole family was raking leaves. Their next-door neighbor, a quiet, retired fellow, offered to take their picture. Although Rob, Allen and Michelle smiled for the camera, their smiles appeared forced. Ana, herself, looked sullen. Her jaw line was set and rectangular. She gazed at the camera with a strange combination of shame and reproach. Before and after Michael, Ana silently observed, her eyes passing back and forth between the last two images her son was gluing to the poster board. The two pictures, lying side by side, captured her emotional oscillations ever since meeting her lover.

Whenever she was with Rob, Ana couldn't help but focus on the accumulation of lies and excuses she had to tell her husband in order to see her lover. Rob was pleasantly surprised that even in the midst of the recession, his wife's paintings were becoming increasingly successful. Ana met with more clients and gallery owners interested in her artwork than before. The fact that she had deposited nearly $ 7,000 during the past few months into their bank account after Michael purchased two of her paintings, made her case appear more credible.

Yet Ana couldn't help but feel remorse when she looked into Rob's eyes and told him such blatant lies.

At the same time, an overwhelming force had drawn her towards Michael from the day they met. Although their mutual attraction excited her, it also frightened her, making her feel like she had fallen under a spell so powerful that nothing, not even love for her children, would be able to break. Ana sometimes wished she could swallow a pill to forget her lover. Oblivion, she speculated, was the only way to resist Michael's inexplicable hold on her. No matter how often she went over her husband's attributes—his loyalty, fidelity, culture, intelligence and sense of duty—they couldn't move her in the way that Michael's puzzling combination of angelic and devilish characteristics did. There was something about the fact that she knew her lover had a dark side that made all of his qualities—his boyish charm, intelligence, humor, fierce sensuality and intense passion—pop out all the more, in full relief.

When she had asked Michael one day over lunch to explain to her why good girls fall for bad boys, he had shrugged with the confidence of a man who's expressing a self-evident truth: "Pure goodness is boring. Besides," he grinned, "I'm a good boy, I swear."

Michael looked so clean-cut, youthful and innocent that Ana almost believed him. Almost. "No you're not," she playfully contradicted him.

He frowned like a child. "Me? I wouldn't even hurt a fly."

She had to laugh. "If you want to convince me that you're a nice guy, please don't quote *Psycho*."

Michael smiled in response, then adopted a more serious demeanor. "My personal hunch is that women want to feel like they have something to tame in a man. If he's already domesticated, it's no fun. You always have to have a challenge. Otherwise life gets too predictable." Ana recalled how Michael had looked at her, with a mixture of indulgence and intensity. "But don't flatter yourself," he said. "You're not a good girl either. Because if you were, you wouldn't be here with me, now would you?" Ana had to concede that her lover had a point. The same one, in fact, that her husband had made when they first got engaged and were discussing their previous relationships. "Nice guys always finish last," Rob had commented. He was referring to his ex-girlfriend, who had left him for a womanizer. Never in a million years, Ana thought, would Rob have suspected that she, the woman he loved, married and had children with, would one day similarly betray him.

Quite often Ana succeeded in deflecting her guilt by painting Rob as an incompatible partner in a comatose marriage. During those moments, she felt entitled to pursue happiness with her lover. Yet as she looked at Rob's face in their family photos, his smile seemed that of an unjustly wronged man. She was drawn to his rounded lips, his triangularly shaped head, his high cheekbones and even to his slightly crooked nose, the result of a deviated septum that he had been afraid to fix. She had always relied upon her husband's loyalty, sturdiness and good character. Whatever his faults may have been, Ana felt, he didn't deserve this betrayal.

Chapter 4

Upon a whim, Michael decided to skip class that afternoon and surprise his girlfriend at her gallery. He peeked in through the glass door, to observe her without making his presence known. Ana stood in front of one of her latest paintings, next to a man in a gray suit. From what Michael could tell, the painting featured two bright figures, a man and a woman, whose profiles blended into each other to form one spherical, sunny whole. Michael couldn't help but smile. He took full credit for Ana's shift towards more cheerful artwork, which seemed to match the lightness of her mood since they had fallen in love. She wore a professional pinstriped pencil skirt and white blouse. He saw her gesture with one hand towards the painting. The dark curves of her lower body eclipsed, with its suggestive silhouette, the fiery burst of color in the painting. The man in the gray suit inched closer to Ana. He grabbed her by the elbow with one hand and pointed towards the canvass with the other. Ana approached to see what he was indicating, then turned to the man and laughed out loud. Michael could hear the ring of her girlish voice even through the thick windowpane. A flash of jealousy moved through him like lightning, as if his girlfriend had revealed an intimate part of herself to another man.

Within seconds, Michael stood by Ana's side. "It's me, Baby, it's me," he whispered into her ear. As she turned around startled, he ostentatiously planted a kiss upon her lips.

Ana tried to pull away, uncomfortable with this gesture of intimacy in the gallery. "Everyone knows me here," she whispered to him.

But her lover only pressed her tighter against him, his fingers interlocked behind the small of her back. "How I've missed you," he said. "I couldn't help myself. I skipped my afternoon classes just to be with you."

Despite the compromising situation, Ana felt touched. "You're such a naughty schoolboy."

Michael looked above her head, appearing pleased with something. She turned around and noticed that her potential customer, the man in the dark suit, was heading out the door.

"I guess he wasn't interested in your painting after all," Michael observed with a sense of satisfaction. "He was interested in you."

"You're so cynical," she countered.

"I just think like a man, that's all," Michael made his way forward, backing his girlfriend into a quiet corner of the gallery.

"I come here regularly with my husband and kids. Tracy knows them," Ana protested casting nervous glances in both directions, like a trapped animal. Although the gallery owner was in her office at the moment, several customers looked at them askance, as if they had never seen people showing affection in public. One elderly woman seemed particularly scandalized by their behavior. Ana silently pointed her out with her pinkie.

"Let them think whatever the hell they wish. Just don't flirt with anyone else from now on," Michael said, looking down at his girlfriend. His mouth plunged to devour hers. Ana felt her heart race with a mixture of excitement and apprehension. Tingles of pleasure made their way from their joined lips, through her chest and abdomen, all the way down to her toes. This man moves me like no other, Ana observed, electrified by her lover's mix of eroticism and assertiveness. Once their lips momentarily unlocked, she took a step back, to admire him. "Let's get out of here," she proposed, her senses ablaze.

But Michael didn't budge. His gaze glided over her, territorially. "Sometimes I wish you'd wear a black dress all the way down to the floor. And cover your head and your hair, so that you'd be invisible to other men," he said, picking up a strand of her glossy black hair between his fingertips, then allowing it to cascade upon her shoulder again.

"I thought you wanted me to wear miniskirts and sexy dresses, not bursas," she retorted with a smile.

"Miniskirts around me, burqas around everybody else," Michael murmured, his voice hypnotic and low.

"I didn't know you were the jealous type," Ana remarked, feeling strangely proud of the passion she had ignited in such an attractive man. It was as if her lover's masculine possessive desire confirmed, and even enhanced, the value of her own femininity.

Michael looked pensive.

"Why the long face?" she pouted flirtatiously.

"Do you feel that what we have is special?"

Ana gazed into his piercing dark eyes. In the obscurity of the corner of the gallery where they had hidden from view, they seemed black as coal. "Of course," she affirmed.

"In what way?" he continued quizzing her.

Ana didn't know how to respond. It was difficult to put into words the sudden, all-consuming passion that had swept over her life. "I don't know... In every way," she replied, somewhat discombobulated. "I've never felt anything like this before."

Michael, however, didn't seem pleased with her vague response. "That's not an answer," he said with an air of impatience. "Just because you've never felt a certain way doesn't mean that feeling is positive. Be more specific."

Ana felt chastised, like a schoolgirl who had given the wrong answer in front of the class. "What do you want me to say?" she asked, taken aback by his severe manner. "I'm just getting to know you. When you put me on the spot like this, it's more difficult to wax poetic about us."

"I'm sorry, Baby," Michael backed off. He wrapped his arms around Ana again, to melt the chilling effect of their exchange. "It's just that I feel so frustrated sometimes. I wish I could have you all to myself. I wish you could come live with me and paint all day long to your heart's content. That way we'd have our own perfect little universe. Nobody would ever try to steal you away from me during the day," he said, alluding to the man in the dark suit. "And nobody would ever take you away from me at night either," he added, alluding to her husband.

"You're forgetting a little detail. Three of them, to be exact," Ana reminded him of her family.

"I know Baby, I know. But a man can always dream, can't he? Sometimes I close my eyes and wish I were all you ever needed. I want to satisfy your every whim," he said, as his gaze flowed lovingly over her body, "and make you perfectly happy." His eyes were aglow. "Because my happiness is your happiness. What my Baby wants, my Baby gets. This will be my motto from now on."

"You're such a dreamer," Ana shook her head. "Perhaps if we had met much earlier, before the kids were born..." her voice trailed off wistfully. But this thought wasn't as pleasant as it should have been. Even for the sake of ideal love, she couldn't unwish her children's existence.

"If we had met before, you'd have everything you ever dreamed of," Michael dove into the flow of her unfinished train of thought. "I'd support you without ever complaining about it. I'd hide you in our little nest and inspire your painting. You'd never have to worry about anything again. Except for what you love best: me and your art."

Ana felt touched by her lover's mixture of idealism and generosity. Momentarily forgetting that they were in a public place, she laid her head upon her lover's chest, to be comforted by his bodily warmth and racing heartbeat. "You're so wonderful," she whispered gratefully.

Michael felt her words as a moist wave of heat moving through him. "And if you ever became famous," he continued enticing her, "I'd be right there, by your side. We'd travel all over the world together to your gallery exhibits." He knew he had touched upon her not-so-secret desire; upon any frustrated artist's dream.

"I wish I could do something to make you feel as happy as you do me," she reciprocated, moved by his show of devotion.

An idea that had been obsessing him for a while suddenly sprung into his mind at this opportune moment. "You can," Michael replied, elevating her head gently, to gaze directly into her eyes. "But I'm not sure that you will," he qualified, appearing to hesitate.

"Try me," Ana encouraged him.

"I'd like to be able to make love to you in the middle of the night," Michael said, his gaze absorbing her into him.

"Me too," she smiled awkwardly.

"No, I mean it," Michael insisted, with a sense of urgency. "Let's do it tonight, when everyone's asleep."

"Are you crazy?" Ana exclaimed, pulling away from him. "With my husband and kids in the house?" The bubble of complicity had burst.

"You said 'anything,'" Michael reminded her.

"I didn't think you'd ask me something so outrageous!"

"I see. You only meant doing what you wanted."

"Michael!" Ana cried out, feeling like he had pushed the envelope too far this time. "How can you possibly ask me to insult my family? Isn't what we're doing to them bad enough? Please!" An unpleasant idea crossed her mind. Was her lover a sadist? Was he so jealous of her husband that he'd want to use her to humiliate Rob?

Responding to her alarm, Michael didn't press the issue further. "Baby, I didn't mean to upset you, alright?" he reverted to his familiar, warm and tender, manner. "I know it was a crazy idea. It's just that I love you so much that I wish we could be together for the rest of our lives. I dream about being free to see you whenever and wherever I want. It kills me to have to share you with another man."

"I share you with another woman," she reminded him.

"Yeah, but the difference is that I'd drop Karen as soon as you give me the word. Your wish is my command."

Ana knew that much was true. Michael would leave his fiancée in a heartbeat, if only she asked him; if only she were free. But that was precisely the crux of the problem, she thought. I'm not as free as he is.

Chapter 5

Ana turned up the volume of the radio with one hand, while with the other she caressed Michael's hair. She sat sideways next to him, her feet tucked underneath her folded legs. She leaned over the stick shift to warm up his ear with little kisses that felt as light, warm and alive as the regular rhythm of her breathing.

"I must say, I've never felt so well-disposed during rush hour traffic in Detroit!" Michael commented cheerfully, turning towards Ana to give her another kiss on the mouth. The car veered slightly into the next lane.

"Keep your eyes on the road!" she exclaimed. "And leave the kissing and caressing to me," she added more quietly. She massaged gently but firmly his shoulder blades until he released those familiar moans of pleasure that were music to her ears whenever they made love. "When I caress you, you go mmm, mmmm like a little kid enjoying a delicious piece of candy," she observed.

"That's because you are my sweet piece of candy," he replied, placing his hand on Ana's leg. "And I'm willing to risk diabetes for you." He reached over for another kiss.

"Let's not have an accident," she cautioned, nervous that Michael never seemed to care about taking risks. But the traffic was moving very slowly. They barely inched along I-96 East.

"And even if we did, so what?" Michael countered. "The best way to go is right after we made love. Carpe Diem, Baby!"

Ana marveled at how Michael was able to be so carefree, with no fears, no inhibitions and no regrets. He savored each moment and each drop of pleasure with a total abandon. Maybe it's better to live this way, she thought. She almost envied her lover's good disposition. "How will I explain myself to Rob if I die in a car accident next to you?" she asked him, only partly in jest.

"It would put an end to this whole charade," Michael replied with a dismissive wave of the hand, returning to his favorite theme. Lately, Ana noticed, he took every available opportunity to imply they were stuck in lukewarm relationships when they could be enjoying the bloom of their youth together. She didn't reply, not wishing to spoil the lightness of their mood. But it was too late. Whenever the subject of divorce came up, she became uneasy and closed up emotionally, curling back into her shell like a snail.

"Hey, I didn't mean for it to come out like that," Michael tapped her reassuringly on the leg. "I've heard this Cranbrook Academy's supposed to be really nice," he changed the subject. "It's in the middle of these woods or nature preserve. Some say it's prettier than Princeton, only much smaller, of course."

"But why are we going there if they haven't even advertised a job in French?"

"No particular reason," Michael shrugged, keeping his eyes on the road. "To give myself a little extra incentive to stick around, I suppose. If I could land a cushy job here, I'd put up easier with six months of crappy Midwest weather."

Ana nodded in silence. She would have hoped that their relationship offered a sufficient incentive for Michael to stick around in Michigan.

"But my best incentive for staying here's you, Baby!" he turned to her, divining her transparent thoughts. He turned off the radio. "You know, if I got a job here, or at some other nice private school in the area, I might sell my house and move closer to you," he said casually, to test the waters.

She looked at him, startled. "Where?"

Michael smiled, as if he were about to reveal a romantic surprise. "I don't know. I was thinking of looking for a house in your subdivision, for example."

Ana's heart pounded with excitement. Lately, during her walks around the block, she had instinctively taken notice of each "FOR SALE" sign in her neighborhood. "Did you know I've been thinking about that also? It would be nice to live closer together. But I was afraid to suggest it, since I didn't want to put any pressure."

"Why the hell not?" Michael burst out. "I put pressure on you all the time. It's only fair."

"I'm so much trouble already. High maintenance, as they say."

"I looove high maintenance women," Michael exclaimed. He turned to give Ana another kiss, only this time, the traffic was moving fast again.

"Watch out!" Ana screamed when the car swerved.

But that only made Michael laugh. He was thrilled that his girlfriend had been receptive to his overture. It meant that she might be ready for his next move. "Supposing that Rob found out about us…" he began.

"Let's not spoil this beautiful day by talking about that again," Ana interrupted him.

"Hold on. I wasn't going to say anything negative," Michael countered. "I was just going to tell you that even in the worst case scenario, if we got caught, if I moved to your subdivision the kids could just walk back and forth from our house to Rob's. That would be so much easier for them than our current arrangement, with me living thirty minutes away."

Ana considered his statement. Although the subject still made her queasy, she saw his point. "Well, I suppose it would be less of a disaster if we lived in the same neighborhood," she conceded.

Her remark had been cautious, but Michael saw it as a local triumph in the battle to make Ana his wife. "I'd love to land a job here this spring," he repeated as he parked the car in the Visitor's Parking lot of Cranbrook Academy. Even from the glimpse they had had, the campus looked breathtakingly beautiful. Its manicured lawns, ivy covered buildings and big stretches of woods called to mind Emerson's vision of transcendental idealism. "After school, I'd come home around four o'clock, to spend time with your kids. That would give you one or even two more hours to paint in peace before dinner," Michael said, sweeping with a dreamy gaze the beauty of the natural surroundings. He then got out of the car and opened the door for Ana with an air of gentlemanly courtesy that she found both quaint and romantic. "And during the nights when Rob has the kids," he continued, "maybe we could take ballroom dancing classes together. You know, salsa and meringue, since you told me you love Latin music. But of course, for now, that's only a dream."

At the mention of ballroom dancing, Ana couldn't help but imagine herself swept up in her lover's arms to the melodious flow of the sensual music she enjoyed: so tastefully abandoned, so elegantly seductive, the very rhythm of desire.

"Either that or we could go out clubbing every night!" Michael punctured her fantasy bubble.

"No thanks!" Ana said as they walked hand in hand down a path leading to a gorgeous contemporary building with long columns marked "Art Museum." They climbed up its majestic set of steps, which were adorned by beautiful nude sculptures.

"These people have great taste in art," Michael commented about the female statues in particular.

"And wealth," Ana remarked, equally impressed.

"They probably pay teachers about 50,000 bucks a year, beginning salary," Michael made a highly educated guess, since he had researched the matter a week earlier. "Enough to feed a family of four quite comfortably," he turned to Ana. Her expression struck him as tense. "If they don't blow it on expensive jewelry and clothes," he took this opportunity to tug at her sleeve and pull her towards him.

As they kissed, Ana felt like she was being energized by her lover's hopes, floating upon his dreams. She could hardly believe that such a romantic, passionate, attractive and intelligent man was so madly in love with her. "It's just not fair," she said afterwards.

"What's not fair?"

"That I get the perfect lover while other women have to settle," Ana replied with a smile.

"Yeah well, other women aren't as wonderful as you are," Michael returned the compliment. But within seconds, a dark cloud seemed to pass over his luminous features. "Sometimes I feel like our love's so perfect, it's almost unreal. I'm afraid we'll do something, or that something will happen, and we'll blow our chances to really taste passion in life."

Ana searched his face for more clues. "What are you afraid of? If we truly love each other, then we should be able to handle anything life throws our way."

"I know, Baby. But what we have feels so right that I sometimes fear we'll screw it up somehow."

"Me too," Ana admitted. Whenever people back in Romania used to praise someone's children, the parents would spit three times into the air, so as not to jinx them. She had caught herself doing that several times when she thought of their affair. It was perfect yet fragile, like a pleasant dream from which she never wanted to wake up. "I hope you'll get a job here," she wished out loud, to show him that she too wanted to keep their dream alive.

Michael crouched down. He took a little twig from the grass and began sketching something in a patch of dirt.

"What are you drawing, little boy?"

"Lookie here," he said as Ana sat down on the grass next to him.

"A square?" she observed. "That's very impressive. Maybe they should devote a whole wing of the museum to your artwork."

"You're cute," he commented, still completely absorbed by his task.

"What do these letters stand for?" Ana asked, noticing that at each corner of the square Michael had sketched a letter: C, S, M, F and H in the middle, at the intersection point of the two diagonals.

"I'm drawing a relationship square," he explained. "C stands for compatibility. S, for sex. M for money issues. F for fidelity. And the H at the center for health. Those are the most important qualities that make or break any romantic relationship. I put health in the middle since if you don't have that, you can't really enjoy anything else." Michael traced an oval around the S and the C on top, then another one around the F and the M at the bottom of the square. He pointed to the top oval. "These are the main qualities we have. We're compatible as all hell and have perfect sexual chemistry," he took this opportunity to seal his comment with a long kiss. He then indicated the lower oval with the twig. "With Karen, we have a healthy relationship to money. We're both frugal, unlike some people," he looked meaningfully at his girlfriend. "And we have fidelity."

"I beg your pardon?"

"She never cheated on me," he clarified.

Ana shook her head. Was Michael that clueless or was he just pretending? "Correct me if I'm wrong, but it takes two to have fidelity."

"That's true. But if I had had the top oval with her, total compatibility and great sex, we'd have mutual fidelity as well," Michael smoothly worked his way around that obstacle.

As they walked hand in hand on the manicured lawn next to the museum, it suddenly occurred to Ana that her lover had missed the most obvious aspect of any romantic relationship. "What about *love*?"

"What about it?"

"Where's love in your brilliant scheme? I don't think you're quite ready to have your own talk show, Dr. Michael," she said, amused by this glaring omission.

Her lover smiled knowingly. "Love's everything, Baby. It's not one single part of the square or even all the elements put together. Love's always greater than the sum of its parts. Mysterious yet real. And you know it when you feel it," he said, looking adoringly into her eyes.

Chapter 6

As Ana drove to their usual rendezvous spot, an outdoor parking garage right outside a circular restaurant with a slowly spinning tower, she spotted Michael running towards her car. His step was buoyant and his face radiant. He smiled with glee from ear to ear like a child each and every time he saw her. Ana simultaneously honked the horn and stepped on the breaks, worried that, in her own eagerness and haste, she might run him over.

As soon as she got out of the car, she felt the warmth of her lover's embrace, his lips pressed upon hers. Then Michael's muscular arms lifted her off the ground, gathering momentum as he began twirling her high up in the air. Ana's peals of laughter and half-hearted protestations rang in his ears, exciting him further.

"You look so damn hot in that miniskirt! How much time do we have?" Michael asked with impatience, putting Ana down gently, only to grab her and nestle her into his arms again.

"Only two hours, unfortunately. I told Rob that I'm going to a *brief* meeting with Tracy," Ana emphasized the word "brief." "Because, you realize, I can't keep on telling him that I'm seeing clients interested in buying my paintings when there's no additional money to back it up."

"That's alright. We have enough time for lunch and a little afternoon delight," Michael focused on the positive.

Given his priorities, the afternoon delight came first, followed by lunch. As they were walking towards the restaurant, Michael deliberately lagged behind, to watch his girlfriend walk in front of him. He was surprised by the sharp contrast between Ana's youthful appearance and her shuffling, uneven gait. "Do I have to teach you how to walk?"

She turned around with a puzzled smile. "What to you mean?"

"You shuffle along like an old lady. Or a geek," he said, emulating her walk, dragging one foot on the ground more so than the other, with his arms dangling by his side.

"That's because I am a geek!" she cheerfully retorted.

"You may be a geek on the inside, but on the outside you're one hot mama. You need to walk more like this," Michael swung his hips to demonstrate the confident gait of models on the runway.

"Very sexy. Now let me demonstrate how you walk," Ana turned the tables on him. She proceeded to mimic Michael's confident swagger, her chin up high, her back arched, moving her upper body with exaggerated turns.

"Fair enough," he smiled mechanically, not amused. "But I still think that your walk doesn't match your looks," he insisted, determined to train his girl-friend to be a proper mate for him.

During the last stretch of their walk to the restaurant, Ana practiced the cat-walk with him, until the muscles around his mouth began to hurt from so much smiling.

"How come it doesn't bother you to lie to Karen?" she asked her lover, once they were in the restaurant together, enjoying their veggie wraps. "I'm almost jealous of your lack of scruples."

"What can I say? It's good to be me," Michael responded, nonplussed. "I mean, what's there to complain about? We just made love. Now we're enjoying a good meal together. Life's good, Baby!"

"Not for Rob and Karen," Ana pointed out.

"You want me to hook them up on a date?"

"Come on, Michael. This is serious."

"As long as they don't find out about us, we're fine."

"And if they do? Then what?"

"Then I'll break up with Karen," Michael announced calmly.

"What if Rob finds out about our affair first?"

"I don't know. That's up to you," he threw the ball back into her court.

Ana took a sip of her soda, to give herself a moment to reflect. "If Rob finds out about us, he'll probably want a divorce," she speculated.

"So he'll divorce," Michael repeated, not seeing any problem whatsoever with that fact.

"What about the kids?"

Michael reached across the table, taking Ana's hand into his own. "If Rob divorces you, I'll be there for you," he gazed warmly into her eyes.

"What do you mean?" she asked, in a slight daze.

"I want to marry you," he said.

Ana shook her head, not willing to absorb the full emotional impact of his marriage proposal. "But I'm already married. My marriage may not be perfect, but I love my husband and he loves me. More importantly, my kids want to be raised by both of their natural parents. They wouldn't be happy if Rob and I divorced. What you don't seem to realize is that this affair's is no longer just about us. In fact, it never was."

Michael withdrew his hand from hers, stung by her refusal. "So what are you trying to tell me?"

"That we should be more careful."

"What does that actually mean? You want to cool it for awhile?" he stared at her fixedly.

"I just want us to keep everything in balance. Like in an ellipse," Ana articulated the model of life that had been crystallizing in her mind during the past few weeks.

"An ellipse?"

"Yes," she confirmed. "Ever since we met, our lives have had two focal points. Each other and our families. Or, in your case, your fiancée. We love both sides of the ellipse. We don't want to hurt anybody, right? So let's do our best to keep this delicate balance intact," Ana pleaded with her eyes as much as with her words.

Michael didn't respond, mulling over the implications of her analogy, which threw him for a spin. For awhile now, he had been contemplating how to tell Karen that he had fallen in love with another woman. But now that Ana was indicating, in no uncertain terms, that cohabitation was out of the question, he realized that he might have to adjust his game plan. "You want to have your cake and eat it too. Unfortunately, that's not possible in real life. Rob wants you for himself. If he knew about us, he wouldn't want to share you. And neither do I."

"But you already have me."

Michael shook his head. "I can't imagine spending the rest of our lives seeing each other in secret. Everywhere we go, we look over our shoulders and hide, like a couple of escaped convicts. We can't even spend the night together. Vacations are out of the question. I don't want to live like this indefinitely. I want us to become a real couple."

"By its very nature, our relationship's illicit," Ana refused to consider his real point.

"And why exactly do you want to continue it like this?" Michael inquired in an irate tone. But he controlled himself and became tender again: "Baby, you know as well as I do that we're meant for one another. I've never felt so happy with a woman before. Besides, what you want is impossible. Passion is by nature exclusive," he declared, relying upon a formulation that any woman in love would easily comprehend. "I'm in love with you. That's why I want you all to myself."

Ana was on the brink of tears. Never before did she perceive the conflict between her two kinds of love—the one for her family filled with affection and a sense of duty, the other for her lover, filled with pleasure and excitement—so poignantly, so painfully. "If only we had met before I married Rob... Or at least before we had Michelle and Allen, it would have been another story. But we don't have the right to destroy the lives of those who love and depend upon us. That would be terribly selfish of us."

Michael had the sinking feeling of being slowly crushed by the weight of her rejection. But he wasn't ready to give up on his goal just yet. Reminding himself that they had been together less than three months, he blamed their fundamental disagreement solely on the factor of time. "I didn't mean to suggest that I'm taking the kid situation lightly," he said, attempting to mask his disappointment. Don't lose your cool. Keep your eyes on the prize at all times, he reminded himself.

Fired up as she was, the terminology her lover used to refer to her children's wellbeing struck Ana as insensitive: "The kid situation?" she repeated. "Michelle and Allen are innocent children who count on having a loving mother and father throughout their childhood."

"Yeah, well, statistically that doesn't happen approximately thirty percent of the time."

"I don't give a hoot about statistics!" she became more incensed. "My kids are not statistics to me."

"I never said they were. Why are you trying to pick a fight?"

Ana made an effort to appeal to her lover's sympathy: "You don't have children. You don't even have a wife. You can't possibly understand what I'm going through; how much I dread hurting my family."

But to Michael's ears, her words sounded accusatory. "Hey, don't try to pin our affair on me. It takes two to tango."

Although they were sitting across the table from each other, Ana had never felt so much distance between them. She looked at her lover as if he were a stranger, astonished by his inability to envision the suffering their actions would cause to those they loved. The two sides of Michael just didn't seem to mesh, so Ana bridged the gap by focusing on his qualities. "I love you," she murmured, scooting her chair closer to his.

Although she meant it, in that instant, her words rang hollow to him. "Yeah, well, you sure don't show it."

Ana had the impression that in the space of only a few minutes Michael had withdrawn several miles. "It's amazing how warm it is outside," she commented after awhile, uncomfortable with the silence.

"We're lucky to get an Indian summer this late in the year," he concurred. The tone and content of their exchange, so conventional and extrinsic to anything they were feeling, reminded Michael of his usual interaction with Karen. He had hit a wall in his relationship with his girlfriend and didn't think that he deserved it. After all, he thought, Ana's the only woman to whom I've given my all. I'm entitled to her devotion and fidelity. By all rights, she should be mine. An overflow of negative emotion saturated his body, escaping through every pore. He tried to control this internal pressure by taking slow, deliberate breaths.

He looks like a bull about to charge at me, Ana observed. "I've never seen you so upset," she said nervously.

"I'll be alright," Michael replied, though his anger was still mounting.

"Have you decided what you want for dessert?" the waitress came by their table.

"We'll just have the check please," he said, without consulting his girl-friend.

"If I said something to hurt you, please let's talk about it," Ana pleaded with him, not wishing to end their date on such a sour note.

Her conciliatory tone only fueled his irritation. "We've said all there is to say at this point," Michael said coolly, following with his eyes the waitress as she returned with the check. "Thanks," he handed her his credit card.

"Perhaps we can arrive at some kind of compromise," Ana suggested. But at the moment she couldn't think of any. She either divorced Rob to be with Michael or she didn't. "Why can't we just stay lovers?" she ended up reiterating her original position.

Michael smirked. "Is that what you call compromising? Having everything on your terms?"

"We see each other so often, we might as well be spouses," Ana weakly protested.

"Well, if we're really like spouses, then I'd like to spend the upcoming Thanksgiving and Christmas holidays with you. And while we're at it, let's throw in this weekend too. How would your husband feel about that?"

"You always forget about the kids..."

"You can bring them along. Just make sure that you leave Rob behind."

"It's not so simple," Ana responded to his sarcastic remark as if it were a serious proposition.

"It sure isn't, because you choose to make life unnecessarily complicated for us." Michael stood up to leave. He'd had enough.

"When will we see each other again?" she asked him, feeling for the first time in their brief yet intense relationship that she was at risk of being aban-doned.

"I don't know." He didn't want to commit to any course of action he might later regret.

"Are you upset with me?" Ana asked him, hoping against hope that he'd say no.

"I'm disappointed," Michael once again showed deliberate restraint in his words. Yet inside he felt the frustration of an animal whose prey is about to es-cape. He attempted to calm himself down by focusing on the shape of Ana's lips rounded into an "o" around his shaft, as she lay on her knees begging his par-don.

"Then why do you sound so cold?"

"Because I'd have liked to see in you the love I feel for you." He looked steadily into her eyes like into a mirror.

"But you do. You know full well that I'm madly in love with you!"

As he saw the raw emotion reflected in her gaze, a new wave of heat rose to his head. To cool off, Michael imagined his girlfriend on all fours, as he was drilling into her, tempted by her orifices, punishing her for sabotaging their rela-tionship. "Yeah, well, apparently not enough," he said out loud, still sullen and distant. Ana was either with him or against him. He wouldn't tolerate being strung along by her much longer, that much was certain.

"What more do you want from me?" she pleaded with a note of despair that reminded him of Karen.

"I want your commitment," Michael said resolutely. "Otherwise, all your nice words mean nothing to me."

"You already have it. I'll be your girlfriend for as long as you love me," she promised him.

Michael felt like flipping over the table when he heard that absurd statement. Once again, he channeled his anger into fantasies bordering on erotic violence. This time, Ana lay prostrate on the ground, inviting penetration by slowly introducing Vaseline into her anus with each finger of her left hand. "Thanks, but I didn't ask you to be my girlfriend. Correct me if I'm wrong, that's what you already are. I wanted you to be my wife."

"Wanted?" Ana focused on his use of the past tense. "So you don't want it anymore?" Never before had she encountered such a strange combination of passionate intensity and extreme conditionality in love, which confused and unhinged her.

"It's not my wishes that pose a problem for us. It's yours," Michael replied quietly, glancing out the window. In its slow rotation, the circular tower had arrived at a position that was approximately 180 degrees away from where it began. "You're the only one who seems to be confused. I, for one, know exactly what I want."

"For now…"

"Pardon?"

"You know that you want me *for now*," she repeated louder.

"Yeah, well, that's a low blow and we both know it," Michael appeared wounded to the quick by her comment.

Ana looked at her lover steadily, ready to meet his challenge. "Has it ever crossed your mind that sometimes I want different things than what you want? Our interests don't always coincide."

"We need to be on the same page on what's important, Ana. Because when our interests will diverge, so will our paths in life."

Michael's tone sounded serious and decisive. Ana didn't know what to say in response. After the waitress returned his credit card, the couple got up to leave.

"You want an ellipse with two focal points, while I want a circle with just one: us," he summed up their situation as they exited the restaurant through its revolving door.

Chapter 7

Feeling like he had overplayed his hand, Michael decided to make a gesture of reconciliation. He called Ana the next day, sounding contrite. "Hey, Baby..."

"Hi," she answered curtly.

"Listen, I'm sorry about how I behaved the other day. Believe me, I'm painfully aware of how difficult it must be for you."

"Actually, I was going to call you if you didn't call me," Ana quickly warmed up.

They agreed to meet at Huron Park. As soon as she saw Michael, Ana felt reassured that all was well between them again. Michael wrapped his arms protectively around Ana to feel her heartbeat through every pore. He rocked gently sideways back and forth, to soothe her nerves. "You're in my bubble now. I won't let anything hurt you." His voice was tender, buttery.

Ana looked up at him. "Your bubble?"

"Yeah. Ever since I was a little kid I imagined that I had this bubble around me. It kept me safe." Michael's features became animated. "Just this past summer for example, I went to a convenience store in Phoenix. That evening, when I was watching the local news, I found out that it was robbed at gunpoint only an hour after I left. The bubble kept me out of harm's way. Now you're in my bubble too. It will keep both of us safe."

She felt like asking him: What about my children? Are they in your bubble too? But she was afraid to spoil their reconciliation.

"Your kids also," Michael read her mind. "I'll take care of them, if it ever comes to that."

They began walking hand in hand along the cement path. But Ana wasn't chipper as usual. She recalled that the last time they were in that park together, she had run ahead of Michael and he had playfully chased after her. The lightness of their courtship was beginning to sink under the weight of pressure. Her gaze was disoriented, scattered like the dead leaves swept away by the autumn wind.

"There's something on your mind," Michael remarked.

She nodded in silence.

"You want to talk about it?" They stopped by a nearby bench and took a seat. He motioned her to sit on his lap, with her legs wrapped up around his torso.

"It's the same old problem. But there's no good solution to it," Ana said quietly.

"Look," Michael began, "I know you don't want to hurt your kids. But even if I weren't directly involved in this, I'd give you the same piece of advice." He swept the bangs away from Ana's forehead, to better gaze into her eyes. "I'd tell you, don't bullshit your kids. Because sooner or later they'll find out about us. Believe me, they'll be much more hurt by the all the lying and sneaking around. You're only compounding the future harm."

"You expect me to tell an eight and a nine year old about our affair?" Ana asked, taken aback.

"Not necessarily. I'm just saying, don't think you can fool them for much longer. Have the courage to reach a decision. I'll understand either way. But you can't sit on the fence forever. In the long run, your indecision will hurt everyone, including yourself."

By way of contrast to their earlier altercation, Michael's words now sounded to Ana like the voice of reason. "I know I'm not a moral person," she replied. "I've wronged my husband and I'm not treating him or the kids fairly. I fell so madly in love with you so fast that I didn't even have the chance to put on the brakes. And my marriage was weak, weaker even than my will. But I know that I don't want to hurt my kids. Just like I don't want to lose you. I'm stuck in an impossible double bind and I don't really know how to escape it."

"I know Baby," Michael pulled her head towards him, so that it nestled upon his chest. She felt comforted by the steady rhythm of his heartbeat. "But it's your kids that I have in mind when I tell you to be honest."

Ana looked up at him again, as he gently stroked her hair. "What do you mean?"

"I don't want them to lose respect for you. Or for us, in the long run. You know, to discover what's going on by accident and then realize that their mom was a cheater and a liar. If you have the courage to tell them the truth, then at least then at least they can't blame you for pulling the wool over their eyes."

Ana felt that what her lover was saying made sense. But the risk of harm was greater than Michael was willing to admit. "Divorce isn't easy on kids their age," she countered. "It can leave emotional scars for life. Especially since they have a stable home environment, with loving parents. I mean, it's not like Rob's ever abusive or anything. He's a good husband and a great father. It's tough to break up our family for purely selfish reasons."

Michael had to fight his visceral irritation at her stubbornness. "I realize that. But we can't live in limbo forever. Look, there's no way to avoid hurting people in our situation," he pursued. "In cheating on our partners, we've done a lot of damage already. The only question we need to answer at this point is how we can minimize the harm, not how to avoid it altogether," he reasoned with her. "That's what we've been quibbling about lately. You claim we'll minimize it by continuing with the lying and the cheating. I say it's by fessing up and embracing our new life together with dignity and courage. The kids would adjust so much better to our situation if we told them the truth right away."

"What about Rob? I don't have the heart to hurt him either."

"But that's exactly what you're doing."

"Yes, but at least he doesn't know it," Ana said, nervously shifting about.

"That's sheer hypocrisy," Michael countered. "They say what you don't know won't hurt you. But they're dead ass wrong about that. It's the lies that hurt most." He sensed Ana's hesitation so he expanded upon his point. "Think of it as hurting Rob now in order to spare him more pain in the long run. Kind of like a father who breaks his son's leg so that he won't be drafted into the war. It hurts the son to have his leg broken. But the risk of worse harm—serious injuries and maybe even death—is so much greater if he goes to war than if he doesn't. At least honesty will give Rob a chance to heal and move on with his life."

"I hate to be in this position," Ana said. "No matter what I do, it feels wrong."

Michael was about to tell her, hey, you decided of your own free will to have an affair with me. Nobody forced you into it. But instead of inculpating her further, he remained diplomatic, to lighten the burden of guilt that continued to pose a barrier between them. "In life it's impossible to avoid harming others," he said philosophically. "Every choice we make is, in some way, at the expense of someone else. Even if you did nothing at all and continued in the lukewarm relationship you have with your husband, you'd still be hurting each other. Because you'd both be losing out on real love with people with whom you're much more compatible. You found someone who's better for you," he said, closely observing her reaction. "Right?" Ana confirmed his statement with a nod. "Well then, don't blow it for us, Baby. You only have one life to live. You owe yourself a chance for real happiness. You owe me that as well. And Rob too. He deserves to be loved as well."

"But I do love him," she protested.

"You have a funny way of showing it."

"I know. That's part of what makes me feel so bad."

Michael gazed lovingly into her eyes. "Ana, I need you much more than Rob does. Because I love you so much more than he does," he said with conviction.

Although Ana didn't reply, Michael felt quite confident that this conversation struck a chord with her. If not now, then in a week, or a month, or maybe even a couple of months. Slowly but surely, he'd chip away at her misguided scruples and misplaced loyalties. Soon enough, his girlfriend would revolve solely around him, just as Karen did.

Chapter 8

Ana arrived home with a heavy heart. For the first time since the beginning of her affair, she realized that she'd soon be compelled to make a choice between her lover and her husband. She attempted to distract herself by doing household chores. Vacuuming, dusting, doing the laundry filled her hours on that afternoon. She folded Rob's clothes with extreme care, even tenderness. When she hung up his work shirts, she caught a whiff of his cologne upon the suits and ties hanging in his closet. The mixture of familiarity, nostalgia and regret made her weak at the knees. Rob had worn the same brand of cologne for as long as she had known him. His clothes were redolent of the first blush of love, when she'd eagerly await every single date with him. But now, the air inside her husband's office seemed saturated with her own anxiety.

"Hi there," Rob entered the room noiselessly and touched her lightly on the shoulder. Startled, Ana turned around. "Do you have allergies?" he asked her, surprised by the redness of her eyelids.

Ana quickly wiped away her tears with her sleeve. "I was just thinking about how much I miss you."

Rob's demeanor changed from serene to apprehensive. Was she going to engage him in one of those draining "us" conversations? he wondered. "Yeah, well, you hardly seem that eager to spend any time with me anymore," he made a preemptive move, unwilling to take the blame for their mutual estrangement.

"With the kids around, it's difficult to find much time for ourselves," she responded quietly, not wishing to provoke an altercation.

"But even when we do, it doesn't change much." Not wishing to dig into the roots of their alienation, he abruptly changed the subject: "Michelle's going to have a sleepover with Natalie tonight."

"That's fine," Ana responded, still contemplating his earlier comment. "What do you think has happened to us over the years? We used to be so close."

Rob shrugged with a sense of resignation. "That's life. We have kids, work, more responsibility, less time for one another. It happens to most couples."

"But does that mean our interaction had to become so..." Ana searched for the right word, "...sterile?"

The harshness of the term wounded her husband. "I wouldn't go so far as to call it sterile," Rob countered. But her comment rang close enough to the truth to trouble him. "Marriage or even just living together for a long time tends to put a damper on the infatuation one feels in the beginning of a relationship," he generalized.

But Ana wasn't convinced. She looked into Rob's amber eyes, those "doe eyes," as she used to describe them back in college. "We were so much in love. We couldn't have imagined this erosion of intimacy ever happening to us."

"Yeah, well, intimacy takes energy and time. We haven't had much of either since the kids were born," Rob reiterated his earlier point, convinced that his wife had a tendency to romanticize reality.

Ana sat down in a yogi position on the carpet. "Do you mind if we continue talking for awhile?"

Rob took a seat on the floor across from her. He wasn't too eager to pursue their conversation, sensing in Ana's tone an emotional neediness that always made him feel viscerally uncomfortable. "Alright," he nonetheless acquiesced. "But I still have some things to do this afternoon. I was planning to use the next few hours to work on a couple of songs."

Ana had a pleasant recollection of their first year together, when Rob had serenaded her with his lyrical, emotionally charged love songs. Back in college, she saw in him a creativity that she had hoped to encourage throughout their marriage. But within a few years, they each went their separate ways. Rob stole a few moments here and there from his overcharged business schedule to squeeze out a few drops of solipsistic inspiration for his music. Ana devoted most of her time to artistic creation, which filled her with a mixture of elation and despair. Although it was pleasurable to paint, material success was much too tenuous. "I'd love to hear your new songs," she said. "You always used to share your music with me. How come you stopped?"

"I hardly have time to compose anymore," he replied, sounding dejected. "Besides, you stopped being interested in my music once you became more involved in your art. It seems that every time I wanted to share with you my songs, you started talking about your next painting. You may not be willing to admit it, but you're more of a diva than a muse."

Ana couldn't disagree with this characterization. It was entirely plausible that she had become so caught up in her own art that she had ignored her husband's timid efforts to reach out to her. "If I've behaved that way, I'm truly sorry. Because I've always admired and wanted to bring out your creativity."

"Apparently not enough to place it on a par with your own," Rob retorted, his inner frustrations trickling out under pressure.

What a waste of so much time together, when we could have been closer, Ana thought. Leaning forward, she gave Rob a kiss filled with a sense of devotion which even years of neglect and months of infidelity hadn't completely dissipated.

He was surprised by his wife's sudden display of affection. "Is anything wrong?" he asked her.

Ana's mood was so fragile that even the gentleness of his tone unhinged her. "I don't want to lose you," she whispered.

"Do you know something I don't? Did the doctor tell you I have a terminal illness?" Rob tried to make light of her strangely dramatic comment.

Ana shook her head. "I just wish we could at least try to focus again on each other. To see if we can reignite the love we felt before."

Rob read her conciliatory statement as a reproach. "And I wish you had a real job with regular hours rather than staying at home to ponder the sad state of our relationship."

"But I'm not blaming you for our problems. I know they're mostly my fault," Ana said reassuringly. "You're the father of my children and our provider. I just wish you had also remained my lover, my fellow artist and my wild child."

"For a long time now, life's crushed the living juices out of me with a ton of responsibilities," Rob retorted, his tone more sad than defensive.

Ana recalled a poem he had written. It had made her realize that there was so much more to Rob than met the eye. "Do you remember that poem you wrote in college? About how having a job, a wife and kids would take over your inner, creative world until nothing was left of it but a worm infested corpse? I thought you were exaggerating ..."

"Unfortunately, I wasn't."

"But couldn't we tap into some of that creativity together?" Ana viewed art as a litmus test that would tell them whether their marriage had any chance of being saved from the grip of her new love.

"Not the way you'd like us to," Rob responded, to her disappointment. "You're so demanding, so intense. You'd like to have hours a day to compose and paint. You want to discuss every spark of inspiration. If we were independently wealthy and childless, maybe we could do that. But even then I'm not sure that I'd get into it quite as much as you do. You need to accept the life we have now."

Ana looked into her husband's eyes: "Do you?"

Rob hesitated for a moment. "Part of me does and part of me doesn't."

"What do you mean?"

"I love the kids and don't mind devoting most of my time to them. But I've always told you that I wish that I had a situation similar to yours. I wish that you had sacrificed your creativity and took on a real job so that I could try to fulfill my artistic ambitions."

"You mean by composing music?"

"Sure," he shrugged. "Or maybe even writing a novel, who knows? When I was young, I had so many dreams. Just like you."

"But you're still young. It's not too late to start now," Ana tried to encourage him.

Rob shook his head. "It's not about my age. It's about our lifestyle. The way our lives are organized. If I did what you do, we'd all starve and our home would be repossessed by the bank."

"Couldn't smaller steps help?" she persisted. "Will you play for me your latest song?" Her eyes implored him to open up to her again.

Rob walked to the closet and took out his guitar, the same one he had used to serenade Ana during their sophomore year in college. She recalled how many dreary winter days in a sparsely furnished dorm room his music had illuminated. And now, as she found herself on the brink of eclipsing their love, her husband's features reassumed their former youthful innocence and serenity. Rob tilted his head slightly upward and to the side as he sang, reminding Ana of a little songbird, as she used to call him. His mouth curled into an oval when he hummed the melody of the refrain, "tu tu ru tu tu." Ana felt the spark of desire reignite. Rob's rounded lips begged to be covered by hers, then slowly licked, then kissed again. The sunlight shone so brightly through the window that it enhanced the brown luster of his hair, its luminous glare masking the "distinguished" white strands that had sprouted the last couple of years above his ears. In that instant, Rob became once again the gentle young man she fell in love with years ago.

Did you ever wonder, he sang,
Why did I go
I didn't have to leave you
Like everyone knows
And do you think about me

When you're alone
Do you ask yourself each evening
Where it went wrong

This wistful song with a soulful melody captured Ana's mood, as if it had been written especially for her. She focused on her husband's delicate fingers, small and thin, moving rapidly upon the guitar strings with a facility that used to mesmerize her as much when he was playing musical instruments as when he tenderly caressed her.

Cause I didn't want to leave you, Rob went on,
I didn't want to hurt you
I didn't want to see you cry for me

"Please let's do everything in our powers to save our marriage," Ana said at the end of his recital with a sense of urgency.

"Why? Are you planning to leave me?" Rob's voice wavered between amusement and concern.

"I'm just touched by your song. It brings back so many beautiful memories," Ana expressed only part of the truth. Ultimately, she lacked the courage to tell him why each note and each word of his song resonated with her current thoughts and feelings.

Chapter 9

Karen surveyed the apartment to decide where to begin packing. The bedroom seemed like the most logical place. She opened the upper hand left dresser drawer and removed all of her underclothes, placing them at the bottom right side of the suitcase. She then pressed them down with her hand, to make sure there would be enough space left for the next drawer, which was filled with tee shirts and nightgowns. Last but not least, there was more than enough room in the suitcase for all of her sweaters: nine total to be exact. She deliberately left two of them behind, for when she'd return to visit him. Going over to the big closet, which they shared, proved somewhat more difficult. Seeing all of Michael's shirts, suits and khaki pants made her wish to put her own clothes back into the drawers. Show some willpower, Karen urged herself. She began removing her shirts, dresses, skirts and pants from the hangers and folding them neatly into the suitcase. All that was left for the second bag were her eight pairs of shoes: two hiking boots, three pairs of pumps, two pairs of black heels and a pair of sandals.

I didn't even need a second suitcase, Karen was surprised to note her own Spartan style. Her modest jewelry collection—consisting of five gold necklaces, including one heart pendant from her fiancé and a gold cross from her mother—

would go into the second suitcase, along with her books. After packing all of her personal belongings, however, the suitcase was still half empty. Karen visually inspected the room, to see what else she needed to take along. All of her makeup, which she rarely wore, fit neatly into an oversized purse. Perhaps some of the cookware could go in here as well, she speculated, walking into the kitchen to confirm that hypothesis. She chose one pizza pan, a skillet and half a dozen plates, along with a few cereal bowls, cups and spoons, knives and forks. Some of them I should ship ahead of time, she thought, carefully placing the fragile dishes into a box filled with shredded newspapers. The flurry of practical activity momentarily distracted her from the reasons behind it. But once she finished the busy work and was faced with the material reality of leaving, Karen broke down in tears.

At this opportune moment, Michael walked in, whistling cheerfully. "What the hell's going on here? Are you going on vacation with your new lover?" he hazarded a tactless joke.

"I've decided to move to Phoenix," Karen announced, assuming the somber expression of someone delivering a eulogy.

"Why?" Is she leaving me? Michael wondered. Part of him felt some relief at this unexpected *deus ex machina* intervention. But another part of him didn't want events to take this turn, at least not yet, since Ana wasn't ready to divorce. "Are you sure you want to do this?"

Karen tried to control her emotions as she began enumerating the reasons for her decision, which she had rehearsed at least a dozen times in her head. "I made a list of all the pros and cons. The pros won. First of all, I'd like to go there earlier than you so I can furnish our apartment. Second..."

"Hold on a sec. *Our* apartment?" Michael interrupted her.

"We talked about moving to Phoenix right after you finish your Masters degree this spring, remember?"

Michael recalled talking about the move several months earlier, but fresher on his mind still was his change of heart since having met Ana. "I told you I'd like to find a good teaching position in Detroit," he, in turn, jogged her memory.

Karen felt compelled to tread more lightly. "I know you were considering looking for a job in the area. But just in case that doesn't pan out, I wanted to set up our nest in your ideal location."

"What if I find the job of my dreams here?" Michael rebutted, substituting the word "job" with the word "woman" in his own mind.

"Then I'll come back. But please promise me that you'll come and see for yourself the new apartment during spring break. It might win your heart, who knows?"

"I seriously doubt it," Michael replied, thinking it was highly unlikely that his relationship with Ana would sour so soon.

"How do you know? A week in paradise might change your mind. Maybe you'll prefer living in an ideal, sunny, beautiful location over a decent job in this dingy ice hole," she tried to tempt him.

"Yeah?" he asked, unconvinced.

Sensing his coolness, Karen approached him and gave him a light kiss on the cheek. "This decision was very hard for me."

"I know, Baby."

"But I've got to do it. I want us to start our relationship from scratch, without all the emotional baggage," she tried to convince herself as much as him.

"You think a new location will erase the fact I cheated on you?" he asked her a little too bluntly.

"I've already forgiven you for that," Karen was quick to assure him, not wishing to reopen that can of worms. "In fact, it cuts both ways. I hope that moving to Phoenix will change your ideas about me. That you'll come there with a fresh head."

"A fresh head of what? Lettuce?"

Karen moved away, hurt that he was making light of such important matters. "I'm being perfectly serious! You have all of these wrong impressions about me."

"Such as...?" Michael's tone now betrayed irritation.

"Such as that I'm not funny. Many people find me hysterical."

"Hey, I can't argue with that," he concurred, thinking of Karen's frequent crying spells lately. "What else?"

"You think that I'm not as cultured as you. When I move to Phoenix, I'll only work part-time. I plan to devote a lot of time to reading and movies, to broaden my horizons."

"That sounds like a good plan," he approved, feeling bored.

"And, of course, I'll also keep up my diet and exercise program."

"Good. Keep me posted, okay?"

"Sure. I was thinking we could talk every night between nine and ten your time," Karen took the cue. "Don't forget, there's a three hour time difference between Arizona and Michigan."

Michael hesitated, wishing to leave his options open. "If I'm not home, just leave me a message on the answering machine and I'll call you back as soon as I can."

"Why wouldn't you be home?" Karen asked, her suspicions easily aroused.

"Who knows? I might want to go out for a beer with some of my buddies."

"You don't have any buddies."

"By that I mean some of my colleagues."

"The only colleagues who interest you are the kind that wear skirts."

Michael couldn't help but smile at this self-evident truth. "You got me there! But I also like shooting the bull with some of my male acquaintances."

Karen's underlying anxiety about Michael's infidelity had been scratched like a wound by their brief exchange. "Don't do anything stupid."

"Don't worry, I won't jump off a cliff," he replied with a smirk.

"I mean it, Michael!" Her tone became beseeching. "At least give us a chance at a fresh start. That's all I ask."

"Okay."

"You promise?"

"Yes."

The following day, at the airport, Karen repeated the same plea, word by word. Her eyes were red from crying, her lipstick smeared by his goodbye kiss. What a lost soul, Michael thought, as if he had already abandoned her. This could very well be our final farewell and she's not even aware of it, he told himself, feeling in charge of their relationship.

"I'll miss you every single day, each minute of each day," she confirmed his intuition.

"Right back at you," he replied, blowing her a kiss.

"I'd never go through with this stupid move if I didn't feel so strongly that's our best chance at a new beginning," Karen excused herself, feeling guilty for initiating their separation.

"May it also mean a better life for you," Michael reverted like a spring back to his original position, of gradually separating the strands of their intertwined lives.

Chapter 10

Since Rob and the kids went to an indoor water park that Sunday and Ana was allergic to chlorine, she stayed behind at home. As soon as she heard the garage door close, she ran to the phone. "It's me," she said.

"Hey Baby!" Michael replied warmly.

"I'm free for the next few hours. Do you have time to meet?"

"Don't I always have time for you?"

It's true, Ana thought. Every time I call him, no matter when, no matter how often, he always sounds so happy to hear from me. Her lover's boundless enthusiasm enchanted her. "What would you like to do?" she asked him.

"I was planning to go furniture shopping this afternoon. Let's just say my old sofa set has seen better days. It would be kind of fun to go there with you."

"Okay..." she answered with slight hesitation. A furniture store didn't exactly sound like the optimal venue for a hot date, but then again, Michael's presence made everything sizzle.

"How about we meet at *Artclub* in half an hour?" he suggested a local furniture chain.

"Sounds good. I can't wait to see you!" she said, punctuated her statement with kisses planted on the receiver.

"Me too, hmm, bye."

Ana went into the walk-in closet to select her clothes, knowing that Michael was very particular about what she wore. She took off her jeans and put on a plaid miniskirt. She then removed her pantyhose and replaced them with the pair of black thigh-highs that Michael had given her the week before. On top, she chose a micro fiber tee shirt with no bra, so as not to leave much fabric between her skin and his roving hands. At first she was hesitant about it, preferring regular pantyhose to the thigh-highs that had a tendency to roll down her legs when the elastic wore out or, if it stayed tight, left red marks upon her tender skin. But, as usual, Michael had countered her objections with the sweet cooing that made her melt inside. "Why refuse me such a little thing? Don't I always do everything you wish?" Then, the melodious refrain she couldn't resist, "Come on, Baby, do it for me please." She did, and not just to please him. Michael's energy and spontaneity made her feel youthful, happy and alive, as if she had spent the past ten years hibernating in a rule-bound, lackluster life that lacked the energy and excitement of their passion.

Michael was already waiting for her in the parking lot. His back was pressed up against the store window, like a spider weaving its net upon a glass pane. He beckoned to her with his index finger to approach closer and closer as she prudently drove towards him.

After parking the car, Ana ran into his arms. As was his habit, he lifted her off the ground in an eager embrace, his lips plastered upon hers, giving her oxygen from his athletic lungs. He gives literal meaning to the expression "he's a breath of fresh air," Ana thought, feeling rejuvenated by her lover's presence.

"It's so good to see you again!" he exclaimed.

"I've missed you so much," she breathed into his ear, under his spell.

"Let's take a little break first," he suggested, opening the passenger door of the car for her.

In the beginning, Ana recalled, Michael's predilection for making love in public places had been a source of tension between them.

"Why does it have to be in public?" she had asked him. She couldn't understand why Michael preferred making love right outside the hotel, even after he had already paid for the room.

"Because it's more fun that way," he had replied with a wink.

"But what if other people see us? We could get arrested for public indecency," she had objected.

"I like living on the edge, Babe. And I don't give a damn about what other people think."

"You act like a horny teenager sometimes," Ana found a ready excuse for Michael's apparent immaturity. Sometimes, however, her lover's silly antics seemed more puzzling than entertaining. She recalled how Michael had boasted about the pranks he played on his parents when they visited him and Karen from Utah. He set the alarm for 2:00 a.m. and 4 a.m. nearly every night.

"Why did you do that?" she had asked him.

"I don't know. To keep them on their toes, I guess," he had responded with an impish smile.

What was even more difficult to comprehend was the pleasure Michael took in duping those who loved him. "For several years I've told my parents that I'm working at an escort service," he confessed to Ana one afternoon, out of the blue.

"Why?"

"Just for fun."

"But why would you lie about a thing like that?"

Noticing the concern on Ana's face, Michael adopted a more serious demeanor. "Look. My mother worships the ground I walk on. Everything I do is perfect in her eyes. But my dad's just the opposite. Nothing I do is ever good enough for him. He wanted me to finish my Ph. D. and become a professor." He shrugged. "But that's not what I want to do with my life. I don't want to spend the rest of my youth rotting in some dusty library. Besides, being a French teacher's nothing to be ashamed of."

"I completely agree," Ana took his side. "And that's precisely why you have no reason to lie to your parents about your chosen profession. In fact, you should be proud of it."

Michael's smile was full of mischief. "I am, but my dad's obviously not. So if I tell my folks I'm the worst thing they can imagine, they'll never dare judge me again." He laughed out loud. "Hell, since I told them I'm working at an escort service, they've been too embarrassed to even ask me about work."

"You're wrong about that," Ana disagreed. "They probably judge you even more, since they're ashamed of your job."

"They'll be alright," Michael brushed off her advice. "Besides, by now, they're used to my shenanigans. Ever since I was thirteen, I started calling them "Bob and Betsy." I had had enough of all the 'Mom and Dad' crap, all that fake parental authority. Since then, they've pretty much realized that I'm my own man and do whatever I damn well please."

"That may very well be, but you're not actually doing what you're saying you are," Ana pointed out.

"I'm just having a little fun with them, that's all."

At the time, Ana felt somewhat uncomfortable with this lie, but chalked it up, once again, to Michael's juvenile sense of humor. "You're such a little boy," she said, assuming the same maternal manner that Karen usually adopted with him. "You play mind games just to amuse yourself."

Ana didn't intend the comment as a compliment, but Michael chose to interpret it that way. "I'm just more independent than most people, that's all. I don't need anybody's approval. When I step into an empty room, I tell myself: I'm here. Where the hell's everybody else? When you step into an empty room, you wonder: Am I in the wrong place? That's the difference between you and me," he concluded.

"Has it ever occurred to you that sometimes you may be wrong?" Ana retorted, not exactly appreciating being called a mindless follower.

"Not really. Let the weak follow the herd. I trust my own judgment."

"You're so cocky," she observed, unwittingly attracted to the very quality that she criticized in him.

"In more than one way," he said with a smile.

Habituated by now to transforming public spaces into their own private love nest, Ana sat on her knees facing the back of the chair. Michael slipped behind her, lifted her skirt and undid his zipper. She felt his moist kisses along the back of her neck, her hair and her cheek. As his tongue traced the inner crevices of her ear, Michael thrust inside her, fast in, slow out, to feel the internal ridges that drove him crazy with desire. He then picked up the pace, pumping faster and faster, until he could no longer contain himself. He burst all over her lower back, in a shower of pleasure and relief. Ana turned around to kiss him. He circularly wiped the grainy, viscous liquid all over the smoothness of her skin, taking great pleasure in this signature gesture, which was simultaneously a demeaning smear and a loving caress that marked her as his.

"I've got good news for you," Michael announced, after they had readjusted their clothes.

"What is it?"

"Karen just left for Phoenix," he informed her.

Ana hesitated, not knowing how to interpret this fact. "You mean you guys broke up?" It occurred to her that this would create an even greater imbalance in their already lopsided ellipse.

"Nope. She went to Phoenix to set up our apartment. You know, to buy furniture for it and that kind of stuff."

Ana hoped she hadn't heard right. "Michael, how can you possibly say that's good news? How often will we be able to see each other from thousands of miles away?"

"Just because she thinks I'll join her in Phoenix doesn't mean I actually will," Michael responded, nonplussed. "Besides, before you were complaining that she's always on my back. Just look at it this way: after she's gone, we'll have a lot more freedom to see each other. Even on weekends," he underscored the positive.

Ana, however, looked downright despondent. "Don't you see what this means? It's like you're putting me on probation. If I don't divorce Rob by this summer, you'll move to Phoenix and marry your fiancée."

"Don't get so defensive, alright?" Michael sharply protested. Then his voice became buttery again: "Baby, it's me we're talking about. You know I'm crazy about you. I know what I want. And what I want is you," he reassured Ana, stroking her hair. His hand moved along her cheek, sliding underneath her jaw, which he gently motioned towards him. He kissed her several times, hoping that his sensual affection would calm her down, as usual.

But she wasn't pacified. "Why didn't you at least try to stop her from leaving?"

"I couldn't. She made the decision unilaterally. By the time I got home, she was all packed, ready to go. Besides, my input wouldn't have changed anything. I have no control over her whatsoever," Michael defended himself.

"Now that's a bunch of baloney!" Ana retorted, pulling away from him. "You've got her wrapped up around your little finger," she indicated with her pinkie.

"You can think what you want," he shrugged. "But you're dead ass wrong about that. Ultimately, she does whatever the hell she wants."

Ana gave him a disapproving glance. "Let's not play games, alright? We both know that her whole existence revolves around you. She's moving to

Phoenix to get you to join her there. She's lost weight for you. Whatever she does, she does it for you. Actually, it's kind of scary."

"Hey, that's her choice, not mine. In fact, it kind of bothers me that she's so damn clingy. I wish she'd lay off a bit and find herself another hobby."

"That's a chicken and egg sort of question," Ana didn't lose track of her main point. "I don't know if Karen was always this way, or if you encouraged her to be so dependent on you. All I can say for sure is that she's really desperate right now. She wouldn't be moving away from you otherwise, since she can hardly spend a few hours without you by her side. It's obvious that she's putting pressure on you to pull you away from me."

"She doesn't even know you exist, the poor woman! Listen to me, Baby," he drew his girlfriend towards him again. "The only thing that matters at this point is what you and I do. Judge me by my actions, not hers, alright?"

Ana remained silent for awhile, contemplating this misfortunate turn of events. "The last thing I needed now was more pressure," she said quietly.

"You take it as you wish," Michael retorted, growing tired of the debate. "Want to help me pick out a new sofa set?" he changed the subject, leading Ana by the hand into the furniture store and periodically planting kisses upon her cheek and hair, to distract her from her worries.

As soon as they stepped inside, a middle-aged saleslady wearing gold-rimmed glasses approached them. "Newlyweds?" she hazarded a guess, noting their public display of affection.

"Yes," Ana answered reflexively.

Michael directed her a look of bemused surprise. "We're looking for a new sofa set. Nothing too expensive. We're just getting started," he addressed the saleslady.

"We have this nice leather set," the saleslady led the way to a dark brown leather sofa and love chair.

"It looks too much like office furniture," Ana commented. "Plus the leather seems wrinkled and worn."

"Lots of young couples prefer this more traditional look for the living room nowadays," the saleslady retorted.

Michael took a peek at the price tag. It cost $4000, which was more than enough to persuade him to take Ana's side. "I don't think leather's for us," he said firmly.

"Alright," the saleslady changed tactics, seeing solidarity. "How about that new micro fiber set? We just got it in stock last week," she pointed to a tan sofa and love seat that, Michael could see from afar, cost a more modest $1000 dollars.

"I love it!" Ana exclaimed, frustrating his intention to haggle. She then plopped herself down on the love chair. Her face beamed with happiness. She rubbed with both hands the micro fiber skin, which left darker and lighter tracks as one does when petting soft animal fur with and against the grain.

Let's compare prices first, Michael was about to suggest. But the image of his girlfriend perched happily upon the love chair momentarily distracted him.

He pictured Ana as he'd have liked her to wait for him at home when he came back from school, once they got married. She was bent over the chair stark naked except for a pair of black thigh-highs and lace gloves. Her light flesh and rosy lips beckoned to quench his desire. Simultaneously, Ana was indulging in her own fantasy of domestic bliss. She imagined herself sitting on Michael's lap in that very chair, watching a romantic comedy together. They no longer cared about the passage of time since they were already married, miraculously, without her even having to get a divorce or hurt her family. In her fantasy, Michael clarified the ambiguities of the movie plot as they periodically fed each other popcorn. Seeing the faraway gaze in each other's eyes, the two lovers exchanged a look of complicity, as if telepathically aware that they were sharing the same dream.

"I'm interested in this sofa set, in dark red," Michael said, thinking that color would go with Ana's pale skin.

"Red? That's a bit bordello, don't you think?" his girlfriend objected.

"That's the whole point," Michael grinned.

"When did you get married?" the saleslady inquired, attributing the young couple's behavior to newlywed syndrome, which a few months of marriage would undoubtedly cure.

"We don't know yet," Ana responded in all honesty. She glanced at her watch and realized that she'd have to return home soon. Her dreamy look and carefree smile were effaced by the awareness that they lived on borrowed time.

"Would you like to purchase it?" the saleslady inquired.

"Not today. But we'll come back for it soon," Michael responded, looking at Ana.

"It will be on sale for the rest of the week," the saleslady informed them. "I wish you a very happy life together."

"Thank you," Ana replied, taking one last breath in the world of make-believe. "Will we ever be that happy couple?" she turned to her lover once they stepped out of the furniture store.

Michael was surprised by the pleading look in her eyes. "It's up to you," he shrugged, feeling like it was a great pity that their future still hung in the balance of her ambivalence. Life would be so much simpler, he thought, if all the major decisions were left entirely up to me.

Chapter 11

"Let's climb up on the roof together!" Michael suggested to Ana, on impulse. He hoped to entice her to make love outdoors, now that his home had become their turf, with Karen thousands of miles away.

Ana shook her head, taking a step back. "No way! I'm afraid of heights."

"Don't worry, I'll hold you," he emboldened her.

"You don't understand. I'm *really* scared of heights. I get dizzy spells even in glass elevators," Ana explained, hoping he'd relent.

Michael stepped into the garage and reemerged with a tall metal ladder. He climbed up to the roof and signaled to his girlfriend: "See? That wasn't so hard. I'll hold on to the ladder, to give it more stability. Come on!"

"It's freezing out here," she objected.

"Trust me. I'll catch you if you fall. Come on!"

"No, I don't want to."

"Don't ever say no to me!" he snapped at her.

When Michael looked into her eyes, Ana felt confronted by a different person. Her lover's usually warm and flirtatious gaze now drilled straight through her. "Why are you talking to me like that?" she asked him, taken aback.

Michael abruptly changed his demeanor. "I'll help you up," he offered with a gracious smile, leaning over and extending his arm to her. "Come on, you little scaredy cat," he taunted her from above.

Ana had an uneasy feeling that her lover was playing a cat and mouse game with her, pawing her around, to see if she'd yield to his will. For a moment, she imagined that Michael was trying to lure her to her death, asking her to climb up on the roof with him only so that he could push her off. With a shudder, Ana dismissed such a crazy idea. "Stop insisting," she said, shielding her eyes from the sun as she looked up at him, leaning over, his boyish face glowing, his dark hair glossy from the shimmering rays. "You look as beautiful as a god," she remarked, hoping that flattery would appease him.

"Then come up here with me, my sweet Aphrodite."

"Adonis, I can't," Ana held her ground, glad that it still lay under her feet. Michael motioned her up with his index finger, with the same gesture with which he brought her closer and closer as she drove towards him during their rendezvous.

A force from within magnetically drew Ana to her lover, nearly overcoming her instinctive prudence. She took a few hesitant steps towards the ladder. She placed her hands on the rims and her right foot on the first rung. When she looked up, she saw Michael's angelic face foregrounded like a beautiful portrait by the stretch of blue sky tinged only by thin wisps of pale clouds. Ana climbed up one step, then another.

"That's my girl!" he encouraged her.

By the third rung, she felt dizzy. "I can't do it," she retreated back to safety.

"You really are a little chicken, you know that?" Michael didn't know whether to feel amused or annoyed by her fear. "Can't you do this for me?" he insisted, determined to push her beyond her comfort zone.

"I'm absolutely terrified of heights!" Ana repeated. His stern expression told her that he wasn't about to give up. "Listen, if you're going to be like this, I'm going home," she threatened.

Michael finally relented. He climbed down the ladder and took Ana into his arms. "You make such a big deal out of nothing," he whispered into her ear. His bodily warmth began to melt her anxiety.

"But you already knew that about me," Ana defended herself.

"I sure did. You're my nervous little Baby," Michael confirmed, rocking her gently back and forth.

"And will you take care of me?" she looked up at him.

"I promise," Michael replied. "But I need your cooperation. I can't do this alone," he said, suddenly aware of the fact that his asking Ana to climb up to the roof with him represented a challenge that tested more than just her nerve.

"What do you mean?"

"We need to present a united front."

"Is this about the divorce issue again?"

"Not necessarily. But we need to remain united whatever we decide to do."

"And what will we decide?" she asked him, genuinely uncertain.

Michael guided his girlfriend into the house, his hand upon her back. He felt the protrusions of her delicate shoulder blades. "It all depends on our strength," he said, acutely aware of her frailty.

"Are you moving to Phoenix this summer?" Ana turned to him suddenly, sensing an implicit threat in his comment.

"You're not getting rid of me that easily, little girl!"

"But Karen will be doing her best to get you to move there with her," she reminded him.

Michael shrugged. "So what? Once I've made up my mind about something, nobody can change it," he said smugly. "Besides, she has no effect on me anymore. She's as familiar as an old shoe."

"Just how many pairs of shoes do you need?" she asked him nervously.

"Only this one," he said, pulling her towards him. "And I want to wear it 'till the day I die."

"Or until you wear it out," Ana would have liked to respond. Once they stepped into the house, she removed her shoes and placed them parallel on the threshold. Michael watched his girlfriend walk barefoot ahead of him to the living room, her gait strangely unsteady, a cross between the walk of a child and that of an old woman. She fell unto the sofa, allowing herself to melt into it as if her muscles had given way to a debilitating torpor. "I'm so worried about our future," she said, gazing at his tranquil features. "How come you're not?"

"Because I care more about the present," he serenely replied.

For her part, Ana found it both reassuring and disturbing that her lover never seemed to worry about anything. Although his carefree attitude offered her some comfort at times, it also made her increasingly aware of a fundamental difference between them. "Will you love me tomorrow as much as you do today?" she tried to bridge the gap through the notion of commitment.

"That sounds like a sixties song," Michael replied with a smile.

Ana took note of his evasiveness. "I'm asking you a serious question. You want me to leave my husband. Why? What will you offer me in exchange? Will you give me love and security ten years from now? Or are we in the midst of a fleeting infatuation that will soon burn itself out?"

"What do you think I am? A fortuneteller? You're asking me to look into a crystal ball and predict the future."

Ana was disappointed by his reply. "I just need to know that there's something more to us than this passion. Because passion's not enough."

"I thought you lived for passion and art."

"There's more to life than that."

"Like what?"

Ana was surprised by his question. "Well, for one thing, there's love for one's children. And a sense of human decency and responsibility towards others. How can feelings based on pure selfishness bring anything good to anyone?"

"You think that what I feel for you is selfish? Then why the hell am I waiting for you? Why am I putting up with all your mood swings and wishy-washiness? Why aren't I pressuring you to divorce right away or moving on, since you won't agree to it? Why does my whole world revolve around you, woman?" he asked, becoming increasingly agitated.

"Because I bring you a lot of pleasure," she answered simply.

"Have I ever behaved in any way that makes you doubt my feelings for you?" Michael's tone wavered between tenderness and reproach.

"You have, indeed," Ana decided to unleash the doubts that had been troubling her for awhile. "You want me to hurt my husband. You want me to hurt my children. And you have been ruthless to your own fiancée. Even though you say your love for her is dead, you're still dragging her along with us. Is that how you'll treat me once you tire of our relationship? Will I be your next back-up?"

Michael wasn't prepared for such an onslaught. "Cut the crap! You know very well that I've never loved Karen like I love you."

"Then why don't you tell her that?" Ana asked him point blank.

His gaze shifted. "Yeah, right. So that if you decide to stay with Rob, I'll be left all alone."

Ana couldn't see the logic behind his statement. "If you decided you don't love Karen before we met, then it shouldn't matter what I decide. Why are you holding on to a woman who's definitely not right for you? Why are you leading her on?" There must be more to their relationship than he's letting on, she speculated.

"Hey, we're in the same boat here. If we're hurting the people we love, it's only because we love each other most. We belong together," Michael reinforced his main message.

Ana's nod reflected irony rather than agreement. "That'll be our excuse when we fall in love the next time. And the time after that. You can't build anything good in life upon the destruction of others."

"I already told you what I think about that. Happiness always comes with a price," he harked back to their earlier discussion.

"Funny how it never seems to cost you anything. Right now, it's mostly Rob and Karen who are footing the bill for our happiness," she commented dryly.

"That's because they aren't as lucky as us. They haven't found the right person yet," Michael retorted, unperturbed. "You need to get your priorities straight and know what you want from life. I certainly do."

Ana gazed at him, struck once again by the contradiction between the angelic sweetness of his features and the callousness of his attitude. "Why is it always about what you want?" she wondered out loud. "I've never once heard you explain that you did something because someone else wanted it."

"Now that's not fair," Michael objected. "I go to movies you or Karen want to see, or to restaurants you like, even if I think they're crappy."

Ana shook her head. "These are trivial compromises and you know it. You always do what you want in anything that really counts."

"Hey, what can I say? I have a mind of my own. I guess that makes me a selfish bastard, doesn't it?" he laughed out loud deeply, from the gut. "And you love me that way, admit it!" he added in response to her disapproving expression.

"I'm not sure that I like that about you."

"Fine, then go ahead and leave me," he said. When put on the defensive or asked to consider the consequences of his actions, Michael instantly retreated into his shell, shutting down. Ana would either be his, or she didn't count, he had decided early on in their affair. After all, he thought, I'm not going to waste my time and energy pursuing a woman who doesn't really want me. I'll be fine without her, Michael told himself whenever confronted with the possibility of losing his girlfriend. The ability to detach with great ease even from the closest human bonds filled him with a sense of autonomy, which translated into the carefree and confident attitude that magnetically drew women to him in the first place.

Ana was no exception. "I can't," she settled back passively unto the sofa.

"Why not?" he approached her stealthily, sensing, like an animal circling its wounded prey, her imminent capitulation.

"Because I'm torn," she replied with a sense of resignation.

Chapter 12

They sat down at the ice cream parlor. Ana was enjoying a chocolate yogurt soft serve while Michael finished up a lemon sherbet in its fruit shell. His gaze lingered on a couple sitting a few tables away.

"It's not polite to stare," she whispered to him.

"I was just thinking…" Michael began.

Ana stole a glance at the couple that had caught his interest. To her surprise, the woman wasn't beautiful, the kind of woman Michael usually looked at, furtively, out of the corner of his eye, hoping she wouldn't notice. Her male companion, on the other hand, was attractive and slim.

"I was thinking about how much I identify with that poor fool," he finished the thought.

"What fool?"

"The one sitting across from that chubby woman over there," he whispered.

"You're judging a book by its cover. That girl might be a very nice and accomplished person. And the guy next to her might be a jerk," Ana pointed out, also in a whisper.

"That's what Karen would like to believe too," Michael replied with a smirk. "But the truth of the matter is that when there's such a big physical discrepancy in a couple, something's definitely off. I began to notice this once we started dating."

"What do you mean?"

"People don't look at us with surprise or disapproval, the way they do when I'm with Karen. If anything, they look at us with envy. Or with this silly grin that says, 'Oh, aren't they cute together!'" He paused for a moment then added, "Once I met you, I realized that I was settling in staying with Karen."

Ana felt flattered, as usual when her lover paid her a compliment. But at the same time, she was somewhat perturbed by his thinking. After all, one could always find a better looking or younger partner than the one currently had. By this logic, would Michael feel like he had settled for her when the next attractive woman came along? "I hope you care about more than just how a person looks," she commented.

"I care about everything," he grabbed her hand. "I care about how she looks, how she thinks, how she acts, how she screws and how smart she is. I want the total package. I want you, Baby."

"And I you," she reciprocated, giving his hand a reassuring squeeze.

"Let's get the hell out of here!" Michael suddenly got up after they had finished their ice creams. "I have a little surprise for you."

"Again? You and your surprises! I hope this time it's not about Karen."

"I'd like to treat you to a little something," he whispered into her ear, walking behind her with his hands covering her eyes, as they stepped out of the ice cream parlor.

"Where are you taking me?" she asked, disoriented from having followed him blindly across the street into a warmer place which, she surmised, was somewhere indoors.

"I did this to test your trust in me," he removed his hands and turned to face her. "Wait. Don't open your eyes yet!" he cautioned, still leading her along by the hand, as they made their way backwards down an isle. "Okay, now you can look."

Ana blinked several times in disbelief. "*Macy's*? This is your big surprise?" she tried not to sound too disappointed. "I come here on my own about once a month," she nevertheless blurted out.

"I want to dress you up like the cute little doll that you are, my Papusica. Any dress you want, if you look good in it, I'll buy it for you," he offered, stepping away a few feet from her.

"Why are you moving away? Are you afraid I might filch your wallet?" she laughed.

"I just want to admire you from afar, like a voyeur," Michael replied, his voice husky and earnest. "It feels so good to know this hot little number's all mine," he declared with a possessive glitter in his eyes. "Other guys can watch you, but I'm the only one who has you."

Ana shook her head. "You've watched that movie, *9 1/2 weeks*, one too many times."

"Maybe. But the truth is that we get to spend so little time together that most of the time we're up-close and personal. All I get to see is fragments of you. Your face, your eyes, your tits..."

"Shhh!" Ana rushed towards him and placed her index finger to his lips. "There are kids in this store."

"You think you're embarrassed now? Wait 'till we get into the changing booth!"

"So what kind of dress should I try on?" she quickly changed the subject, knowing full well that, for once, Michael was being perfectly serious.

"I don't know," he shrugged. "Just pick out whatever you like. In the meantime, I'll feast my eyes on you."

"Suit yourself, but you'll die of starvation." An expert at shopping, Ana nimbly passed her hands through the racks. Michael paced back and forth, observing his girlfriend from different angles: now tantalized by her curvy behind wrapped up in the gray pencil skirt she often wore to her art exhibits; now enchanted by the her dark flowing hair narrowing down to a point on the small of her back; now yearning to taste the nipples he could barely discern through the thin fabric of her white blouse.

"What do you think of this one?" Ana pressed up against her body a black sequin dress cut slightly above the knees.

Michael contemplated it in silence for a moment. "Nice, but a little too cabaret. Can't you find anything hotter?"

"You must be joking! This dress is as sexy as it gets without being illegal!" she pulled demonstratively at its clingy fabric and sparkly sequins.

"It's too predictable. Let's find something more striking. Like you are," Michael approached her stealthily. He took Ana into his arms, his hands plastered on her behind, with reawakened desire.

"Have you no shame?" she pretended to chastise him.

"I sure do! It would be a damn shame to let any opportunity to make love to you go to waste," he responded playfully and kissed her again, this time on her throat, sucking her tender skin between his teeth and tongue.

"Stop it, you little vampire!" she protested, her eyes shifting nervously. She noticed a few women observing them. "Can't you see that they're looking at us funny?"

"So what? Let them. They're just jealous. They want what we have."

"Oh yeah? Then why don't more couples make out in public like us?"

"Because, as the song goes, they've lost that loving' feeling."

"But then why do they stare at us with such disapproval?" Ana rebutted.

"Because they don't want to be reminded of that fact," Michael concluded with confidence.

"So should we buy this dress or not?" she returned to business, seeing it was no use trying to persuade her lover to show some common decency in public.

"And by 'we' you mean..."

"You, of course," she completed his sentence.

"I think we should look for a sexier outfit," he decided. Taking matters into his own hands, Michael began to search among the racks. After a few minutes, he emerged victorious: "This is the one!" he announced, exhibiting a black micro fiber minidress with a crisscross shoelace design along its plunging neckline and on the sides.

"This isn't a dress. It's lingerie. Somebody must have placed it here by mistake."

"Nonsense. This dress is perfect. Sexy yet tasteful. Quirky and unique without being weird. Plus it's short enough not to overwhelm your petite frame."

Ana directed him a look of profound skepticism. "I'll try it on, but only to please you. Because I still think it's way too revealing, even for an evening out."

Once they stepped together into the dressing room, he watched her unzip her skirt, letting it slide smoothly down her thighs and legs. With one swift gesture, Ana swung her blouse over her head. Her dark hair cascaded over her shoulders, framing her pale breasts.

"You're so beautiful!" he said.

Encouraged by his compliment, Ana slipped on the black dress he had selected. After taking one look at it, however, her immediate instinct was to remove it. "It's way too short and tight. It looks like I'm tied up by a pair of ugly shoelaces. I look stupid."

"Not at all!" Michael disagreed. "You look so appetizing in it," he approached and began kissing her.

"I much prefer the sequin dress," she maintained between his kisses.

"That's too bad. Because that one's more common. I've seen dozens like it. This one's intriguing and unique."

"Maybe, but I still don't like it."

"Then could you please wear it for me?" he asked her very sweetly.

Ana felt torn between giving in just to please him and the uneasy feeling that sooner or later, kiss by kiss, plea by plea, Michael always got his way on everything.

"Don't wear this dress for anyone but me, okay? You're my pretty little doll," he unwittingly confirmed her intuition.

"But I prefer to be my own person," Ana objected, sliding her tank top over her head. Michael stopped her with his hand, just at the moment when the shirt covered her face and her naked breasts lay exposed.

"You're my sexy little doll," Michael repeated. He bent down to suck each nipple, one at a time. Ana hoped that the security camera inside the changing booth didn't record what happened next.

As she drove back home with the new dress Michael had bought her, Ana couldn't help but wonder how long her lover would derive pleasure from his new doll before moving on to others. What perturbed her even more than these vague fears of infidelity, however, was the sense that her own wishes were so often ignored: only in such a sweet and seductive manner that she herself was beginning to forget what she wanted and who she was.

Chapter 13

Ana and Michael stood side-by-side, naked. At his sweetly voiced request, she wore only a red heart shaped apron wrapped around her waist. They washed together the dishes after having finished the paper-thin crepes filled with *Nutella* chocolate butter that Michael prepared for brunch. In an assembly line fashion, he washed the dishes while Ana dried them. From time to time, he planted little kisses upon her cheek, her hair, behind her ear and lightly caressed with the tips of moist fingers her nipples, the curve of her waist and the smoothness of her thigh. As soon as they were done, Michael took Ana by the hand and pressed her up against the wall. "Not again! So soon?" she feigned protest. He got down on his knees and lifted her apron. His avid mouth left round wet marks upon her skin while his tongue traced an uneven trail of moisture all over her stomach, her pudendum and her legs. His touch tickled and tantalized her. Her hands grasped his short-cropped hair. She drew his head closer to hers and covered his face with kisses. He delved into her with a sense of desperation, as if he hadn't made love to a woman for years.

"How long had it been?" Ana inquired with a smile afterwards.

"Too long."

"A whole hour?"

"Like I said, way too long," Michael took her into his arms again. They began kissing, probing and pumping with their tongues, consuming each other anew. "Hey, you know what?" he asked once he came up for air. "I'm in the mood for some dark chocolate. Want some?"

"Sure. But, personally, I prefer milk chocolate."

"You're such a little baby!" he taunted her, adding, "Baby." He got up and Ana admired his athletic body, as he made his way through the hallway into the bedroom.

"Wrong way!" she called out to him. "Don't you keep the chocolate in the kitchen, like normal people?"

"Nope," he returned with a small package in his hands. "Karen hides these little gifts for me all over the house."

"That's so nice of her!" Ana said somewhat peevishly.

"Not really. It's kind of like a bitch marking its territory. She wants these gifts to remind me of her," Michael said dismissively.

"She's just trying to be romantic," Ana replied, surprised to hear herself defending her rival.

"In our relationship, I'm the one who pampers you," Michael countered. "Call me old-fashioned, but I think that's the way it should be."

"But I like to be romantic too."

Michael took a deep breath. "You know the only kind of romance I like?" He broke off a small piece of chocolate, placed it between his teeth, then slowly slid it with the tip of his tongue into Ana's mouth like a benediction. After allowing it to melt a little, she returned the favor. They kissed, savoring the bittersweet flavor from each other's tongues and lips. At that moment, the phone rang. Michael reluctantly picked it up.

"Yup!" he responded as usual when he thought it might be Karen. Ana felt a sense of triumph thinking about how her lover always answered tenderly "Hey Baby!" whenever he thought that she was calling him.

"What's up? Basking in the sunshine?" Michael asked his fiancée. He removed the cordless phone from the receiver and lay down on the kitchen floor, next to his girlfriend. "Yup, everything's fine in my neck of the woods," he said in response to Karen's question. "Get this. You won't believe who I had lunch with today," he said, to Ana's surprise, since they had spent the entire day together. She hoped her lover wasn't about to launch into a confession. "Nope. You'll never guess," he continued.

"I certainly hope not," Ana whispered nervously into his ear.

He smiled. "I told you that you wouldn't guess. It was Paul! The guy we met up with in Chicago. Yup. That's the one…" After a pause, he laughed out loud: "He wasn't a scumbag! He just liked women, that's all. Can't blame a guy for that," Michael placed his free hand on Ana's breast and started teasing her nipple between his thumb and forefinger. "Well, it looks like he's having girl problems again. Are you surprised?" he continued. "His new girlfriend just left him. Apparently, she was sick and tired of his philandering," he winked playfully at his girlfriend. Ana couldn't understand how Michael could feel so at ease in such an awkward situation. She gently removed Michael's hand and inched away from him, to indicate her discomfort. He scooted over next to her again and began stroking her inner thigh.

"Well, we just went to the Chinese restaurant near campus. Yeah, the cheap one with the crappy lunch buffet. I know, it sucks. But hey, what do you expect from two cheapskates like us, right?" He laughed out loud. "We had General Gao's chicken with broccoli. We ordered one dish and split it, how's that for cheap? The whole thing cost only five bucks."

An image of Michael preparing the crepes they had for brunch flashed before Ana's eyes. How in the world did he come up with Chinese food? she wondered. And who's this Paul, the guy he supposedly met for lunch?

"So how was your day?" Michael asked his fiancée. "Hm, hmm," he approved of whatever she was telling him. "Did you do your morning workout yet?" He listened for a moment, then burst out, "Good. Jogging and swimming already. Wow… You're a regular exercise beast!" The inviting softness of his girlfriend's skin contrasted with his fiancée's bland account of her exercise routine aroused him. He took Ana's hand and placed it upon his hardened member. She withdrew it. Looking at her with an impish smile, he placed her hand on the same spot again.

"How about your knees and feet?" Michael inquired. He enjoyed the sensation of heat around his midsection, barely listening to Karen's reply. "That sounds like a pretty decent plan," he approved. "Just avoid the pavement. And make sure you put on a lot of sunscreen before heading out," he advised her, his hand over Ana's, to set the right rhythm. "The kids are great!"

Ana became even more confused. Kids? What kids? This conversation's getting curiouser and curiouser, like in *Alice in Wonderland*, she thought.

"Yup. Ray's right here, next to me," Michael smiled reassuringly at his girlfriend, whose bewildered expression amused him. "He had a little spat with Peanut earlier this morning. That's alright. They worked it out and they're best buddies again. What? It was about the chocolates. Peanut said he preferred milk chocolate to dark. Hey, by the way, thanks. I found the ones you hid in my drawers." He paused to move Ana's hand more vigorously up and down his shaft, his mouth still savoring the bitter sweetness of the chocolate he had enjoyed with his girlfriend. "I thought of you when I ate it," he said out loud to Karen. Ana felt his erection moving, as if it were a living creature, in the moist palm of her hand. "Yeah, I miss you too. Listen, I was just about to go mow the lawn," he announced, eager to wrap up the conversation and return to more entertaining activities with his girlfriend. Apparently, however, Karen wasn't quite ready to let him go. Michael began shifting about with impatience. Ana removed her hand. Being no longer aroused, Michael didn't place it back. "Yup," he said in a flat monotone. His fiancée must have picked up on his hint, since he replied, "Of course I enjoy talking to you," in response to her reproach. "I was just ready to haul my ass out of here and cut the grass, that's all."

After a brief pause, Michael cried out, rather aggressively, "I'm not trying to get rid of you, woman! Geesh...We'll talk again tonight if you want. All right?" he tried to pacify her. But Karen must have been unsettled by his tone and the unusual brevity of their conversation, since she still refused to release him. Michael rolled his eyes and made a gesture of despair with his free hand, to suggest to his girlfriend that his fiancée was driving him crazy.

Ana tried to smile sympathetically in response. In her mind, however, she went over the same perplexing phenomenon. Never in her life had she encountered anyone so at ease with lying and cheating.

"Alright. I love you too," Michael's voice betrayed impatience to the point of rudeness. "I'll call you later. Mmm hmm. Bye," he hung up the phone. Despite his earlier irritation, Michael's mood radically shifted, like sunshine re-emerging after a brief thunderstorm. "Now where were we?" he reached for Ana.

She placed her hands upon his to fix them in place. "Hold on. Something's bothering me."

"Whatever it is, I can fix it."

"How can you lie so easily to Karen?"

"You do it too," Michael replied nonplussed. "It's not like you tell Rob about everything we do together." His smile was full of complicity.

"I don't, but I feel pretty bad when I see him right after meeting with you. And if he asks me any questions, I do my best to be brief and evasive."

"Well, as you can probably tell, Karen doesn't give me that option. I guess you have it much easier than me." But Ana didn't look convinced. "Why? You think you're more ethical?" A glimmer of malice lit up his eyes.

Ana shook her head. "No. You're just far better at being immoral than I am. I still can't understand how you can lie so easily."

"It's a gift. I make up all that crap on the spot. The words just flow right out of my mouth whenever she asks me any questions," he boasted.

"But why did you lie about Paul and the Chinese restaurant? I mean, why didn't you say you ate crepes at home, which was the truth and wouldn't have compromised anything?"

Michael shrugged. "I don't know. Sometimes I prefer to make the stuff up. It makes life a little more interesting. But usually I blend in part of the truth with the lie, to make it sound more plausible. It all depends. I don't really think about it in advance. I just wing it."

"I've never met someone who lies as well as you do," Ana reiterated her conclusion, simultaneously fascinated and repulsed by that fact.

"It's all in the details," Michael said, as a tennis pro might boast about his technique by saying, it's all in the wrist.

"It kind of scares me that you're such a good liar."

"Why?"

Ana looked at him with an air of disbelief. "Why do you think? Because you could lie to me as easily as you do to Karen."

"And you to me as you do to Rob," Michael established, once again, a perfect symmetry between them.

"Except that I'm not as good at it. I'm more of an average liar. You, on the other hand, are a maestro."

"What can I say? I'm gifted in all sorts of ways," he grinned.

But Ana wasn't amused. "A relationship can't survive without honesty," she said.

Michael burst into laughter. "Sorry, but this statement sounds funny coming from you."

"I know what I'm talking about precisely because I see it in my rapport with Rob," Ana countered in a serious tone. "That's part of why our relationships with our partners are dying. All this lying kills the trust and destroys whatever's left of the intimacy in a couple. It's toxic."

Michael assumed a more serious demeanor as well. "Listen to me, Baby," he gazed steadily into Ana's eyes. "I promise to always tell you the truth. There will be no bullshitting between us. Ever."

"But how can I trust you, when I know how well you lie?" she asked him. "In fact, you're probably lying to me right now, but I can't tell the difference. Basically, with you, I'll always be faced with the liar's paradox."

Michael looked at her so lovingly that his gaze itself seemed to offer a promissory note. "You need to take a leap of faith. Just like I'm taking one with you. Besides, we've both learned our lesson from this whole fiasco. We know now that lying and cheating ruins a relationship. And we love each other way too much to screw up our special bond."

"I really hope so," Ana liked what she heard and wanted to believe him. "But, no matter what you say, I'll never trust you," she was obliged to admit, since, after all, they had just promised each other total honesty.

"Nor I you," he retorted flirtatiously, as if their mutual lack of trust somehow bonded them further.

"That's very reassuring!"

Michael pulled his girlfriend close to him. "Hey! Stop it. You've got to believe me," he insisted. "I love you more than I've ever loved anyone before. I'll never lie to you, alright? You can start suspecting me of misconduct once you see me behave with you the way I do with Karen. But, so far, I've treated you pretty well, don't you think?"

"Yes," Ana relented, but only for a moment. "Who's Peanut?" she asked him, not yet done with her inquiries.

"He's our imaginary kid. An elephant," Michael said matter-of-factly.

"You and Karen have imaginary children?" Ana asked, thinking that even her eight-year-old son had outgrown that stage two years earlier.

"Yeah, that's our way of compensating for not having any real ones. Kind of in like in that movie, *Who's afraid of Virginia Woolf.* Have you seen it?"

"No." This bit of information introduced a new worry into Ana's mind. Apparently, Michael wanted kids. If her lover had a child with Karen, their affair would be over or, at the very least, seriously compromised. "But you could always marry Karen and have kids," she said, to test him.

"I don't want any kids with her." His voice had a hard edge that gave it a note of certainty.

"Why not?"

He looked sad. "You know how cold and reserved she is. How could I possibly want her to be the mother of my kids?"

Ana touched his shoulder, to comfort him. Although she felt somewhat relieved that her lover had no intention of having children with her rival, part of her also felt bad for him. He had been stuck with such a cold-blooded woman, when he, himself, was so nurturing and affectionate. She also sensed the contrast between the energy he generated when he communicated with her and its complete absence when he talked to Karen. It confirmed her impression that Michael and his fiancée were a mismatched couple, as he had told her from the very beginning.

As if reading her mind, Michael said: "Plus it's too much of a commitment. Kids tie you down."

"And you don't want to be tied down?"

Michael had an instant flashback to the last family get-together. Karen's sister had announced that they were expecting a third child. He recalled the heat of envy that suddenly rose within him, taking him by surprise. At such moments, he too longed to be a father. He wanted to have what so many other men his age already had: a kid to call his own, who'd follow him around and worship the ground he walked on. But all it took was one peek at Karen for him to realize that it couldn't possibly be with her. "Right now, I prefer to tie you down," he retorted playfully, grabbing both of Ana's wrists with one hand and pinning her down under the weight of his muscular body.

Chapter 14

Ana heard her husband open the garage, unlock the back door, then take a few steps on the creaky hardwood floor towards the closet. She sat by the phone, frozen in a state of disbelief. Rob removed his coat and placed it neatly on a hanger. He then greeted his wife, barely looking at her. But even that cursory glance told him that something was wrong. "Are you okay?"

She didn't respond.

"Have you had dinner yet? Where are the kids?"

"Yes, we ate. The kids went to play for a little while at Katie and André's house," Ana replied mechanically, staring blankly ahead.

"Have they finished their homework?"

"They'll do it when they get back from their friends." Ana stood up and headed to the bedroom to avoid further conversation.

As she was about to turn into the hallway, Rob asked her again: "Is anything wrong?"

Even that minimal show of concern transformed her state of shock into one of pain: "Tracy won't be showing my art in her gallery anymore," she turned to her husband, mortified by the bad news she had just delivered.

"What do you mean?"

"She said my paintings are too depressing. People want more cheerful art nowadays."

"How many times did I tell you to stop painting those corpses?" her husband snapped at her.

Ana stared at him in silence.

"You've blown your only opportunity to sell your paintings. Now you'll be spending your time down in the basement doodling only for yourself," Rob summed up the situation. Then he went into his office.

Ana followed her husband's receding figure with a gaze filled with contempt. This man has no heart, she thought to herself. Whenever I'm down, he only pushes me lower. As for pleasure, he doesn't even know the meaning of the word. Recent memories of her romantic dates with Michael momentarily displaced Ana's sense of defeat. She went into the bedroom, looked the door and quickly dialed her lover's number. "Michael?"

"What's wrong, Baby?" he immediately picked up on her anxious tone.

"Tracy threw me out of her gallery. She said my paintings are too depressing," Ana told him in one breath.

"Oh, sweetie, I'm so sorry... I wish I could be there right now to hold you in my arms and comfort you. Do you want to come by my place for a few minutes?

"Yes," she replied without hesitation. "I'll be right over."

As soon as Ana stepped into his apartment, Michael wrapped his arms around her. He rocked her gently back and forth. "It will be alright, Baby. You'll see. We'll find you a much cooler gallery."

"You're just saying that to make me feel better," Ana protested, though his tender demeanor instantly improved her disposition.

"You don't believe me? Alright then, I'll put my money where my mouth is," Michael responded to her challenge. He led her by the hand to his computer. Ana sat on his lap. They began to look on the internet for local galleries. They narrowed down the search to ten places—seven in the Chicago area and three in downtown Detroit—all of which featured some artwork similar in style to Ana's.

After they made a list of their contact information and submission requirements, she felt somewhat relieved. "Well, it's a start," she remarked. "What would I do without you?" she turned around to look gratefully into his eyes.

"You'd be just fine. You're like a cat always landing on its paws. You'd find yourself another lover in no time. Probably one who owns a gallery," Michael replied with a smile.

"You're the only man I want," Ana declared, sealing her words with a kiss. "Do you believe me?" she asked him afterwards, quizzing him with her dark eyes.

"Maybe..." he responded playfully. "And you're the only woman for me," he reciprocated.

Touched by her lover's affection, Ana's thoughts turned, by way of contrast, to her husband. Her resentment quickly resurfaced. "Not only did Rob not help me, but he also blamed me for the whole fiasco."

"Don't pay any attention to him. Rob doesn't know anything about the art world. He's in a regular profession, not this arbitrary zoo of taste," Michael shrugged off the comment.

"You wouldn't believe what he said! That I should paint cheerful stuff that sells. He doesn't care at all about artistic creation. All he thinks about is material success," Ana pursued.

"Well, doesn't Tracy care about the same thing?"

"Yeah, but only after selling my work in her gallery for how many years now? At least she tried," she exculpated her friend.

"But, ultimately, it boiled down to money for her as well," Michael stuck to his point.

"I'm so tired of depending upon the taste of others," Ana commented with a sigh. "I wish people respected real art rather than wanting to put up boring pictures of pretty flowers on their walls."

Michael examined her face, which, it occurred to him, resembled a flower. His glance moved over the petal-softness of her cheeks and lingered upon the delicate stem of her neck, framed by the bloom of her luxurious dark hair. "I love you so much," he declared. "And I believe in your talent."

Ana's smile was grateful yet skeptical, as if she were accepting an empty compliment.

"I mean it," Michael insisted. "You have a rare ability to convey human suffering without making it unbearable. You're a damn good artist. Don't worry about what others say or about what they buy and don't buy. Just keep on painting your way."

For several years, ever since college, Ana hadn't heard such compelling words of encouragement. "What if I fail despite my best efforts?" she asked him.

"I won't respect you one bit less," Michael assured her. "What matters most is creating something that has value for you. If others like it, that's great. If not, just think of it as their loss, not yours."

"Mine too, if I don't make any money," Ana responded more pragmatically. "You know, sometimes you really surprise me, Michael. I wouldn't have pegged you as an anti-materialist."

"If I ever have the fortune of marrying you, you won't have to worry about how much money your artwork makes anymore. I'll support you and the kids. Your only job would be to produce the best art you can create. I believe in you, Ana," he gazed steadily into her eyes.

Her lover's words were music to her ears. For as long as she could remember, Ana longed to be an artist. With or without the money. With or without the external recognition. Michael was the only person she had met who not only respected that dream, but was also willing to support it. There was only one little glitch in this perfect picture. "How would you be able to support me and the kids, when all you make is 12,000 dollars a year from your teaching assistantship?"

"You forget that I'm getting my degree this spring," he reminded her. "Hopefully, I'll get a teaching position in French at a decent prep. school. They generally pay about 50,000 bucks a year. Money would be tight, no doubt. But we'd have enough for a family of four. Especially since, I presume, Rob would chip in and help support his kids," he calculated. "But there's no way in hell that I'd ever be like him and discourage your goals," he underscored his main point, which seemed to have left a deep impression upon his girlfriend. "I know how important painting is for you and I promise to do everything I can to make you happy."

"… and, above all, to make yourself happy," she added with a smile, recognizing a hedonist when she saw one.

"Hey, I look out for number one!" he unabashedly admitted.

Strangely enough, behind Michael's every declaration of love, Ana sensed the ominous potential of its undoing. She couldn't help but wonder if with the same fortuitous ease with which her lover became entirely devoted to her, he wouldn't attach to some other object of affection and forget her in an instant.

Noticing the unsteadiness of her gaze, Michael thought that he had been too forward, forcing her hand once again on the divorce issue. "If you wish, I'll wait ten years to marry you. Until Allen goes off to college," he said, moved by a blend of spontaneous verbal generosity mixed with the cunning intuition that was exactly what Ana needed to hear at the moment.

She looked up, surprised by this concession: "Do you really mean it?"

"Absolutely. In fact, I'd wait for you my entire life," he continued, encouraged by her grateful gaze. "That's how sure I am that you're the only woman for me."

"That's got to be the sweetest thing anyone has ever said to me," she responded, moved.

Michael proceeded to prove the depth of his feelings through his usual show of tenderness and sensuality.

But after only a few minutes, Ana jumped up from his lap. "Oh my Gosh! I've got to get home right away. I was so upset, I left without even telling Rob that I was leaving. He's probably looking for me as we speak."

"Don't worry about it. He might just be enjoying a few minutes of peace and quiet at his computer."

"Not likely, since the kids are back home from their friends' house. They probably need my help with their homework," she pulled away, picked up her coat and hastened towards the front door. "I love you!" she turned to blow her lover a kiss. "You've made me feel so much better, you know that? You're absolutely wonderful."

"We'll finish up those gallery applications next week," Michael poked his head out the door, following his girlfriend with avid eyes, his desire fanned by their interrupted caresses.

Chapter 15

When Ana stepped in the door, everything seemed normal at home. Rob was sitting at the dining room table, helping Allen with his math homework. The boy was complaining about it while demonstratively hitting his forehead with the palm of his hand, to protest the level of difficulty of the multiplication problems.

"Oh, come on. It's not that hard," Michelle chimed in, more to irritate her little brother than to assist him with his homework. "Look, six times seven means six plus six seven times. Get it?"

"I don't want her to help me!" Allen objected, now feeling provoked by his sister in addition to being distracted from a very important game of Nintendo by the homework in question.

"Michelle, would you mind working on your own homework?" Rob suggested in a tired voice.

"I already finished it. All I had was reading." Michelle said, scooting her chair closer to her brother's, to be able to peer over his shoulder.

"Daddy, tell her to go away!" Allen screeched.

At this point, Rob noticed that his wife had returned. "Where were you?"

"I went shopping," she replied, then thought her answer must sound implausible.

"I could have used a little help with the kids," Rob responded, resenting the fact that after a full day's work, he had to spend the rest of the evening tending to the children on his own. "Sometimes I feel like a single dad around here."

"Usually, I pick up the kids from school, make them dinner and help them with their homework," Ana pointed out in her own defense.

"Yeah but while I'm at work, you get to relax in your studio all day long," Rob commented irately.

Ana felt her cup overflow. Enough was enough. Without saying a word, she ran up the stairs to her bedroom, taking two steps at a time.

The first thing that caught her eye was the neon light of the alarm clock, indicating that it was 9:34 p.m. After washing her face with cold water in the bathroom, Ana changed into the animal print teddy that Michael had given her and slipped under the covers. The softness of the down blanket soothed her weary body, enveloping her in a physical comfort that felt almost maternal. Her head sunk into the pillow. She closed her eyes and tried to clear her mind of all worries. As she was beginning to relax and drift off to sleep, the room suddenly turned bright red through her closed eyelids. Ana opened her eyes. The overhead light blinded her at first, but after a few blinks she discerned her husband's approaching figure.

"Sorry if I was so hard on you earlier. I had a tough day at work myself," Rob said apologetically. He got under the covers and touched Ana's shoulder, hoping to make peace with her.

"I'm really tired tonight," she assumed the cold manner that had become a constant source of humiliation to him.

He took the hint but didn't leave the room. If only out of principle, Rob decided to reclaim his bed: the rightful place he had relinquished for years. For the next few minutes, husband and wife lay quietly side by side. Neither of them could fall asleep.

Rob stared blankly at the ceiling, contemplating the sad state of their marriage. Ana's hardly a wife to me anymore, he thought. I'm not even welcome in the same bed with her. She doesn't have a reliable career, yet still leaves too much of the childcare upon my shoulders. And what about her constant meetings? If she has so many clients for her paintings, then how come she got kicked out of Tracy's gallery? Rob began nursing his suspicions, which had grown in direct proportion to the frequency of his wife's absences.

Lying on her side, her back turned to her husband, Ana was considering the reverse side of the coin. He doesn't love me anymore. Instead of being supportive like Michael, he blames me for my failures even when I do my best. We've grown too far apart to stay together, she concluded.

"Where were you *really* this evening?" Rob asked her.

Ana's nerves were stretched to the maximum. "I have something to tell you," she turned to him, ready to disburden herself, out of an incongruous mixture of guilt and contempt. "I fell in love with someone else. I've been seeing him for months. I was with him this evening."

Her confession was greeted with silence. Rob felt too stunned to respond. Although the thought that his wife might be having an affair did occur to him, he had always dismissed the idea. He told himself that a frigid woman wouldn't take a lover. But now the clues began falling into place. His chest felt constricted and his thoughts were a blur.

"Who is he?" he asked after a few moments, seeking clarity.

"He's a grad student in the French department at the university."

"Do you love him?" Rob's voice sounded faint and strained.

"Yes." Everything that had been so muddled in her mind became, all of a sudden, crystal clear. "Rob, I want a divorce," Ana stated resolutely.

Part III

Chapter 1

Rob stared up at the ceiling, which even in the darkness of the night seemed ghostly pale. He placed one hand upon his heart, as if to monitor its slow, irregular beats. To Ana, who looked at him out of the corner of her eye, her husband appeared still as a corpse.

"Why are you doing this to us?" he asked her, feeling nauseous. His mind struggled to absorb the information that his body viscerally rejected.

"We weren't much of a couple anymore..." she started to explain.

But, in Rob's mind, that familiar refrain didn't justify anything. "If you thought our marriage was that bad, then why couldn't you talk to me about it before throwing yourself into the arms of another man?"

"I tried to, several times. But you just thought I was nagging you."

Rob looked at his wife. Even with her disheveled hair and tired eyes, he still wanted her. In that instant, he felt ready to do anything to save their marriage. "Oh, God. I never thought it was that bad..." he responded, trying to recall if he had ever taken seriously any of Ana's warning signals. A sinking feeling seemed to turn his body to mush. He couldn't believe that his wife of ten years would pick up and leave him one day in such a backhanded and cowardly fashion, for another man. It occurred to him that he didn't know anything about this stranger yet, presumably, Ana would expect him to trust him with their children. "How long have you known this guy?"

"For almost a year."

"And you've been cheating on me with him this whole time?"

"Yes."

Rob felt the heat of anger rise to the surface. "Why didn't you tell me about it earlier? I can understand falling in love with someone else. I can understand being unhappy with our marriage. But I can't understand all the lies. Why did you have to deceive me for so long?"

Ana looked away, to avoid seeing the pain in his eyes. "I didn't want to lose you or to hurt anybody," she tried to convey her initial ostrich policy towards her affair. "Michael pressured me to do this."

"What do you mean?"

"He kept telling me how hard it was to keep up the intensity of our relationship in these difficult circumstances. He complained that we're hiding like prisoners. Basically, he made me feel like our relationship might not last unless we moved in together."

"And you didn't find his behavior in the least bit manipulative?" Rob prompted her, already starting to cultivate a negative impression of his rival.

"Not really. I could understand his perspective. He said that he loved me much too much to share me with another man."

All Rob heard in her words was a selfish justification revolving around the pronouns "me" and "he." "What about me? Where did I fit into your sordid scheme?" he demanded. "Did you ever stop to consider my feelings? Would you want to be deceived for a year? Or would you prefer to know right away?"

Ana remained silent.

"In depriving me of knowledge," Rob pursued, "you've deprived me of the power of choice that both you and your boyfriend had."

"I didn't want to hurt you or the kids," Ana said. "For the longest time, I thought I could handle the situation. I wanted to keep everything with Michael under control and our family intact."

"Then why did you tell me tonight?"

She finally turned to him. The whites of his eyes glistened in the semi-darkness. "Because everything spun out of control. The pressure became too much. I wasn't even planning to tell you tonight. It just came out."

"It just came out? So you were planning to lead me on indefinitely?" For the first time since he could remember, Rob became conscious of an impulse towards physical violence, which he curbed by looking away from Ana.

Her temples pounded, like a heartbeat. "I don't know. I felt pressure from all sides. In fact, I was torn from the start."

Rob felt not only deceived, but also unjustly abandoned. I've wasted my entire life with a woman who doesn't love me, he thought, regretting ever having met his wife. "All these years I've been a decent husband to you, Ana. I've provided for you and the kids. I've never once cheated on you. I could easily have done to you what you did to me. But I made a deliberate choice to build my life around our family." He placed his hand to his forehead in a futile effort to stop a splitting headache, which emanated from the inner schism he felt: the sense that he had done the right thing but maybe he shouldn't have. "That turned out to be the biggest mistake of my life," he concluded out loud.

"No it wasn't. You should be proud of your choices. You're a better person for them. Besides, nothing that happens between us should ever make you regret your love for the kids. You've been an excellent father."

"And husband!" Rob added, stung by her omission. This woman has never appreciated anything I've done for her. All these years, all my efforts to make her happy, were all for nothing. Wasted on a faithless... he had to struggle to repress the hateful word that was on the tip of his tongue. What would be the point of resorting to insults? They wouldn't fix and they couldn't heal anything.

"Yes, but we've neglected our marriage for several years," she returned to the leitmotif that made her actions seem more justifiable in her own mind.

Rob looked at her with disgust. How easily she rationalizes her vicious actions! he marveled, incredulous that this was the woman he had loved for so long. "What makes you so sure that he'll treat you better than I have?" he asked her.

Her demeanor became wistful. "Because he loves me. He always listens to me. He's extremely affectionate and attentive. And he accepts me for who I am, flaws and all."

Rob felt sick to his stomach upon hearing her words of praise. His anger veered off from Ana to her lover. "Is he also married?"

"No, but he's been engaged for several years to a woman he doesn't love."

This formulation struck Rob as bizarre. "Then why did he stay with her?"

Ana shrugged. "Convenience, I guess. Plus, she really clings to him."

What makes you so sure that he won't do the same thing to you, once you move in with him? " Rob countered. "He might very well tell the next woman he falls in love with that he's been with you just out of convenience. It's a very *convenient* excuse."

Ana felt more confident about her reply this time. "Michael never felt for Karen what he feels for me. Our bond's *special*," she emphasized. "We're much more compatible than he ever was with her. We have similar interests in art and literature." She noticed that her husband looked skeptical. "It's not that he criticized her to me or anything," she hastened to add. "Actually, he told me that she's a nice person. It's just that Karen's personality's way too cold for him. She's distant and not all that attractive."

"Is that what you told him about me?" Rob asked her, recognizing in his wife's answer the classic excuses people generally offer for cheating.

"No, of course not. Because that wouldn't be true about you."

Rob struggled for a moment to adjust to the new truth he had discovered about his wife. She's a cheater and a liar, he reminded himself. "Since when has the truth stopped you from lying?"

Ana looked at him reproachfully, as if this allegation were somehow unfair. "I told him that we've grown apart. I also said that you're a decent man and a great father and that I don't want to divorce you. But he insisted. He said a love like ours couldn't be shared."

How disgusting! Rob thought, embittered. "Well then the two of you deserve each other!" I'm not going to give up until I open her eyes about that bastard, he nevertheless told himself, not sure why he remained invested in having Ana see the truth about her lover. "But you're naïve to assume that he'll treat you better in the long run just because you're *special* to him at this moment," he added, since his wife's reasoning struck him as simultaneously self-serving and self-defeating.

Of course Rob would say something like that since he never saw anything special in me to begin with, Ana told herself.

"Has he told his fiancée about you?"

"Not yet. He was waiting for me to make the first move with you."

"How considerate of him!" Rob exclaimed. Then he paused, still bewildered by Ana's choice of partner. "You trust a man who's been deceiving another woman and leaving her over you?"

"Karen's not right for him, but she's very clingy. She's doing everything within her powers to make sure that Michael doesn't leave her. He's just trying to let her down easy."

"It sounds to me like he's stringing her along."

"You're interpreting everything I say so negatively," Ana protested.

"That's because it *is* negative!" It occurred to Rob that a guy who was so manipulative towards both his fiancée and his girlfriend could be stringing other women along as well. "Just how many girlfriends does this guy have?"

"He *had* lots. If you can even call them girlfriends," she placed emphasis upon the past tense. "He was a bit of a player before we met. But he was totally upfront about it. He told me from the start that he had one-night stands and flings with dozens of women. About two hundred in all."

"You mean twenty," he corrected her math.

"No, it was hundreds," Ana stuck to her original estimate. "He kind of overreacted when his first girlfriend, Amy, left him for another man." Ana read the disapproval in her husband's expression. "But ever since we met, he's been completely faithful to me," she hastened to add.

Rob's eyes widened with dismay. "How can you trust a single word this guy's telling you?"

"Because he's changed. He acted that way before only because he hadn't found the right woman yet."

Rob marveled that his wife would even listen to such drivel, much less believe it. Something's not right with her head, he concluded, seeing no other logical explanation for Ana's uncharacteristic gullibility. "And you assume you're the one? For the rest of his life? If you believe that, I have some ocean front property in Ohio to sell you."

"Yes, I believe him."

Rob couldn't repress a skeptical snort. "Are you out of your mind? You're leaving an honest and faithful husband for a cheating sex addict?"

"He was that way for awhile because the woman he loved left him. Then he ended up with a frigid fiancée. He feels extremely frustrated with their relationship," she mechanically encapsulated Michael's version of events.

"Nobody's chaining him to her."

"You don't understand their situation. Karen's so needy and desperate that he didn't have the heart to leave her yet. He's been giving her a chance to get back on her feet in Phoenix," Ana continued elaborating her lover's perspective.

"How considerate of him! I'm sure you'll appreciate his kindness when you find yourself in his fiancée's position," Rob retorted, his anger being slowly displaced by indifference. Let her do what she wants. Why should I care? Soon, her fate won't even matter to me anymore, he predicted, longing for an early liberation from the disaster his wife's actions had created.

"He's promised that he'll never be dishonest with me. He says I'm everything he's been looking for in a woman," she insisted. She didn't know anymore if she was trying to persuade herself or him.

Upon hearing the kind of cheesy baloney sleazy men feed credulous women to get them hooked, Rob looked at his wife like one does at a stranger. He felt like he had never really known Ana. Everything he had assumed to be true about her and their marriage turned out to be false. All these years he had believed that they had settled into a comfortable relationship, built on mutual love and commitment, even if the heat of their passion cooled off once the children were born. But, as it turns out, he now reflected, I've been worth so little to her that she's ready to leave me for a jerk. "A leopard doesn't change his spots," he cautioned. "Who knows what he told his fiancée. She was probably the love of his life too. Until you came along."

"No, she wasn't," Ana stubbornly maintained.

Rob looked at his wife once again with a sense of disbelief. Part of him was still hoping that this episode would turn out to be surreal: a nightmare that would disappear as soon as he opened his eyes. The new Ana he had just discovered was not only dishonest, but also completely delusional. What he found most depressing, however, was how strongly his wife seemed to feel about her decision to leave him. Her reasons for wanting to leave me, Rob reasoned, are premised on the belief that the intensity of her affair, in which she's spent so little time with her lover, will continue unabated forever, after living together and marrying him. How could such a seemingly intelligent woman be so blind? he asked himself, scrutinizing Ana's features in search for an answer. Her eyes glowed feverishly, confirming his intuition that she was must be overtaken by some kind of delirium. "Don't you think it's at least possible that this guy originally told his fiancée, and probably other women too, similar things to what he's been telling you?" he asked her. "I mean, it's all too convenient. He makes up some lame excuse to dump his current partner once he's tired of her so he can hook up with the next woman he's interested in for a while. This guy's completely untrustworthy."

"I believe in giving people a second chance. Especially since Michael hasn't given me, personally, any reason to doubt him," Ana stuck to her perspective.

"You've been completely brainwashed. Otherwise you wouldn't be half as blind."

Yeah, right, Ana answered only in her own mind.

Whether or not our marriage can survive this storm, I think she's in desperate need of therapy, Rob observed. Then his thoughts traveled from his wife back to himself. Feeling deeply wounded by his wife's attitude and betrayed by her actions, it occurred to him that, ultimately, he'd be happier if Ana carried through with her plans and went to her likely doom with her lover. But the next moment, when he thought of having to tell the children that their mother was leaving him for another man, Rob's mood switched again. I don't want to see our family broken, he told himself. If anyone had asked him before what he'd do in such a situation, he'd have answered that he'd never be faced with it because his wife wouldn't be unfaithful. If that person had insisted on such a hypothetical, he'd have said that he'd be so upset that he'd immediately ask Ana for a divorce. But reality often turns out different from what you'd expect, in the abstract, before it catches you off-balance and hits you like a tidal wave with its brute force. Rob looked into Ana's eyes and took her gently by the hand. "You're taking a very serious step that will affect all of our lives. Please think about it carefully before we reach the point of no return. I love you and am willing to work with you on our marriage. But you must decide what you want: our family or that man."

"No matter what happens, I'll still be a good mother to my kids," she replied, unwilling to acknowledge how much her children as they were now—happy, safe and innocent—belonged to the intact family she was about to sacrifice to her lover.

Chapter 2

On her way to Michael's house, Ana prayed silently to discover some major flaw in him: anything that would give her the strength to back down, resist his magnetic pull and do what was right for the sake of her family. As soon as he heard her car pull into his driveway, Michael ran to greet her.

"I told Rob about our affair," Ana announced right away.

"You what?" Michael's eyes opened wide. A rush of emotion rose to his head and his ears turned crimson with heat. He had finally defeated his rival and won over his girlfriend, as he always knew he would. He just didn't think it would happen so soon. . . .

"I had to," she said almost apologetically. Michael led her into the house, one hand placed upon the small of her back, the other opening the door for her. "It's been weighing on me for months. I couldn't hold it in anymore. Are you mad at me?" she asked him, unsettled by his silence.

Michael stopped in the middle of the living room. "Are you kidding? You're finally mine!" He picked Ana up and began twirling her, spinning around faster and faster, holding her high above his head, like a trophy.

The walls mixed in with the brown of the furniture and the white of the ceiling as the whole room became a dizzying whirl. "Michael, stop it!" she exclaimed, feeling like she was no longer in control of her senses.

After a couple of more revolutions, Michael put her down, in front of him. As he admired her bright eyes and flushed cheeks, he couldn't help but smile. Ana looked at her lover indulgently, as she did whenever he acted so young. Michael beamed with delight, like a child receiving a much-awaited Christmas gift. His pleasure made her smile too, only with traces of sadness. "It was pretty tough on Rob. And we haven't even told the kids yet."

"We'll deal with all that later. Now it's time to celebrate!" Michael rushed into the kitchen to uncork the bottle of champagne he had saved for a special occasion.

Ana followed him there. She accepted the drink, sipping it gingerly while examining his expression. "I'm happy that you're happy."

"Aren't you happy for yourself?" Michael asked her, his own bubble of elation punctured by her somber mood.

She hesitated a moment before replying, "Yes, I am."

Michael grabbed her free hand and pulled her to him. "What's wrong, Baby? You don't seem that happy," he commented, becoming attuned to her guarded reaction.

Ana looked to the side, focusing on the diamond pattern of the linoleum floor, to distract herself from her own mixed emotions. "I dread telling the kids about this," she said quietly.

Michael placed his wine glass on the kitchen counter and took a seat, pulling Ana unto his lap. "Look at me," he gently commanded. "You need to get a hold of yourself. What's done is done. We finally took the plunge. Now we need to stay united. Let's keep our eyes on the prize at all times, alright?"

"I'm worried that it's going to be hard on them."

"So where's the news here? We already knew it wouldn't be easy. But are you going to fall apart at the finish line? Or are you going to carry the day for us, like a champ?" he slipped into life coach mode.

"I'll do my best," she said without much conviction.

"Did you discuss with Rob any of the practical details yet?" Michael asked, a sense of pragmatism displacing his initial elation.

"Like what?"

"Like the custody issue."

Ana nodded. "It's one of the first things we agreed upon this morning. We're going to draft a divorce settlement that stipulates joint custody. Fifty-fifty, with alternating weekends and split vacations. That way Michelle and Allen can feel at home in both places. But they're staying at their current schools, since that's where all their friends are. We don't want to uproot them."

"Good," Michael approved, in a business-like manner. "What about the money?"

"Since we just bought the house, we don't have that much left in savings. But we co-own it, so I'll probably get half its value. I'm not really sure yet."

"How much will you get?"

"About 150,000 dollars," she estimated.

"Not bad... We can use part of that for our vacation," Michael proposed. His eyes lit up at the prospect of traveling again. "I was thinking this summer we could spend a few days in Paris. And maybe also visit Provence for a few weeks, since it's cheaper and less crowded."

"Actually, I was planning to put those funds in a money market account. I wasn't going to touch them until we buy a bigger house. You know, so that the kids can each have their own room," Ana shared with him her own plans.

"Nah, they'll be fine," Michael brushed off her suggestion. "At any rate, they're not mutually exclusive, the new house and a nice vacation." He approached Ana until she could feel the warmth of his breath tickle her cheek. "Our little honeymoon," he enticed her. It suddenly occurred to him that he might even be able to get Ana to fall in love with Arizona. "We don't even have to travel abroad. I know this wonderful little place in Arizona, which I'm sure you'd love. Have you ever heard of Sedona? It's an artists' town filled with galleries and surrounded by mountains and canyons. It's really spectacular. The landscape changes color with the sun." Maybe once Ana saw the beauty of Sedona and got her paintings into a gallery or two down there, she'd be instantly seduced by it. Rob would be just fine taking care of the kids on his own. After all, hadn't she told him ad nauseam that he was a responsible father?

"We can't count on the settlement money," Ana proceeded with caution, oblivious to the reference to Sedona. "First of all, because the divorce might not go through by this summer. Plus, even though Rob and I co-own our house, I don't really know how much of it is actually mine."

"Why not?" Michael frowned.

"Because I bring in less income than he does. At any rate, we never discussed these matters before. We weren't planning to divorce," she directed him a meaningful glance.

"That kind of crap, not having a clue about who gets what, won't happen if we ever get divorced!" Michael assumed an air of authority. "We'll draft a nice prenup, so that it's clear that my house stays in my name, no matter what happens with us."

Ana's gaze clouded. "Why do we need a prenup?"

"To protect our assets. Even when madly in love, one has to keep one's feet firmly on the ground."

It occurred to Ana that before, during all those months of courtship, her lover had made the opposite argument. He had tried to persuade her, through both words and actions, that when one's passionately in love, reality itself is lifted unto a higher plane of existence. "I just can't believe that you're already thinking about divorce when we haven't even gotten married yet."

"Hey, if you don't like the deal, then the marriage's off!" Michael retorted. "We can always live together, if you prefer," he added, adopting a cavalier tone that he had never used with her before. But it sounded very familiar to Ana because she had heard him talk that way to Karen on the phone. She jumped off his lap and stood facing him, with arms akimbo. "All these months you've been pressuring me to divorce Rob so that we could marry. Honorably, with lifelong commitment. You never once mentioned anything to me about a prenup or cohabitation. I'd have never agreed to any of that! I certainly didn't want to leave my husband, whom I still love despite our problems, and traumatize my kids, just so that the two of us could live together, with no commitment, no nothing, like a couple of hippies."

Ana's voice had a high-pitched edge that grated on Michael's nerves. He had never noticed it before, during their previous disagreements. "Calm down, alright? We're not Romanian peasants and this isn't the nineteenth century! Co-habitation isn't a dishonor in this country. I assure you that they won't stone us for it here."

"You never mentioned any of this to me before. I'd have never agreed to it!" Ana insisted. She couldn't help but think that her lover had dangled the marriage proposal, along with the promise of lifelong commitment, as bait, to lure her to divorce her husband.

"That's because we never discussed any of these practical details before. The best relationships are those where both parties choose to be together on a daily basis."

For Ana, his answer felt like a slap in the face. And a brazen lie at that, since she recalled that Michael had certainly discussed the practical details of their marriage, even telling her how they'd buy a house in the same neighborhood, what a loving husband and stepfather he'd be and what activities they'd do together as a family. She scrutinized his face, attempting to pierce through to the core of his innermost thoughts and feelings. But Michael's expression remained perfectly serene, except for a glimmer in his eyes that struck Ana as more malicious than mischievous. He's enjoying toying with my feelings, she observed. "Not for me. For me, the best relationships are based on mutual trust and commitment. I trusted your offer to marry me and I can't accept having a relationship with you under these changed conditions."

Michael appeared suspended, like someone in a video right after you press "pause." Given that, so far, Ana had always given in to his wishes, he hadn't expected such a vehement negative reaction from her. "I guess then I'll just have to go through with my original plan and move to Phoenix. Or maybe even try out California," he mumbled. During one of Ana's spells of ambivalence about divorce, he had looked up Amy, his first girlfriend, on the internet. He found out that she lived in a small town in California and still looked pretty hot. If things didn't work out with Ana, he had made a quick mental note, he might be tempted to give Amy a second try. And if that wasn't an option anymore, he calculated two moves ahead, then perhaps the combination of Karen and Phoenix might not be so bad after all. Michael mentally congratulated himself for not having burned that bridge just yet.

"What are you talking about?" Ana asked, in a daze.

"I was just thinking out loud about what I'd do if we broke up."

"At this point, shouldn't you be thinking about how to make our relationship work?"

"Hey, don't try to pin this one on me! I'm not the one backing out on us. You are."

"That's only because you're backing out of our commitment!" Ana protested. Michael looked away to hide a sardonic smile. "Look at me!" she commanded. "From the very beginning, you pressured me to marry you. You always said *marriage*. You never said anything to me about living together. I'd have never agreed to it," she tapped the floor with her foot.

She's having a freaking meltdown, Michael noted with irritation. Not willing to give up on Ana right at the moment when he had finally seized her from her husband, however, he felt obliged to back down momentarily. "Baby, chill out, okay? I still want to marry you," he reassured her. "But I refuse to get myself in the situation Rob's in right now, not sure as to how to divide our property. This house is mine and it will stay mine," Michael defended his main point, his eyes shining with the possessiveness dogs have towards their food dish when they perceive another dog approaching it.

Ana looked at him with dismay. It's as if she couldn't recognize her lover anymore. She had definitely expected that telling Rob and the kids would be a challenge. But she didn't imagine that Michael himself would suddenly back down from his seemingly rock-solid commitment the very instant when the reality of marriage displaced the fantasy of their affair. He had always told her that he lived in expectation of that reality. But now that they were about to live together, Michael was hedging, protecting himself from her. Erecting a barrier between them. A wall made of qualifications, divided assets and, worst of all, divided interests. Ana couldn't help but smile at one of the sad, self-defeating ironies of human nature. As soon as you finally get what you want in life, you no longer want it.

"What are you smirking about?" Michael asked her.

"It just seems a little strange that you already had a backup plan all lined up in case our plans fell through."

"Hey, you know me! I always come prepared," he replied, it occurred to him, in the same way he had to Karen when she made the same charge.

"Would you forget me that easily?" Ana struggled to contain her emotions.

"Of course not," Michael replied more tenderly. "I was only talking like that in self-defense, because you're pushing me away. But, quite frankly, I feel like if you ever decide to leave me, I'll be spending the rest of my life searching for another you. Let's face it. If we ever make the colossal mistake of breaking up, neither of us will find this kind of passion again. As they say, lightning doesn't strike twice."

Michael's tone was so warm and his demeanor so gentle that Ana really wanted to believe what he was saying. Even a day earlier she'd have believed him. But on that afternoon, the mood had changed. She couldn't dispel a sense of unease. "I don't know," she replied, still shaken by the perfunctory manner in which Michael had withdrawn his earlier promises. "It seems to me like you loved me so much more when you didn't have me," she said with a note of regret. Ana thought about what Michael had told her months earlier; about the protective bubble that surrounded him ever since he was a child. "All of a sudden, I feel like I'm not in your bubble anymore."

"That's a low blow and you know it!" Michael protested. "I had always envisioned drafting a prenup to protect my assets. I just never mentioned it to you before because I saw no point in it. Our marriage was just an abstraction then. Now it's becoming real. Hey, speaking of reality, do you want to get a new living room set? That nice, bordello red micro fiber sofa and love chair we looked at a few months ago? I wouldn't mind making love on it right there at the store, when nobody's looking, to test it. What do you say?" he added playfully, hoping to lighten her mood.

Ana had a flashback to the early days of their affair, to her own fantasy at the furniture store, of sitting in Michael's lap in the love chair in the same position she occupied a few moments ago on the kitchen chair. Only in her mind they weren't arguing about cohabitation, prenups or money. They were watching movies together and planning fun activities with the kids.

"Is Rob giving you money for your half of the furniture?" Michael interrupted her pleasant reminiscence.

"I don't know. Why?"

"Because we could use it to buy new furniture."

"I'm glad to see you have your priorities straight," Ana remarked coldly. It occurred to her that her generous lover was rapidly morphing into Karen's stingy fiancé.

Noticing her defensive attitude, Michael decided it was time to switch gears, back to romantic mode. "I can't wait for us to move in together!" he declared excitedly.

His statement struck Ana as incongruous with their earlier exchange. "Are you sure about that?"

"Of course, Baby. I've been trying to get my paws on you for almost a year now," Michael said, his hand slipping surreptitiously underneath Ana's shirt and gently fingering her nipple. Inspired by the giving softness of her skin hardening under his touch, he recalled his own vision of their future, which he had turned over and over in his head during the long, frustrating months when they were obliged to live apart. "I'll call you from school at lunch, to let you know ahead of time what I want you to wear when I come home and in what position you should wait for me," he whispered breathlessly, barely containing his arousal. "On some days, I'll ask you to wear the thigh highs and corset I bought you and wait for me by the door, with your legs open," he motioned apart her thighs with the tips of his fingers, "while on others, I may want you to wait for me wearing nothing but a pair of black lace gloves, bent over our new red micro fiber sofa," he added, attempting to remove her shirt.

But Ana resisted, keeping it firmly in place with both hands. "Hold on a sec. You expect me to wait home for you wearing certain clothes and in certain positions?" she repeated with an air of incredulity.

"Hey, it will be my little treat for bringing in the dough for our family," he crudely articulated what so far had been only an implicit assumption.

Ana was troubled not so much by what her lover was asking her to do as by his peremptory manner. Michael had never behaved this way with her before. It's true that sometimes he bought her lingerie or sexy outfits that he wanted her to wear when they were together. But they were always offered as a gift and accompanied by kisses, caresses and sweet nothings whispered in her ear, which made her happy to wear them, just to please him. "Michael, what did you think

I'd become once we lived together? Your kept woman? I'll be your partner, your wife. I hope that you'll continue to treat me with respect."

At that moment, she realized that, up to now, she'd have done almost anything for this man. Just because of the manner in which he asked her, so cajoling, tender and seductive. Just because of the manner in which she loved him, so completely, with such ardor. She'd have sold her soul to please Michael, since he seemed to love her like she had never been loved before. But now that he was practically giving her orders, treating her as if she had no mind of her own, for the first time in their relationship, Ana felt her will tighten inside of her like a muscle being flexed, resisting overt domination.

"Of course I'll respect you," Michael moved her chin up with his hand, to look into her eyes again. "Haven't I treated you well?"

"So far you have," she cautiously admitted. "Let's keep it that way."

"What's that supposed to mean?" he asked, not pleased with her qualified response.

"You've spoiled me as a girlfriend, that much is true," she acknowledged. "But it's a whole different story to treat me well as your life partner, once we actually move in together."

"Just tell me what you want and I'll grant your wishes in an instant," Michael responded with an air of indulgence, like Santa Claus asking a little girl what she wanted for Christmas.

Ana was encouraged by his receptiveness. "I was thinking that during the weekends when we'll have the kids over at our house, we could have one day in which we cart them around to their lessons. Allen has guitar and Michelle has horseback riding on Saturday mornings. Then we'll drive them to their various play dates with their friends, which are really important to them. We could make Sunday our special family day, you know, go to the zoo or the movies and have fun together. That way the kids can grow to like you and adjust to our situation."

"Like that will ever happen!" Michael snapped back. He had expected that Ana would share with him her sexual fantasies, not all the freaking errands he was supposed to run for her brats.

"What do you mean? You always told me that you'd do your best be a good stepfather to Michelle and Allen."

"Sure, I'll try," Michael said unconvincingly, with a shrug. "But no matter what I do, they'll still hate my guts. Especially Michelle, since she's older and a girl. Girls are more precocious and sensitive than boys. Plus they tend to worship their real dads. So I guess, I'll be shit out of luck with her."

"Michael, don't be so negative!" Ana protested. "You never used to talk like this before."

"Yeah, well, before none of this crap was real."

"But you wanted it to be real. You insisted on making it real," she reminded him. For her, Michael's attitude towards her children functioned as a litmus test. "If you love me, you'll be good to my kids."

"Of course, Baby, I'll do my best. It's just that my best may not be good enough. I'm more realistic than you are," Michael smiled gently and stroked

Ana's hip with a circular motion. "I was thinking that the nights we don't have the kids over at our house, we could go out to clubs."

"To clubs?" she repeated, with obvious disappointment. "I don't get into that modern stuff, rap, hip-hop or whatever they call it. I'm too old for it and even when I wasn't, back in college, I still didn't like it. Earlier, we were talking about taking salsa lessons together, remember? What happened to that idea?"

"Hey, why waste the money on lessons when we can go dancing for free, right?" Michael countered cheerfully.

"That's one way of looking at it."

Michael realized he had to say something to preempt her withdrawal before they reached the finish line. Her took Ana by the hand and gazed steadily into her eyes. "Listen to me, Baby. After everything we've sacrificed to be together, let's make sure that we're still on the same page. If you agreed to divorce Rob, given your misgivings, it's obviously because you love me more. You told me you want to spend the rest of your life with me. I feel the same way about you. Nobody's more important to me than you are. We may face some difficulties at first in adjusting to our new circumstances. That's only to be expected. Nobody said divorce was going to be easy. But if we stay united, we'll make it. This is our one chance in life to really live out passion in marriage. Let's not blow it, alright?"

"I don't intend to," she assured him.

Yet as she drove back home, Ana couldn't help but dwell upon Michael's earlier comment, about dancing for free. It sounded analogous to the popular saying, why buy the cow when you can get the milk for free, which seemed to sum up her lover's reaction to her news. It also reminded her of a scene she witnessed quite often at the beach, where a man sucks in his stomach when a pretty young woman walks by, only to let it go back to its natural beer gut in front of his own good old wife. Before Ana had been the girlfriend to impress. But now she had become the future wife in front of whom Michael could let all his flaws hang out, his flabby selfishness and unbecoming stinginess. Above all, it was the suddenness of his transformation that made her feel uneasy.

Ana recalled how one day, early into their relationship, Michael had described to her his game-like attitude towards one-night stands. Before he scored, he explained, all of his energy was focused on seducing a given woman. But after he had sex with her, he lost all interest and didn't "waste" an ounce of energy on pleasing her anymore. One anecdote stuck out in Ana's mind. Michael had told her about his date with a girl with wavy, auburn hair whom he had picked up at a bar and invited to a movie. It took him more than half the movie to coax her gradually, kiss by kiss and caress by caress, into eliminating the divide between them, crouch unto his lap in the back row of the movie theater and make love, in the blend of semi-obscurity and public display that never failed to arouse him. But as soon as they consummated the act, Michael disconnected. When the girl tried to caress him again, he moved her hand away with the impatience with which one swats off an annoying fly. Once his sexual desire was satisfied, he wanted to watch in peace the rest of the movie. "But how can you switch just like that, from charming and seductive to cold and disinterested, in a matter of seconds?" Ana had asked him. "Because I was done with her," he replied with a shrug. "And didn't you ever become attached, you know, because of the sexual intimacy, to any of the women you dated?" she pursued. "To those sluts? No freaking way! I just used them and tossed them away like a bunch of dirty condoms. Back then, before we met, it was all about the scoring, Baby!" he boasted with an air of smugness that bordered on cruelty.

In some ways, this episode reminded Ana of how Michael had acted with Karen. Although his relationship with his fiancée had been more serious, a similar pattern of behavior emerged. Once Michael decided he was done with a woman, her needs, her actions and her entire personhood no longer mattered to him. Initially, Ana had felt a certain pride that her lover had placed her in a different category of women, since he had often told her that he had never loved anyone so passionately or needed anyone as much as her. She was the exception that confirmed the rule, he had repeatedly assured her. No doubt, part of her enjoyed the challenge of taming a man who had been so wild with every other woman in his life.

Yet now that she had observed her lover's reaction to the news that she'd finally become his partner, Ana began to wonder if she, herself, wasn't just a score for him. A different kind of score, a seduction of body, mind and soul. One that took more time, energy and patience, but with the same inevitable end result. Once he had won the match, Michael would move on to the next challenge. This idea greatly perturbed Ana, hitting too close to her husband's warning. For that very reason, she tried to dismiss it. Michael loves me, she told herself. He wooed me for months. He gave me all of his attention and affection. He promised to take care of me and the kids.

By the end of this rehearsal of Michael's loving words and gestures, Ana felt somewhat pacified. But a trace of distrust towards her lover lingered. She was now on the alert for any future warning signals. Because she knew that when he was really interested in a woman, his focus on her and on everything associated with her was total and intense. It resembled a powerful beam of light that illuminated only one spot at a time. For almost a year, Ana had been that spot.

But now she began to wonder for how long she'd continue to attract his undivided attention. Because once Michael's interest diminished, the light dispersed. Afterwards, there was no energy left in the relationship, except perhaps for the unreciprocated, desperate efforts of a discarded partner: which is to say, a total waste of energy. Emotions poured into a black hole. Although Michael may not have been honest with anybody else, Ana sensed, he always remained true to himself. He lied disturbingly well, with an uncanny glibness and ease. But he was much too selfish and, in that sense, much too honest, about his own needs to convincingly fake interest in someone else. Which is why, despite his seductiveness, deceitfulness and charm, Michael was actually quite transparent if you were willing to open your eyes and take a good look at him. And once you did, you saw the man Ana was beginning to see. You saw the seducer.

Chapter 3

The storm had passed, yet the calm state in which Ana and Rob found themselves seemed more like the eye of a tornado. The room vibrated with the stillness of tension. They had told the children as diplomatically as possible the bad news. They tried to explain that they both loved them very much, but didn't get along as well they should, which is why they were getting a divorce. At least Ana had framed the issue in such a conveniently neutral manner. Feeling like a hostage in the whole situation, Rob had added that he was completely against the divorce, but that Mama fell in love with someone named Michael and was leaving him for that man. Michelle was the first to respond, with a shrill scream, "Mama, how could you do this to Daddy? I hate Michael!" She stormed out of the room and locked herself into her bedroom, to release in solitude the pain of her newly shattered world.

Allen didn't react at first. He stood still, trying to comprehend what was happening between his parents. He looked in silence at his father, then at his mother. After a few moments, he decided that he loved them both equally. In his mind, they were the greatest parents in the world. "I love you," he said to them. Then, seeing that his sister had defended his father and that his mother was in tears, he gave Ana a hug. "Don't worry, Mom. No matter what happens with you and Daddy, I'll still love you," he said to her.

Rob resented the fact that his wife would be selfish enough to hurt her own children. Enough was enough. "When are you moving out?" he asked her.

"I don't know," she replied, dazed by her children's opposite reactions, both of which tugged at her heartstrings. "I wish I could take this pill, like in that science fiction movie, and just forget about him. I wish we had never met," she said in all honesty.

"You say this now. But as soon as you see him again, you change your mind and forget all about us," Rob countered.

"He's got this weird hold on me," Ana said, placing her hand upon her heart, as if trying to relieve a muscular ache that accompanied her oppressive, conflicted emotions. She thought back to the melodious sound of Michael's voice, to his mesmerizing gaze, to the overpowering fierceness of his desire. They lulled her conscience, controlling her will, as if by some inexplicable hypnotic force. Ana didn't know how to explain this strange phenomenon to anyone, not even to herself. She felt like a willing captive, a contradiction in terms. Because Michael wasn't just pleasant or charismatic. He was *intensely* charming. Ana felt gripped by the force of his personality, swept up by the whirlwind of his desires, uplifted by his vows of love.

Seeing the faraway look in his wife's eyes, Rob felt disheartened. If even seeing the pain she's causing their children couldn't stop her, nothing would. "You're free to do as you wish." A flash of anger passed through him when he realized that Ana was hedging not because she felt genuinely torn, as she claimed, but because she didn't fully trust her lover. "But let me make one thing very clear: if you chose Michael, it's all over between us for good," he decided it was time to draw some clear boundaries.

Ana nodded mechanically in agreement. She had made such major life decisions, yet she felt like she hadn't chosen anything at all. It was as if a hidden force had been pushing her from behind or pulling her forward, towards her lover. "I don't want to go but I can't stay either," she replied, stuck in the impasse that had paralyzed her from the start.

Rob stared at her unsympathetically. "I can't feel sorry for you, Ana. At least you have no one to blame but yourself for your pain. The rest of us are suffering because of you." His eyes flashed with hatred. But the emotion didn't last long. Ana looked so lost, defeated. She didn't look like a woman leaving an unhappy marriage to live out her dream with the love of her life, as she claimed. "Why are you doing this to us?"

"He loves me. I owe him this chance."

Her answer triggered Rob's anger again. "How does he love and respect you more than I have?" he demanded. "I've been loyal and faithful to you all these years. I've taken care of you and our kids. What has he done to prove his love? Other than declare it with words? Words are cheap, Ana."

"The day I got kicked out of Tracy's gallery, I felt horrible," she recounted. "And you just blamed me for my bad break, as usual. But Michael was there for me. He helped me find other galleries."

"Any man who wants to be with you for awhile will tell you what you want to hear," Rob countered.

"His interest in my art is genuine," Ana insisted.

"It may very well be, but I'm sure it's no coincidence that he gave you all that attention right at the moment when he was trying to win you over from me. Only time will tell if he'll be as supportive of you once you actually move in with him."

"I believe that he will be."

How it sickens me to hear this, Rob thought. She wants me to match Michael in devotion to her art. How could I possibly do this? When would I have the time? he asked himself. Should I quit work, apply for a government check and spend my time tending to her needs? And what about my own needs? "How much do you encourage me and my ambitions?" he turned the tables on her.

"You never want to share anything with me."

"You're not interested in what I do."

The same old Catch-22, Ana observed. In that instant, she felt almost relieved to escape this vicious circle by moving in with her lover.

"If you had real confidence in your art, you wouldn't need his goddamn flattery!" Rob burst out. "Look at the guy's actions, not his words. If he had any genuine respect for you, he'd see how torn you feel and let you make your own decisions, without pressuring you."

Ana bristled at this accusation precisely because it rang plausible. "Michael doesn't control me. And he doesn't flatter me either. He just encourages me to create the kind of art I want."

She's blind, blind as a bat, Rob thought. "All I can say is watch out for excessive flattery, Ana. Because those who feed your vanity generally want something from you," he warned her. "I don't understand what this guy wants from you, since you're neither rich nor famous. All I know is that you've wrecked our marriage for a very shady character. Only time will tell if I'm right or wrong about him. But if things don't work out between the two of you, I won't be there to save you," he repeated, hoping to get through to her.

"Yes, only time will tell," Ana repeated.

When he went to sleep on the living room sofa that night, Rob contemplated their earlier conversation. She regards me as a safety net, not as her husband, the man she loved. I could never take her back even if she changed her mind, he resolved. There's no way I could continue living in a marriage where I linger as the pale image of Ana's one true love. How often, and how pathetically, must I keep on telling her that I want to feel loved exclusively in our relationship? The fact that I have to point this out to her is a sign of incredible weakness and dispensability; an emasculated cry for a love that can never be forthcoming from the brutally selfish woman who forces me to ask for it in the first place.

Chapter 4

The next day, after Ana called him to confirm that she and Rob had told the kids about the divorce, Michael took a few moments to gather himself. He wanted to make sure that he was in an appropriately contrite mood to tell Karen the bad news. He sat down on the couch and attempted to think of something depressing, but nothing occurred to him. What the hell, I'll just wing it, he decided and picked up the phone. "Hey, you!" he greeted Karen.

"Hey..."

"What's wrong, Baby?"

Hearing him call her "Baby" in such a tender manner, Karen instantly let down her guard. "I don't know what to do anymore," she complained. "I've tried everything. I exercise four hours a day, like a maniac. I follow our strict program. I walk in the morning, then go swimming after lunch, do cardio and weight lifting at the gym in the evening. I eat fresh fruit, lean meat and vegetables. I cut out sugar and carbs," she became increasingly upset as she recounted the Spartan nature of her diet regimen. "But in spite of all this, I've gained three pounds this week," she sourly concluded her report.

"Did you check to see if the scale was set on zero?"

"Yes, it's set where it's supposed to be. I weigh myself about once a week, like you suggested."

"No more than that!" Michael counseled. "You don't want to become too obsessed with your weight. It could backfire."

"Yeah, well, it's a little too late for that."

"You're doing everything right, Babe," he reassured Karen, usually sympathetic when her distress wasn't demonstrably his fault. "Don't beat yourself up over nothing. You've lost so much weight already. It's normal to gain a few pounds just from the exercise itself. Remember what I said earlier?" he quizzed her.

"What?"

"Muscle weights more than fat. Since you've been weightlifting almost every day, it's likely all that weight gain's pure muscle. In fact, you've probably lost some more fat weight. So, actually, congratulations are in order!"

"I'm not so sure about that," Karen replied, not ready to uncork the champagne bottle just yet. "My clothes don't fit any looser than they did last week. In fact, they seem a little tighter."

"You might be bloated from p.m.s.," Michael offered another charitable explanation.

"Maybe," Karen hesitantly conceded. "My period's so irregular since you made me get off the birth control that I don't have a clue anymore when it's supposed to come."

"That's alright. The pill screws up your hormones and makes you retain water. And you know I didn't propose this for selfish reasons this time!" he laughed out loud.

"Yeah, well, it's hard to tell since we've been living apart. And I miss you so much... I think about you all day long," she launched into the real topic she wanted to discuss.

"I know," Michael said without reciprocating, however. He used this occasion to allow his fiancée to pick up the scent of his detachment, without having to express it explicitly himself. His philosophy of communication was: when it comes to anything unpleasant, let your interlocutor do the work. That way you'll get much less of the blame in the end.

"Do you miss me?" Karen fell right into his net, sensing evasiveness.

"Of course," he blandly affirmed.

"You know, I've been thinking about giving up on this whole Phoenix idea," she tested the waters for a potential change in plans. "It's so lonely out here without you. And who knows if you'll move to Arizona this summer. You may find the job of your dreams around Detroit."

Michael was not expecting this twist. "I don't think you should make any hasty decisions just because you had a bad week," he assumed the tone of a disinterested observer. "Look at all the progress you've made in such a short time. You're exercising several hours a day. You're eating healthy. Even your attitude seems much brighter."

"The truth of the matter is that I'm not happier here by myself," Karen confessed. "I try to sound upbeat on the phone since we talk so little. But there's not a single day goes by without me feeling sad that we're apart."

"Let's not exaggerate!"

"I'm not exaggerating," Karen insisted. "If anything, I've been doing my best to downplay the whole situation. I know how annoying it is when people complain ..."

"You never annoy me."

"I wish that were true! You're very patient," she added, knowing full well that Michael responded much better to flattery than to blame.

"Hey, what can I say? I aim to please." She was fortunate to have me for as long as she did, Michael told himself whenever he tried to put himself in Karen's shoes. She had a great life while we were together.

"You're so much more independent than I am," Karen returned to her initial concern. "Sometimes I feel like you don't miss me as much as I miss you." She hoped that Michael would deny this claim.

But he didn't. He said nothing at all, allowing his fiancée to draw her own conclusion from his eloquent silence.

"I go on walks to many of the places we visited together last summer," she prodded him. "That way I feel like part of you is still here with me."

"Which part?" Michael quipped, glad to have spotted a pun.

"You always mock me!" Karen snapped back. But she caught herself. "I'm sorry, honey. I'm a little on edge today. I think I'm gaining weight just from depression. My metabolism must be slowing down."

"I highly doubt it," Michael countered, as comfortable as ever with the subject. "Genetics, exercise and diet determine metabolism much more than mood does," he expertly pointed out.

"Yeah, but my mood's pretty bad," she emphasized, hoping that Michael would finally see how miserable she felt away from him and encourage her to return promptly to Detroit. "Why don't we just forget about this stupid Phoenix idea, sweetie, and live together in Michigan, as before? We can always visit Arizona whenever we want," she tried to tempt him.

"It seems to me that you're so much happier in Phoenix," Michael countered since, as far as he was concerned, Karen was moving quite literally in the wrong direction.

"I just miss you too much to enjoy living out here without you." She hoped her confession would move him.

Michael exhaled with frustration. Karen was coercing him into becoming brutally explicit, something he preferred to avoid. After all, he didn't want to look like the bad guy in this whole scenario. "I'm afraid I have some bad news," he announced in a somber tone.

"What is it?" she asked with trepidation, dreading his reply.

"I've fallen in love with another woman. Her name is Ana. She's leaving her husband for me," Michael came out with it all at once.

At first, Karen was too shocked for words. Thinking back, she sought hints of this disaster in her fiancée's behavior during the past few months. In all honesty, she couldn't see any. There was nothing unusual about their interaction lately. After all, she recalled, Michael had tried to discourage her from moving to Phoenix in the first place. He talked to her on the phone every evening. He expressed interest in her concerns, as usual. He advised her on the diet and exercise routine, same as before. And he told her that he loved her, same as always. She was left with only one possible conclusion: "Is it because you were horny?"

Michael latched on to that promising lead. "Maybe," he said, hoping that she'd develop on her own the explanation of their tragic undoing from this minimal justification.

Karen didn't disappoint him. "I shouldn't have left you on your own," she turned the blame back upon herself. "Even my mother warned me that you couldn't leave young men on their own. They have their needs."

"That much is true," he concurred.

"My depression was like an internal alarm signal. It was telling me that it was a huge mistake to come out here on my own," she repeated, momentarily forgetting that the reason she had moved to Arizona in the first place was to try to resuscitate their comatose relationship.

Michael remained silent. After a rather unpromising beginning, the conversation was progressing surprisingly well.

"Is she pretty?" Karen pursued, her curiosity aroused after the initial shock.

"Yes."

"Is she a student in your department?"

"No. She's an artist."

"How did you meet her?"

"We met in church," he stated, without elaborating.

"Since when do you go to church?"

Michael refrained from commenting.

"How long have you been seeing her?" Karen pursued.

"Since a few weeks after you left." Will she buy that? he wondered.

"I bet you didn't even let our bed get cold before you replaced me!" Karen let out only a tiny fraction of the spleen building up inside her.

But Michael couldn't tolerate an unsubstantiated charge. "Yeah, well, you're dead ass wrong about that! I was alone for a whole month before I even looked at another woman," he lied with panache.

"I'm sorry," Karen backed off. "I made such a huge mistake," she reverted to self-blame. "Even my own sister said you were too good looking to be left alone. But I didn't listen to anyone. And now everything's ruined," she concluded, devastated.

"Yeah, well, you couldn't have known. Some things in life are beyond our control," Michael said philosophically.

"Do you love her?" she asked with trepidation.

"Yes," he affirmed.

"Why?"

"Who the hell knows? Why do people fall in love?"

"Do you feel like you're more compatible with her?"

"In some ways," Michael responded noncommittally, not wishing to alienate her. "Like I said, she's an artist. She's pretty and smart. We have a lot in common."

"You always thought I wasn't good enough for you," Karen commented without any hint of reproach.

Michael could now afford to be gallant: "That's not true. Don't put yourself down."

"What's going to happen to us now?"

"I'm afraid it has to be over, Baby," he said tenderly.

Upon hearing this statement, Karen broke down in tears. "Can we still be friends?" She felt crushed by the thought of never being close again to the only being she had ever needed and loved.

"I doubt it," Michael replied, thinking that Ana would object to him remaining close to Karen, especially while being strictly forbidden herself from establishing friendships with other men. "But we can exchange a few greeting cards a year, like for birthdays and Christmas," he kindly offered her a fair substitute for marriage.

After a brief pause, Karen said: "I'm too upset to talk right now. I'll call you back as soon as I gather myself, okay?"

"Sure, take your time," Michael obliged, thinking that the whole unpleasant business was concluded much more expediently than he had anticipated. He knew that the discussions with Karen would continue, of course. But at least the worst was over. Relieved, he went into the kitchen to make himself an ice cream sundae.

Meanwhile, Karen threw herself on her bed to melt into a pool of emotion. What a heavy price I've paid for one stupid move! she thought, going over and over in her head the counterintuitive decision to save their relationship by moving away from her fiancé. Eventually, however, some solace trickled out of the obsessive rehearsal of her own misjudgment. She began focusing on the figment of the other woman. Michael must have been desperately horny. A hot-blooded young man, left on his own, will sometimes make mistakes. Out of loneliness and desperation, he'll jump into bed with the first attractive woman that crosses his path, she told herself. Once she identified the trivial source of the problem, Karen felt somewhat more confident about finding an adequate solution to it. I'm not giving up without a fight. I'll go back to Michigan and reclaim my future husband, she resolved.

When she called Michael back, Karen sounded almost poised: "Don't you think it's kind of unfair of you to break up our engagement over the phone? At least we should discuss it in person."

He quickly calculated the cost of such a move. If I agree, Karen will feel like I'm kind enough to grant her wishes. Ana will probably freak out at first, but she'll calm down eventually. After all, Karen was my fiancée. "Sure. It's the least I can do," Michael said, proud to display his generosity.

Chapter 5

Karen got out of the airplane, having mentally prepared herself for the worst. She had repeated to herself over and over again that Michael would now be cold to her. He'd treat her like an acquaintance or, at best, an old friend. I have to be strong, she emboldened herself. I had nothing to do with his horrible decision and now it's entirely out of my hands. But in her heart of hearts, she didn't really believe this. After the initial shock, Karen reverted to her usual pragmatic mode. She planned to do whatever it took to save their relationship. It worked before and it could work again, she reminded herself, to boost her own moral. Less than half an hour after Michael delivered the bad news, Karen jumped on the computer and did some Internet research on Ana, to dig up some dirt on her rival. Although she found nothing particularly incriminating, Karen retained the hope that, upon further skillful questioning, Michael himself might deliver some helpful clues against his girlfriend.

She spotted her fiancée in the crowd, as radiant and disarmingly handsome as always. He waved to her and flashed a bright white smile. He's still so friendly to me, Karen noted, surprised by this unexpectedly positive reaction. What should I do? she wondered. Shake hands with him? Do nothing? Michael quickly resolved the matter by giving her a peck on the cheek and hugging her, as if nothing happened. Although Karen had mentally prepared herself a cold reception, his warmth threw her off. "I'm... why are we hugging?" she managed to stutter.

"Why not?" he smiled unctuously at her. "We're not enemies, are we?"

Is he flirting with me? she wondered, with genuine confusion. "I don't know what we are anymore."

Michael noticed that Karen was carrying only a small tote bag. "Where's your suitcase?"

"This is all I brought," she shrugged. "I didn't know how long I'd stay. Plus, I still have some clothes left at my mother's house."

"You can stay with me for a few days. Maybe as long as one or two weeks," Michael informed her, still planning to part ways with her on the best of terms. "However long it takes us to sort things out."

"Is your girlfriend okay with this?" Karen asked him, surprised that Ana would accept such an unusual arrangement.

"I've told her that you're coming so we can discuss everything in person."

"And what did she say?"

"She wasn't too thrilled about it, as you can imagine. But in the end, she understood. I didn't tell her how long you'd stay with me though," he made a slight grimace, to claim ignorance. "We hadn't worked out the details yet."

"I doubt that she'll put up with it," Karen commented, feeling slightly triumphant. Through this tiny and seemingly innocuous deception, the solidarity between the two lovers was beginning to crack.

Despite this note of optimism, however, once Karen and Michael stepped into the car, an air of awkwardness settled between them. On the drive back, they hardly exchanged a word. Karen, herself, didn't know what to say. She was overcome by the painful awareness that this was the first time she and Michael sat so close together without being romantically involved. She gazed out the window at the scenery they had passed so many times before, in happier circumstances. Her mood shifted from sadness to jealousy. As soon as they arrived at his house, Karen asked him: "Do you have any pictures of her?"

Michael looked at her with apparent compassion. "Yeah. But are you sure you want to do this to yourself?"

"Yes. No more lies. I want to know everything."

Michael deposited Karen's tote bag in the guest room. He then went into his office, to take out a bunch of photographs of Ana from his desk drawer. "Here she is," he extended her the pictures.

Karen examined each one closely: one in front of their house, with Ana standing between the two largest pine trees; another taken in a parking lot near a Chinese restaurant; the third inside the revolving restaurant where, she became painfully aware, Michael had always taken her on special occasions. Without making any comments, Karen returned the photographs to him with a look of disgust. She didn't just feel betrayed. She felt replaced.

Michael placed the pictures back neatly into his desk drawer. "Have you had dinner yet?" he asked her matter-of-factly.

"I'm not hungry." Karen thought that Ana was pretty but not stunning. Looking at her, you wouldn't have thought she was the home wrecker type. Nonetheless, as she had suspected all along, it was all physical between them. Yet, somehow, this assumption didn't make things any easier for her. "You did me a favor. I've lost five pounds just since you told me," she tried to make light of her own distress.

"I'm sorry," Michael apologized, gazing steadily into her eyes. "I didn't mean to hurt you."

His apology only stirred up Karen's anger, however. "Yeah, well, you obviously did."

He approached her and took her hand in his tenderly. "I didn't mean to hurt you and I'm sorry," he repeated. "You're a great person. You deserve better." His gaze remained steady, to recapture her emotionally.

"Actions speak louder than words," Karen threw back at him the phrase he had often used himself, to reproach her for occasionally rebuffing his sexual advances. "I want to find out more about the situation with Ana," she gathered the strength to return to her original strategy.

Michael led her to the sofa, where they sat next to one another. "Anything you wish. What would you like to know?"

"Is she worth sacrificing our whole future together? Do you really love her?" Her unsteady gaze trembled with emotion.

"I do."

"What is it that you have with her that we didn't have?" she persisted, trying to figure out the secret recipe to his heart.

Michael had a dreamy look. "She's creative and intense. She's really passionate and not just in bed, but in every way and everywhere. As you know, I usually go for tall, athletic type. But Ana's frail and small yet still turns me on. I don't want to blow this unique opportunity. I feel this is my one chance in life to really seize passion and see how long I can make it last."

A mental image of Michael twirling his petite girlfriend flashed before Karen's eyes. "I bet you love cradling her in your arms," she said, feeling all of a sudden inadequate for being so tall and large-framed, even though that was what drew Michael to her in the first place.

"She's like a little doll," he confirmed. "In fact, that's one of the pet names I gave her."

Although Karen had asked for more information, once presented with it, it was more than she could handle. "That's enough," she stopped him. "I guess I'm not ready to hear about this woman after all." A knot of emotion constricted her throat. "I thought we really had something special," she said, as tears rolled down her pale cheeks. "You made me feel like you really loved me."

"I did, Baby, I did," he replied in a buttery voice. "It's just that life's difficult to predict sometimes."

"Don't blame this on life, Michael! For once, take responsibility for your actions," she burst out, infuriated by his subterfuge.

"Fair enough," he agreed, to pacify her.

Although feeling more discouraged now than when she was working out everything in her own head, Karen wasn't prepared to give up just yet. She knew from experience that every relationship had its soft spots. "I must say, I'm a little surprised by your selection," she said, pursing her lips as she often did whenever she expressed what she considered to be perceptive criticism.

Michael hadn't expected this reaction; not after he had spoken so highly of Ana. "Why?"

Karen began to feel more in her element, like the discussion was back on her turf. "Well, for one thing, I thought that you'd pick someone who was free, not a married woman with two kids," she began with the facts.

"You don't really choose who you fall in love with," Michael countered fatalistically.

"How does her husband feel about this?"

"Pretty bad."

"What about her kids? What was their reaction? She has a girl and a boy, right?" she pursued, on a roll.

"Yup," he confirmed. "Eight and nine years old. From what Ana tells me, the girl's angry about the whole situation. The boy's a guy, so he's more or less okay with it."

"You'll see once you become their stepfather. Neither of them will be *okay with it*, that's for sure!"

"I realize that," Michael reluctantly agreed. "But I'll do my best. What else can I possibly do?" he raised his shoulders with an air of resignation.

"Maybe chose a partner who isn't already married with kids?" Karen suggested. "Anyway," she moved on, feeling like she had made her point, "how does Ana herself feel about the divorce?"

"She's kind of ambivalent about it," Michael was obliged to admit. "In fact, at first she didn't want to go through with it. Because even in the best of circumstances, it would still mean shuttling the kids back and forth between parents and having them only half the time," he elaborated, to highlight the fact that his girlfriend's misgivings had nothing to do with him or the quality of their relationship.

"Sure. Divorce is always tough on the kids. Unless the relationship between the parents is so bad that separation's preferable," Karen reverted to the objective approach she generally adopted when discussing the lives of others. "Is she ambivalent even now?" she probed another promising weakness.

"Somewhat. I mean, she's still shaken up about it. In fact, she sometimes gets downright hysterical."

"I see... A regular diva!"

"Kind of," he said with an indulgent smile. "She tends to be very dramatic."

Karen peered straight into his eyes: "Are you sure that's the kind of woman you need? I thought you enjoyed your peace and quiet."

"It gets me so hot, Baby!" Michael quipped. "Not a dull moment."

Karen, however, duly ignored his facetious remark. She preferred to stick to a no-nonsense perspective. "Yeah, but if she's so emotional and ambivalent about getting a divorce, they'll soon be trouble in paradise," she helpfully predicted.

Michael didn't reply.

Confident that she had driven home the previous point, Karen moved on to the next. "Does Ana plan to work? Other than on her art, I mean?"

"Nope. That was one of the things we agreed on from the very beginning. She wants to devote herself entirely to painting." Karen didn't comment, so Michael went on. "As a matter of fact, that was one of the sore spots in her marriage. Rob complained that she didn't make enough money from art. So I told her this wouldn't be an issue between us. It was a major selling point for her."

"Well then, for your sake, I hope that she becomes wildly successful real soon. Cause it's hard to imagine how you'll manage to support a wife and two kids on your current teaching assistant fellowship," Karen assumed an air of maternal wisdom, alluding to the fact that so far, in their relationship, she had been the main breadwinner.

"I'll be looking for a teaching job in the spring," Michael reminded her.

"And I pray that you find it," Karen retorted. "But even if you do, money will be a problem. Didn't you say the prep schools pay only 50,000 dollars a year? For a family of four, that's a little tight, don't you think?" She didn't wait for his reply, however, since the question was purely rhetorical. "Is Ana a big spender?" she smoothly transitioned to her next point.

"Yup," Michael reluctantly admitted. In the past, he had contrasted his fiancée's plain attire to Ana's understated elegance. But now it suddenly occurred to him that these qualities came, quite literally, at a cost. Ana loved spending money on clothes, shoes and jewelry. Especially his money, since he'd been quite generous with her, spoiling her with all kinds of gifts while she was his girlfriend. But, then again, he didn't have to support two kids before. "We'll have to renegotiate her spending habits," he articulated his conclusion out loud.

"As you'd say, Mazeltov Baby!" Karen said almost cheerfully. "Let's see if I've got this right. You're leaving a responsible, loyal and faithful woman for a volatile artistic diva type who's already cheated on her husband."

Although not one prone to worrying, Michael was somewhat perturbed by some of the points raised by his former fiancée. Given Karen's insecurity, he had been fully prepared for another sort of conversation. He thought that she'd ask him details about his affair, see that Ana was a better match for him and conclude, much as he had, that he couldn't really be blamed for following his heart and choosing his girlfriend. He was also prepared for Karen becoming upset and insulting Ana, out of jealousy and spite. But he hadn't expected that their conversation would deftly turn to Ana's flaws and the weak spots in their relationship. Preferring to focus on the here and now, the future was something Michael rarely contemplated. However, since living with Ana would become his reality within a matter of days, Karen's arguments sounded ominously relevant.

Would he be able to support an artistic diva and her two kids? Michael began to wonder. Would Ana's children ever view him as anything other than the unwelcome intruder who broke up their family? Would he be able to get her to become more fiscally responsible, perhaps even frugal, like his fiancée? Could he ever really trust her? If Ana had cheated *with* him, what would guarantee that she wouldn't cheat *on* him? After all, sometimes even players got played. That evening the rosy picture of the future he had envisioned with his girlfriend dimmed somewhat, as if he were seeing it through a pair of dark sunglasses. "Eh, what the hell! We'll manage," he said out loud to Karen. Yet, in his own mind, the idealized image of his girlfriend began to fissure, like the fine, hardly detectible wrinkles of a beautiful woman on the cusp of the bloom of femininity and the wilting of maturity.

Chapter 6

That morning, Michael woke up early. He peeked into the guest room to see if Karen was awake yet. He had gallantly offered her their bed the night before, but she had refused. "I'm only a guest here now," she said, turning away from him. The blinds were closed. Her curved shape formed a hilly relief underneath the white sheet.

Michael slipped into the room and kneeled in front of Karen. He traced with the tip of his index finger the trail of wetness upon her cheek. "Baby, don't cry," he whispered in her ear. His tenderness provoked an almost imperceptible convulsion underneath the sheet, as Karen released a guttural cry. Her heartfelt suffering flattered and aroused him. He began caressing the curve of her body with the flatness of his palm.

"Please don't!" she protested. "You're torturing me."

"Come on. You know you want it as much as I do," he said under his breath. With one swift motion, Michael whisked the sheet away, covering her with his voracious gaze. Karen's body lay helplessly exposed in a fetal position, like an overgrown child in need of comfort and protection. Sensing her vulnerability, he mounted her. She wriggled underneath, struggling to budge him away.

"Stop it. You're depraved," Karen managed to say. "Why are you doing this to me? Why now?" Nothing about Michael's behavior made any sense to her anymore. He hadn't manifested such desire for her in years. Now that he had broken up with her and replaced her with another woman, here he was, bent over her, devouring her neck, like a vampire.

His arms fought against hers, while his knees pulled her legs apart like a pair of muscular forceps. He wasn't about to be rejected by his woman. "I want you now," he hissed.

"You must have me confused with your other girlfriend," she replied. This statement, right out of a melodrama, burst the tension between them. Michael laughed out loud and Karen smiled the first genuine smile since he had delivered the bad news. "Honestly. What's come over you?"

"I don't know," he gazed fixedly into her questioning eyes, stimulated by the novelty of this chiasmic reversal. In the span of one day, his fiancée turned into his girlfriend while his girlfriend became his legitimate fiancée.

"How do you think she'll feel about this?" Karen asked him with a nervous yet naughty sparkle in her eye that reminded him of Ana.

"She doesn't have to know about it," Michael breathed into her ear. He delved into her, encountering no further resistance.

When it was over, he felt spent and she felt used. "I still don't understand you," Karen said, disappointed by her own disappointment.

Michael got up and pulled on his pants. "You think too much about things. It was no big deal."

"No big deal? I'd be curious to see if your new girlfriend agrees," she taunted him.

Michael turned and peered straight into Karen's eyes, with that unblinking gaze which became a focused beam when he meant business. "Ana can't know about this. Ever," he emphasized.

"You think she'd be jealous?"

"You bet your ass she would!" He slipped on his periwinkle tee shirt, Ana's favorite. "In fact, I'm going to see her right now," he announced. "If she asks me about you, I'll just tell her the truth."

"Namely?"

"That you slept by yourself in the guest bedroom," he coolly replied.

"I'm sure she'll appreciate your honesty as much as I did," Karen couldn't resist the sarcasm. She felt deflated. The moment of vengeful elation had been short-lived, like a drop of sweat during dry, hot Arizona weather. No sooner has it reached the surface than it's already evaporated.

Michael rushed into the car to make his breakfast meeting with Ana at *Panera's*. Since he was a few minutes late, he anticipated that his girlfriend would already be there, growing impatient. Let her wait, he told himself. She needs to get used to waiting. I can't always be at her beck and call. I've spoiled her while we were lovers. But things will be different from now on. As soon as he stepped into the restaurant, sure enough, Michael saw Ana sitting at a corner booth. Her elbows were planted on the table, her face rested upon her hands. He could tell from her brooding expression that a difficult morning lay ahead.

"Why so glum?" he asked her in a deliberately cheerful tone. "Rob wasn't in a good mood last night?"

Ana looked up at him, wondering how Michael could be so chipper in such tense circumstances. "It's not just about him. It's about you and Karen too. I couldn't sleep last night knowing that she's back at your place again."

Michael slipped next to his girlfriend on the bench, his thigh pressed up against hers. He placed his arm around her shoulder. "My poor Baby! Nothing's going right, now is it?" he said in the kind of condescending, indulgent tone one uses to pacify a grumpy child.

Although Ana generally appreciated her lover's levity, this time his light-hearted attitude bothered her. "You never take anything seriously, do you?" She scrutinized his face for signs of a more normal human reaction.

But instead of reassuring her, Michael confirmed her charge by laughing out loud. "Why should I worry? Life's good. In just a matter of weeks, you'll be all mine."

Ana recoiled slightly, as if she hadn't heard right. "Why a matter of *weeks*? I thought I was moving in with you *this week*."

Michael's expression became serious all of a sudden. "Actually, I'm glad you brought this up, since that's exactly what I wanted to talk to you about. I have some good news and some bad news. Which do you want to hear first?" he asked her in the playful manner a magician might ask the audience which trick they wanted him to perform.

"The good news. Because I need some right about now."

"That one you've already heard. We'll soon belong to each other."

"Okay, then the bad news," she said, not amused by his rhetorical games.

"You've heard that one too," he announced with a grin. "Karen will be staying at my place for a couple of weeks."

Ana felt butterflies in the pit of her stomach. "Why? Did she convince you to give your relationship another chance?" She held her breath while waiting for his reply.

"God no!" Michael burst out. "Nothing can change my mind about us. You're the woman of my life. It's just that Karen's in a lot of pain right now. She doesn't understand why I broke up with her."

"So did you see what she was wearing?" "What would you like to drink?" "When did you get here?" "We still have time" "This bagel seems a bit stale." The background noise of the restaurant and the bustling movement of people around them assailed Ana's senses, closing in upon her. She felt overwhelmed, no longer able to distinguish inside from outside. "But I thought you were going to explain to her our situation in a day or two," she managed to say, attempting to bring into focus her lover's blurry face.

"I did explain it to her, Baby," Michael said soothingly. "But that was a lot of information to absorb, all at once. I need to help her through this difficult time. I owe her that much at least. I'm not an ogre, you know!"

Something about this whole arrangement just didn't sound kosher to Ana. With a quick, nervous motion she placed a wayward lock of hair behind her ear. "I don't get it. Why exactly will it take you several *weeks* to explain to Karen our situation? Telling her in person, I understood. I was kind of nervous about it, since I'm sure her intention is to get you back. But I agree that you owe her discussing the situation face to face. Spending one or two days to comfort her, I understand as well. But a few weeks?" She stared at him. "Is there something else you want to tell me?"

"It's you I want, I promise," Michael repeated, wrapping both arms around her and drawing her to him. Ana felt the beat of his heart against her eardrum as she lay curled up against his chest, like a kitten. "Don't be jealous, okay?" he peered down at her. "There's no reason to feel jealous. I'm not in love with Karen anymore. I'm only in love with you. In her place, you'd want me to do the same thing. You wouldn't want to be dropped without explanation, like a hot potato. It's inhuman."

His melodious voice sounded caring and sincere. It resonated in her ear, making its way through her chest, down to the butterflies in her stomach, soothing everything along the path of its sound waves. "I know," Ana replied, momentarily embarrassed by her outburst of jealousy. "It's just that we're so close to finally being a couple, like you wanted from the very beginning. I didn't think it would take you so long to explain to her our situation," she repeated, beginning to feel unsettled again.

"It won't be that long, you'll see. After all, what's two more weeks when we have the rest of our lives together?" Michael pulled her face up towards him and began kissing her eyelids, which instantly fluttered shut, then moved on to her cheekbones, her forehead and her lips. "Time will fly and soon we'll have exactly what we wanted."

What *you* wanted, Ana silently reformulated his phrase. "Are you trying to compare us?" she peered into his eyes. "To see which one of us you want to marry?"

"Come on!" Michael recoiled. "What do you think I am?"

"Then I don't understand your behavior."

"It's called tacking," he explained.

"It's called what?" she grimaced.

"Tacking," Michael repeated. "It's a term used in sailing, for when you allow the wind to move your sailboat in the wrong direction from your intended destination. Because sometimes if you go against the wind in the direction you want, the sails will rip and you won't be able to go anywhere anymore."

"Why is it that we need to be moving in the wrong direction at this point?" Ana inquired, since his analogy hadn't clarified much.

"Because otherwise I'll look like an asshole, that's why!" Michael exploded, losing his cool. He decided to confide further, since Ana was obviously acting paranoid. "Karen's in touch with my parents and complained to them about our break-up. She's also told her parents that our engagement's off. Nobody really understands what the hell happened. Needless to say, they all blame you and me for it. I need some time to smooth things over with Karen."

"Why couldn't you have done this stalking, or whatever the heck you call it, during all those months when you were pressuring me to divorce my husband? Why are you stalling now that I've already told Rob about us and we're supposed to be moving in together?" Ana demanded.

Michael sighed, as if he were about to disclose something against his better judgment. "Alright, I didn't want to tell you this, to protect your feelings, but you're forcing it out of me." He paused for a moment, to generate suspense. "Karen apparently talked to my folks on the phone several times already. She blamed the whole fiasco on you. She told them you're a heartless seductress and a slut. She said our engagement fell apart because of you."

"And did you set the record straight? Did you tell your parents how much we love each other and how committed we are to making our relationship work?" Ana inquired with a note of alarm. Michael laughed out loud. "What's so funny?" she asked him with dismay.

"The first thing my mom asked me after her little chat with Karen was if you were one of the call girls from work! Cause remember, I've been telling my parents for several years now that I work at an escort service," he managed to say, attempting to contain his amusement.

A wave of prideful indignation rose into Ana's throat, constricting her breathing. Her body stiffened. "And you didn't defend me? You didn't explain that I'm an artist and tell her how much you love and respect me?"

"Frankly, I didn't get the chance to talk much about you," Michael said. "My mom was on a roll, as hysterical as you can get sometimes. Besides, all she cared about was the break up with Karen. She thinks Karen's the only woman who can 'tame' me, as she puts it."

Ana stared at her lover with a sense of stupefaction. Couldn't Michael see how his mother, how any mother, would feel when told that her only son is leaving a stable relationship with a decent woman for what's presented to her as a temporary fling with a slut? And how could he possibly allow Karen to present her and their love affair in such a negative light, without at least trying to undo some of the damage? "What in the world is wrong with you, Michael?" she exploded, pushing him away from her with both hands. "I can understand Karen criticizing me, even if what she said is petty and mean-spirited. But I thought you and I were on the same side here. Any man who respects his girlfriend and plans to marry her does everything possible to defend her to his parents, to create a positive impression." Ana gazed at her lover, who looked so boyish in his preppy outfit and it occurred to her that the clean-cut image Michael projected might be only a mask. Maybe it was a way to hide from others his real self and his actual desires, which seeped out only in his fantasies and lies. You're the one who slept around with dozens of women. You're the real slut, not I, Ana thought. These words vibrated on the tip of her tongue as she saw her lover with new eyes.

Michael's air of levity vanished once confronted with his girlfriend's indignation. "Hey, I can't control what Karen tells my folks."

"Right. But you can control your response."

"Just like I'm sure you defend me to Rob every time he criticizes me," he volleyed back.

"At this point, I don't really care what Karen thinks about me or Rob about you. But you should have defended me to your parents. Their opinion matters to us," Ana insisted.

Michael shrugged. "It doesn't to me. But I must admit, I'm a little surprised by my mother's reaction. My dad's a jerk, so I kind of expected he wouldn't approve of us. He said our relationship shows that I'm thinking with my dick."

"Excuse me?" Ana hoped that she hadn't heard right.

"Yeah, he thinks it's all about the sex between us. But I really thought my mom would take my side. Especially since she's been suffering at the hands of that cold-blooded bastard all her life. I thought she'd value real love by now, since she never got any from him. Even as a kid, I hoped she'd wake up and divorce his sorry ass."

"I've never heard you speak so negatively about your father," Ana remarked. She was taken aback by the contempt she heard in Michael's voice. Not only towards his father, whom he openly criticized the way you wouldn't even speak about an enemy, but also towards his mother, whom he seemed to praise in a back-handed manner, which combined flattery and disdain. It's as if Michael felt betrayed by her; as if he suspected that his mother had turned against him by momentarily siding with Karen. Ana wished she could persuade her lover that his sense of betrayal was misplaced. In fact, neither parent had turned against him. Given the kind of information Karen had relayed, they reacted as any normal parents would: with deep concern, warning their only son for his own good. Why couldn't he put himself in their shoes?

"He's never been such an ass with me. This time he really outdid himself," Michael added.

"But you said it's your mother who disapproved of our relationship," Ana reminded him.

"Yeah, but he's the one who told Karen, 'My son's a person who's always disappointed everyone around him.' My mom, on the other hand, thinks I'm perfect. She only blames you for the fiasco."

Ana was about to say something, but Michael interrupted her. "Babe, don't worry about it. She's a bit of a gossip, but she'll get over it. I know how to handle her. I'll have a little chat with her to explain why Karen wasn't right for me," he declared with confidence. But the truth of the matter was that his mother's negative reaction got to him. Initially, it stunned him that she disapproved. Later, however, he reinterpreted her response not as a negative reflection on himself, but as a bad reflection on Ana. Which was kind of disappointing. After all, Michael had been quite confident that a more attractive and cultivated woman would make him look better, like he finally had a partner worthy of him. When confronted with his mother's disapproval, however, Michael began to sense that his new girlfriend was not such a good catch after all. Instead of making him look better in the eyes of others, Ana's volatile temperament and tarnished reputation made him look worse. He was downgrading rather than upgrading his partner, as he had originally intended. And if Michael adhered to one principle in life, it was to always upgrade.

It struck Ana that the only time her boyfriend said anything positive about anyone other than himself was when he commented on how much that person worshipped him. His mother was all right because no matter what he did, she adored him. His father was a bastard because he occasionally saw a small fraction of Michael's flaws and dared criticize him. Karen was fine too. Although she couldn't always do everything Michael wanted, at least she idolized him. The students who fell under his spell were his favorites. He never even mentioned the rest. *When will he stop seeing himself as the center of the universe and realize that if we're going to have any chance at a happy life together, he'll have to start thinking in terms of us, as a couple?* Ana wondered. "I also want you to tell your mom why I'm right for you," she told him. "I don't want Karen's negative description of me to stick."

Michael peered at her coldly. *Who the hell does she think she is telling me what to do?* "You're so selfish," he sneered, returning like a boomerang Ana's own thoughts about him. "You always think only of your image, don't you?"

"This isn't just about me, Michael," she protested. "We've traumatized everyone in our lives. Now we're all in limbo. I'm talking about my family too."

"And I about mine."

Ana felt too upset to reply.

"We both need to handle this difficult situation in the most diplomatic way possible," Michael continued more calmly, interpreting her silence as consent. "Through tacking, not attacking," he found a convenient play on words. "Don't turn against me, Powderpuff. Don't bite the hand that feeds you."

Ana winced at the word "Powderpuff," which had been one of his terms of endearment for her. Now she took it as an insult, as if Michael considered her a lightweight in general. She then thought about his analogy. *This tacking, or whatever he calls it, doesn't make any sense. I'm sure that Karen's manipulating him, to weaken his love for me so that he'll return to her. She's poisoning our relationship and sabotaging my future rapport with his parents.* Nonetheless, what bothered Ana most was the fact that Michael allowed that to happen.

That's his choice, not Karen's, she told herself. "I understand what Karen's doing and why. She's doing everything within her powers to turn us against each other in order to get you back."

"And can you really blame her?"

"I don't blame her," Ana struggled to remain calm. "Because it's clear to me that she's a desperate woman. No matter how badly you treat her, she still clings to you. It's as if her whole world has become this box of your relationship. She can't even imagine life outside the box anymore."

"Just because she's less vain than you doesn't make her more desperate," Michael said. Pretty soon I'll have you spinning in my box too, he thought to himself, casting a territorial glance over his girlfriend.

Ana decided to go ahead and tell him exactly what she thought of Karen all along since, she safely surmised, the gloves were coming off on both sides. "This isn't about vanity or even love. It's about dependency. Karen needs you for her self-esteem. I've overheard enough of your phone conversations and you've shown me enough of your email exchanges to see how she functions. If you praise her, she feels good about herself. If you're indifferent, she worries and doesn't know what to think. If you're brief, she's anxious and suspicious—and for good reason, mind you. If you disapprove, she tries to change to please you. Even in those emails you showed me, remember?"

"Which ones?" Michael perked up at the intrigue.

"Well, like the one where she wrote you a chatty note about everything she did on a given day and whom she talked to. Then, when you wrote her back a brief, disinterested comment, she shot back another email, with the heading, 'email: Michael style,' and five succinct bullet points of her daily activities."

Michael smiled, simultaneously flattered and amused. "Oh, yeah, I remember now. You've got a pretty good memory."

"I paid attention to everything you said about Karen."

"Why? Because she's your competition?" he arched an eyebrow.

"Not only that," Ana looked straight into his eyes. "Because she's my precursor. I want to avoid being treated by you the same way that she was. Whatever she did, it didn't work. And I think that's because she showed you how vulnerable she is. How much she needs you. You saw that as a weakness and took advantage of her."

"So now you're saying she's weak?" Michael asked, entertained by this indirect catfight. Up to recently, Ana had refrained from overtly criticizing Karen while Karen didn't even know of Ana's existence. Now that both women were identifying each other's faults and fighting over him, all he had to do was sit back and enjoy the show.

"I'm saying that she acts like your puppet," Ana pursued. "She's an egoless egocentric, if you will."

"I won't, since I have no clue what that means," Michael said dismissively.

"It means that pretty much all she thinks about is herself. She needs your approval to have a sense of identity," Ana clarified, not backing down.

"Dang! We're feeling feisty today, aren't we?"

Indeed, I am! How dare that woman, that spineless jellyfish, call me a slut to people I hope to impress? Ana thought, indignant. She was going to give Michael a piece of her mind, quite confident that he'd go back and relay her kind compliments to Karen. "I think in some ways, though, she feels superior to all the other women you've been with. Superior by association," she continued her analysis.

"How so?"

"Well, it's pretty clear to me that Karen worships the ground you walk on and thinks you're the most special man on Earth. The fact you stuck with her longer than with any other woman must make her feel special too. Like, somehow, she's better than the rest of us just because you, God's gift to womankind, loved her longer and, she assumes, deeper than you've loved anybody else," she concluded her statement in a mocking tone.

"Great observation, Dr. Ana. But how's that so different from how you feel?" Michael served her criticism back to her. He felt like he had both women right where they belonged, wriggling in the palm of his hand. Pitted against one another, each saw only the other's faults and predicament. Which was all right with him. After all, the more they focused on criticizing each other, the less they noticed his maneuvers.

Ana smiled, being fully prepared with an answer that, she hoped, would keep Michael on his toes. "I can tell you this much: if you ever cheated on me, I definitely wouldn't grovel to get you back."

"What would you do?" he asked, titillated by the knowledge that he had already cheated on her.

Ana gazed at him coolly. "If I found out about it, I'd kick you to the curb."

Michael's mouth curled into an ironic smile. "And if you didn't find out?" he brazenly carried the game a move further.

"It would soon become apparent," she replied with confidence. "You're not that good at faking interest."

"But how would you know for sure that it's because I cheated? What would you do? Spy on me?"

"I doubt it. Because if it came down to that, there'd be nothing worth saving." She placed one hand upon her stomach. "My gut instinct would tell me that you don't really love me anymore. And then I'd stop loving you too."

"That's what we always tell ourselves before the fact," Michael replied, unfazed. "But when it comes right down to it, when we love someone, we love them for life, no matter what they do."

Ana examined his tranquil features. "Funny. This is the first time I've heard you speak of unconditional love." She then thought for a moment and changed her mind. "But then again, it's not that surprising after all."

"Why not?"

"Because you said it in the context of expecting it from me. When it comes to you, everything's conditional. I bet if I cheated on you, you'd drop me in an instant."

"You're damn right about that!" he replied. "But I'd still love you and cherish our memories together, the way I do those with Amy and Karen. I just wouldn't be your partner anymore."

"Spoken like a man who thinks he'll be the cheater, not the cheated," Ana remarked.

Michael didn't like this formulation. "I don't trust you either, if that's what you mean," he responded, put on the defensive. "But it doesn't really matter. If you cheat, I leave. It's as simple as that."

"So much for cherishing our memories!" she pounced on the contradiction.

"Hey, you know me. I prefer to enjoy life rather than dwell on what could of, would of, or should have been," he boasted, confident that he could rebound from any failed relationship with great ease.

Ana thought about her past. "Unfortunately, my memories aren't so easy to erase. When I fall in love, I love with all my heart. And when I'm mistreated, I hate for life, the way I do Nicu. I'll never cherish a shred of memory with him for as long as I live. We probably had some happy moments together. But for me, the bad always erases the good."

"That's because you're a pessimist while I'm an optimist. You see the glass as half empty when I see it as half full," Michael pointed out.

Ana shook her head. "It's not a matter of optimism or pessimism. When people abuse you physically or emotionally, like Nicu did me, it erases everything good they ever did. It makes all the positive seem phony," she delivered a warning with her gaze as well as her words. "At any rate, what I'm trying to tell you is that if you ever cheat on me, I'll never act like Karen."

"She just loves me."

"You have way too much power over her, Michael!" Ana gestured with both hands, becoming heated once again against her rival. "She needs you so much that she's giving you the reins to her life. All you have to do is tug at her strings," she mimicked the motion, "and she reacts in whatever way she thinks will please you. You're walking all over her."

"And you're caricaturizing her," Michael retorted.

"I'm afraid you're the one who has turned her into a caricature," Ana countered.

"It's not my fault. Karen is who she is. That's her personality. She's clingy and dependent. We've known this for a long time," Michael exculpated himself.

"Sure, but you encourage her dependency. So, somewhere in there, you must enjoy it. Otherwise you'd have broken up with her once we fell in love."

"Let's not go over that again," he said in a tired voice, growing weary of the whole conversation. "We're going round and round in circles. We've already covered the argument of symmetry."

"Alright then," Ana conceded, eager to get a satisfactory answer for her more pressing concern. "Now we have symmetry. I'm divorcing Rob to marry you. So then why are you still encouraging Karen to spend a few more weeks at your house, in our current circumstances?"

Michael fidgeted with impatience, feeling backed into a corner. "I already told you. I'm trying to minimize the damage. For your sake and ours. I don't want Karen to freak out and criticize us to my parents."

"Even though she's done that already."

"I've hurt her enough, alright? I'm not going to be even more of an asshole to her just to please you!" Michael lost his cool.

Ana gazed at him. She noticed that his regular features were distorted by anger. "Whatever you say..." she responded, unwilling to pursue their altercation any further. She saw no point in it. Whenever Michael had made up his mind about something, nobody could dissuade him. Ana gazed at his small, fragile hands with unusually rough nails, which had dingy brown crescents underneath: peasant nails, her grandmother would have said. It occurred to her that Michael never really showed his hand. The only thing you could do is play the game to the very end, like Karen did, and risk losing everything or cut your losses and fold. Lately, Ana had been often tempted to fold. But she didn't have the heart to go through with it. She recalled her father explaining to her, a long time ago, Newton's first law of motion. A body in motion tends to stay in motion unless an external force is applied to it. By now, inertia was the main force that still kept her moving, within her lover's orbit. The unbridled attraction that had them gravitating around each other for almost a year had all but disappeared. Yet after having gone so far already, Ana felt like she had to pursue with courage the path she had chosen.

Chapter 7

Karen recalled that she had left one of her favorite sweaters in Michael's drawers. She especially missed the one he had given her on her last birthday, a tiny white angora sweater that went down to her navel. He said it reminded him of something Audrey Hepburn might have worn. She opened the second shelf on the left. When she spotted it, she experienced a sense of delight, like someone reuniting with an old friend. There it was, bright white and speckled with touches of silver. It lay neatly folded into four, just as she left it almost a year earlier. Karen lifted it gently and placed it next to her cheek. She breathed in, allowing its softness to embrace her face. Its scent haunted her with the aroma of days gone by, when she and Michael were happy and in love, or so she thought, because she was. She recalled that Michael had handed her a golden bag with a silver bow. "Put it on for me," he had told her. When she reemerged from the bathroom wearing her black skirt with the white angora sweater, his glance radiated admiration. He approached her slowly and removed it with one swift motion, pulling it with both hands over her head, effortlessly. The memory of the last time she wore that sweater became almost too painful to bear. She placed it back into the drawer, to bury it in their past, where it belonged.

Karen noticed a sliver of white lace. She peered more closely and spotted a pair of white lacy thigh highs that were still attached to a matching garter belt. She pulled out a red bustier with a shoelace design in the front, whose hook was accidentally caught on the fabric of a black dress made of stretchy fabric. Underneath them lay a red and black plaid miniskirt, completing the picture of the kind of gifts her fiancé must have purchased for his girlfriend while he refused to spend any money on her. Karen crammed the lingerie back into the drawer and slammed it shut. The flash of anger took her by surprise. Before this moment, Ana had been more or less an abstraction to her. Now, however, the other woman became tangible and real, embodied by these fetish objects. The air in the room stifled her, redolent with the perfume that another woman wore, with memories that weren't hers. Enough is enough! Karen decided. She walked resolutely towards the door.

As she was stepping out, Michael walked in. He seemed surprised to see her going out this late. "It's past ten o'clock," he observed, then added, since old habits die hard, "Sorry I'm late. I had a meeting."

Karen glared at him. "I know all about your meetings. I'm surprised that you didn't bring her over. That way we can have an even bigger meeting together. Maybe your *darling* would entertain us with a fashion show."

"What the heck are you talking about?"

"I'm talking about all the stuff you bought her! The thigh-highs. The bustier. The miniskirt. The black dress," she listed each item emphatically, like a prosecutor enumerating evidence in court. "What kind of a person would leave all this stuff behind for me to see?"

Michael said nothing in response. He waited calmly for her anger to subside.

"You two deserve each other!"

"That much is true," he agreed with an insolent smile.

"I'm going out," Karen announced, heading for the door.

"Wait. It's really cold outside," he grabbed her arm. "Where are you gonna go at this hour, in the dark?"

"It's not like you care," Karen pulled her arm away and left.

Michael sighed. Women. They're so jealous, he thought, as if he had never experienced that emotion before. He opened the refrigerator and removed the tuna casserole. This will have to do, he decided to settle for leftovers. He warmed up the dish in the microwave. For dessert, he treated himself to a scoop of fat free vanilla ice cream that Karen had purchased for herself but hadn't even opened yet.

The phone rang. "Hello?" It was Ana again. Didn't I just see her? Michael asked himself, annoyed. He was hoping to finish correcting the last of the student essays before Karen returned for round two of their altercation. "Hey," he said flatly.

"What happened to 'Hey, Baby'?" Ana asked him, her tone between playfulness and reproach.

"Karen just had a fit," he told her, to justify his sour mood.

"What happened?"

"She found some of your stuff in my drawers."

"Why was she looking in there?" Ana asked, unsympathetic. "Is she from the *Securitate*?"

Of course. The mandatory reference to communist Romania, Michael thought. By now, he could predict Ana's comments. Does she read from a script? he wondered, all of a sudden aware that he was becoming as bored with his new girlfriend as he had been with his former fiancée. "Well, the Romanian Secret Police sure could have used her. She conducts very thorough inspections," he commented blandly. "Honestly, I don't know what the hell she was doing rummaging through my drawers. Maybe she was looking for her clothes, since she left some over here. She prefers to pack lightly," he said by way of explanation, hoping to conclude the cross-examination.

"But she already knows about our affair. So why is she getting so possessive all of a sudden?" Ana wished she could eliminate the suspicion in her voice. Maybe that was part of what was driving Michael away.

"Listen, speaking of the *Securitate*, I don't need this interrogation from you also. What can I possibly tell you that you don't already know? She's jealous. She's upset. I was waiting for the shit to hit the fan. I knew I had gotten off way too easy. I just didn't know what, specifically, would set her off. Now we know."

"I'll call you in a little while to see if she got back home safely," Ana said. "It's so dark and cold outside. Not the best time to go out for a walk."

"Why the hell do you care? It's not like Karen's your best friend."

Ana was about to comment on his tone, but she refrained. "She's a human being. I'll talk to you later." After hanging up the phone, she felt uneasy about the whole conversation. It's as if Karen and Michael were having a lovers' quarrel and she was the unwelcome intruder who had unwittingly stepped in the middle of it. Somehow, she felt superfluous. She nevertheless called her boyfriend an hour and a half later, as promised.

"She's not back yet," Michael announced preemptively as soon as he heard Ana's voice.

"What do you think happened?"

"I have no clue. She's probably walking around the neighborhood, like a headless chicken."

Ana envisioned a despondent woman walking aimlessly in the dark, lost in the suburban maze. "Then why don't you go search for her? Aren't you worried?"

"This isn't exactly a high crime area," he retorted. "Don't forget, we live in one of the safest suburbs of Detroit."

"I know, but still... How long has she been gone?"

She could hear the static of the phone line while Michael checked his watch. "A little over two hours," he estimated.

"I think you should go look for her."

"Yes, Boss!" Michael responded, not accustomed to taking directions.

"Will you call me once you find her?"

"Sure. But won't it be too late for you?"

"No. I haven't been sleeping well lately."

"Join the club!"

After hanging up the phone, Michael went into the kitchen to pour himself a glass of cognac. He decided that if Ana called to nag him again, he'd tell her he had gone to look for Karen but hadn't found her. Heck, he might even tell her that he went to the police station to file a report, to look like he was really concerned. As soon as he stepped out of the kitchen, glass in hand, he noticed that Karen's tan coat was back on the hook.

"Hey!" he called out, mustering a friendly tone.

She didn't reply. The door to the guest room remained closed.

Michael cracked it open and peeped in. Karen was sitting at the desk, writing something. "I'm glad to see that you're back okay."

Her glance was like an arrow, filled with poisonous reproach. "I hope I'm not interrupting a hot date with your Gypsy girlfriend."

"Where the hell were you? I was getting worried."

"Yeah, I'm sure you were worried to death about me. I should have called the paramedics, in case you had a heart attack or something."

Ah yes, the familiar sarcasm. Where would we be without it? Everything's back to normal, Michael observed. He attempted to think of something constructive. "You could wear her lingerie if it will make you feel better," he proposed with a suggestive grin.

"What did you say?" she squinted at him.

"You know, if you wanted to get back at Ana..." he began to explain. But before he could finish his statement, Karen stood up and took deliberate steps towards him. "Michael, you're the most insensitive person I've ever met!" she declared, pushing him with the tip of her fingers out of the room before shutting the door in his face.

That's the thanks I get for trying to help, Michael thought, steadying himself with one hand on the wall, so that he wouldn't spill his drink.

Chapter 8

They reconciled by making love. If you could call their constant tension fighting since, in point of fact, Ana and Michael rarely fought. Yet there was a negative energy vibrating in the air from her side and from Michael's, increasingly, Ana began to sense detachment. They washed each other's bodies, using the flat of their palms covered in foamy soap, with slow, circular motions, somewhere between functionality and caress. The lightness of their touch, along with the warm flowing water, seemed to wash away the tension, allowing it to flow into the drain and evaporate elsewhere, liberating them.

"I love you so much, Baby," Michael wrapped his arms around Ana's naked waist, his voice raspy and sweet, filled with nectar.

This is the man I know and love, Ana reminded herself, beginning to feel safe again. "Should we go out for lunch to the Joyful House?" she suggested the ambiguously named Chinese restaurant they used to frequent, located only a few blocks away from his house.

Michael's well-disposed smile was replaced by a scowl: "I hate that place!" he said with a vehemence that startled her. "It's so freaking expensive and the food's too greasy. Plus it's dim as hell in there. I can hardly see you when you're sitting across the table."

Ana didn't recall her lover ever complaining about that restaurant before, the scores of times they had eaten there together. "Why didn't you tell me that you didn't like it?"

"I went there just to please you."

Ana was left to conclude that Michael wasn't that concerned with pleasing her anymore. But she refrained from reproaching him, for fear that his reply would only confirm her growing suspicion that their best times were already behind them, the honeymoon over before it began. "We don't have to go there," she relented, stepping into the bedroom to dress.

"You're wearing that skirt again?" Michael directed her a disapproving look as she slipped on her pencil skirt.

This question, too, took her by surprise. She recalled that only a few weeks earlier, when they were having lunch together at *Panera's*, Michael had asked her very sweetly to get him a fountain drink. He said he wanted to watch her walking in that "hot, tight skirt" that, he had claimed, made him "drool with desire." "It may come as a shock to you, but sometimes I wear what I want," Ana retorted. He should buy himself a lap dog if he needs someone to obey his commands, she thought.

Michael took a deep breath, in and out, as if this small act of defiance was part of a larger, and much more significant, battle of wills that he fully intended to win. For now, however, he didn't insist. He chose instead to bide his time and lose this battle in order to win the war: "We can go to the Chinese restaurant if you like. One last time. Because if it were up to me, we'd have never gone there in the first place."

"How kind of you!" Ana no longer bothered to contain her sarcasm. Michael's bossy attitude bothered her less than his growing indifference, which cast a pall over their lives. It's too late to turn back, Ana reminded herself. We've already taken the plunge, jumped over the precipice together. Now I have to do whatever it takes to land safely on the other side. Don't bite the hand that feeds you, Michael had warned her. In a sense, Ana felt that he was right. She had lost her parents long ago. She had alienated her husband and in-laws. Her own children felt betrayed by her actions. Michael was the only ally she had left. Besides, having chosen her lover based on their spell of all-consuming passion, Ana now wanted to rise to the challenge. She wanted to prove to herself that she could care about a man and remain loyal to him when they lived through the real-life difficulties of an actual relationship, not just the pleasant diversions of a love affair. Even small compromises, she hoped, might reflect a mutual willingness to make their relationship work. "We don't have to go there just for me. We can go anywhere you like," she told him.

Michael felt obliged to exhibit some graciousness as well: "No, let's go to the Chinese restaurant."

"Thanks," Ana forced a smile.

They put on their coats and walked hand in hand to the restaurant in silence. As of late, they had little left to say to each other. Most of the substantive topics of conversation—their relationship, the kids, money, the divorce, their current partners, their future activities together, the pain they were causing or felt—had become subjects of contention. Michael opened the door for his girlfriend. As Ana stepped into the familiar restaurant, it occurred to her that, in this instance, her lover was right. Its atmosphere was redolent with the smell of sauce wafting up to the sticky ceiling. The dim light of the Chinese lanterns oozed a sense of cheapness. Ana had never noticed any of this before. But then again, she told herself, when we were happy together, even a greasy joint like this became a place where you flirted and fed each other with chopsticks bits of chicken and rice. She marveled at how her concept of time had become so elastic. They had told their partners about the affair only two weeks earlier, which now felt to her more like two months, or even two years. From that moment on, everything between them changed dramatically for the worse.

When is she finally going to get over it and stop bitching about the breakup with Rob? Michael wondered, noticing Ana's sullen expression. He was annoyed that the woman he fell in love with, his doting and sensual girlfriend, had been replaced by a depressed neurotic who drove him daily to the end of his rope. Seeking a welcome diversion from Ana's company, his gaze surveyed the restaurant. It lingered upon a cute little blonde with the loveliest blue eyes who sat across from a plain looking boyfriend who'd certainly be no rival for him, Michael speculated. Out of the corner of his eye, he noticed Ana looking at him reproachfully. "That girl's so annoying. She's got the most irritating giggle," he remarked in a conspiratorial whisper, moving his head in the direction of the blond who had caught his attention.

"I didn't hear her laugh even once," Ana commented dryly. "I guess I'm not as observant as you are."

Michael wondered where this ever-present sourness he had never noticed in her before came from. It reminded him of Karen, when she was in one of her passive aggressive moods. He wasn't too thrilled that his girlfriend was turning into his fiancée.

A family of four, the mother being a petite brunette about Ana's age, the father somewhat older, and two small kids, one a toddler, the other still a baby, sat down at an adjacent table. The mother struggled to situate the baby in a highchair. When the latter began complaining, the mother quickly removed a pacifier from a napkin in her pocket and swiftly placed it into the baby's mouth, which quieted her down.

"That's what I should do to you when you get fussy. Only not with a pacifier," Michael said suggestively. Suddenly, he was overcome by a rush of new-found hope. "That's what we need!" he exclaimed, excited by the epiphany.

"What? A pacifier?"

"No. A baby. *Our* baby," he emphasized. "That way we can create our own family." His eyes glimmered as he looked at his girlfriend as his future wife, with complicity and affection again.

Ana winced as if Michael had mentioned the unmentionable, what she had feared all along. "You want me to have a baby with you to separate me from my own children!"

"Our baby would be your child too," Michael pointed out, irritated by her defensive attitude. He was sick and tired of women telling him what to do, of women saying 'no' to him and frustrating his desires. He was sick and tired of having freaking jokes of imaginary animals instead of real children, his own kids. "I decide if and when we have a baby," he said under his breath.

But Ana barely heard his statement. Preoccupied with her own thoughts, she nervously twirled a napkin between her thumb and forefinger. "When will the waitress take our order? We've been waiting for fifteen minutes already," she commented with impatience.

"What's really bugging you?"

She hesitated.

"Come on. Out with it!" Michael urged.

"Lately I've been filled with doubt," Ana obliged, not one to contain her emotions for long. "And not just about the divorce. About our relationship too. Ever since we told our partners about our affair, everything between us has changed. Haven't you noticed? Before, pretty much everything I said and did used to please you. You were so ecstatic about me, it was almost embarrassing since, God knows, I'm far from perfect." She paused to regain her breath, then went on. "But now you're so cold and aloof that I can hardly recognize you anymore. Every night I go to sleep worried about my family and about whether or not you still want me or love me."

"That's your fault, not mine," Michael commented dryly, unmoved. "You choose to focus on the negative. You create all this drama over nothing."

"It's not over nothing, Michael!" Ana protested. "It's over *everything*. Because if we're going to leave our partners and traumatize my kids, it better be for a damn good reason!"

"Don't raise your voice at me," he said sternly.

"And that's another thing," she continued, undaunted. "Your tone with me is different too. You don't ask me sweetly anymore. You command me. And I don't like it one bit," she tapped her foot on the floor, for emphasis.

This Latin gesture used to remind Michael of his favorite opera, *Carmen*. Now it just annoyed him. "Yeah, well, right now you're the one who's screaming at me."

Ana sighed, feeling exasperated. "Thanks for the reminder. You just brought up another excellent point," she went on, on a roll. "You don't listen to my issues anymore. You automatically dismiss them. It's as if my feelings were completely irrelevant to you. Meanwhile, I wake up every morning worried about what you might want from me and about how to make you happy. I'm starting to feel like Karen, bending over backwards for you. What in the world's happened to us, Michael?" By the end of her statement, which cascaded out of her unstoppably, Ana was downright hysterical. She cried into her napkin, her shoulders heaving with irregular convulsions.

As if confirming her charges, Michael didn't rush to console her. Instead, he observed her coldly, with undisguised disdain. Even Karen doesn't lose it like this, he observed. And she certainly has more class than to do it in public. Looking at Ana now, with her features distorted by tears, Michael couldn't help but see her as a defeated woman. He could hardly believe that he had wanted her so badly for all those months. "Get a hold of yourself, alright?" he said in the patronizing tone with which one chastises a volatile child in the midst of a temper tantrum. "I don't know what lines Rob's been feeding you lately or where all these stupid accusations are coming from. But I'll go ahead and refute them one by one, just *to make you happy*," he deliberately mimicked her phrase. "First of all, you wanted this affair as much as I did. So don't play Little Ms. Innocent with me cause I ain't buying it. Second, you enjoy the sex as much as I do. So cut the crap and don't play the prude either. It's not a role that suits you. Third, you, yourself made the decision to tell Rob about us and ask him for a divorce. I didn't even know you were going to do it when you did. Personally, I think it was a bit rash. We didn't get the chance to work out all the practical details first. Finally, as far as my own behavior's concerned, I'm a little more stressed nowadays because of our circumstances. That's all there is to it. As usual, you're making a mountain out of a molehill," Michael was about to conclude, but he noticed Ana's skeptical expression and decided to pursue his argument further. "And while we're still on the subject, I certainly don't find your behavior the same as before either. There's always something with you lately. You're worried or stressed or hysterical or cranky or, more often than not, all of the above. I realize that it's tough to divorce a man you've been with for so long. But I can't have much sympathy for you when you bring most of the stress upon yourself. Like all of the crazy things you're accusing me of. They're all in your head. None of them are real. I wanted to find a solution to your worries, a way to prove to you my commitment. I thought that starting our own family would bring us closer than ever. Remind me never to make any constructive suggestions again, okay?"

Ana glared at him. All of her former gushing feelings of love that had overflowed into their relationship condensed into an all-pervasive sense of resentment that bordered on hatred. "Michelle told me you'd do this. She warned me that you'd ask me to replace my own children."

"You're completely nuts! How the hell did the two of you geniuses come up with such a crazy idea?" Michael exploded. "I can understand how an immature kid might say something that preposterous. But you, Ana? How could you possibly think that I'd want you to replace your kids? I've never heard of anything so absurd in my whole life!"

Thinking that she might have overstated her case, Ana attempted to calm down. "I'm not saying that I'd ever abandon my kids. Nobody and nothing could make me do that. I'm just saying that they, themselves, would feel replaced if we had a baby. Think about it. Put yourself in their shoes," she pursued, more reasonably. "Even as things are, since Rob and I will share custody, I'll be with Michelle and Allan only half the time. If on top of that my time's taken by our new baby, my kids will feel like I'm not giving them the love and attention they deserve. And could you really blame them?"

"Bogus!" Michael retorted. "Many couples divorce and start their own families. That's very common. It doesn't mean that you're replacing the kids you had from a previous marriage. That's got nothing to do with it."

"That may very well be, but that's how Michelle, and to some degree Allen too, would see it. And given how much I've hurt them already, I don't want to risk doing anything to damage our relationship further," Ana explained, appealing to his sympathy.

"Children are malleable and their perceptions can change. Parents have influence over them," Michael countered in the staccato tone he generally assumed whenever his innermost desires were frustrated. "I'm not going to let your kids rule our lives. We're the adults here. We'll make decisions for them."

"You used the plural form, 'parents,'" Ana coolly observed. "That obviously means that your Royal Highness acknowledges that I, too, have some say in whether or not we have a baby together. Especially since, presumably, I'd be the one getting pregnant. And I say NO. I don't want to have a child with you."

Well then, the rules of the game have just changed little lady, Michael decided, telling himself that if Ana wouldn't always put him first, then he no longer owed her anything at all. Through her obvious disregard for his wishes, she had removed whatever trace of good will he had left. "If that's the way you want it, then that's how it will be," he said in a deeper voice, coming from his chest and the back of his throat. This statement, uttered as a concession but delivered as a threat, rang ominously in Ana's ears.

Chapter 9

That morning, as Rob was about to leave for work, Ana glanced at his wrist. She noticed that his watch looked dingy and old. The dial was slightly cracked and the watchband appeared worn. By reflex, she made a mental note to buy him a new watch that day, as she'd have done if they were still a couple. She made sure that the new watch had a small round dial and a smooth black leather band, as her husband preferred. When Rob arrived home that afternoon, she offered him the gift. "It looked like you needed it."

Rob looked down at the watch, then up at Ana. He could hardly believe the normalcy of her gesture. A rush of emotion overcame him. The gift reminded him of their ordinary life together. He turned away, not wishing to betray his feelings. Michelle silently observed the exchange between her parents. She had become very attuned to their interaction lately. As her father moved away, the girl approached Ana. "This is the first time I've seen Daddy cry. How could you do this to him, Mama?" she hissed under her breath. She was unwilling to accept that her mother would ever want to hurt her father for some stupid man she despised that she'd never in a million years accept as her stepfather. She already had a father. She wouldn't even speak to that dude, the girl resolved from the moment she heard of Michael.

Ana's heart sank upon witnessing her husband's reaction. A few days earlier, they had met with a lawyer to draft the divorce settlement. As Rob had promised, it stipulated joint custody and a fair division of their marital assets. They didn't quibble over any of the details. All of their tension centered on the decision to divorce in the first place, not on the terms of the settlement itself. Rob's fairness, his reliability and all of his other good qualities, which he manifested even during this period of great tension, only emphasized in Ana's eyes the sharp contrast between her husband's good character and her lover's increasingly transparent selfishness.

To distract herself from her mounting anxiety, Ana turned to her son, to help him with his homework, as she usually did before dinner. She rummaged through Allen's overcrowded backpack and removed, as if from a magician's bottomless bag of tricks, a seemingly endless supply of crumpled papers, worksheets, graded assignments, PTA announcements, candy, smashed pop tarts and pencils and pens. After scrimmaging in that messy pile, she finally found his last homework assignment. She recalled that particular essay, whose subject was, ironically, "My Family." The students had to select a theme—something that defined their family life—and develop it into an essay that included descriptive adjectives, illustrative examples and a main message. Ana read over the second grader's childlike print, with its uneven characters and predictable misspellings:

"My family. By Allen B. Have you ever wondered what will happen next in life? I have come to know it is impossible because everybody gets surprised. Once on vacation, I was in Louisiana and I saw someone was celebrating there birthday. I was so excited for my birthday to come! And I said 'too bad it's not even my half birthday.' Then my dad said 'it's your half birthday' and he was serious. That was a good surprise for me!

But a few days ago I also had a bad surprise. My parents told me they want to divorce. They were mad at each other. That makes me sad because they are nice to me. Both love me very much. They don't even ground me or scream at me. They only yell at each other. That's why there getting a divorce. Lots of my friends have stepmothers or stepfathers. But I'm still sad about it. I want to keep my real parents.

I think if you're nice to people, people will be nice to you! When you care for your friends, they will care for you. If you be nice to people, they will like you. If you share your toys with them, they will share there toys with you. I think it's great to make friends and the only way to do that is to be nice. Being nice is an important life skill to have. Because if you don't be nice, you will never make any friends. If you be nice, people will want to hang out with you and you will be able to learn more and more things about that person. If you be nice to people, you are a great person. I wish everybody could be nice to each other. My parents also. I wish them to get along and not fight and not get a divorce. Then there would be lots of love and happiness in our family. Being nice to each other is very important. There would be no more war and weapons if people were nice. Everything would be great in our family and in the world. We would all live peaceful, happy lives."

Ana raised her eyes from the essay, which contained such untainted wisdom, to look at her son. With his closely cropped hair and a lopsided mustache of chocolate ice cream, the boy looked like the picture of innocence. "I'll always love you and take care of you. We'll do homework together after school, as usual. Nothing will change between us," she said reassuringly. Ana then took Allen by his slim little hand, still sticky with traces of ice cream, and enfolded him in a maternal embrace. She felt his warmth and rapid heartbeat. The closeness of this somatic bond filled her with renewed hope. Maybe she could escape Michael's grasp. Maybe her marriage was still salvageable. Maybe the damage done by her affair was not unfixable. She rushed to her husband's office and knocked on the door.

When Rob opened it, she could hardly recognize him anymore. Her usually calm, rational husband had the feral look of a wounded animal. She glanced at his computer screen and saw pictures of women, in neat little squares. "What are you doing?" she asked him, stunned.

"You've made it perfectly clear to me that it's all over between us," Rob coolly replied. "I need to move on with my life. At first, I didn't want you to leave me. I was devastated by your decision. But now I don't want you to stay anymore. I've seen too much in you that I don't like."

"So what are you doing?" Ana repeated.

"I'm looking on a dating website. I don't want to suffer anymore. I look forward to falling in love again, with someone who'll treat me right."

"*Before* I even left our house?"

"*After* you cheated on me and asked for divorce," he emphasized.

"I thought we were getting along pretty well, under the circumstances," she alluded to her gift.

Instead of being appeased by this reminder, Rob became flushed with anger. "You can't hold me in reserve. I'm not some damn library book!"

Ana retreated to her room. She told herself that she should have expected that her husband would try to rebuild his life without her. But she was completely unprepared for it happening so soon. The flash of jealousy hit her hard, sneaking up on her like a fist punch from the side. I still love Rob! she belatedly realized.

Chapter 10

"Yup!" Michael answered the phone in a flat and uninviting manner that sounded disturbingly familiar to Ana. She had heard him answer that way when he was expecting a call from his fiancée. Only Karen was already there, so Ana deduced, with a sense of disappointment attenuated only by the viscosity of denial, that this time he was expecting her call.

"It's me," she said.

"Hey, you! What's up?" he attempted to sound chipper.

But Ana noticed traces of anxiety in his tone. She suspected that Karen must have been working on him again. "What's the matter? Did I catch you at a bad time? Were you in the middle of another one of those 'us conversation' with her?"

"We had a tough day," Michael confirmed. "We went through our photo albums and split up the pictures. She's letting me have most of them. She doesn't want to be reminded of our past. It's too painful for her."

"Is she trying to persuade you to stay with her?" Ana asked, threatened by Karen's unshakable attachment to her lover.

"Nope. She's just upset. She's been crying so much that the whole area around her nose is red, like she has the flu or something."

Ana detected a note of pride, but no sadness whatsoever, in Michael's voice. "She must really love you," Ana articulated the logical conclusion to his statements.

"Yup. She keeps on telling me that she wishes she could fall out of love with me or love me less."

Once again, Ana was struck by Michael's smugness. She reminded herself that his emotionless reaction to Karen's pain was the result of his having fallen out of love with his fiancée long ago. Yet part of her refused to believe that her lover could experience such utter indifference towards a woman that he used to love. Perhaps he was hiding something... "Did you try to comfort her?"

"Of course. I'm not an ogre you know," Michael ignored her innuendo. "There were a couple of times when I was in tears myself and had to look away."

"Why did you have to look away?"

"So as not to be inconsiderate, of course," he calmly informed her. "I mean, we're the ones who caused this whole mess. Our pain's nothing compared to theirs. The least we can do is not rub it in their face."

"It's not a matter of respect or disrespect. I'm genuinely upset about leaving Rob."

"Are you changing your mind?"

"No," Ana was quick to reassure him. "But the situation we've created is painful for everyone involved. Including ourselves."

"Yes, but *we're* the ones who created it," Michael underscored their underlying complicity.

Ana had noticed her lover's "us" versus "them" mentality when it came to his outlook on the world. They were the passionate free spirits, while the others followed conventions like sheep. They were the ones who conspired against their partners, so they couldn't pretend to share their feelings of pain, nostalgia or regret. Although she generally sided with Michael, his "us" versus "them" dichotomy didn't fully capture her emotional landscape. "Sometimes it's really difficult to stay strong, if by strength you mean lack of emotion." She decided to come clean with what was really bothering her. "Rob told me that he's starting to look for another partner on a dating website."

"So what? Are you jealous?"

"No. Well... Maybe a little bit," she reconsidered. "But, in a way, I'm also happy for him. I mean, I think it's healthy that he's moving on. He obviously deserves a better wife than me."

Michael remained silent for a moment. "Our partners definitely aren't made of the same stuff. Karen just told me that she'd wait for me however long it takes."

"However long what takes?"

"For our relationship to end." He hoped that telling Ana that Karen saw their relationship as a short-term fling would rile up her competitive spirit.

"But I was under the impression that we were marrying for life."

"I know that. You know that. But Karen doesn't. She hopes against hope that I'll soon wake up and see the error of my ways," he released an ironic little laugh.

Ana was not amused, however. "So I'm a mistake in her mind?"

"She thinks I'm with you mostly because of our physical attraction. But she believes that on a deeper level I'm more compatible with her."

"How come you didn't refute that assumption?"

She could almost see Michael shrug in the momentary pause, before he replied: "She wouldn't understand if I tried to explain the nature of our relationship. Besides, what does it matter what our partners think about us? Let them believe whatever the hell they wish if it makes them feel better. The only thing that matters is how we feel."

"Right now, I feel sad," Ana took the cue.

"What is it this time?"

"I miss Rob even though haven't even left him yet. He'll be a great catch for just about any woman. He's a wonderful family man. Responsible, principled, has a good, stable job and a decent income. Let's face it, he's a divorcée's dream come true! He'll fare better on those dating websites than the rest of us put together." Ana could hear Michael's deliberate, controlled breathing. She stopped herself, realizing a little too late that she was being tactless.

"Oh yeah? How much do you want to bet that I could beat him?" her lover asked her in a tone that, surprisingly, showed no trace of irritation or anger whatsoever: only eagerness.

"Beat him at what?"

"At how many women we can get on the dating website."

"I'm sure you could get more women quantitatively since you currently hold the world record of one night stands," she conceded. "But Rob will treat the woman he loves better in the long run. Because he's a decent human being."

"So you don't think I could fake decency?" Michael asked her with such earnestness that it made Ana smile.

"If you have to fake it, you ain't got it."

"Don't play dangerous liaisons games with me, little girl!" he taunted her.

"What games are you talking about?" she asked, troubled by his cavalier attitude. "I was just telling you that my husband's trying to move on with his life. I wasn't daring you to enter a dating contest!"

"I know. I was just kidding, Baby," Michael said. However, he was unable to let go of the idea. An instinctive surge of vanity coupled with the perverse need for preemptive vengeance welled up into his throat, like acid reflux. "Get this! You know what we could do? Put ourselves on one of these dating websites. Out of curiosity, to see if they'll match us up," he proposed, deciding that he'd had enough of Ana's whining and negativity and paving the way for finding her replacement, with her unwitting consent no less.

Fasten your seatbelts ladies, because the player's back in the game! Michael thought, feeling completely justified in his shift of attitude towards his girlfriend. If she considered her husband the better man, he reasoned, then there'd be literally hundreds of women eager to take her place, who'd appreciate him far more than she did. Ana's thoughtless remark, coupled with the tedium of her constant complaining, had just bought her a one-way ticket to the end of the line, replacing Karen as his backup, in case he couldn't find a better mate. Besides, now that even her own husband no longer wanted her, his girlfriend was much less desirable in his eyes as well. If Rob was enjoying the benefit of seeking new women, Michael thought, then why the hell shouldn't I, when I'm so much better than him? Why should I end up with some other man's reject?

Ana took a few moments to process Michael's suggestion, which struck her as bizarre. Even the way he had introduced his statement, "Get this!" rang unpleasantly familiar to her. That was the verbal tick he used with Karen on the phone before spinning his web of lies. "Since I'm divorcing Rob and you're leaving Karen so we can marry, as you've insisted all along, I think it's safe to assume that we're already matched up. Besides, I thought that you were Mr. Independent. Who cares if some impersonal dating website deems us compatible?"

"It was just a silly idea. I was curious to see how we'd match up according to so-called objective criteria, that's all," Michael replied matter-of-factly, to avoid raising any more red flags.

"It's the subjective ones that count," Ana retorted. With that comment, she hoped to close the debate. "When's Karen moving out?" she changed the subject to a more pressing concern.

"In a week. I'm helping her move her furniture from her parents' house to her apartment in Phoenix." Since Ana remained disapprovingly silent, he added, by way of explanation, "It's the least I can do after breaking her heart."

"I'll be so relieved once we can be together," Ana focused solely on the fact that her rival would soon be thousands of miles away from her lover, where she belonged. "This situation of us living apart and still being with our significant others is very difficult on all of us."

"Just remember: especially on them," Michael reiterated his main point. "So don't be heavy-handed about showing emotion in front of Rob. He's suffered enough already. You're only pouring salt on his wounds."

"Alright," Ana replied wearily. "I better go to bed now since I'm tired."

"Try to chill out, Babe. Get some rest," he advised her. "We only have a few more days of this drama, after which it will be smooth sailing for us."

"Thanks for putting everything in perspective," Ana felt momentarily grateful to have a partner who kept his cool in such heated times.

"Stay positive and focused. Keep your eyes on the prize at all times," Michael repeated his mantra.

That night, Ana fell asleep picturing her lover's angelic features, which used to sooth and reassure her. As she slipped into the visual richness of the R.E.M cycle, Michael's face became transposed unto a computer screen, along with a description of his assets, the languages he spoke and the sports he enjoyed. Michael had chosen to display the portrait of himself where he resembled a Romantic hero: his dark hair swept away from his brow; his cocky, playful smile appearing like a flirtatious challenge; his penetrating gaze oozing sensuality. Ana moaned in her sleep as she realized that literally hundreds of women could be contacting him on dating websites. In the agitation of her troubling dream, she heard the echo of her lover's voice declare, "I keep my eyes on the prize at all times." She relived the moment he triumphantly lifted her high up into the air like a trophy on the day she announced to him that she was divorcing Rob. The image vanished, leaving as its only somatic trace the impression of a sharp sting in her side.

To ease the discomfort, Ana shifted her position in bed. She lay flat on her stomach, her head turned to the side upon the pillow. "You're my little doll, Papusica," she heard Michael's voice once again. A collage of images of their numerous shopping trips together unfolded with the visual richness of a Chinese fan. Ana's eyelids fluttered restlessly like butterfly wings as various scenes of making love with Michael in public places—parks, malls, parking lots, cars, garages—danced before her mind's eye. She was dressed up in his gifts—the schoolgirl plaid miniskirt, the shoestring black dress, the variously colored corsets and thigh-highs her lover had offered her—and moved about in various places and positions to his liking, like a marionette. "Just be a good little doll," Michael said as he cradled her into his arms on his couch, proceeding to unwrap like a gift the layers of clothing.

As this scene faded out, another took its place. "You're my fragile little bird," her lover said, only not lovingly as usual, but hissing between his teeth as he pinned her down under the weight of his athletic body. Ana felt nearly suffocated in her sleep as she pictured herself struggling underneath him, her arms and legs helplessly flailing about. Once she managed to free herself from his grasp enough to look to the side, she recognized pieces of furniture from his house: the tan sofa, the cherry wood dining room table, and the mattress lying in the middle of the bedroom floor. When Michael finally released her, Ana ran towards the entrance. The door was shut with a golden lock. Looking for another escape route, she noticed that every piece of furniture in his house had turned to gold. She, herself, hopped around like a wounded bird from one room to the next, trapped inside her lover's gilded cage.

A picture of Karen and Michael on the day of their engagement flashed next before her eyes. Michael looked cheerful and happy but Karen seemed weary and dejected. Ana recalled that the photograph was positioned on a counter between several athletic trophies that Michael had won in college. The image of Karen and Michael then dissolved, to be replaced by a picture of herself and her lover on their future wedding day. The couple wasn't wearing any clothes. Michael was smiling, but Ana's eyes were closed.

The scene shifted again. In the next image, Michael and Rob were engaged in some kind of a race. Ana waited at the end of a road while both men were running as fast as possible towards her. At some point, Michael cheated. He tripped Rob and the latter fell down. Her lover exerted his athletic body to its limits and reached Ana first, sweeping her up into his arms. When he put her back down again, she noticed a throng of women crowding around her lover, perhaps to congratulate him for his victory. As Michael talked and flirted with them, Ana stood alone on the side of the road, watching her husband hobbling away. "Please don't go!" she shouted, but Rob kept on moving ahead, as if he couldn't even hear her anymore.

"You know what we could do? Put ourselves on a dating website just for fun, you know, to see if they match us up," Ana had an instant replay of Michael's suggestion earlier that evening. "I keep my eyes on the prize at all times," her lover repeated as he sat down calmly at his computer to answer emails from dozens of women, with Ana perched upon his lap like a kitten. The pictures fell all over her, in an avalanche of images.

She couldn't take it anymore. She tore away the blanket and stood up from bed, her heart racing and her brow covered with sweat. As she woke up from her nightmare, Ana was tormented by a single thought, which emerged with a painful thrust from the folds of her unconscious. Everything's a game to Michael. EVERYTHING. Including our love!

Chapter 11

On the following morning, Ana called Michael to set up a meeting with him. "I had a nightmare about us last night," she said as soon as she saw him, her eyes anxiously seeking his for signs of concern.

The look she saw in his eyes, however, was one of voracious desire. "You and all your worries. Get in the car!" he opened the door for her.

Ana didn't step in, however. "We need to talk," she insisted.

Michael's desire morphed into impatience. "About what?" Ever since Ana had spilled the beans to her husband, she needed his reassurance ten times a day. He hadn't had so many damn "us conversations" with Karen in three years as he'd had with his girlfriend during the past three weeks.

"My love, don't be annoyed with me," Ana pleaded. "We've been going through a tough time lately. Please remember that my situation's more complicated than yours."

Michael looked away, to contain his mounting irritation. "How many times have I heard this sob story already?"

"It's not a sob story, Michael. It's our lives." Ana walked over to cling to him, hoping that their physical contact could somehow translate into emotional intimacy, as before.

"What is it that you want from me?" he asked her, exasperated.

"A little empathy."

"Get a hold of yourself, woman! Show some god damn strength!" he shook Ana by the shoulders, using both hands.

"That's so much easier for you to say. I need your support. After all, we're supposed to be life partners now!"

"I'm sorry, Baby," he folded her into his arms. "I had forgotten I was dealing with my little Powderpuff."

Feeling safer, Ana reiterated her request: "Can we please talk about this?"

"Talk to me," Michael obligingly agreed this time, guiding her into the car.

"I had a nightmare about what you said to me last night. You mentioned joining a dating website," she went straight to the point.

"What about it?"

"That comment really bothered me."

Michael made a dismissive gesture: "It was just a silly idea. I wanted to see if they'd find us compatible. You always make such a big deal out of nothing."

"Not this time," Ana disagreed. "I sensed something in you yesterday," she gesticulated, struggling to express her troubling intuitions. "You were like a bull about to charge. Or like a vulture smelling death. I don't know how else to describe it. But something in your attitude said to me that your hunger for other women was about to resurge. It was just a matter of time as to when." She looked into Michael's eyes, hoping that her lover would deny these charges and that she'd be entirely convinced by his claims.

"I don't know what the hell you're talking about," Michael responded, annoyed. "What kind of a marriage will we have if you can't even trust me? If every time I make some stupid remark about other women, you automatically suspect me of infidelity? A relationship can't exist without trust," he turned the blame back unto her jealous ways.

"You must admit, you don't have a very good track record."

"Hot damn! That was before we fell in love! Since we met, I've only had eyes for you. What more do you want from me, woman?"

To Ana's ears, her lover's words sounded more like a violent outburst than the declaration of love she needed to hear. Not daring to provoke him any further, however, she retreated into the seat and stared at him, perplexed. Who was the real Michael? she asked herself, feeling torn again. This man yelling at her or the man who held her tenderly in his arms only a few moments earlier? Now Michael was looking straight ahead at the windshield and, it occurred to Ana, with the same air of apparent unawareness with which he had caressed her during the first days of their affair, he now tapped the dashboard with the palm of his hand.

His gesture seemed vaguely familiar. She tried to recall when she had seen it before. Ah, yes.... It was during one of his phone conversations with Karen that she had witnessed, when she was lying naked next to him on the kitchen floor. As the conversation began, Michael was his usual charming self, bantering with Karen while gently caressing Ana's naked breast. But at some point, when he tried to cut the conversation short, Karen began reproaching him for not wanting to talk to her. Although that was obviously true, he became furious and defensive, as if his fiancée had accused him of something of which he was entirely innocent. He abruptly stood up and began tapping the kitchen counter with a steady staccato motion and later hung up the phone, annoyed. Yet only a few seconds after the altercation with Karen, Ana recalled, Michael's mood changed. He playfully took her into his arms to make love to her again. At the time, Ana took that conversation as yet another confirmation that her boyfriend loved her, not his fiancée. But now that she was observing his defensive aggression when confronted with her own charges, she began to believe that her misgivings couldn't have been that far off the mark. Ana made a conscious decision to voice them bluntly, to push Michael to reveal his true colors, whatever they turned out to be: real love for her, as part of her still hoped, or the callous indifference he manifested towards Karen. "It was terminal," she enigmatically observed.

"What was?"

"Our fight over the baby issue. It started the whole domino effect."

"What are you talking about?"

"The moment I refused to have a baby with you, I was history. You began looking for my replacement," Ana stated calmly.

Michael breathed in, a little impatient sniff, like a hound following a trail of trouble. "How the sound of your voice turns me on, Baby," he reached out to stroke her shoulder, hoping to distract her.

Ana backed away from him with a self-protective gesture, as if he were about to deliver a blow, not a caress. "It's very important that we settle this right now," she said with a sense of urgency.

"Alright," he relented, stung by her withdrawal. "But don't be so defensive. It's not like I was going to bite you."

Even the way he said this, with a flash of a smile and a malicious glimmer in his eyes, reminded Ana of all the kisses Michael had planted on the softest and most vulnerable part of her neck, leaving bluish green spots, like a vampire.

She no longer recalled the pleasure of those kisses, the tingles of desire she had felt when he pressed her skin between his tongue, teeth and lips. She only remembered the fierce, possessive look in Michael's eyes afterwards, when he gazed with satisfaction at the bluish patches that spread like a rash all over her neck. "Come on, admit this much at least. You're much too selfish and much too poor to want to take care of a newborn baby, on top of my two kids. You wanted to make sure that I'm completely tied to you. The bonds of love weren't enough for you. You wanted to create bonds of blood between us."

"Yeah, so? What the hell's wrong with that?" Michael asked with a dismissive shrug. "Many couples become even closer after they have a baby together. The fact I wanted a kid with you rather than Karen should flatter you. It only proves I love you more."

"No, it doesn't," Ana vehemently contradicted him. "Because I suspect that if I had really wanted a child with you, you'd feel trapped, like you did with Karen, and you wouldn't want it anymore. You want to have a child with me only because I don't want one with you." As she was saying this, a sound bite echoed in her mind, when Michael had snapped at her "Don't you ever say 'no' to me!" when she had refused to climb up on the roof of his house with him. "If I say 'no' to something you want," she articulated her intuitions, "you see it as an act of defiance and you feel unloved. Because for you, love means getting everything you want from someone. And even then, when you get a really compliant person like Karen, you're still not satisfied. You still want better and you still want more. That's why our fight about having a baby turned out to be so important. You want to control me completely, if possible, even more so than you did Karen. If I'm not under your thumb, then I'm totally worthless to you. But if I am under your thumb, like Karen obviously was, then I'm disposable too, the way she is. There's no way to win with you. I'm damned if I do and damned if I don't."

"You're completely paranoid!" Michael exclaimed.

Part of her wanted to back down, to dissipate the tension and restore their precarious harmony, as so often before. But a dominant part of her told her to allow her fears to rise to the surface, pushing them to their logical conclusion. "Am I? Or is it that I'm finally starting to open my eyes and see the truth about you? All those castles in the air you promised me, about lifelong faithfulness and happiness together, were nothing but a house of cards," she said, placing her hands together in the form of a triangle. "Flat and easy to topple," Ana folded one hand upon the other. "All it took is me saying 'no' to you once and our whole relationship crumbled."

"You're quite a magician yourself, I must say, since you're amazingly good at creating drama out of nothing!" Michael became animated, as if engaged in a game that finally got interesting, with a real opponent. "I've noticed this for quite some time now. You're constantly provoking Rob, provoking me and provoking your kids. You've been doing everything in your powers to alienate everyone around you. It's like you're looking for excuses to destroy our love. Hey, let's face it. When it comes right down to it, you're too much of a coward to take a leap of faith and live with me the passion you've always wanted."

Ana contemplated Michael's features. Initially, they seemed expressive and alive. But by the end of his statement, they became incongruously calm, given the intensity of their exchange. It was as if his voice came from behind a mask. "You know what I think? I think that pursuing me was just a game for you. Now that you won the match against Rob, you've grown tired of me and are eager to move on to your next conquest," she continued baiting him.

"Oh yeah? You think if all I wanted was some piece of ass, I couldn't have gone after easier targets?"

"I didn't say all you wanted was sex," Ana corrected him, trying to contain her raw emotions. "I said you viewed me as a challenge. I was a prize to be won. Just like you saw Karen, at first. She was a challenge to you because she was colder and more virtuous than the other women you pursued. You viewed making her enjoy romance and sex like a game. But you didn't succeed, so you went on the prowl for a more hot-blooded woman. That's when you found me. But now that you finally have me, you've stopped wanting me as well. You've come to the conclusion that I'm too much of a headache, especially under the circumstances. Now you're ready to move on and play the field again, as you did before we met."

Ana half-expected Michael to refute her narrative, which seemed to emerge out of her with the automatism of an unwitting revelation rather than the clarity of a logically thought-out conclusion. She waited for him to deny her charges and declare, as before, how deeply he loved her; how special she was in his eyes; how engaging in loveless sex with loose women was the furthest thing from his mind now that they were finally about to marry, as he had wanted all along.

But Michael didn't deny anything at all. Instead, he just smiled at her with the silly grin of a naughty child caught in the middle of a harmless prank. There was no trace of anger, irritation or even mild embarrassment reflected in his tranquil features. The former show of emotion, when he was furiously tapping on the dashboard in response to a much milder challenge from his girlfriend, magically disappeared once he was faced with this more serious accusation. "I didn't expect it would happen so soon," he said quietly, as if speaking mostly to himself.

"You didn't expect what would happen so soon?"

"Any of this," he gestured vaguely.

"You mean you expected us to break up?"

Michael didn't reply.

"But then," Ana pursued, becoming increasingly perturbed by the implications of his silence, "why did you pressure me to get a divorce in the first place? Why put me, my husband and my children through all that pain?"

"Like I told you from the start, I don't share."

"Why did you ask me to make such huge sacrifices for you?" Ana insisted with a sense of desperation, hoping against hope that sooner or later her lover would offer some kind of a satisfactory explanation for his inexplicable behavior. "What comparable sacrifices are you making for me?"

As if she had pushed a hot button, Michael suddenly switched from passive to active mode: "Cut the crap! You can't tell me I wasn't doing anything for you when I was going to do my best to support you and to be a decent stepfather to your kids."

Ana shook her head, unconvinced. "You're comparing my real life sacrifices to your mere promises. You were *promising* me that you'd support me or try to be a good stepfather to my kids," she emphasized. "But in divorcing my husband and seeing my children only half the time, I was making a real sacrifice for you. The moment I told Rob about our affair and asked him for a divorce I began making that sacrifice for you, for the sake of our relationship," she insisted upon their underlying asymmetry.

"*Noblesse oblige!*" Michael replied cheerfully. "I guess you're a much nobler creature than I am. I bend down to kiss your little feet, princess. Hey! I hope you cut those toenails!"

Ana looked at her lover in utter disbelief. She was stunned by Michael's playful insolence, when her whole life and the lives of her children were at stake. She felt anger slowly rising into her throat, then something snapped inside her brain: "You never loved me at all. You never loved any woman in your life because you're utterly incapable of love. To you, love's only a weakness that you can exploit in others. You're a selfish, heartless bastard and I never want to see you again!"

In response, Michael continued to smile at her, with an impudent Cheshire cat grin. "Then get the hell out," he said coolly, opening the car door in anything but the gentlemanly manner he usually assumed with her. "If you can't keep up, get out of the way!" he added louder. Ana lunged out of his car, overcome by the mixture of confusion, anger and dread that a small critter must feel after having just been swallowed whole and regurgitated alive by a snake.

Chapter 12

"When are you planning to move in with Michael?" Rob asked his wife, perturbed by the fact that their separation was dragging on in no-man's land, neither still married nor clearly heading for divorce.

"Never," Ana replied.

"What's that supposed to mean?"

"I broke up with him," she announced.

Oh God, this can't be happening to me! Rob thought. I had just gotten over the hump, used to the idea of divorce. "Why in the world would you do that now?"

Ana noticed that her husband sounded anything but pleased with the news. "Something's gone terribly wrong. I don't know what's come over Michael. He's like a whole different person from the man I fell in love with."

"Not really," Rob disagreed. "He's the same person who cheated on, lied to, manipulated and then dumped his fiancée once he got tired of her and got a hold of you. The love of your life. Everything you've ever wanted in a man. Ideal lover... right... You were so blind, it made me sick! This guy gets more ass than a freaking toilet seat!"

"Please. You don't need to launch into a character assassination of him."

"There's nothing to assassinate since he's got no character," Rob retorted.

"Just remember that Michael's also been under a lot of pressure lately," she reminded him.

I can't believe she's still defending that jerk! Rob fumed. "The poor guy... After he deceived and manipulated everyone. Now I'm supposed to feel sorry for him?"

"Nobody's asking you to feel sorry for anybody." The moment didn't feel right. But when would it feel better? After a slight hesitation, she gathered the nerve to ask him: "Do you still want me to leave?"

"I'm not going to throw you out into the street," he circumvented her real question. He wished he had the strength to tell her that it was too late; that they had reached the point of no return. But would it be true? he wondered, still feeling divided.

"Would you like me to rent an apartment?" she reformulated her question, sensing ambivalence.

Rob didn't know how to respond. He knew that probably any other man, any normal man, would tell her to go ahead and leave, as she had originally intended. But something inside of him prevented him from closing the door on their relationship. My worst fears have been confirmed, he reflected, considering his love for Ana as a terrible, self-defeating weakness. Now I'll be stuck in a hopeless marriage for the rest of my life, with a woman who needs me but can't love me. What did I ever do to deserve this? he asked himself, filled with self-pity. "You do what you want. You always do what you want," he finally said, unwilling to be the one responsible for the break up of their family.

This wasn't the reaction Ana hoped for, but it was the one she expected. "I want to give our marriage another chance," she said quietly.

"You want to give *me* another chance?" Rob asked, disturbed by her ambiguous formulation.

"I didn't say that." Ana breathed in and out to gather the courage to tell him what was really on her mind. "I want to work on our relationship. To make it what it should have been in the first place. For us to have our meals together, sleep together, be mutually faithful and be more loving and appreciative of each other than we were. I want a fresh start," she pleaded with her dark eyes.

Is this another ruse? Rob wondered. "How do you expect me to believe any of this when you're still defending him?"

"I won't defend him if you don't attack him anymore."

"So now it's my fault," Rob observed under his breath, incensed again. A sordid idea occurred to him. "You're just as sadistic as he is! You want to give me and the kids hope that we can be a happy family and once we begin to believe you, you'll turn around and go to him anyway."

Ana had been prepared for a downright refusal, but not for this accusation. "What? No! I'd never do something like that. I'm telling you, it's all over between us."

Rob didn't know what to believe anymore. "And I'm telling you that I don't trust you," he said, to test her reaction and gather more evidence, for or against her.

"How can I make you trust me again?"

"By not praising him anymore, for starters. By not comparing us at all. By being faithful to me. By loving me," he said, exasperated. "You should already know this. I shouldn't have to tell you!"

"Okay," Ana agreed, eager to pacify him.

Okay? That's it? If only things were so easy to fix in real life. "We'll need some serious counseling to even begin to undo some of the damage to our marriage," he said, feeling drained.

Rob retreated into the bedroom to contemplate this new development. He threw himself on top of the bed, his arms behind his head, his heart slowing down to the tempo of discouragement, of a profound sense of hopelessness. She won't let me move on in peace, he disconsolately observed. Then it occurred to him that Ana would probably reconcile with her lover if he rejected her at this point. His blood boiled when he imagined his children raised by such a conscienceless man. This is a guy who has admitted to his own girlfriend that he slept with dozens of women, Rob recalled. Strangely enough, Ana sees no problem with this fact. Could he hide his sexual addiction from my children? Would he convince her that it would be "for the good of the children" to initiate them into the ways of sex? He wouldn't be the first stepfather to do so. What would there be to stop him? Certainly not his conscience, since he's got no scruples. Would Ana be capable of standing up to him to protect our kids when she's yielded to everything he wanted so far?

His thoughts reverted to his wife. Ana had stated that she wanted to work on their marriage. She had told him from the very beginning that she didn't want to leave him; that Michael had pressured her into divorce. But the problem remains, Rob thought, how can I ever trust her again? One thing's become transparently clear to me: Michael would be sheer destruction for her. If she moves in with him, all of her previous pining for him would become pining for the wholesome family she left behind. His so-called charm would turn into domination. Eventually this would become sheer torture for her, since she's so willful and proud. It probably already has and that's why she broke up with him. But I wanted Ana to choose me rather than to reject him! Rob thought with a sinking feeling.

Yet a decision has to be made, since we've already had several weeks of limbo, he continued reasoning. I'll take her up on her offer to work on our marriage, for the sake of our children and because I still see potential in it, he resolved. But his heart wasn't really into it. Everything will stay in balance for as long as Ana remains under his spell, Rob qualified. And I don't want to be strung along anymore if divorce is inevitable. Oh, God... What a shitty existence! We've got to see a marriage counselor right away, he concluded.

Chapter 13

Michael parked the car in the garage. Within a few leaps, he was inside the house. "Hey," he greeted Karen. She was sitting at the kitchen table, licking the last traces of fat free yogurt from her spoon. "Still eating only fruit and yogurt?"

"I don't have much of an appetite lately. I might as well take advantage of that for my diet," she got up to place the spoon into the sink.

Michael followed her tall figure with his eyes, weighing in his mind the pros and cons of what he were about to propose to her. When she turned around to face him, he saw that the area around her nose was rosy, as if she had been crying again. "Do you have a cold or something?"

Karen looked at him reproachfully. "It must be my allergies."

Michael breathed in, as he often did when he was about to raise a point he considered particularly important. "Do you want to stop by *Andrea's*?"

Karen winced at the suggestion. That was their favorite restaurant, where they used to celebrate special occasions. "Why go there now?"

"I have a surprise for you." He looked around slyly. "But I prefer to reveal it somewhere special."

"What is it?" Karen asked, without much enthusiasm. She had had more than enough surprises from Michael lately.

"I'll tell you when we get there," he took her by the hand and led her out the door.

She followed him blindly. "What kind of a surprise?" she asked him again once they stepped into his car.

"If I told you, it wouldn't be a surprise anymore, now would it?"

Karen's heart sank. Michael's behavior reminded her of the days when he used to love her, when he'd surprise her with fancy dinners and bouquets of flowers and boxes of the dark chocolate she preferred. But those days were now forever gone.

Michael stole another glance at her. He seemed pleased with her sad expression. Once they arrived at the restaurant, they squeezed together into the same compartment of the revolving door, like he used to do with Ana. He asked for the same table he had occupied with his girlfriend only a few weeks earlier, which happened to be available. He wanted everything to be as it had been with Ana. "*Pinot noir*," Michael ordered two glasses of wine when the waitress came by. "And scallops with bacon, please," he named Karen's favorite *hors d'oeuvre*.

She smiled at him quizzically until the corners of her lips began to quiver. "What's going on?"

"It's over."

"What is?"

"The whole fling with Ana. We broke up."

Karen couldn't believe her ears. "Come on..." she said skeptically, examining his face. But Michael's expression remained perfectly serious. He didn't burst out into laughter, like he usually did after making some cruel comment or inappropriate joke.

"Why? What happened?"

Michael shrugged. "She was freaking out about the divorce. Plus, she didn't even want to have a baby together. It became quite obvious to me that she wasn't ready to commit to our relationship. You know me. Screw that! If you can't keep up, get out of my way. In fact, that's exactly what I told her."

In spite of everything that had happened, Karen felt sorry for Michael. He must feel so hurt, she speculated. She could tell from the start that Ana never really loved him. But she deliberately refrained from saying anything that would sound like 'I told you so.' She knew how proud Michael was. Besides, he needed comforting right now. "I'm so sorry," she said. Strangely enough, at that moment, she meant it.

"No you're not," he contradicted her, putting himself in her shoes. "You're happy about it. Don't bullshit me."

Men mask their disappointment so much better than we do, Karen speculated, surprised by Michael's lack of emotion about the recent breakup with his girlfriend. After all, he had been completely obsessed with Ana for almost a year. But what does all this mean for us? she wondered. That question must have been reflected in her eyes, since that's precisely the point Michael addressed next.

"Thanks," he looked up to thank the waitress who had returned with their drinks, then turned to his fiancée. "To us!" he raised his glass.

"To us?" Karen repeated and slowly raised hers as well. She took a sip of wine and waited patiently for an explanation. Her hand trembled lightly upon the stem of the glass as she set it back on the table.

"Maybe you were right all along," Michael finally uttered the words she had longed to hear ever since he had told her about the affair.

"What did I say again?" Her heart raced uncontrollably.

"That Ana wasn't right for me. That I needed a woman who was patient and calm and frugal and virtuous." His gaze lingered over her, calming her frayed nerves. "A woman like you."

"A woman *like* me?" Karen repeated, perturbed by the generic formulation.

"You," he looked straight into her eyes, not so much lovingly as possessively, to reclaim his rightful territory. Then his gaze relaxed. "Of course, that's entirely up to you. Given how I've behaved, whatever you decide, I'll understand." The waitress stopped by with two empty plates and a little tray filled with scallops wrapped in bacon, which she carefully placed at the center of the table. "Thanks," Michael said to her with a friendly smile.

Karen sighed. So the ball's now in my court, she observed. She had hoped for this moment, prayed for it, and even had tantalizing dreams about it that felt more like nightmares, during the hellish period when she was coming to terms with their breakup. "I don't want to be second best again," she replied, surprising her own self. She had assumed that she'd return to Michael in an instant if he asked her. But now that she was confronted with that reality, she was overcome with genuine ambivalence. "I want to be the only woman you love. Not the woman you settle for because your top choice let you down."

Michael nodded. "You are Baby, you are." He paused, looking discouraged. "Of course, how can I convince you of that now?"

"It will be difficult," Karen agreed. "I'm extremely hurt by what happened. I don't know how I'll ever trust you again. I know I've said this to you before. But now it's more true than ever."

"Please know that I'm willing to wait on you however long it takes you to decide. Our future's in your hands."

Michael's tone was so earnest and warm that Karen felt touched. "How do I know that you won't use me as your backup until you find your next true love?" she asked him nonetheless. "I never want to live again in another woman's shadow."

"I guess I really fucked up this time. Pardon the pun," he grinned.

Karen looked at his boyish face. How can he be so immature? she wondered. Here he is, a man in his late twenties who still speaks and acts like an adolescent boy. She sighed. That's part of his charm, she thought, her maternal attitude overtaking her instinct of self-preservation.

"Why are you smiling?"

"Because I'm starting to feel a little better about us," Karen confessed. Despite this moment of hope, her anxiety resurfaced. "I just want you to be sure this time," she emphasized.

"What does this actually mean? Practically speaking?" Michael inquired. You lead the way, he seemed to suggest, enjoying this psychological game of chess.

Karen felt uncomfortable with what she was about to propose. But better now than later, she told herself. "You're on the rebound now. I think you need some space to figure out what and, more importantly, *who* you want. You seem confused," she chose to interpret his recent actions as generously as possible.

"And you? How come you're not confused?" he asked her, knowing in advance what she'd say in response.

Karen's smile was sad, making her appear prematurely aged. "I've been ready practically since the day we met. I knew from the beginning that you're the only one for me. It's you who's always looked around and strayed. You're the one who doesn't know what he wants."

Michael burst out laughing at her blunt expression, amused by its apparent perspicacity. But, in point of fact, he knew exactly what he wanted. He wanted it all. The maximum possible. "So what does this actually mean for us?"

She hesitated. "I probably should return to Phoenix for awhile. To give you some space," she said, struggling with her own ambivalence. "Even though I don't want to risk losing you again."

Michael reached for her large hand and held it reassuringly. "I don't need space. Let's stay together through this, Baby. We belong together."

"I've always thought so too. But I think we need to be apart for a little while, so that you can be sure that's what you really want, before we actually..." she paused for a moment before bringing up the concept that seemed to scare him away, "...marry."

To her surprise, Michael didn't withdraw. "I could come visit you every other weekend," he offered.

"What about the other weekends?"

"You can come visit me here," Michael said, knowing full well that such an arrangement would be prohibitively expensive and impractical.

"What if you fall in love with someone else while I'm away?"

"You don't have to leave. We can work things out here, together."

Karen shook her head. "Not until you're absolutely sure you want to commit to me."

"So what are you saying? That, for now, we're together yet free?" Michael attempted to control his glee.

Karen smiled at him only with the corners of her mouth while the rest of her features remained fixed. "You're the only one who needs to be free, Michael. Not me."

"What makes you say that?"

"I can't compete with your torrid affair." She intended to sound sarcastic, but ended up sounding jealous.

This time, he didn't contradict her. With the manipulative man's instinct, Michael sensed that to denigrate Karen's rival would mean to lose one of his most important game pieces. He planned to milk the rivalry he had fostered between the two women for all its worth, long after Ana was out of the picture.

"If you don't get that woman out of your system, we have no future together," Karen continued. Her eyes pleaded with him. "You need to do whatever it takes to flush her out completely."

They exchanged a complicit glance. "You mean the way I got over Amy?" he alluded to his bout of promiscuity after his first girlfriend had left him.

She looked away. This decision was excruciating for her.

Few women would accept such an arrangement, Michael thought, looking at Karen steadily to ascertain what was really going on in her head. He didn't know if he should disdain his fiancée for agreeing to this new humiliation or admire her for confronting it so boldly. One thing is certain, he observed. This woman loves me. "Anytime you want to come back home, you'll be welcome," he declared wistfully. To distract her from scrutinizing his reaction, Michael pushed the plate of scallops towards her. "Have some before they get cold."

Karen took a little bite of a scallop. After not eating much of anything for so long, its lukewarm chewiness turned her stomach. Even after this unexpected twist of fate, she still felt dejected.

Michael grabbed a scallop by its toothpick and popped it whole into his mouth. He chewed with his whole face, cheeks full and pumping. His heart pounded with glee. Screw all that cheating and hiding crap, he thought. What a coup! An open relationship on his side alone. And, in case things didn't work out with someone new, Karen would still be there waiting for him, closing her eyes to his player lifestyle, just so that he'd forget about her rival. Forget who? Michael jokingly asked himself recalling Ana's mystified expression when he had told her to get out of his car. The past was already behind him, the present filled with promise, while the future looked brighter than ever.

Chapter 14

"I don't believe psychiatrists can help unless you're clinically insane," Ana said to her husband as they pulled into the parking garage. "There's a place over there," she pointed to an empty spot.

"Then he should be able to help you," Rob commented.

"How so?" Ana pretended not to get the unflattering innuendo. "I've already broken up with Michael."

"Yeah, but if he comes to get you, which he still might since I don't think we've heard the last of him yet, I'm not sure that you won't leave me for him again. Besides, there's so much damage this affair's done to our marriage. We don't really know how to fix it. If left to our own devices, we'll just go back to ignoring each other."

Ana directed him a skeptical glance: "And you really believe that paying a shrink two hundred bucks an hour to tell us that we're in love with our parents will fix all our problems?"

Rob took Ana's cool hand into his. For the first time since she could remember, he chivalrously helped her out of the car. "This isn't just about us." His gaze shifted nervously. "I can't even look my own parents and colleagues in the eye, given what you've done to me. At least now I'll be able to tell them that we're making some genuine effort to work on our marriage with a professional therapist. Otherwise, I'll look like a chump who doesn't have the guts to break up with his two-timing wife."

Ana contemplated her husband's statement as they climbed down the staircase that led them out of the garage. "I didn't think you cared so much about appearances," she said, without masking her disappointment.

"Yeah, well, you'd care more too if you had gone through the humiliation I have. But you're incapable of putting yourself in my shoes," Rob reproached her.

"It's not like your colleagues necessarily have more empathy than I do," Ana countered. "And I feel terrible about what I did. That's part of why I changed my mind. But, frankly, I don't care about what your colleagues and their secretaries think," she stuck to her original point. "Ultimately, it's our lives, not theirs. We'd be the ones to suffer had we separated. And we'll be the ones to suffer if we stay together and our marriage is unhappy."

"That's the whole point of therapy," Rob took her argument in the opposite direction. "I don't want to stay in an unhappy marriage. And obviously neither do you. We need to work together to improve our relationship."

"I agree," Ana replied looking directly into her husband's eyes as she squeezed his hand in solidarity. "But I seriously doubt that a shrink can help us," she reverted like a spring to her initial prejudice.

"Dr. Emmert is an experienced marriage counselor, not just any therapist," Rob defended the psychiatrist, who had been highly recommended by two of his colleagues at Ford Motor Company. "We're here," he opened the gilded front door of a tall, posh-looking building.

Ana stepped in first. "This is like a mini skyscraper. For Ann Arbor, at least," she remarked, being easily impressed by the air of opulence.

"His office is on the fifth floor," Rob pressed the elevator button.

"Promise me that if we don't get anything out of this session, we won't schedule another one," Ana whispered into her husband's ear once they stepped out into the hallway. She paused before the mirror outside the psychiatrist's office to adjust her hair.

"I promise," Rob agreed, since he wasn't a proponent of throwing money out the window either. "And you, in turn, promise me that you won't try to seduce him," he said, noticing that his wife was applying a fresh layer of lipstick.

"When do I ever?"

"Don't get me started on that!" Rob warned her. "I've seen how you behave with clients at your gallery. You always try to draw men into your orbit."

"That's not ..." Ana was about to object, but she didn't get the chance to finish her sentence since the therapist opened the door.

"Please come in," Dr. Emmert invited the couple into his office. Ana noticed that he was tall, younger than she had anticipated and, somehow, less German looking. Stereotyping psychotherapists, she had envisioned a Freud look-alike with a white beard. Not only was the therapist more handsome than her mental picture, but also he had these large, expressive brown eyes that, ironically, reminded her of Michael.

"Hi, I'm Rob," her husband shook hands with the psychiatrist. "And this is my wife, Ana," he introduced her.

"Nice to meet you," she smiled at him.

"Please make yourselves comfortable," Dr. Emmert gestured towards the two chairs facing his desk. "So how can I be of help?"

Rob gazed briefly at his wife, to see if she wanted to begin. But Ana didn't give any such sign. She was busy visually inspecting the room, to see what she could tell about the psychiatrist based upon the objects in his office. Not much, she decided after a brief examination. Dr. Emmert's office was sparsely furnished: two wooden bookshelves filled with books on developmental and child psychology; a chair that didn't look particularly imperial; no fancy Persian rugs like she had expected; a computer and no ornaments on his desk whatsoever. One of these days I'll have to bring him a couple of Moldavian vases to spruce up the place a little, Ana made a mental note, as if the psychiatrist were an old friend.

"We're here because my wife almost left me for another man," Rob began.

Dr. Emmert nodded, encouraging him to go on. He had heard that story dozens of times before although, in all fairness to Ana, usually it was the men who cheated.

"Basically," Rob continued, "A few weeks ago my wife informed me that she's been having an affair. She told me that she's in love with a man named Michael and that they want to marry. She asked for a divorce." Rob spoke quickly as if to get the unpleasant business over with. He paused briefly, to gather the strength to continue. "At first, I was unbelievably hurt by this news. Not just for my sake, but for the whole family, especially our kids, Michelle and Allen, who are eight and nine. But after awhile," Rob went on, "I got used to the idea of divorce. In fact, I even looked forward to having a spouse who'd treat me better than Ana did, which, I figured, wasn't setting the bar that high. And that's precisely when she changed her mind and told me that she wants to leave her lover and stay with me," he pursued. "Initially, I was almost as devastated by her change of heart as by the news that she wanted to leave me. Because I wanted to start a new life with someone who wouldn't hurt me the way she did." He took a deep breath before completing his statement. "But I still love Ana and she claims she still loves me. We're here because we'd like to save our marriage," he concluded his summary.

"Okay," the psychiatrist replied. He had listened carefully to Rob, then switched his attention to Ana, to hear her side of the story.

"Part of the problem we're facing right now is that it will be difficult for Rob to trust me again," she took the cue. "And even before, our marriage had serious problems. Also, emotionally speaking, I'm still not completely over my lover. He's probably not given up on me yet either, even though we've broken up, of course."

Dr. Emmert shook his head, as if something didn't quite mesh in these two complementary descriptions: "What's the point of even trying to work on your marriage if you're still in love with another man?" he asked Ana, then turned his attention once again to her husband, to observe his reaction.

"That's what I can't figure out either!" Rob concurred. "Frankly, I never understood why Ana changed her mind. And how do I know that she won't change it again?"

"Can you try to answer this question?" Dr. Emmert looked directly into Ana's eyes with his calm, penetrating gaze.

"The answer's simple, but Rob doesn't believe me," she replied. "It's because, ultimately, I still love him. It hurt too much when I tried to leave him. Plus I didn't want to see the kids much less, since he and I would be sharing custody. I was crying every day about that," her voice started to crack with emotion just from the recollection of those trying weeks.

"Those seemed like crocodile tears to me," Rob remarked flatly.

"They weren't!" she protested.

"Ana's reasoning struck me as similar to that of the Nazi doctors," her husband elaborated. "Some of them may have had genuine empathy for their victims, but they continued inflicting the damage. She complained every day about leaving me, but she was still going through with that decision anyway."

"Yes, but the fact remains that I didn't," Ana insisted. "I couldn't. My suffering wasn't innocent, obviously, because I was the one causing it. Yet it was real, in that I genuinely felt it."

"Sorry, but it was tough to feel any sympathy for you under the circumstances," Rob retorted.

"Then why did you reconcile with her?" Dr. Emmert asked him. "Many husbands wouldn't have, under the circumstances."

Rob shrugged as if unsure, even though he had been contemplating this question for days. "I don't know. Part of me believes that it's because I have no backbone. Another part of me believes that it's because I have this idealized image of the nuclear family." He took a furtive look at his wife, then directed his comment to the psychiatrist. "But another part of me believes that it's because I still love Ana. We have over ten years of history together. I also think I wanted to save her from a man I considered very dangerous for her." As he said this, Rob enveloped his wife in a protective glance, his own pain momentarily eclipsed by a concern for her wellbeing. "I realize that I'm biased given my position as a jilted husband. But I honestly thought that she was making the biggest mistake of her life."

"He thinks that Michael's a horrible person." Ana's tone reflected skepticism rather than agreement.

"And you don't?" Dr. Emmert asked her.

Ana shrugged. "I'm ambivalent about him. During most of our relationship, Michael treated me better than any other man. But towards the end he acted pretty badly. I couldn't even recognize him anymore."

"Then why didn't you go through with your decision to leave your husband?" the psychiatrist pursued, beginning to pick at the thread of her narrative.

"Mainly because I love my family. I couldn't build my happiness upon its destruction. Even though Rob was getting used to the idea of divorce, it still broke his heart," she said, looking at her husband. "And mine too," she turned again to the psychiatrist. "Our children were also pretty devastated. They're old enough to realize what was happening and to suffer because of it. We had worked out a divorce settlement that stipulated joint custody. But kids don't particularly enjoy being shuttled back and forth between parents."

"How come these concerns didn't prevent you from having the affair and asking for a divorce in the first place?" Dr. Emmert pursued.

"That's what I'd like to know," Rob chimed in.

"Because I didn't have them at the time," Ana replied in all honesty. "When I first started seeing Michael, I focused mostly on what was lacking in our marriage," she launched into the main topic of discussion she had been having with her husband. "For many years, I've been feeling that our marriage was sterile." She noticed that the psychiatrist didn't seem particularly sympathetic to her characterization. "Don't get me wrong, Rob's a good man and a great father," she qualified, not wishing to seem unfair. "But as a couple, we didn't have that much intimacy left in our marriage. I mean, for a number of years, we haven't even slept in the same bed anymore. We also didn't talk much, except about practical matters and the kids. For quite some time, Rob and I have been estranged. And I, for one, felt pretty hopeless about it."

"That didn't justify you cheating on me and leaving me for another man!" Rob interjected, his anger aroused all over again by what sounded to him like a self-serving rationalization. "Our estrangement was mutual, but I didn't deal with it as selfishly and dishonestly as you did."

Ana nodded. "I realize that," she said calmly. "And I'm not trying to justify my actions. I'm just answering Dr. Emmert's question by explaining why I was susceptible to Michael's advances." She hoped the psychiatrist would see that every marital crisis had two sides, even if they weren't always equal. "For almost a year, Michael showered me with attention and affection. I mean, it's rare to find someone who cares about you, your dreams and frustrations to the point where he *wants* to hear about them," she emphasized, leaning slightly forward in her chair. Then she relaxed again, feeling deflated. "With Rob, I often had the impression that telling him about what's on my mind was kind of like pulling teeth. And when he does communicate with me, it's mostly out of duty. He rarely seems to enjoy it."

"I think Ana's exaggerating," Rob objected, also addressing Dr. Emmert, as if they found themselves before a judge in court. "We don't have such horrible communication, as she claims. We do talk. But I have a full time job so I can support my wife and kids. Ana has the luxury of focusing full-time on her art. When I come home tired from work, I prefer to unwind on the computer or watch a game. I don't feel like engaging in some heavy duty conversation about her frustrated ambitions or our marital problems or God knows what."

"…or about movies or literature or art or anything at all," Ana supplemented his sentence.

"What leads you to believe that such ample communication would have lasted with Michael once the two of you moved in together?" Dr. Emmert asked Ana.

Ana had a flashback to the fight she and Michael had had at the Chinese restaurant, recalling how little they had to say to one another during the last few weeks of their relationship. But she felt put on the defensive by both her husband and the psychiatrist, as if they were ganging up against her and her former lover. "Because we *genuinely* shared the same interests—in art, movies and literature—and didn't have to force ourselves to communicate. Everything came effortlessly with Michael," she focused on everything except the end.

Upon hearing this, Rob got up. "Listen, I didn't come here to listen to you sing praises to your lover!"

"Come on, Rob! I'm just trying to explain," Ana tugged at his hand, attempting to get him to sit down again.

Rob pulled his hand away. "Of course you are!" he said, but sat down anyway, determined to find in the therapy session a resolution to his ambivalence. "She talks as if this guy walked on water," he addressed the psychiatrist. "If you only knew how devious and selfish he is! I haven't personally met him, yet from everything Ana's told me about him, even when she tries to praise him, he sounds like a horrible human being. The lowest of the low."

Dr. Emmert nodded to him sympathetically. "It would be interesting to know how his fiancée would describe him," he sought another angle to reach Ana, since the direct approach didn't seem to work. "Would she describe him in negative terms, like Rob just did, or glowing terms, the way you did?' he asked Ana.

"You're referring to Karen, his fiancée?" Ana corrected him. "Probably not. But they didn't have as much in common as we did."

"Or so he told you..." the therapist said skeptically.

"She bought into everything that guy told her to get laid!" Rob heatedly declared.

"There's no need to be crass..." Ana replied.

"I'm being crass? What about your actions?"

"My actions were wrong," she admitted. "But my motivations weren't what you think they were."

"Sure they were. They were completely selfish."

"And perhaps also based upon false assumptions," Dr. Emmert added. "Apparently, you assumed that the honeymoon phase with Michael could have continued forever."

"Are you saying that my relationship with him would have eventually turned into his relationship with Karen?" Ana asked him.

"I don't know," the therapist replied in a detached, nonjudgmental manner. "But it seems to me like it wasn't just your love for your husband and children that made you change your mind," he looked probingly into Ana's eyes. She averted her gaze, uncomfortable with the scrutiny. "I'm sure that had a lot to do with it," he added, to put her at ease. "I certainly don't wish to minimize that. But I suspect you had other compelling reasons. I'm a big believer in the unconscious. Somewhere in the back of your mind you must have realized that the honeymoon period with this man would be pretty short-lived. Something must have scared you away from him." He observed closely her reaction, as she nervously fidgeted with her bracelet.

Ana felt obliged to nuance her claim: "I hoped that Michael and I wouldn't tire of one another," she said quietly. "Because our relationship wasn't just about mutual pleasure, as Rob and Karen seemed to think. Our compatibility was on all levels—intellectual, emotional and psychological—not just sexual."

"For you maybe. Not for him," Rob emphasized.

"Do you think that mutual pleasure and compatibility are sufficient to form a lasting bond between two people?" Dr. Emmert came to his aid by reverting to the Socratic approach, which had brought some of Ana's misgivings to the surface.

"No. You also need principles," she responded.

"And where do you believe principles come from?" the psychiatrist pursued his line of questioning.

"Ethics," Ana replied tautologically, feeling confused.

"I suspect that empathy might also have something to do with it," Dr. Emmert suggested. "Scruples are inseparable from love. They depend on caring enough about another person to put yourself in their shoes. Given his attitude and behavior, do you think Michael would have been capable of empathy? I mean, over time?"

"Not a chance!" Rob answered on his wife's behalf.

"Well, up until the last few weeks together, Michael was very supportive of me," Ana found her husband's statement too harsh. "How can I put it? At first, he showered me with love and attention. When I was upset about getting thrown out of my gallery, unlike Rob," she directed her husband a reproachful glance, "he comforted me and helped me find other galleries."

Rob turned to his wife. "Are you completely blind? He didn't live with you, Ana. He wasn't supporting you and the kids. It didn't cost him much energy or time to *sound* supportive to you. But the point is that I actually *was* supporting you, in every way that counts! Because of me you could afford to be an artist, full-time, and do what you wished."

"That's true," Ana was obliged to acknowledge. She would have liked to add that Michael had promised to support her too, without ever reproaching her for being an artist, even when the market for art waned. But it occurred to her that any defense of Michael was pointless in this context. It only incensed Rob, while the psychiatrist deliberately asked her leading questions that went against the grain of her replies.

As if confirming her impression, Dr. Emmert inquired: "And when did Michael express interest in making a serious commitment to you?"

Ana paused for a moment, thinking that his question was somewhat of a non sequitur. "Almost immediately," she said. "We fell in love pretty fast. But it wasn't love at first sight. It went deeper than that. A total compatibility. 'The whole package,' as Michael liked to say."

Rob felt like getting up to leave again. "The only package that guy cared about was the one in his pants," he commented.

"How soon did he want the package in question delivered to his front door by wrapping up the divorce?" Dr. Emmert indulged in a little play on words of his own.

"Within a few weeks, a month at most," Ana estimated, thinking that the therapist was evidently on Rob's side, as the wronged spouse. But, in spite of that, she liked him. At least he hadn't told Rob that she's a lost cause, even if he may have thought it. "Michael tried to persuade me that our love was special and that we belonged together. He argued that our passion couldn't be shared. He wanted us to become a normal couple. By that he meant living together, not hiding 'like prisoners,' as he put it."

"Did you agree with him?"

"In principle, yes. If I hadn't already been married with kids. But our circumstances, particularly mine, changed everything."

"It didn't change much at all!" Rob objected. "You jumped into bed with him anyway and destroyed our marriage."

"Did you find it strange that Michael was pushing for commitment so soon? I mean, given that the two of you barely knew each other?" Dr. Emmert asked her, more diplomatically.

Ana hesitated. "Yes and no. No, because, like I said, we fell madly in love from the start. I suppose I did find it a little strange that he didn't want to wait for our compatibility to be confirmed over time. But I interpreted it a sign of love, which is how he presented the whole thing to me."

"How could you possibly imagine that a guy who pressures you to destroy your family would want what's good for you, Ana?" her husband asked her. "And don't you think that a guy who wants to have sex with you right away is likely to behave that way with other women too?" he pursued.

"I think Rob's right about that. It seems to me that Michael's impatience should have been a warning signal," the therapist concurred. "Because normal, healthy relationships take some time to develop," he elaborated. Most people don't make such a serious commitment right off the bat, when there's so much at stake. Especially given the fact that, as you pointed out to him, you're a married woman with kids. Such a decision would have impacted the lives of your entire family."

"But why would falling madly in love be a warning signal?" Ana objected. "Sometimes it can be a positive sign. It means that you're right for each other."

"It makes me sick to hear the phrase 'madly in love' applied to that jerk," Rob said.

"Sometimes relationships that begin with love at first sight, as they say, end up with a less exciting but deeper attachment," Dr. Emmert sought to remain objective. "But based on my clinical experience, a rapid warm up, coupled with the demand for instant commitment, tends to be a very bad sign. It usually means that the person has shallow emotions. So they're likely to detach from you as quickly as they attached."

Ana wasn't prepared to accept such a negative conclusion. In her mind, that was like throwing the baby out with the bath water. Clearly, she told herself, Dr.

Emmert, like Rob, didn't understand much about the mysterious workings of passion. But she decided to focus on finding common ground rather than engaging in a futile debate about the nature of love. "I didn't want to commit in the way Michael asked me to because I felt attached to my family. He and I argued quite a bit about this issue."

Rob shook his head. "You proved to us that your attachment to your family was trivial, if you left us for him."

"I wasn't going to abandon my kids!" Ana objected.

"But you abandoned me."

Ana didn't know what to say in response. Rob was right. She was planning to leave him, despite her ambivalence.

"So why did you give in to Michael's pressure?" Dr. Emmert asked her.

She didn't reply immediately. This was a question she had asked herself repeatedly during the course of her affair. She still didn't have a clear answer to it. "It's not that Michael ever forced me to do things I didn't want to do. I mean, he didn't order me around or give me any ultimatums," she gestured, struggling with the vagueness of the information she was trying to convey. "He could have easily blackmailed me about moving to Phoenix with his fiancée. But he never did that, at least not explicitly. Yet, somehow, it was an undercurrent between us, like an implicit threat or something. Whenever I didn't go along with his wishes, I sensed that he withdrew from me. It was as if our mutual affection and all the good times we shared were instantly erased from his mind, like they never existed," she recalled the emotional vacuum she felt whenever she and her former lover disagreed.

"And how did that make you feel?"

"Horrible," Ana began unburdening herself of some of the negative recollections. "I mean, with a more normal man, the difference between closeness and detachment doesn't feel that big. In most relationships, you just go from lukewarm to cool," she measured a miniscule distance between her thumb and index finger. "But with Michael, the difference was staggering," she extended her arms wide open. "Whenever we disagreed, we'd go from boiling hot to ice cold within a matter of seconds. And I dreaded the coldness. So I almost always gave in to his wishes. Because I didn't want to lose him."

"All this is very flattering to our marriage!" Rob exclaimed, stung by the fact that his wife had referred to their marriage as 'lukewarm.'

"I think I understand what she's trying to say," the therapist intervened on Ana's behalf, to attenuate, once again, the tension between husband and wife. "Michael didn't behave like a normal man. He lavished upon you an inordinate amount of attention and compliments, right?" Ana nodded in confirmation. "But only if and when you did what he wanted," Dr. Emmert pursued. "Which, I presume, was most of the time since you claim that he treated you well."

"That's right," she agreed.

"He *pretended* to treat her well!" Rob emphasized. "I treated her well, with genuine love and respect. I showed it through my actions, not just empty words," he addressed the therapist.

"It seems to me that Rob's bringing up another good point. Michael treated you well in a manner of speaking," the psychiatrist qualified. "Because people like him push the envelope. The more you give in, the more they claim as rightfully theirs. Apparently, when you disagreed with him, Michael withdrew his approval. It was a form of Pavlovian conditioning. The carrot and stick."

"Except for the fact that, for the most part, the stick was merely the absence of the carrot and the carrot was always so sweet," Ana reworked the analogy, to give it a more positive spin. "Rob called Michael domineering. But, actually, up until our last days together, he never behaved that way with me."

"Michael's carrot was covered in shit," Rob encapsulated his personal opinion of his rival. "But you were so smitten with this guy, and he filled your head with so many lies and empty promises, that when he told you it was candy, you believed him and even thought it tasted sweet."

Dr. Emmert smiled, appreciating the Freudian slip. He decided to lead Ana to this unpalatable conclusion more gently, however, by reexamining her own experiences. "You keep on saying, 'until the last days,' or 'up until the end,'" he observed. "Did Michael change his pattern of behavior with you?"

"Yes. During our last few weeks together, right after we told our partners about the affair," she recounted, "he become much colder and bossy with me. But that's in part because I also became moody, since it hurt me to hurt my family. We all went through a difficult time during those last few weeks, for obvious reasons," she didn't want to target her lover in particular.

"The reasons *are* obvious!" Rob concurred. "When real life hit you, your boyfriend showed his true colors."

"I'm sure that the difficulties you experienced with your family affected Michael's change of attitude towards you," Dr. Emmert commented, attempting to steer a middle course despite his sympathy for Rob, as the wronged spouse. "But I suspect that was only an accelerant." Ana stared at him blankly. "By that I mean that the stick would have probably come in due time, once you were more fully under his control. Because manipulative and controlling behavior, which is what you've described so far, tends to increase in severity over time."

"That's what I've been trying to explain to her," Rob responded. "The guy's a bully."

Ana reflex was to refute his claim. But, this time, she resisted that instinct. "Possibly," she breathed out, more of a sigh than a statement. "I know that if I had continued to refuse to marry him, I feared that Michael would leave me. He often told me that I was irreplaceable to him and that our love was special. But I still felt like if I did something that displeased him, the punishment would be disproportionate to the crime, so to speak."

"This sense of entitlement is the foundation of emotional abuse," Dr. Emmert said, jotting down some notes. "Controlling individuals always want to be the ones in charge. Their demands are sometimes disguised as polite requests. But, ultimately, they aren't requests, because when you don't do what they ask, they retaliate." He paused for a moment then added, to jog Ana's memory, "By lying, cheating on you, or doing something else to hurt you."

"Not that you're incapable of behaving that way yourself," Rob turned the tables on his wife.

"I realize that I'm no angel either," she readily conceded. "But what I'm trying to describe is somewhat different and…" she looked to the side, searching for the right word, "… more general." The therapist's explanation made perfect sense to her. "As Dr. Emmert said, Michael had a sense of entitlement towards everyone and everything. He lived life according to his own rules, which he made up as he went along," she imperceptibly began to switch sides. She paused to glance out the window, at the light gray haze of that overcast spring day, which seemed to capture the nebulous nature of her misgivings, then turned back to the psychiatrist: "Even in the beginning, when he acted so nice to me, something about Michael's behavior led me to believe that his affection was entirely conditional."

"… upon you doing everything he wanted," her husband completed her sentence.

"Or nearly," Ana cautiously agreed. "He definitely wanted to get his way on pretty much everything. He even tried to prescribe the clothes I wore around him. It always had to be short skirts or mini-dresses. Never pants or jeans, not even when it was cold outside." Ana felt ashamed, as soon as she voiced the idea out loud, that a grown woman would take instructions on what to wear from a man. But during the months when Michael was wooing her, she recalled, she rarely felt like she was being pressured to do anything against her will. She felt like a spoiled girlfriend indulging her lover with little favors intended to please and excite them both.

"Then you see," Dr. Emmert responded, "This form of positive conditioning can be even more powerful than overt domination."

"I guess when his controlling behavior came in the form of niceness and affection, it was hard for me to recognize it as a form of abuse," Ana replied.

"Sure. But you did everything Michael wanted for as long as he acted nice to you," the therapist pointed out. "And when you didn't, I presume, you saw his true colors. The man behind the mask, so to speak."

"There was no mask!" Ana protested. "Michael was really in love with me."

"I don't doubt it," the therapist conceded. "In his own way. . . ."

Ana looked at him, intrigued by this qualifier, which she had been tempted to use herself on a number of occasions. "What do you mean?"

Dr. Emmert leaned forward in his chair and gazed probingly into her eyes: "Have you ever wanted a piece of jewelry really badly?" he asked her. When Ana came in, he had noticed that she wore a diamond ring as well as a pair of aquamarine earrings and a matching pendant.

"She wants jewelry all the time," her husband commented. "For every special occasion—Christmas, her birthday, Valentine's Day, our anniversary, you name it. She always asks for jewelry," Rob observed, his hand moving defensively towards his wallet.

"Guilty as charged!" Ana admitted with a smile. "What can I say? I know what I like."

"But if you like each piece of jewelry that much, then why do you keep on wanting more?" the psychiatrist pursued.

"Because I like each new piece even better."

"Well, that's exactly how Michael desires women. As possessions. His need to possess you was quite genuine but shallow. Without any real consideration for your wellbeing. In a few days, weeks or months after you moved in with him, he'd have become obsessed with someone new. Of course, since I don't personally know this guy, I can't make a firm diagnosis. But from what you, yourself, have told me about him, Michael seems to have emotional intensity without depth," the psychiatrist observed.

This explanation oversimplifies everything, Ana attempted to protect the integrity of her pleasant memories. "I'm not sure I entirely agree with your jewelry analogy. While we were together, Michael only had eyes for me. All of his attention was focused on our relationship."

Dr. Emmert smiled knowingly. "Sure. That fits with the psychological picture I was sketching. Or at least, it doesn't contradict it. People like Michael have a kind of predatory hunger for what they want. Lately, that happened to be you. They have an uncanny ability to focus on that person or goal to the exclusion of everything and everyone else. And this powerful obsession generally lasts for as long as they don't yet possess what they want. But once their target is within their grasp, they get bored. Once they lose interest they move on to someone—or something—else."

Ana considered his statement. She recalled that Michael acted like he loved her during the entire year together. He changed only after she too became more difficult. "I sometimes tell myself that if I hadn't become so moody and impatient with Michael at the end, he'd also have behaved differently towards me," she said, thinking out loud.

"So you're saying that you regret staying with me?" Rob asked her, stung.

"Not at all," Ana replied, obliged to go on the defensive again. It occurred to her that it was difficult to strike the right balance in this session. She couldn't be completely honest with the therapist while also remaining tactful towards her husband. She opted for erring on the side of honesty. Without it, she sensed, the therapy would be meaningless. But antagonizing Rob didn't help matters either. It defeated the whole purpose of couples' counseling. "It's just that Michael's change in behavior towards the end really puzzled me. And sometimes I blame myself for it."

"Why so?" Dr. Emmert asked her.

Ana shook her head, as if to dissipate the haze. "I feel guilty towards everyone. Rob, the kids and even Michael."

Rob couldn't believe his ears. "Towards Michael? He's the one that manipulated and hurt everyone, including you!"

"I hate to say this so often, but in this case I think Rob's right. I can understand why you'd feel guilty towards your family," Dr. Emmert commented calmly, to diffuse the tension. "But it seems to me that feeling guilty towards Michael is a distortion of your conscience."

"He reproached me that I'm the one who bailed out on our relationship."

The therapist nodded. "And why did you?"

"Because I love my family. And because I became frightened by Michael's behavior," she admitted more openly. "Ultimately, I couldn't place my trust in him."

"What were you afraid of?"

Ana gesticulated vaguely. "Towards the end, I became afraid of everything." Thinking of how to describe that fear most succinctly, she recalled something her lover had told her early on in their relationship. "His first girlfriend called him a snake," she said out loud, as if that epithet were particularly relevant.

"She was quite perceptive," Rob commented.

"Michael told me that she's the one who left him. Which made me wonder why she called *him* a snake…"

"Why do you think?" Dr. Emmert threw the question back at her.

Ana looked out the window trying to think of a way of formulating her intuition. "Because what I've come to realize is that with Michael you never know when he'll turn around and bite you."

"Then why do you blame yourself for leaving him? Especially given everything at stake for you and your family?" the therapist inquired.

"I don't know," she sank once again into ambivalence.

"The reason is clear," Rob stated. "She was completely brainwashed by that guy."

"I'm nobody's puppet," Ana protested.

"Do you feel that if you had behaved differently at the end, he'd have been good to you?" the therapist pursued, steering the dialogue away from mutual insults.

"That's what I hoped. I thought that if I treated Michael right, loved him with all my heart and did my best to make him happy, he'd never hurt me."

"Love can't solve everything. Especially if it doesn't exist in the first place," Dr. Emmert commented. "But the metaphor you used is quite helpful. Just look at Michael as a pet snake. No matter how nice and loving you are to him, he won't grow fur and become a puppy. Sooner or later, he'll attack you." He stole a glance at Rob, who from the very start had intuitively struck him as a decent fellow. "If you became Michael's partner, you'd have seen the difference between the dominance bond he established with you and real love."

"His fiancée didn't see it. She still loves him," was the only defense Ana could muster.

Dr. Emmert shrugged. "Women who stay with such men generally suffer from low self-esteem or have some kind of martyr complex."

"That's Karen alright!" Ana whole-heartedly agreed. "She does everything she can to please him. *Everything*," she emphasized.

"And look how he nicely he's rewarded her for her efforts," Rob said.

"But Rob, Karen's not exactly perfect either," Ana objected. She recalled Michael's explanation, during one of their early encounters when they had confided in each another like old friends. He had told her that no matter how hard he worked on their relationship, Karen remained reserved towards him. "She's cold and distant."

"Or so he claims..." Dr. Emmert supplemented her sentence. "At the same time, you said that she does everything to please him," he pointed out the contradiction.

"That much is true," Ana shrugged, as if there was nothing she could do to resolve this apparent paradox. "She does everything within her powers. But the fact remains, she's not all that powerful. Like Michael said, Karen lacks the qualities to make him happy," she concluded. "No matter how hard she tries, she's not warm, sexy or interesting enough for him."

Rob shook his head. "When you say things like this, Ana, I don't even recognize the smart woman I fell in love with. Most men who cheat say that about their wives to their lovers. It's just words. Ready-made, cheap excuses."

Dr. Emmert smiled cynically. "To pursue Rob's point in a slightly different direction, don't you think that if you had become his partner you would have eventually run up against the same wall?" he asked Ana.

"Maybe..." she hesitated, instinctively placing her fingers to her forehead, to sort through a painful recollection. "Our relationship became so confusing and stressful at the end that I couldn't tell who was to blame for what anymore," she attempted to soften the picture.

Seeing her stubbornness resurface, Dr. Emmert folded his hands. "Just out of curiosity. Why is it that you believed everything this man told you? Why did you accept his side of the story about Karen? Did Michael ever give you any compelling reason to trust him?" he reverted to the Socratic approach, which seemed to yield most progress.

Ana leaned slightly forward in her chair. "It's not just about *what* he said to me," she explained. "It's more about *how* he said it. He spoke in this calm, soothing voice and looked straight into my eyes. It was really hypnotic. At any rate, he seemed very sincere. There was no fidgeting, no looking away, no nervousness whatsoever, like when people lie to you."

"My point exactly! The fact this guy could lie as easily as normal people breathe should have made you run away from him as fast as possible," Rob remarked.

"It sounds to me like Michael's slick style obscured your reason," the psychiatrist concurred. "You were so distracted by this guy's smooth manner that you didn't pay enough attention to the content of his words. Because if he had, indeed, concluded that Karen wasn't compatible with him and that he didn't love her, then why didn't he leave her?"

"I asked him this very question on a number of occasions."

"And?"

"He never really gave me a satisfactory answer."

"That's because he couldn't admit right off the bat that he wanted to string along both of you, plus several more women on the side," Rob said, running out of patience with his wife's inexplicable naiveté, which, he felt, bordered on stupidity. That's not the Ana I knew, he thought, once again having the eerie sensation that his wife had become a different person, a stranger, as a result of this experience.

"What did he tell you?" Dr. Emmert asked her.

"He said that it's because he didn't want to be left all alone," Ana replied mechanically, as if citing an answer in a foreign tongue that she didn't fully comprehend.

The therapist smiled knowingly. "I see. And, given that he already had you and thus wasn't all alone, that explanation didn't ring false to your ears?"

"Sure it did," Ana admitted. "I never quite understood why Michael wanted to hold on to a woman that he didn't love anymore."

"Maybe that's because he always needs to have someone to control and manipulate," Dr. Emmert offered his own hypothesis. "Sexual conquests may not be sufficiently stimulating for him."

Ana considered his reply, then her eyes lit up with a recollection of a more generous interpretation. Given how all of the therapist's explanations were systematically unsympathetic towards her lover, she felt like she needed to point out the other side of the coin. "Early on, Michael gave me an answer that kind of made sense to me at the time. He said that he was a hopeless romantic, like me. That's why he never lost hope on the relationship with Karen. I guess he was still trying to make it work," she half-heartedly suggested, since this answer no longer rang convincing to her.

"By cheating and lying to her?" Dr. Emmert asked, raising an eyebrow. "Did his answer seem even remotely plausible to you?"

"It sure did, since that's exactly how Ana worked on our relationship!" Rob sullenly interjected.

Ana had no reply. She couldn't defend Michael's behavior. She couldn't even defend her own, for that matter.

Dr. Emmert sensed they had reached an impasse. "It seems to me like you're engaged in a few denial strategies of your own," the psychiatrist observed, gazing in passing at his watch. He needed to bring the session to a close in the few minutes they had left. "Unfortunately, for some reason, and only you can tell us why, you're still struggling to hold on to an idealized image of Michael and of your relationship with him. This will make it practically impossible for you and your husband to work on your marriage in good faith."

"That's what I've been telling her and why I persuaded her we needed therapy," Rob commented. But the session hadn't been as helpful as he had hoped. He felt ignored yet also validated during this therapy session, which had revolved around Ana and her former lover rather than their marriage.

"For as long as you believe that Michael's the perfect standard by which to judge all other men, including your husband," Dr. Emmert pursued, "you can't focus on improving your relationship with Rob." The psychiatrist's gaze passed back and forth from husband to wife. "So if you guys are interested in having another meeting with me, I'd like to suggest the following exercise: think about what was missing from your marriage that you'd like to accomplish together.

Also," he addressed Ana in particular, "ask yourself what was missing in Michael as a partner. In other words, continue to de-idealize this fantasy you've constructed of the perfect love story. Because, as you're no doubt beginning to see, your relationship with him wasn't nearly as perfect as you initially believed. In fact, in many respects it was the opposite of what it seemed to be."

Once again, Ana felt like the psychiatrist, her husband and probably anybody who hadn't lived through a similar experience couldn't really comprehend it. "You're implying that I was blind for not seeing through Michael. And in some ways I was. But things aren't so simple when you actually live through them. I mean, when a man gives you so much affection and support for months on end, it's hard to see him as selfish and malicious."

"I'm not saying that you were blind," Dr. Emmert calmly responded. "But clearly you ignored the red flags that revealed early on Michael's core self-centeredness and insensitivity." The therapist seemed lost in thought for a moment. "In fact, the more I hear about him, the more convinced I become that Michael's a textbook example," he concluded.

Ana meant to ask him a textbook example of what, but Dr. Emmert continued, sounding somewhat rushed, "Listen, our time's almost over," he informed the couple, to wrap up the session. "But from what you've been telling me about him," he took a quick glance at his notes, "Michael seems to be seriously lacking the two qualities that are essential to love: the capacity to form emotional bonds with others and empathy. Without forming genuine emotional bonds, people have no compelling reason to stay together over time. They don't need each other when they're together and they don't miss each other when they're apart. And without empathy, or the ability to put yourself in another person's shoes and care about their feelings, they lie, cheat, con and manipulate people easily, for profit and fun," the psychiatrist observed, examining Ana's reaction to his statements. She seemed to be contemplating his statements. "I'd like to suggest that you take a look at a few psychology books," he extended her a note on which he had jotted down three titles. "You don't have to read them from cover to cover. Just browse through the parts that seem most relevant to you. These studies will help you recognize some of Michael's personality traits. After reading this material, it will be even harder for you to see him as an ideal partner."

"Thanks," she took the note and slipped it into her coat pocket: ironically, exactly where she had placed Michael's phone number on the day they met.

"Would you be interested in setting up another meeting with me?" Dr. Emmert asked the couple.

Rob looked uncomfortable. He didn't think he could suffer through more blow-by-blow analyses of his wife's affair with another man.

"We have to decide if it wouldn't be more useful for me to have a few individual sessions with you," Ana replied, after exchanging a quick look with her husband, who seemed hesitant. "It looks like before Rob and I can work on our marriage, I have to get Michael out of my system."

"And I'd rather not be a part of that process," Rob hastened to add. "I've heard more than I ever care to find out about that guy."

"Alright, then how about you figure out together which configuration you prefer and get back in touch with me to schedule an appointment?" Dr. Emmert proposed.

"Sounds good," Ana agreed.

Once they were alone in the elevator, she burst out: "He's straightforward and has a lot of common sense!" She was pleasantly surprised by the discovery that sometimes her prejudices, not just her idealizations, turned out to be mistaken.

"Yeah, he's good. But I thought he was going to help us work on our marriage, not rehash your sordid affair," Rob responded somewhat less enthusiastically.

"Like the Dr. Emmert said, we can't do one without the other," his wife reminded him.

Chapter 15

"What are you doing with Kitt?" Ana asked her daughter. They had purchased the 1930's doll, complete with her art nouveau bedroom set, only last summer.

"Nothing. I'm just moving her to the basement."

"You're bored with her already?"

"I've outgrown dolls, Mama," the girl rolled her eyes.

With her diminutive frame, large blue eyes and delicate features, Michelle herself looked like a doll. "You're only nine years old. How could you have outgrown dolls already?" Ana objected.

Her daughter's eyes suddenly clouded. "I've grown up faster this year, I guess."

Ana blushed at the allusion. "You never let us know you were so upset."

Michelle placed the doll on the living room sofa. She sat down next to her, a little doll and a bigger doll side by side, both with blond hair and blue eyes, only Michelle's gaze was so much more expressive than Kitt's. "I saw how you and Daddy were upset. I didn't want to make you feel even worse. Besides, you were sure you wanted to leave us. There was nothing I could do about it." Her usually sparkly voice trailed off with sadness.

"You mean leave Daddy," Ana corrected her.

The girl shook her head. "Not just him. Me and Allen too. I don't think that man would have ever cared about us. He wouldn't have liked us coming by his house."

A few weeks earlier, Ana would have insisted that Michael's house would have been theirs as well. But now she was much more inclined to agree with her daughter. "Maybe. But he couldn't dictate my actions. And I'd choose to be a good mom to my kids."

"You say that now. But before, you chose him," Michelle retorted. She approached her mother to give her a conciliatory hug. "It's okay, Mama. You made the right decision in the end. That's all that counts."

"Yes, but I'm afraid I've hurt everyone too much. Especially your father," Ana replied.

Suddenly, Michelle's face lit up with an impish smile and she became a child again: "I have only one thing to say to that," she replied, then paused for dramatic effect.

"What?"

"Build a bridge and get over it!"

"Easier said then done."

Michelle once again assumed a more grown-up demeanor. "Think of it this way: at least things are better now between you and Daddy. Before all this happened, I used to pray that you wouldn't get divorced. You and Daddy were so cold to each other. But now I don't have to pray about that stuff anymore. My wish came true."

"What do you pray for now?"

"For Allen to stop bugging me," Michelle replied. Then she suddenly remembered that she was about to take Kitt to the basement, where she kept all the toys she had outgrown, unwilling to make the more decisive move of giving them away to charity. She glanced evaluatively at the doll. Kitt's demeanor seemed pretty mature. After all, the doll was older than she was, being eleven already. She also dressed okay, considering her clothes were almost a century out of date. "I might keep her in my room for a few more months," Michelle reconsidered her decision.

Ana knew better than to approve too enthusiastically. "It's up to you," she said. But deep inside she was glad that her daughter was holding on to her childhood for a little while longer.

That evening, when they were all sitting down to dinner, Michelle said a brief prayer for her reunited family: "Dear Lord, thank you for this meal, for keeping us healthy and for getting my parents back together. Amen." Then they all dove into the chicken alfredo.

"Chew with your mouth closed," Michelle advised her brother.

"I am!" Allen objected, as bits of chicken burst out of his mouth like fireworks.

Ana could hardly believe that only days after her break-up with Michael, life was beginning to return to normal. Only this was a new, more normal normality, one which they never really had: with all the conventions like eating together as a family and sleeping with one's spouse and nobody else's, which they had skirted before, since after all, Ana was a subversive artist and Rob was too busy to be conventional.

But later that night, when she and her husband lay side by side in bed, there was an aura of tension around their bodies, shielding them from physical intimacy. Rob wondered when he'd be able to make love to his wife again. Ana still emanated another man's touch, another man's scent and another man's kisses. Would he be able to touch her without thinking of him? When he looked at his wife, Rob saw a desirable woman who still looked attractive and youthful. But the difference between finding her desirable and desiring her wasn't yet bridged. The other man continued to lie between them.

For her part, Ana felt surprisingly at ease given the tension that still vibrated in the air. It was nothing compared to the tension of remorse and regret, of hurting those she loved. The thought of Michael made her think once again about Rob, in an association of opposites. Ana sensed that it was still too early to show any overt signs of physical affection towards her husband. It would seem fake after everything we went through, she speculated. When he's ready to make the first move, he'll make it, she decided. She nonetheless appreciated the comfort of lying in bed next to a man who hadn't bedded hundreds of women and who wasn't plotting whom to seduce next. A man who didn't manipulate her or ask guilt-inducing questions like "Don't you trust me?" or "Who was that man I saw you with the other day at the gallery?" A man who allowed her space and freedom, maybe to a fault. With Rob, it's the real deal, Ana told herself. No bells and whistles, no ideal promises, no romantic gifts, no public displays of affection or wild declarations of love repeated dozens of times a day. But whatever he says or does, I can always count on it to be true and real. And that, she thought as she began drifting off to sleep soothed by the warmth of her husband's presence, is what now matters to me most.

Chapter 16

Michael felt something tickle his back. He brushed it off with a somnolent, half-conscious gesture, but the sensation persisted. He turned over and opened his eyes. A young woman with pale blue eyes and platinum blond hair lay by his side in bed. "Morning sleepy face!" she whisked away the sheet from her body. By now fully awake, Michael's gaze went straight to her large, semispherical silicon breasts, white as powdered milk, with protruding, rosy nipples. His mouth gravitated to one of the inviting nipples, which he suckled greedily, then to the other, so that it wouldn't become jealous. He slid her body towards him and gestured unambiguously toward his erect member. As she was slowly, skillfully undertaking to bring him to orgasm, like trained professionals do, by using both her hand and her mouth in a synchronized, rhythmic motion, he tried, absurdly, to remember her name and how they met.

Was it "Hallie?" or "Hollie?" That sounded about right. She was his second pick up on the previous evening, as he made his rounds to the clubs. Despite the lack of adequate sleep, Michael recalled that she had mentioned something to him about being an advertising major. The one before her that evening, a cute little oriental doll whom he nailed in the parking lot near another local bar, had also been a business major. These business majors sure know how to get down to business, Michael thought, looking down at his partner. Her mouth was opened into a perfectly shaped oval, her cheeks caved in from the sucking efforts which were beginning to arouse him. "Stop!" he said, motioning her to get on all fours. At the sight of her rounded, athletic posterior and the parenthesis of her slim legs revealing a set of pinkish-gray partially unfolded lips, Michael could hardly contain himself. He quickly placed on the condom he had left on the counter. After a few deep, violent thrusts that made her whole body plunge back and forth like a piston, he exploded inside her in a sequence of diminishing spasms, releasing a series of grunts that gradually dissipated into a complacent silence. Though Hollie might have been the business major, after he was done with her, Michael was the one who became all business. He sprung from bed and hit the shower.

"Mind if I join you?" she coyly peeked in through the plastic curtain.

"Actually, I'm in a big hurry," he spoke louder over the running water. "I have to teach a class in a few minutes."

"I understand."

As he lathered up, Michael considered how to get rid of Hollie and make sure she understood that she wouldn't be visiting him again. Going over her assets, he thought that she was hot and a pretty good lay. But she was too ditzy to be girlfriend material. In fact, he couldn't recall having had much of a conversation with her other than a volley of flirtatious comments culminating in the classic hook up line, "Do you want to go somewhere else?" that led them straight to his place. An easy score, Michael summed her up, drying himself with a large white towel he had taken as a memento from a hotel where he had once been with Ana, in the early days of their relationship, when Karen was still in town. A light current of nostalgia passed through him at this recollection. He still found his former girlfriend more interesting and sensual than the women he was currently hooking up with. He catalogued each of them in turn. He was back together with Lisa, thanks to her horny disposition and big tits. Mireille also occasionally kept him busy at the office, though she was more moody and less reliable lately. In the evenings, he went out for an early tryst at the local bars. Then, between nine and ten, he had daily phone conversations with Karen, who was back in Phoenix, attending six different support groups plus a pole dancing class, trying to figure out how to boost her sex appeal and save their relationship. Afterwards, he made his rounds at the bars once or twice, depending on whether or not the first session had been a quickie. Michael was somewhat amused by the fact that Karen, so plain, wooden and solid, was trying to compete with the practically professional hoes—or "prohoes," as he facetiously dubbed them—he was dating. Even the previous evening, during their conversation, Karen told him that she was reading erotica, to learn how to please him.

"Will you make love to me in the park?" Michael asked her, to test her new openness.

He could hear Karen hesitate in the awkward silence.

"Ana did," he prompted her. He knew that button never failed to arouse his fiancée's competitive instinct, if nothing else.

"What a slut!" she commented.

"That's what a woman's supposed to be with her man."

"Yeah, well, some of us have self-respect."

Michael had to bite his tongue. Given the way Karen was bending over backwards to please him, her self-respect wasn't exactly in evidence. "I'd respect you even more if you become a little more flexible," he tried to entice her.

"We'll see," she said reluctantly. "I have to learn to become more comfortable with my body first."

"I can help!" he graciously offered.

"You're being very helpful nowadays. A regular humanitarian!"

Rather than making Michael feel guilty, Karen's wry comments only titillated him, reminding him of his recent victory. "What can I say? I'm selfless in that way."

"I don't care to discuss your whoring around, okay? It's very difficult on me."

"Hey, don't blame me. You're the one who came up with this stupid arrangement," Michael shot back, putting the blame squarely on her shoulders. "Besides, it's not like I'm taking advantage of it. I'm not even 'whoring around,' as you so eloquently put it."

"Don't add insult to injury by lying to me!" Karen exclaimed. "I'm sorry," she added more quietly, struggling to control her temper. "But I'm really uncomfortable with this topic."

"The pole dancing classes should help," Michael suggested, returning to their earlier, more pleasant, discussion.

"How so?"

"Because once you become more comfortable with your own body, you'll also be less inhibited with me. And that will make us both happy," he pursued, still wishing to squeeze out, like from a nearly empty tube of toothpaste, the remaining sexual use-value of his fiancée.

"I hope so," Karen replied, her tone not quite matching his in optimism. When they hung up the phone that previous evening, he really needed a pick-me-up. Or rather, a pick-her-up, he thought, easily amused, as usual, by his own puerile play on words.

Later, as he looked into the mirror and combed his dark, shinny hair away from his forehead, Michael felt satisfied with himself. The reigns of power are back in my hands, he observed, feeling like he had handled the breakup with Ana pretty well. No depression, no mourning period, no nothing. He had jumped right back into the saddle. This thought reminded him of Hallie, or Hollie, or whatever her name was, who was probably still waiting for him in the bedroom.

Michael stepped out of the bathroom still in his boxer briefs and noticed that the young woman was already dressed. If you could call the halter-top that emphasized her most impressive assets and the jean micromini that had initially attracted his attention to her long, lean legs being dressed, he observed with a smile. He was almost tempted to give her his number for a future rematch. But as soon as she opened her mouth to say, "I really had a great time last night. Wanna go out to dinner?" with a slight drawl and a needy edge in her voice, Michael recalled why he had ruled her out. "Why don't you give me your number?" he proposed. She hastily opened her silver sequin purse and took out a dingy piece of paper on which she scribbled her name and number.

"Hallyie. That's an original spelling," he observed.

"My mom chose it," she said almost apologetically.

"Thanks," he said, putting the note on top of the dresser, fully intending to toss it away later. "Do you need a ride back to campus?"

"Sure. I left my car at *Zephyr's*," she named the bar where they had hooked up.

"See you around sometime," he said noncommittally once they pulled into the parking lot of the bar where he had been so eager to lure her the night before. By the absent look in his eyes and the flatness of his tone, Hallyie could tell that nothing else would follow. A look of disappointment clouded her pale features as she said goodbye to him. Her sadness led Michael to experience a fleeting sense of triumph. *That's what you get bitch for fucking around with me!* he said to himself, feeling like each woman he used and discarded was in some indirect way payback for Ana leaving him.

Generally speaking, however, Michael focused on the positive. After all, his girlfriend had done him the favor of expanding his taste palate. Before dating Ana he used to go only for the tall athletic blondes like Amy, but now he also enjoyed a taste of shrimp cocktail. Petite brunettes had become his newest fetish. Plus, he was glad to get back into the swing of things, after a hiatus of near-monogamy. Seducing a woman to the point where she was itching to sleep with him. Man, what a rush! Then, the sex itself, since nothing compares to a good lay, with no strings attached. And now that Karen wasn't around to cramp his style, he could afford to be pickier. He stuck around longer at the clubs and chose only the hotter chicks. Dumping them once he was through didn't feel too shabby either. He had become such a pro at the letdown phase that he didn't even need to be explicit anymore. All he had to do is say in a neutral tone "See you around sometime" and even airheads like Hallyie usually got the picture. His schedule now overflowing once again with women, Michael felt in control of his life, like an orchestra conductor directing an orgasmic symphony. Schedule this woman here, that one there. Squeeze the third one between the date with Mireille and the phone call to Karen. Make some women feel used while giving others false hope. Michael always remained the one in charge.

The only thing that was missing from this picture was ending it with Ana the right way, on his terms. But, he consoled himself, *at least she hadn't even made a dent in my good disposition.* He recalled the visceral pang of pain he felt one afternoon, very early into their relationship, when he and Ana had shared a chair at the library while looking up art galleries on the computer, since there were no other empty seats available. When someone left the adjacent cubicle, she moved to it to have her own chair. He felt as if a piece of his flesh, the part of his thigh that had touched her leg, was torn away from him. He wanted her so badly on that day, more than he'd ever wanted anyone before. But by the time Ana left him, Michael was no longer infatuated with her. Their breakup didn't hurt him one tenth as much as on the day when she moved only a few feet away. The thin layer of passion having been scraped off by exposure to reality, all that was left of Michael's emotions for his girlfriend was what he felt for everybody else: layers upon layers of contempt that went to the very core of his being, the hole around which revolved in a dizzying vortex all of his insatiable hunger for pleasure and control. Sometimes he surprised his own self with his immunity to loss, nostalgia and pain. Whatever material other human beings were made of, Michael knew one thing for sure: he was much stronger than them.

Chapter 17

"I got you a little something," Ana announced with a coy smile, extending her husband a greeting card.

Rob looked quizzingly into her eyes as he tore open the envelope. "What's the occasion?"

She shrugged. "There isn't one. It's just because you're so sweet."

Rob didn't know whether to be grateful or weary as he peered down at the card. It had a picture of a little kitten and a sleepy puppy with its floppy ear over the kitten's head, protecting her underneath it like a cozy cover. The caption read, "And yet it works...." He smiled at her. "Thanks."

Ana approached him to give him a hug, then a peck on the cheek. "You really are a good person," she said and this time she meant it, unlike during the days she was planning to leave him for another man, when her husband's good character was just an abstraction to her. Rob sensed the difference. He heard in Ana's voice a sense of conviction, which perhaps accompanied the freshness of a new discovery, of falling in love all over again with the person you have ignored for too long.

As Rob reciprocated, wrapping his arms around Ana, he felt her soft breast upon his chest and sensed her rapid heartbeat through the thin texture of their shirts. When she looked up at him gratefully with her lively brown eyes, he bent down to kiss her. He explored her mouth with his tongue, as if she were simultaneously distant and familiar, a stranger and his wife, the new woman he desired and the one he had always loved. Rob led Ana by the hand to the bedroom and locked the door. She leaned back on the bed and he pulled her towards him by the feet and dove into her body, which had a clingy, viscous sweetness of honey that, at the moment, could make him forget the past. The rhythm of her quickened breathing merged with his accelerated movements, as her moist lips periodically met his cheek, his lips, and his ear. "I love you," he said, letting go of the hurt, releasing the betrayal, allowing it to flow back into her and become re-assimilated into their love.

That night, the aura of distance that had separated them even during sleep melted away. They lay side by side, spooning each other, his arm crossed over her naked waist, as he cradled her body protectively into his own. Ana couldn't even close her eyes, she felt so excited. The man she thought could never desire her again had made her feel both wanted and loved. Unlike the other one, who, she now realized through the contrast between her lover and her husband, had made her feel so intensely wanted that she had confused lust with love.

Ana recalled the feral look in Michael's eyes whenever they made love, especially when he twisted her into a position that hurt or asked her to try something new to reignite his senses, never satisfied with the same, always needing more. She closed her eyes to make those images disappear. Go to sleep, forget about him, she advised herself. But the fugue of memories persisted, paradoxically reignited by the renewed intimacy with her husband, which made her see her experiences with her lover in a new light.

Ana recalled how once, when they had stopped by a hotel, she had noticed a stain on the bedspread and commented to Michael that she'd remove the blanket, since there was no telling who had done what on that bed. Before she even had a chance to pull away the dirty cover, he gently pushed her body into it, face down, lifted her skirt and took her from behind. At the time, she had interpreted his gesture as a sign of his arousal. But later, as he coaxed his way into getting her to accept unacceptable acts, she realized that what excited Michael most was bending her to his will and pushing the envelope.

Where would it have stopped? she now wondered. "Please try this for me, Baby. I promise it won't hurt," he had once told her as he slipped a smooth, anointed finger into her, then quickly removed it and attempted to inch his way in. But he had lied, as usual. Because it did hurt, as much as when Nicu took her against her will the first time and almost as much as when she was giving birth, only without the reward. "Stop it!" she kept crying out until the searing pain drowned out both her own protests and his inducements. Through tear-stained eyes she could see that Michael's expression was disgruntled.

"It wasn't too much to ask of you," he said to her afterwards. "Lots of women get into it."

"Well I don't," she countered, still aching. "It hurts."

"Only at first, Baby. Just like when you first made love. But with proper lubrication, it doesn't hurt anymore. I promise."

"I don't want to do that again."

Michael looked her in the eyes and said, "Karen said no to me. I don't want to hear you talk like her. We're too much in love to deny each other these little pleasures. We'll take it nice and slow next time."

Even back then, Ana began to suspect that her lover's desire to engage in a given act grew in direct proportion to the vehemence of her refusal. "There won't be a next time," she maintained.

It looked as if Michael was about to get angry, but then he changed his mind. "You say that now. But you'll see. One eventually gets used to everything in life."

"There are some things that I don't want to get used to," she had replied. Ana vaguely imagined her lover asking her to do more and more painful acts just to please him. She dismissed those disturbing visions, since after all, she wanted to believe that Michael loved her and wouldn't want to harm her. "If something you enjoy causes me pain why would you want to do it at my expense? Why would you want to hurt me?" she asked him.

Michael approached stealthily and whisked her into his arms. His mouth was pressed to her ear when he said, "Because I like to feel your tightness against my shaft." As he spoke, she felt the heat of his breath through the strands of her hair.

"But is your pleasure worth my pain?" she backed away to look probingly into his eyes.

And then Michael had smiled with a disarming air of boyish innocence and replied, "Of course not, Baby. You're my frail little doll. I'd never want to break my little Papusica." Afterwards, they made love the way she liked it, softly and tenderly, with the unbearable sensuality that made caresses feel like kisses and kisses feel like the cool gentleness of an evening breeze against naked warm skin. But now she understood that Michael had misled her once again on that afternoon. Because, in his eyes, even his slightest pleasure would be worth her greatest pain.

Poor Karen! Ana whispered to herself, thinking that her lover's perversion would now become her rival's misfortune. "You two deserve each other," Michael had told her that Karen had commented when she had discovered Ana's lingerie in his drawer. That may very well be, Ana now felt like answering her, but once we saw the real Michael, I'm the one who left him and you're the one who kept him, honey. Because in spite of everything he had done to her, Karen still colluded with him, Ana thought, her sympathy diluted by bitterness. She filled his head with warnings and criticisms of me. And he, in turn, filled hers with false promises framed as conditionals—if only you had done this, that or the other thing, we'd have never found ourselves in this situation—so that she'd be there in reserve for him, a safety net to his spills and a slave to his wishes.

They'd never let go of each other, it dawned upon Ana. She feels incomplete without him and he never fully releases a willing target. I'd be caught between them like in a vice. A cold shiver traveled down the curve of her spine. "A vice in both senses of the term," she said under her breath, almost forgetting that she lay safely in her own bed, beside a loving husband, with her children sleeping peacefully next door. "What?" Rob mumbled, awakened by the sound of her voice. "Nothing. I love you," Ana nestled into him, seeking his body's protection against the nightmare she would have endured.

Chapter 18

The bedroom door was shut, but Karen could still hear her giggles, her half-hearted protests, his tender inducements and his grunts. They kept her up at night, like a mocking echo in her brain, making her wish that Michael would do something more drastic, something overtly brutal, so that she'd hate his guts and find the strength to leave him. Karen didn't even know who was with him in the bedroom. She hadn't seen the woman go in and hoped to God that she wouldn't have to watch her leave. The less she saw and heard and felt, the more numb and deaf and blind she became, the lesser the pain. But sometimes it was impossible to ignore all the new ways he found to hurt her. During those moments, she was almost ready to cut the perverse umbilical cord that bound her to Michael in a mixture of pleasure and pain that kept her constantly hovering on the edge of despair. Just when she thought she had enough and could take no more, Michael would back off temporarily. He'd take her out to a fancy restaurant, or make love to her tenderly again, or tell her in that sweet melodious voice of his that he loved her more than ever and that those sluts meant nothing to him. Sometimes he'd promise her that he'd join her soon in Phoenix. There they'd live out her dream of a happy life together, which had originally been his dream, if she recalled. That's when the unbearable would become bearable again. Until the next time she discovered traces of another woman in his in his life, in his house, in their bed. Then the whole cycle of pleasure in pain would start anew.

"You're the one who wants to come visit me here all the time," Michael retorted when Karen objected to his out of control cheating. But she was only sticking to their initial agreement, of coming to visit him every other weekend, since she found herself unable to weather the distance between them and he almost never visited her in Phoenix anymore. Given that Arizona was Michael's idea of heaven on Earth, she knew exactly what was keeping him so busy in Michigan. Short of begging him to come see her, which she knew in advance wouldn't work anyway, Karen learned to become more creative about earning the right to see him regularly. Each time she was obliged to invent a new excuse for why she needed to return to Michigan, which she presented from his perspective, having understood long ago that her desirability to him was measured in terms of utility rather than pleasure. "Your house needs painting," was the comment that had bought her one weekend with him. "It looks like you have a termite problem. I can take care of it," had gotten her another weekend together. When she ran out of things to do for him, she had to resort to more neutral and generally less effective justifications, to the effect of "I'll drop by since I'm visiting my mother anyway." But in her heart of hearts, it greatly pained her that Michael didn't want to see her just for herself, without expecting her to offer additional inducements. She was no longer welcome in his house. It was no longer their home. It was his alone and she was only a reluctantly accepted guest.

Whenever Karen complained about their current arrangement, Michael would kindly remind her that she was the one who had proposed it in the first place. "You gave me no choice," she'd try to defend her largely involuntary decision. "What could I do? I found myself between a rock and a hard place. It was either Ana or other women. I chose the lesser of two evils. You didn't really give me the option of an exclusive relationship."

"You never asked for it," Michael countered.

Karen felt that was sheer sophistry on his part. He knew full well that was exactly what she wanted. A simple, normal, exclusive relationship with him where she'd be once again the center of his life, like during the days when he had courted her so romantically in the beginning. She wanted the whole she-bang. Commitment. Trust. Marriage. Maybe even children. Everything that still seemed possible until that woman came along and destroyed everything between us, Karen thought with bitterness. "Ana's husband chose Ana. And so did you," she reminded Michael a few days after the break-up with his girlfriend.

"I said I was sorry. She seduced me. How long will you harp on this? It's over," he replied with an air of impatience.

"You're not really sorry. You're just offering excuses."

"Excuses? Hell no!" he said.

By now enough time had elapsed since the end of the affair. It was time. Was he ready? "How much more time do you need to get over that woman?" Karen would ask him periodically. She avoided using Ana's name, not wishing to personalize her memory.

Michael's answer was usually vague, non-committal: "I don't know," or "I can't predict the future," which was his way of avoiding dealing with the whole gangrenous issue.

Why do I still want him so much? Karen wondered, perplexed by her own tenacity. As she beat the pavement walking around for hours to keep her body toned and trim, there was not a single day when she didn't ask herself this very question. Because I love him, was the only answer she could offer. Then she turned the question around, putting the onus on him. Why does this man hurt me constantly? The obvious answer boomeranged back to her. Because I let him. I love him more than anything in the world, she kept repeating, as if this basic truth could somehow justify all her pain.

Each day she hoped it couldn't get much worse, yet it always did and she got used to the new mistreatment. What she had found appalling only a week earlier, she eventually came to accept. She began to see Michael's compulsive womanizing as a sign of his immense desirability. In a weird twist that reversed the poles of pleasure and pain in her brain, his philandering made her feel that being with a man that so many other women wanted was a reward, not a pun-ishment. Karen recalled the anger she felt on the day she found Ana's lingerie in his drawers. Now, barely a month later, she witnessed Michael luring other women into their house without even batting an eyelid, as if that were normal behavior. How did this happen? Karen tried to recall the downward spiral which made her head spin with a disorienting mixture of hope and shame. She recalled the withering remark which made her fear that he'd throw her out for good if she objected too much, "You're always free to leave, you know," he said coolly. "Nobody's tying you down here."

But in point of fact, Michael did, on a couple of occasions, since he was always exploring new fetishes when the old ones began to bore him. They had already gone through all the "non-negotiable" positions he had practiced with Ana. They had made love in every room of their house and even up on the roof. They made out in parking lots, behind trash dumpsters, in the changing rooms of stores, at the cinema and in men's restrooms. He had already penetrated every orifice except maybe for her ears. Karen passively submitted to everything, hoping that if she pleased him he wouldn't need all those other women. But Michael's appetite for sex was insatiable. Each time they crossed a new boundary, he'd get this flicker of a smile, a moment of triumphant glee. She'd feel encouraged by the sign of approval, as if this time was it, he loved and wanted her the way he had wanted his girlfriend, if not more so, since he'd have to be blind not to see that she loved him far more than Ana ever did.

If only she did everything he asked her, however painful or humiliating, then she'd eventually get the prize he constantly dangled before her eyes and that prize was *his love*. But after they had engaged in a certain activity a couple of times, Michael would become dissatisfied again. He'd look at Karen's naked body as if it were nothing more than a sack of potatoes and tell her in a dispassionate tone that he wasn't in the mood anymore and that, at any rate, he had a few "errands" to run later on that evening. She knew exactly what he meant since his code was crudely transparent. Once she even insisted that she join him on a so-called "errand," just to observe his reaction. He wasn't phased at all. "I thought you weren't into threesomes," he taunted her.

"Why aren't I enough for you, Michael? I've done everything you've asked me."

"It's not about *what* you do. It's about *who* you are," was his devastating reply.

At night, Karen silently prayed she could become younger and prettier at the snap of a finger. She wished she could magically change the color of her hair and eyes, to become a different shade of woman every day. She longed to have the plasticity of a gymnast, the grace of a ballerina and the poise of a ballroom dancer. Maybe then Michael would love her again. But each time she tried harder to please him, he only raised the bar higher, or simply changed the rules of the game, and never in her favor. All I'm asking for is that the man I love love me back, she'd tell herself when they were lying in bed together the night before she was supposed to return to Phoenix, missing him already. As Michael turned his tight body into hers, Karen marveled that he could sleep so well at night, with the oblivious innocence of a child, in spite of the constant upheavals he created in their lives.

Chapter 19

"I love you! See you after school," Ana kissed her son on his ruddy cheek.

"Alright, Mom," Allen mumbled. He turned away from his mother, to indicate to his peers waiting by the bus stop that he wasn't a mama's boy. Although it was already spring, it was still very cold.

Ana noticed that Allen had left the house without a coat. "Are you sure you'll be warm enough? I could run back to get you a jacket," she offered.

"I'm sure, Mom. I'll be fine."

Ana got the picture, but couldn't resist giving him one last hug right before the school bus stopped in front of them. As she waved goodbye to her son, she was overcome by the feeling that she had backed away from the edge of a precipice. As soon as she stepped back into the house, she heard the phone ring. "Hello?"

"Hey, Baby! I'm sure glad to hear your sexy voice again," Michael said in a light and melodious voice. "I've missed you like hell."

Ana's heart pounded as she hesitated between hanging up immediately, as she knew she should, and tying up loose ends with her former lover. "I told you it's over between us," she said after a slight hesitation.

Michael picked up on her ambivalence. "Why? Our fight was just a snafu. We both know what we feel for each other."

The word "snafu" bothered Ana. "Then why did you act so casual when I broke up with you?"

"You're dead ass wrong about that!" he sharply contradicted her. "I was in total shock."

"Not really. You were calm and flippant about it."

"Come on now! You know that's how I react to bad news. I become defensive and shut down," Michael switched tactics, granting her recollection but giving it a different spin.

"It doesn't matter anymore. All of this is water under the bridge now…"

"It doesn't have to be," he challenged her. "I can come pick you and all your stuff up even today if you want. I'm ready when you're ready. Karen's moved out of the house. She's back in Arizona now."

This news surprised Ana. "When did she leave?"

"Right after we broke up. She's giving me space to mourn the end of our relationship." His own artificial sentimentality aroused him. "Just say the word and I'll be there," he repeated.

"The word is no. I'm staying with my family," Ana held her ground. She sensed, however, that it would remain slippery under her feet for as long as she continued communicating with Michael.

"Are those Rob's orders?" he turned the blame upon the wronged husband, to reestablish complicity with her.

"No, it's my own decision. I want to work on my marriage," Ana countered.

"Now that's a sham that won't last very long!"

"It's not a sham at all," she calmly contradicted him.

"Sure it is," he insisted. "Because we both know that Karen and Rob bore us to death. Nothing will ever pump any life blood into those corpse-like relationships."

"I can't speak for you and Karen, but you're wrong as far as my marriage is concerned," Ana objected, struggling to maintain her cool in the face of provocation. "Rob and I are seeing a couples' therapist. And he's really good," she added, to buttress her argument. "I've realized that Rob is the right man for me. And, conversely, that I blocked out so many danger signals from you. You're not the man I thought you were."

Out of all the information Ana had conveyed, Michael focused solely on the fact that she was seeing a therapist. "And you're not the woman I thought you were either. The woman I knew detested crackpot, psychobabble therapy! You used to be so strong and independent."

"What you called strength was me being pressured or coaxed by you into doing everything you wanted," Ana replied. "And I assure you that Dr. Emmert doesn't practice crackpot therapy. He's very competent and helpful. He doesn't use any jargon or psychobabble whatsoever. He just tells it like it is, using a lot of common sense. Which is precisely the quality I've lacked ever since falling in love with you."

Ana's defense of her therapist only confirmed Michael's suspicion. "I'm sorry to hear you were brainwashed by the same bowdlerized psycho-babble Karen read," he said, knowing that any comparison with his fiancée would bother Ana. "She bought this stupid book, *Manipulative people,* and liked it so much that she recommended it to my folks. Of course, the irony in all this is that they began finding manipulative traits in themselves."

"What else could they do? Take her side against you? Blood runs thicker than water," Ana offered her own interpretation.

"Either that or, which I believe is far more likely, their lesson carries a valuable reminder to us all. Any person who doesn't recognize themselves in these psychological maladies is probably the most screwed up," Michael pontificated. "If I were you, I'd start by interviewing your shrink about his own disorders, before you open up any further and maybe even decide to open your legs for him!"

Ana was taken aback by Michael's crassness and disdain. "Please don't talk to me in this way!" she snapped back. "I'm not interested in my therapist as a lover. I don't want any lovers anymore. I've learned my lesson. But the fact that you're speaking so casually and crudely about me taking on another lover really offends me." Her voice quivered with emotion.

Sensing the resurgence of her feelings, Michael changed his demeanor again: "I'm sorry, Baby. I didn't mean to insult you. It's just that my heart's really heavy. When you spoke so highly of your therapist, it made me jealous. By now we were supposed to be already living together, celebrating the beginning of the rest of our lives. You know that I love and respect you most in the world," he added in a whisper, to evoke their former intimacy.

But everything Michael said rang hollow to Ana. "No, actually, I don't know that at all. You're not the person I thought you were," she repeated the leitmotif that had been obsessing her lately.

"Yeah, well, neither are you. You're obviously buying into the bullshit your shrink's been feeding you," he reverted to the insolent manner he had adopted earlier.

"Do you have an on and off button or something? You switch from sweetness to contempt in a matter of nanoseconds," she observed, almost intrigued by his vacillations.

"What the hell do you expect me to do? You're pissing me off, woman! You don't need to take a dump on our love just because other men are telling you to do it. They don't know our history together. And I'm willing to bet they don't understand the meaning of passion. Babe, they hardly even have a fucking pulse! You want to end up like them, the living dead?"

"It's not necessary to be vulgar," Ana attempted to restore a modicum of civility to their communication. "After all, we're not peasants or hoodlums, as my grandmother used to say."

"Sorry, Baby," Michael retreated again. "It's just that I'm so sick of all these people putting barriers between us. Getting to you is like going through a damn obstacle course. First Rob, then Karen, next my parents and now you've added a shrink to the mix. Wasn't our situation already complicated enough? Why did you have to screw up everything when we were so close to the finish line?"

"Our lives aren't a race and we're not in a competition to win anything," she replied, by now attuned to Michael's game and racing metaphors.

"Then why do I feel like I lost you?"

His feigned emotion irritated Ana. "Don't you find something wrong with the fact you lie so much and manipulate others?"

"Not at all," he replied in a cool tone, this time. "I mean, no more than you do. After all, you lied to Rob so you could be with me. We're in the same boat here. Everyone lies. It's human nature," he observed, her criticism slipping off him like water off a duck's feathers.

"Yeah, but not everyone does it as easily and as well as you do."

"I'm just more Machiavellian, that's all," Michael chose to interpret her criticism as a compliment.

"Most decent people who lie actually feel bad about it. But you don't. You're proud of it. Doesn't that bother you?" Ana insisted, hoping to puncture through his thick skin.

"Bad men do what good men dream," Michael answered philosophically.

Ana paused for a moment to consider his reply. "Bad men's dreams are good men's nightmares," she countered.

"Haven't you read Nietzsche?" he took their conversation to a loftier plane. "That's just the kind of bullcrap the weak tell the strong. If I lie better than others, it's only because I think quicker on my feet. And if I don't feel guilty, it's because I'm not wishy-washy like some people. When I make a decision, I stick to it."

"So now you're calling me wishy-washy and weak?"

"Hey, if the shoe fits…"

"You have a topsy-turvy view of reality," Ana retorted. "And for as long as we were together, so did I. People who lie and cheat without remorse aren't stronger or better than everyone else. In fact, they're weaker and more dependent. Because they need to use and mistreat others in order to feel superior to them. And they're not more decisive either," she went on venting her spleen. "You constantly change your plans and violate your promises. When one has strength of will, one doesn't do that. The strong stick to the words that come out of their mouths."

"Yeah, well, what's coming out of your mouth is total garbage, so I certainly hope you won't stick to it," he replied.

Ana got the distinct impression that nothing she said actually reached Michael. In fact, she had come to realize that nothing anybody said ever reached him. "I obviously became involved with the wrong person," she voiced her conclusion.

"I'm not the wrong person," Michael objected. We're going round and round in circles, he thought with impatience. "Not that long ago, you, yourself, called me the love of your life. Do you remember how happy you were in my arms?"

Ana hesitated for a moment. "Yes," she replied. Because, in all truth, up until the end, she really did feel elated in her lover's presence.

Michael was encouraged by her response. Promise her whatever she wants and she'll be yours again, he calculated. "Listen, if what you want is a damn ellipse, you can have it. You can have anything you wish. Like I always told you, 'What my Baby wants, my Baby gets.' If you don't want to divorce Rob because of the kids, we can stay lovers for as long as you wish. Until Allen graduates from high school," he reiterated the offer that had made the best impression on Ana. But, in his own mind, this concession wasn't free. Before articulating his thoughts out loud, Michael performed a quick cost-benefit analysis. If she doesn't want to marry me, he told himself, then I'll keep Karen as my fiancée, Ana as my girlfriend and continue giving myself extra treats, for a little fun on the side. During the time he confidently awaited her response, he also reveled in the idea of posting his application on several dating websites, to see how many women he could line up for his personal enjoyment. And in the off-chance, which was becoming increasingly unlikely, that Ana would decide to leave her husband, Michael thought a few steps ahead, he'd hang on to her until he found someone who didn't carry quite as much emotional baggage. Then he'd let her down easy, like he had done to so many others. He'd tell her that she was obviously too depressed about breaking up her family to be a good partner for him. That way their break-up would seem to be her fault rather than his.

Without even suspecting the profound cynicism of Michael's design, Ana was not even remotely tempted by it. "I don't want to be either your wife or your lover anymore," she said to him.

"What exactly am I being accused of? Thought crimes, like back in Romania?" he challenged her. "Even if looking on some dating website crossed my mind, so what? It's not like I was actually going to do anything about it."

"For you, the distance between thought and action is infinitesimally small," she remarked. "You have about as much impulse control as a starving dog in front of a juicy sirloin steak."

"You know what? Screw you, Ana! I'm sick and tired of all your freaking accusations. I always knew you were unstable. But your paranoia really eats the cake!"

She didn't respond to this escalation in their argument. She regretted having engaged in any discussion with Michael. It was completely pointless, like talking to a wall.

"When are you going to finally come to your senses and realize that we belong together?" he asked, believing that she had caved in under the weight of his denials.

"I already did. And once I woke up from my dream, I realized that I was living a nightmare. What I thought was mutual love turned out to be, at least on your side, just an extended one-night stand."

"That's total bull crap and you know it!" he objected, incensed by her stubbornness. "You've been brainwashed by people who don't understand us. Because of them, you've turned our lives into some damn science fiction in your head. All you have to do is look at our past to know that I'm a passionate man and that you're *my* woman. I love you like I've never loved anyone before and I refuse to let you go. If I have to come rape you and get you pregnant for you to finally open your eyes and see that we belong together, I will. Don't push me to extremes, Ana!" His voice vibrated with anger.

"You've completely lost it," she quietly observed. However outrageous Michael's threats might have sounded, however, Ana sensed that they weren't empty. Part of her still wanted to believe that they arose from the profound, frustrated passion he avowed. Yet a growing part of her suspected that they came from his controlling nature and a fierce desire to possess her, like her therapist had told her. "I'm not your property. You don't own me," she declared.

"When I come to get you, just make sure you open the door!" Michael advised her before hanging up the phone.

Instead of feeling intimidated, however, Ana felt indignant. *He thinks he owns me, the way you own a dog,* she told herself. She had a flashback to Nicu, her first boyfriend. She recalled how one afternoon Nicu's sheepdog, Ciobanu, a little mutt who followed him around with slavish devotion, suddenly took off. Nicu seemed genuinely worried and looked everywhere for his dog. Finally, after a few hours of searching, he saw Ciobanu digging behind a tree, from a distance. He called him very sweetly, "Come here Ciobanu. Come here little doggy," holding out his hand, as if he had a treat waiting for him. Ciobanu rushed back eagerly to his master, his tail wagging with friendliness and anticipation. As soon as he held the dog firmly by the collar, Nicu began hitting him with a stick, hard and without mercy, over the head, the back, the legs, despite the dog's desperate yelps and Ana's tearful protestations.

During their whole conversation, Ana had the impression that Michael's sweetness had the same phony ring as Nicu's voice when he called his misfortunate dog to him. When he acted nice, it's as if her lover was trying to lure her back, but only so that he could punish her for having had the gall to leave him in the first place. Her fingers instinctively went to her throat as if searching for a collar. She felt the black silk cord with the aquamarine pendant Michael had given her a few months earlier. Ana removed the necklace and tossed it into the trash, as if the gift itself enchained her to her lover. It reminded her of the way he had so often consumed her with that disconcerting vampirism of the flesh and soul that feasted upon her emotions and marked her as his momentarily privileged possession. All those beautiful presents—the jewelry, the clothes, the expensive meals and even the more precious gift of time itself—were never a sign of any real generosity, she now thought. They were his way of buying me: a down payment for future abuse. "You don't own me," she repeated to herself the phrase that would become her liberation from a love that had existed only in her own mind, as the fantasy of a faithful and adoring lover that Michael never was and never could be.

Chapter 20

If anyone had listened in on the lovers' quarrel that had just taken place between Ana and Michael, they wouldn't have believed that they were witnessing the end of "the love affair of the century," which is how the two protagonists, recently turned antagonists, had previously regarded their relationship. As Ana hung up the phone, her hand trembled on the receiver. It's as if two Michaels existed in her mind: the one before they told their partners about the affair and the one after. A small part of her still refused to believe that the tender, affectionate, charismatic, reliable and doting lover she had known, whose stated objective in life was to make her happy—"what my Baby wants, my Baby gets"—had morphed into one of those hollow men profiled in the psychology books her therapist had recommended.

Logically speaking, the two sides of Michael, the one she had known and loved, the other she feared and despised, couldn't be reconciled. She recalled Michael running to greet her with unbridled enthusiasm each and every time they met. Even those over-the-top romance novels couldn't quite capture the intensity of his real life passion. The tactile memory of his touch gently exploring her body before consuming her with an insatiable hunger still sent shivers of desire up and down her spine. Michael's patience throughout her professional struggles and emotional vacillations still attested to the depth of his feelings.

The ease and comfort with which they communicated struck her as unique. And the interest he took in her art, which he not only encouraged, but also inspired, made her feel like in losing her lover, she'd be losing a soul mate. She recalled a moving, jazzy song she used to listen to with Michael. It described a woman letting go of her lover gradually, piece by piece, trace by trace, memory by memory. She now felt like she too had to let go forever of Michael's passionate kisses, of the way he cradled and twirled her in his arms, of his excited 'Hey, Baby!' greetings, of his sensual caresses, of his desirous, flattering gaze that had made her feel beautiful and feminine, and, most painfully of all, of their joint dream of a happy future together.

Of course, had he listened to that love song, Dr. Emmert would have said that it didn't apply at all to her situation. One doesn't let go of a psychopath piece by piece. One runs away as fast as possible in the opposite direction. That's what Karen should have done also. She recalled a photograph Michael had shown her, which featured him and Karen on the day of their engagement. Michael's smile looked so beautiful, with his pearly white, perfectly aligned teeth, that it seemed almost plastic. By way of contrast, Karen had struck her as rather plain, reinforcing the point Michael had made on a number of occasions that his fiancée was not pretty, or cultivated, or sensual or affectionate enough for him. If he was cheating on her, he implied, it was only because he belonged with a woman who measured up to his good looks, eroticism, intelligence and talents. That woman was his girlfriend. Not one to remain immune to flattery, Ana had bought his argument. Now that she had caught a glimpse of the darker side of Michael, however, she recalled the sadness of Karen's expression in the photograph that was supposed to celebrate their engagement. Her smile wavered somewhere between meekness and melancholia, while her deep-set eyes expressed a sense of resignation that Ana had rarely seen in someone so privileged and young.

From the day they met, Ana sensed that Michael couldn't live without danger, without risk, without dream. His life had to be a perpetually thrilling fantasy. So far, Ana reflected, I've been his dream, while Karen was his reality. I've lived somewhere else and was his escape from the mundane existence he lived with his fiancée. She recalled Michael's excitement and eagerness whenever he'd call her during their first few months together, before Karen had moved to Phoenix—"Hey Baby. Gosh, I miss you so much!"—while his fiancée was asleep or away on an errand. Looking back at the last few weeks of their relationship, Ana realized that those excited calls had all but disappeared. After telling their partners about the affair, it was generally she who called her lover, while Michael greeted her with a flat "Hey" rather than the eager "Hey, Baby!" that used to make her heart flutter with anticipation. Which meant, Ana retrospectively deduced, that it was the manipulation, the cheating, the lying and the risk that were most exciting to Michael, not she, herself. This presaged a disturbing pattern that inextricably bound pleasure with infidelity. Had he taken full possession of me, she extrapolated, absence would have become presence and the ideal would have switched sides. Someone else would have become the spoiled girlfriend while I'd have turned into the duped and neglected spouse.

Clue after clue began seeping into Ana's consciousness as a more multidimensional image of her former rival foreshadowed her own likely future. She recalled the dismissive air with which Michael had described the pointlessness of Karen's efforts to make him love her again: "She's doing everything to please me: losing weight, exercising like a freak four hours a day; reading books she thinks I might like, but nothing works. When you've got it you've got it and when you don't you don't." He had gone on to explain how everything about Ana, from the inflections of her voice to her slightest gesture, excited him naturally and effortlessly. Yet those weren't the words that echoed in her mind at the moment. "When you've got it you've got it and when you don't you don't," Ana repeated to herself the phrase that Michael had used to describe Karen's Sisyphean task.

Would any woman "have it" for a lifetime, she wondered, beginning to intuit that lasting attachment was relational, having much more to do with the attitudes of the lovers than the inherent qualities of the beloved. Was Michael even capable of lifelong loyalty and commitment, as he had repeatedly avowed? And what did any of his promises mean, when he had shamelessly violated all the ones he made to Karen?

Ana felt that she had loved Michael as passionately as anyone could love anybody else. But she had never really trusted him. During their conversation, Michael had reproached her for her distrust. He maintained that their partners, his parents, her therapist, her own neuroses were to blame for her lack of trust in him. But Ana didn't see it that way. Michael's reassurances simply didn't ring convincing, while his dismissal of her doubts only fueled her suspicion. The moment you let down your guard, she speculated, you became another Karen; a pawn of his capricious will and a victim of your own vulnerability.

Ana recalled the crass, demeaning manner in which Michael had described his fiancée's generosity on another occasion: "She hides chocolates and other silly little gifts throughout the house for me, like a bitch marking its territory." At the time, that comment had provoked Ana's jealousy. All she could think of was that another woman was competing for her lover. Only Michael's reminder that in their relationship it was he who showered her with presents had reassured her then that she had the upper hand. She had also bought wholesale Michael's description of Karen as a needy and possessive woman who clung to him so fiercely that the poor man felt suffocated. But now Ana could easily imagine finding herself in the pathetic position of fighting desperately to reclaim his affection, while he was busily pursuing another woman with the same single-minded fervor with which he had seduced her.

Whenever Ana felt threatened by her rival, Michael was quick to reassure her: "Don't worry, Baby. Once I've made up my mind about something, nobody on Earth can change it. There's nothing Karen can do to win me back. It's you I want. You're the woman of my life." In the past, such declarations of love were music to Ana's ears. Now, however, they sounded cacophonous, striking the

wrong chord. If even a woman who loved Michael with such unconditional devotion couldn't make the slightest dent in his attitude and feelings towards her,
what did that say about his capacity to love? From Ana's perspective as a
spoiled girlfriend, Karen's efforts to win back Michael had seemed as pointless
as a fish struggling to survive on land. It was transparently obvious to her that
Karen's logic—if only she tried harder, cooked better, became thinner, wore
sexier clothes and acted more tender, Michael would fall in love with her all
over again—was at best misguided and at worst delusional.

"Dream on!" Michael had commented with contempt one afternoon, de-
scribing his fiancée's desperate efforts, as he lay stretched out like a cat on his
girlfriend's lap. "I want you so much," he had told Ana over and over again, his
eyes filled with desire. But even back then, in the midst of her willful blindness,
the detached, arrogant way in which he talked about his fiancée had made Ana
feel like her lover was capable of discarding a woman with the same insouciance
with which a child tosses away an old toy. What she had refused to believe back
then was that she, herself, could ever be that discarded toy. Now, however, Ana
couldn't help but wonder: if I had chosen the same path as Karen, would her
vain hopes and agony have become mine? Would I also bury my head in the
sand and explain away Michael's disinterest in the most implausible ways in the
humiliating and futile attempt to revive his nonexistent love? Would I, like her,
remain so attached to our past, to the memories of the days when he doted on
me, that I'd be incapable of letting go?

Why didn't Karen let go? Ana began thinking about what might induce a
woman to stick to a man once he gives such incontestable evidence of mistreatment. Because even now, after he had nearly left her for another woman, Ana
felt quite sure that Karen still clung to Michael with all her might, from thousands of miles away. Ana recalled one of his explanations for his fiancée's tenacity: "She thinks that my love for you is intense, but ephemeral. She doesn't
think we'll make it three months once we actually move in together." Karen
must have convinced herself that what she and Michael shared was true and lasting love, while what he experienced with other women was merely temporary
and superficial. The memories of how well Michael treated her in the beginning
of their relationship—all the wooing, the romance and the charm that were his
natural trademarks—must have obliterated the avalanche of uncaring words and
actions that had followed. And in that avalanche, Karen's identity and self-
respect were crushed.

Ana wasn't about to make the same mistake. He offered heat without
warmth. Attachment without bonding. Passion without love. Before, Ana would
have considered these phenomena impossible. But with Michael, everything
became possible. His appetite for self-gratification was insatiable and his cha-
meleon-like personality, adapting to any woman's needs in order to control her,
incomparable. Yet underneath that pliable layer of charm, Ana had discovered a
hardened egocentric personality that allowed no woman to get close to him and
capture his attention for long. The heart of the problem, Ana believed, was that
Michael viewed love only as a game. For each match, there had to be a winner

and a loser. The winner, of course, could only be him in the end. "Keep your eyes on the prize at all times," he often told her. But once you won the prize, what then? You hung it up on the wall and sought the next target. I don't want to be vanquished, since I'm too proud and independent, Ana told herself. And I don't want to be a victor, since I don't need to dominate anybody. The only viable solution is the one I've chosen, she concluded. Leaving him.

Easier said than done. Turning over at random one of the books her therapist had suggested, Ana glanced at its back cover description: "He will choose you, disarm you with his words, and control you with his presence." That's definitely Michael! she confirmed. He had an electrifying, almost inescapable, charisma. No matter what he talked about, even when discussing the most trivial topics like what he ate for breakfast, Michael's voice had the soothing feel of silk and the husky, soft texture of velvet. "He will delight you with his wit and his plans. He will show you a good time," she continued reading, recalling all the plans for travel around the world and boundless artistic creativity he had conjured up for the happy days when they'd finally live together. "He will smile and deceive you," she went on reading, her nostalgia displaced by the intuition that one day, sooner rather than later, she too would have been replaced. "And when he's through with you, and he will be through with you, he will desert you and take with him your innocence and your pride." And no amount of effort will ever change his mind, she added to herself, thinking of Karen. "You will be left much sadder but not a lot wiser," the author predicted, "and for a long time you will wonder what happened and what you did wrong." Getting involved with and, worse yet, staying with him, that was the error, Ana answered, her thoughts turning once again to Karen. "And when the next one knocks on the door, will you open it?"

Ana pondered this question. First things first. At the moment, she didn't even feel confident in her reply concerning this one, let alone "the next one." Her lover's smoothness, persistence and passion had profoundly shaken the foundations of her being and her life. Her conscience had been leveled by largely uncontrollable emotions, impulses and desires. Her marriage would have to be reborn from the ashes, like a phoenix bird. Her children had just been taken for an emotional roller-coaster ride that might have scarred them for life.

Ana was interrupted from her thoughts by a loud knock on the door. She went to see who it was, surmising that it was probably the mail carrier delivering the package of books she had recently ordered online.

Instead of the mailman, however, she was faced on the other side of the glass panel by the door with Michael's friendly smile, as if they hadn't had an altercation less than an hour ago.

"Come on, Baby, open the door," he urged her in such a lighthearted manner that he seemed to be laughing off their earlier lovers' quarrel. "I'm more in love with you than ever after the stunt you just pulled on me. That only proves we're meant for one another, you spunky little girl!"

Ana hesitated. Every rational fiber in her being told her to resist all of Michael's advances henceforth. Yet part of her remained drawn to her lover's familiar charm as well as their former complicity, welded by months of intense passion, forbidden pleasures and—she thought—friendship. Ana's whole being trembled with the ambivalence that the prey must feel when it's caught in the mesmerizing gaze of its predator, as it absurdly hesitates between life and death, between capitulation and escape.

Chapter 21

"I can't talk to you anymore," Ana said, without opening the door. She felt a tingling sensation, shortness of breath and a rush of adrenaline as her body kicked into combat mode.

"So all those times you said you loved me meant nothing to you? So much for living for passion and art!" Michael said with a note of reproach.

Through the rectangular glass panel on the side of the door, she could see him make a theatrical, sad face; an inverted smile like a masked figure in an ancient play. He may have wanted to appear sincere, but he looked grotesque. "What about you?" she challenged him. "Would a passionate man ask the love of his life to sign a prenup?"

"I was only trying to protect our assets. Yours too, not just mine."

"Yeah, right! Your paws would have been all over my money while you kept the house in your name alone. Would a passionate man become stingy all of a sudden?" she continued. "I said 'yes' to my generous lover only to end up with Karen's stingy fiancé!"

"Hey, it cuts both ways. You became petty too."

"Did I also require you to wear a certain uniform for me?" Ana let out some of the bile that had been building up inside. "I didn't appreciate being told to only wear skirts around you or how I should wait for you when you came home from school. Even my daughter has been choosing her own clothes since the age of seven. You need to buy yourself a Barbie doll if you want to play dress-up!"

Michael seemed amused by her anger. He was tempted to kindly inform her that he had had plenty of real-life Barbies, only he preferred to play dress-off rather than dress-up with them. "All you had to do is say 'no.' I always listened to your wishes and did exactly what you wanted," he answered instead.

His seemingly conciliatory statement only incensed Ana further. "Always, of course! Like when I told you that I didn't want to have a baby with you and you decided to look for someone else on a dating website?"

Michael's calm demeanor changed. He became agitated and started to gesticulate, marking each phrase with abrupt, vertical hand beats. "You're completely nuts!" he exclaimed. "I've explained all of this to you before. I never intended to replace you. I just wanted to prove to you, since you're so goddamn stubborn, that even those silly websites would match us up."

Upon hearing this absurd explanation again, Ana became downright furious, picking up steam as she vented her anger. "Like you ever cared about what others thought! You must think that I'm a total idiot. You're lying through your teeth and it's obvious. The gig's up!"

Michael looked up, as if appealing for divine intervention: "I give up! I've refuted your paranoid charges before. What's my incentive to go over all that crap again?"

"You've got none since you won't get anything out of me anymore," she concurred. "What hurts so much is the fact that you're still lying to me," she said. "You promised that you'd never lie to me the way you did to Karen. You said that no matter what happened, we'd never poison our relationship with deceit. I always hoped that even if things didn't work out between us, we'd let each other go honestly."

Despite the anger in her tone, Michael viewed the emotions behind it as the beginning of Ana's capitulation to him. "I haven't lied to you, Baby," he said gently, glad to see that he still kept her guessing, on her toes, her thoughts and emotions wrapped up around him. "Your worries are the product of your own imagination and all the pressure we've been under lately. They have nothing to do with my actions. Haven't I shown you how *passionately* I love you, Ana? Haven't I?" He gazed tenderly into her eyes, as if the anger and irritation had already washed over him, having barely touched the surface of his being.

Ana nodded in mock agreement. "Yes you have. You've shown exactly how *passionately* you love me by looking for my replacement a few days before we were supposed to move in together. I'm very touched by your passion, indeed!"

"What the hell?" he cried out. "I didn't come all the way out here to conduct yet another postmortem of our relationship! Nothing happened, alright? Since we met, I never wanted any woman but you. You're imagining things."

Ana looked away, to indicate that she didn't want to listen to his futile denials. All of his mind games wore her out, but they couldn't wear her down anymore.

"Baby, listen to me," he continued. "This is mostly Rob and Karen's doing. They manipulated us, to turn us against each other. Karen constantly nagged me about how you'd spend all my money, how I couldn't trust you, how you'd leave me for another man just like you did your husband. No doubt, Rob worked on you in the same way. We played right into their hands."

Instead of ranting against Karen as before, Ana just smiled at him. "Nice try. But it won't work this time."

"What are you talking about?"

"Setting me against Karen. Blaming her and Rob for all our problems. You're doing it to distract me from my real enemy," she glared meaningfully into his eyes.

"How the hell am I your enemy?"

Ana allowed her deep-seated resentment to seep out, like puss from an infected wound. "You tried to do me what you did to Karen. To isolate me from my family. To make me emotionally dependent on you. To erode my boundaries and my values. To destroy my self-confidence, so that I'd be at your mercy, doing your bidding and buying into your lies, the way she did. But I can't do that anymore. You duped me for awhile, but you'll never fool me again."

Michael didn't feel like listening yet again to Ana's hysterical diatribes. When he was in love with her, he liked her feisty, Latin temperament. Now, however, she just struck him as a drama queen. Let's turn the tables on her and see how she likes it, he decided. "Listen, instead of only looking into what I did wrong and whether I wanted to replace you, you should start considering why I might have wanted to do that. You always put the blame on me. But, as they say, it takes two to tango. When a couple runs into problems, both partners are at fault," he explained in the calm, deliberate manner he assumed whenever he wanted to appear reasonable and fair.

Ana was amazed by his talent for deflecting blame away from himself and displacing it unto those he was hurting. Michael seemed able to modify the past just as easily as he changed his future plans. She approached the glass panel on the side of the door and placed her open palm on it, in a last appeal to their mutual vow of honesty. "Would a passionate man lose interest in the love of his life the instant she was about to become his partner in life?" she asked him. "Please admit this much, Michael. Admit it's the taboo of our affair that excited you. Not me, not our relationship." She hoped that he'd finally tell the truth, to release her forever from the last traces of doubt she might experience in those moments of weakness when she still believed in the illusion that he once loved her.

Michael placed his open palm on top of hers, so that only a sliver of glass separated them. "Would a passionate woman become hysterical over divorce once she agreed to it and chicken out at the last moment?" he retorted, in the same vein.

Ana smiled at the absurdity of the situation. Their dialogue had become a volley of rhetorical questions; a mirror of mutual blame for their aborted relationship. This was the closest thing she had experienced to what the French called a *dialogue de sourds*. But she knew it was much too late to listen to one another. Reproaches were futile and explanations fell on deaf ears. As Michael stood there, only a few inches away from her, Ana's gaze lingered on his dark almond shaped eyes shaded by long eyelashes, his delicate nose and his full lips. She saw the angelic face of a man with a diabolical soul that almost made her forget the best interests of her children, who truly were innocent. As impossible to resist as her lover had been at the beginning of their relationship, so impossible to love he had become by the end. "I just no longer felt any human warmth from you," she said quietly.

"What?" Michael asked. Ana had spoken so softly that he couldn't make out the words through the glass panel.

She removed her hand from it, allowing her arm to fall limply by her side. "I lost faith in our love," she repeated louder.

"Did you really, Ana?" He recalled the fire in her eyes on the day they met; the abandoned look of longing whenever they made love. "You used to say that you adore me. You told me that your life was in my hands. What happened to that trust? What happened to your love?"

"They were misguided and misplaced," she answered as honestly as she could. "When you had the chance to show me that you cared about me and my kids, you chose instead to look out for number one. As always."

His eyes narrowed. "And you didn't?" he countered. "Who bailed out on us? You or I?"

"I did," she admitted, straightening out her back, now taking pride in that decision. "Because it became quite obvious to me that you wanted a slave, not a partner," she declared, approaching the glass panel until the warmth of her breath left a circular haze upon its clear surface. "You know what I think? You act like a hero, but, in fact, you're really a coward. Because if you had any balls at all, you wouldn't stab people in the back the way you do."

Michael's eyes were completely devoid of emotion. Then Ana heard a shrill, older voice, as if he were channeling another creature from within. "Shut the fuck up, woman! I'm tired of listening to all your goddamn accusations!" he shouted at her, with clenched fists at his side.

She laughed in his face. "You think I'm scared of you? There's nothing to you, Michael. You're a trivial human being who can't even love. You're empty to the core."

"Yeah, well, if by love you mean the way you treated your husband, no thanks! I can do without it. By the way, good luck with your new chastity belt!" he sneered. "Let me know if you need any help putting it on."

Ana's eyes narrowed. "You know the only thing that's bothering you now? The fact that I dumped you, not you me. If it had been the other way around, I wouldn't have seen trace of you anymore. But you're a control freak and you always want to be the one in charge."

Instead of exploding, as she expected, Michael's tense features relaxed into a silly grin. "Hubba, hubba! Aren't we feeling feisty? I know how we can fix that little problem," he directed her a salacious glance. He then paused for a moment, not willing to accept that Ana meant half the words she said. This must be just another one of her emotional tirades. "You're saying all these nasty things about me so that you can convince yourself to get over our love," he said. "Because, in your heart of hearts, you're still in love with me the way you'll never be with Rob."

Ana was even more disturbed by his cavalier attitude than she had been by his earlier displays of anger. She began retreating backwards, to indicate that their discussion was finished. "You're wrong about that. Because there's nothing and nobody to get over. I don't like you, I don't respect you and I don't love you anymore, Michael. I'll never look back fondly upon you or any of our memories."

Time stood still as they glared at each other. Ana's gut instinct told her to walk away. At the moment when her body pivoted on her left heel to turn around, Michael leaned back and kicked in the glass panel with his foot, with a powerful, swift movement. She watched him break the glass as if in slow motion. She saw it shatter into bits and pieces right in front of her eyes, so fast that she barely had time to shield her face with her hand. He slipped his arm through the jagged hole and unlocked the door from within. Her heart pounded as she confusedly considered what to do next. She thought of running to the phone. But before she got the chance to take a single step, Michael was already in the foyer, his gaze alert and furious. He grabbed her arm and twisted it behind her back, both of her hands fitting uncomfortably, with the fingers pressed tightly together, into one of his. He placed his free hand around her throat, strangely enough, reminding Ana of one of their first intimate encounters, of his unbearable tenderness on that day, of how he had cradled her neck in his hand and convinced her that he enjoyed feeling the smoothness of her skin against the roughness of his palm, so that she began abandoning herself to him, seduced by the lightness of his touch. Whereas now, the veins in her throat pounded as she awaited like a sacrificial lamb the constricting motion of his fingers, the sense of suffocation, possibly even death, although she couldn't imagine it just yet.

"We'll see who's so tough now, Powderpuff," Michael hissed into her ear. Yet he remained patient, not yet tightening his grip, enjoying her fear and the sense that her life was once again in his hands, where it belonged.

Panicked ideas flurried in her mind as she stood there in his grasp. She glanced sideways towards the door to see if any of the neighbors would be close enough to come save her in case she screamed for help. That's when she saw them: her saviors, a scene right out of a dark comedy. The navy blue van with flowery pink letters *"Dolly Maid Service"* had parked in her driveway. Two women, dressed in navy uniforms, made their way to the door, one armed with a vacuum cleaner, the other with a mop and bucket.

Michael promptly released his prey. He walked towards the door and courteously opened it for them, like an old-fashioned gentleman. "Sorry about the mess. The kids were playing ball earlier," he said in a friendly tone, nodding apologetically towards the shattered glass. The maids smiled, grasping only his tone, not the meaning of words since they only spoke Spanish. "See ya later, Babe!" Michael turned to his former girlfriend with a meaningful, though no longer menacing, glance.

To Ana's ears, those were ominous words uttered in the lightest of manners. She had asked Michael to remove her last glimmer of hope that he might be a decent human being. He gladly obliged, by attacking her. Now she knew that there was no point in trying to sort out the truth from the lies. Michael himself was the lie. From beginning to end, from love to indifference, from tenderness to violence, from "You're the woman of my life" to "See ya later, Babe!" their whole relationship was a sham. A single word seemed to capture what she felt, after all those months of passion, followed by the weeks of torment: *disenchantment.*

When she recovered from the initial shock, Ana's first impulse was to call her husband. She tried Rob's cell phone, knowing that would be the easiest way to reach him at work.

"What's the matter?" he asked her. He could tell from her faint voice and strange tone that something was wrong.

"Michael showed up at our house today. He attacked me."

"Did he hurt you?"

"I'm fine. The cleaning ladies came by so, thank God, nothing really happened. He just frightened me."

"What did he do? And how did he get in?"

She heard the suspicion in her husband's voice. "He kicked in the glass panel on the side of the door with his foot. Then he shoved his hand through it and opened the door himself, from within."

Rob tried to imagine this scene. It occurred to him that the first thing he'd do in such circumstances is run to the phone and dial 911. "Did you call the police?"

"I didn't get the chance. It all happened so fast."

"What about after he left?"

"No, not yet."

Rob had the impression that his wife's behavior didn't make any sense, given everything they had learned about Michael. "Why didn't you call the police as soon as you saw that creep at the door? Before he even kicked in the glass panel?"

"Because at first we were just talking calmly. Only at the end he attacked me all of sudden. The whole thing took me by surprise."

The phrase "talking calmly" triggered Rob's recurring doubts. "But you just told me that you didn't open the door for him," he pointed out what seemed to be an inconsistency in her story. He was afraid of catching his wife in a lie yet at the same time wanted to get to the bottom of things, once and for all.

"I didn't. Like I said, he kicked in the panel. But before that, we talked through the glass. He seemed pretty calm, overall. I mean, there was nothing unusual about his behavior. He was just telling me that he wanted us to get back together."

"You had *a conversation* with him?" Rob asked, incensed that his wife would engage in such reckless behavior. "After Dr. Emmert explained to you how dangerous this guy could be?" She's far from being cured of her sick love for that loser, he thought, feeling simultaneously angry and discouraged.

It struck Ana that her husband seemed to be blaming her for Michael's attack. They always blame the victim, she thought. "It's not like we were having a pleasant discussion. In fact, I told him that I wanted nothing more to do with him. I didn't think he'd freak out all of a sudden, break into our house and try to strangle me!"

Rob couldn't believe his ears. "He tried to *strangle* you? My God, Ana... I'm calling the police. This guy should be arrested."

"Maybe it's not necessary to go that far," Ana hesitated, having heard that in many cases police intervention only eggs bullies on.

"It certainly *is* necessary!" Rob countered, becoming increasingly alarmed as the information his wife relayed to him started sinking in. "I'm not going to stand idly by while this creep harms you or any member of my family! Ana, listen to me. Get out of the house... now! And meet me at the police station."

"Why?"

"Listen to what I tell you, for once in your life! Meet me at the police station," he repeated emphatically.

Before she could respond, Ana heard a click and the dial tone. She felt ambivalent about filing a report about the attack. What could the police do? Issue a restraining order? Could that piece of paper really protect her? She had seen this situation before. They'd label the incident a "domestic dispute." Since she had no visible marks on her body, it would be his word against hers. Besides, even if arrested, Michael would be out of jail in a matter of days and even more incensed against her. The whole cycle of hatred would go on and on, indefinitely. Ana saw no easy solution to the problems a chance encounter in a church had created. Life would be so much simpler, she thought, if Michael would move far away, preferably across the globe, or somehow magically disappear from her life—him and every shred of memory of him—as if they had never met.

Chapter 22

When she stepped into his office, Dr. Emmert could tell that Ana was unusually agitated. They had scheduled an emergency session the day before, following Michael's attack. Somehow, Ana thought, looking around her therapist's familiar office, the restraining order she filed against Michael didn't seem as much of a protection as processing this event in her own mind. She didn't sit down as usual. Instead, she paced back and forth across the room, filled to the brim with nervous energy.

"Why don't you take a seat?" the psychiatrist suggested.

But Ana acted like she hadn't heard him. She turned to him and announced abruptly, "I hate Michael. Last night, I dreamt of killing him."

Dr. Emmert gazed at her without any show of surprise. "You had this dream after his last visit?"

"Yes."

"Why don't you tell me about it," he motioned towards the empty chair.

Ana plopped herself down, tossing her purse on the ground with uncharacteristic carelessness. She forced a smile. "It was funny. In a sad kind of way. It would have been comical, if it weren't so tragical, as my daughter would say. I feel so angry."

"Was it his last visit in particular that makes you feel this way?"

Ana paused to think for a moment before answering him. "Not really. It just pushed me over the edge. But I've been feeling angry ever since I began to realize I was this close," she pinched a few millimeters of air between her thumb and index finger, "to destroying my life and compromising my children's lives for a man who isn't even worth a second glance. His last visit sealed the deal. Now I definitely hate him."

There was something feral in Ana's demeanor that made the psychiatrist believe her statement. It came from the gut, from the spleen. "Passion often turns to hate. Just as love turns to indifference," he remarked, used to dealing with broken relationships. "What did Michael do in particular to make you feel so angry with him?"

Ana snorted with disdain. "He attacked me. But I wasn't intimidated," she said defiantly, almost believing her own words. She had already forgotten the visceral panic she felt when Michael wrapped his hand around her throat. She only recalled the resentment that followed.

"Can you tell me what happened?"

"He came and knocked on my front door two days ago, in the early afternoon," Ana said, becoming slightly calmer now that she focused on facts rather than feelings. "I didn't open it, of course, since I'm not that stupid. I just communicated with him through the glass panel next to our door," she sketched a rectangle into the air. "At first, he was nice, like the old Michael I used to know. Baby this, Baby that, Baby the other. But I'm not his Baby anymore so I refused to open for him."

"Good for you," the therapist approved.

"That's not what bothered him. What really got under his skin was that I no longer believed him. I couldn't be brainwashed and bamboozled anymore."

"What was he trying to sell you? I mean, tell you?"

Ana ignored the pun. "Oh, you know, the usual lies. That he loved me. That I'm the woman of his life. And it made me really angry."

"What did?"

"The fact that Michael was still trying to dupe me even after he'd been so thoroughly unmasked."

"Perhaps he didn't think he was unmasked," the therapist speculated. "Because, in his own mind, he never wore a mask to begin with. In fact, he probably feels betrayed."

"*He* feels betrayed? What about Rob? What about Karen? What about me?"

Dr. Emmert shrugged. "When it comes right down to it, Michael doesn't care about any of you. He only sees things from his own point of view. From his perspective, you wronged him. After all, he was prepared to leave his fiancée for you."

"How can he feel betrayed when he doesn't care about anybody but himself?" Ana asked, perplexed.

"Well, it's not the kind of betrayal you, Rob or Karen feel," Dr. Emmert explained. "For most people, betrayal means a violation of trust in the context of a close, interpersonal relationship. For psychopaths, however, it means something entirely different. Since they don't have the ability to form genuine emotional bonds with others, they don't feel any violation of real trust. To trust someone, you have to be close to them. Psychopaths never get close to anyone to begin with. Instead, they experience betrayal as a violation of their control over certain individuals, especially those who had previously admired them. Since you escaped his control, from his distorted perspective, Michael doesn't think that he mistreated you. Most likely, he believes that you mistreated him."

Ana recalled how contemptuously Michael had spoken of his parents when they had dared engage in the slightest criticism of him. He seemed particularly stunned by his mother's disapproval. After all, she was the one who idolized him most. "But that's just it. He did mistreat me and everyone close to him," she replied, arguing against Michael in her own mind. "Everything about him was a sham. Everything." She began counting by her fingers: "The fact that he can love. The fact that he can care about another human being. The fact that he can be faithful or honest. The fact that he would have been good to me and my kids. He's incapable of being good to anyone. He's a psychopath."

"Yes, but he doesn't know it," Dr. Emmert emphasized. "Just as he has no real connection to others, Michael has only a tenuous rapport with his own self. He lacks the self-awareness to see the workings of his own disorder."

Ana's hand trembled upon her lap. "He never loved me."

"No, he didn't," Dr. Emmert agreed. "He temporarily saw in you the fulfillment of his sexual fantasies. What psychologists call the fantasy of the 'omniavailable woman.' A woman who's always aroused, always available to fulfill a man's desires, always pliable to his will."

"I was just being myself," Ana responded, feeling far from a fantasy woman. "I was always real with him."

"Sure," the therapist agreed. "But once you told your partners about the affair, you showed him another part of you. One that was just as real, but that he didn't like quite as much. You reacted normally to the trauma you were causing yourself and your family. You became difficult and depressed. And once you became a real woman, Michael's interest in you diminished. Because a cranky and depressed woman is much less fun. And if a woman's going to be less fun, then he might as well get his supply of pleasure elsewhere."

"During the last few weeks together," Ana recounted, "Michael started behaving really bossy with me. When he cooed and cajoled and gave me gifts, I didn't realize just how controlling he could be."

Dr. Emmert smiled. "It's funny that you didn't see him as bossy during our first session together. When your husband described him that way, you became defensive and took Michael's side. What changed your mind?"

Ana looked at him with frankness: "I stopped defending him to others only once I stopped defending him to myself. Then I started to see Michael for what he is. A bully, a control freak and a pervert," she added. "Once our relationship started to unravel under pressure, it struck me how much Michael talked about sex. Everything revolved around sex for him. And I took that as a bad sign."

"Good. Because it was," the therapist confirmed. "It meant that he was oblivious to other dimensions of life. That wouldn't have been a solid foundation for marriage or any real life partnership. More importantly, it meant that the person," he gestured towards Ana, "was far less important than the act. Because the act, you can do it with anybody."

Ana absentmindedly twirled her wedding ring, which she had placed back upon her finger a few days earlier. "You know," she said very quietly, as if speaking mostly to herself, "being lovers masked Michael's sexual addiction. Because it's normal for lovers to focus upon sex, romance and pleasure. It goes with the territory, so to speak. But once we began planning our future together, I expected to see other sides of him."

"Such as?"

"Well, like concern for my children, for instance. And concern for me, in both the practical and emotional aspects of life. But I didn't see any of that. In new and more complex circumstances, I saw the same sex-obsessed Michael, minus some of his best attributes, such as his charm, good humor, generosity and patience, all of which pretty much went out the window."

"That's perfectly normal," Dr. Emmert remarked, then qualified, "for someone so abnormal, that is. Michael lives exclusively for his self-gratification. Nothing else matters to him."

"Yes, but I didn't see that at first."

"You didn't want to see it," the psychiatrist corrected her statement. "Your blindness, in fact, was part of initially drew him to you."

"What do you mean?"

"Well, early on in your relationship, you indicated to Michael that you were vulnerable and that you lacked clearly defined boundaries. You confided in him about your marital problems right away. You agreed to divorce Rob despite your serious misgivings. This behavior, in which you gave in to him bit by bit, inch by inch, gave Michael the impression that you'd be a perfect target."

Ana couldn't help but smile as she imagined herself with the word "target" imprinted on her forehead.

"You were reticent enough to present a challenge to him, yet, ultimately, he was the one in charge of the relationship," the therapist pursued. "With minimal effort and finessing, he could do with you as he pleased. That's why, for as long as you put up just enough resistance to stimulate in him the thrill of the chase but not enough to frustrate his desires, he saw you as the fulfillment of his fantasies," Dr. Emmert encapsulated the dynamics of the affair.

There was something about Michael's behavior that, in hindsight, was even more disturbing to Ana than the fact that he preferred fantasy to reality. "You know, I believe that even if I weren't married with kids, and even if I were his 'omniavailable woman' as you put it, he'd still cheat on me and eventually leave me, like he did Karen. Honestly," she blinked, as if trying to convince the psychiatrist of her earnestness. "Even if I could magically become a different nationality of Miss Universe every day, he'd still get bored with me. Because, as I've come to realize, Michael needs the cheating, the lying, the variety and the risk to get really turned on. Just like he prefers the taboo of sex right outside the hotel room rather than inside, even after he's already paid for the room. He thrives on transgression."

"It's never a good sign when the excitement in a relationship is provided mostly by the circumstances, not the person," Dr. Emmert commented.

"But I didn't see it this way until he cooled off towards me, after he told Karen about us. Overall, he was pretty patient with me during our debates over the divorce issue while he was still in the process of winning me over. But once we told our partners about our affair, it's as if his incentive to remain patient with me instantly evaporated. Then I began to see the real Michael: a man who's selfish, calculated, deceptive, manipulative and ice cold."

"You didn't frame it quite this way during our last two sessions. It seems like the more you think about your past with Michael, the harsher your assessment of him becomes."

"That's because now I have the benefit—if you can call it that—of 20/20 hindsight."

"And you didn't before, when you came here with your husband a few weeks ago?"

Ana was obliged to amend her statement. "I guess it took me awhile to come to terms with what happened. Because for the longest time, up to the last few weeks we spent together, Michael had me convinced that he loved me," she said with renewed bitterness. "Part of me still can't believe who Michael turned out to be. I mean, did he fake it all? The sensuality, the passion, the interest in art and literature?"

Dr. Emmert shrugged. "I don't really know, but somehow I doubt it. I've never met a psychopath who didn't do exactly what he wanted. I suspect he probably wanted to inspire your art and whatever else he did with you. But whether or not Michael's interest in you was genuine at the time doesn't really matter. The bottom line is that he was in the relationship only for his own advantage."

Ana thought for a moment. "But what could he have possibly wanted from me? I'm neither rich nor famous, as Rob so kindly pointed out."

"That's very likely part of why he targeted you. You're an aspiring artist. Psychopaths generally look for people with vulnerabilities that they can exploit."

This explanation made only partial sense to Ana. "But I don't have low self-esteem, at least not the way Karen does. If anything, Rob tells me I'm too wrapped up in my own artistic ambitions."

"Sure," the therapist agreed. "But being wrapped up in your art doesn't exclude the fact that you needed external validation. In fact, that's exactly what you were looking for, right? Someone to encourage you to paint the way you wanted to and tell you that you're going to make it."

Ana nodded, recognizing Michael's lure. "Above all," she pursued the thread of the psychiatrist's narrative, "I wanted someone to tell me that it didn't really matter if I made it. At least not in the conventional sense of the term, of getting money and fame, which seems so important to Rob and just about everyone else. I wanted a man who loved me for myself."

"Isn't that what you told Michael that your husband wasn't willing to do?" Dr. Emmert asked. "You showed him your soft spot from the start. He knew that for as long as he pretended to support you the way no other person ever had, he could ask anything of you in exchange."

"But what exactly did he want from me?"

"He wanted power. You said so yourself. He wanted to control how you dressed, when you saw him, how you made love, where you did it and even what you painted. Psychopaths never do anything for anyone for free. They conduct deals, not relationships."

"And what did I get from this whole transaction?"

"That's something only you can say."

Ana looked down at her hand and mimed the gesture of someone trying to grab a fistful of sand and hold on to it as it slowly trickled between her fingers. "I got nothing. Because everything I thought he gave me—true love and friendship—was an illusion, at least on his side. Which made it false on my side too. I never loved the real Michael. I fell in love only with the phony image he projected."

Dr. Emmert cocked his head to the side, appearing skeptical. "On some level, that's no doubt true. But are you sure you didn't get anything out of this experience?"

Ana thought for a moment before she replied. "I got burned, if that's what you mean. Now I know not to put my hand into the hot oven anymore."

"You probably learned something about yourself in the process too," the therapist attempted to lead her to a more positive conclusion.

"Like what?"

"You tell me."

After a few seconds, Ana's face lit up. "I suppose I learned that I don't really need him. I don't need Michael or anyone else to tell me that I'm 'hot' in order to feel attractive. I don't need him to tell me that I'm a good artist in order to paint. Above all, I don't need him to know who I am and to find meaning in my life," she repeated what she had told Michael on the day when they were fighting over Karen, believing these statements were now more true than ever.

Dr. Emmert smiled. "Those are important lessons, don't you think? I mean, as you've come to realize, this whole episode could have ruined your life. It could have ended your relationship with Rob and even with your kids. It could have made you weaker and more insecure. But it didn't. You may still be suffering right now, but on the whole, this whole fiasco has made you stronger. So Michael didn't end up getting what he wanted either. Because, ultimately, he wanted to destroy you."

Ana shifted uncomfortably in her seat. Everything her therapist said rang true. Michael wanted to destroy her. He was a social predator. Someone who targets and devours those who trust him. And for such a man she had risked everyone and everything that mattered to her. "I'm angry, above all, with myself," she finally admitted. "I have a wonderful family. A husband who cares about me. Even if he doesn't always know how to show it, at least Rob's a decent human being. And he loves me. I have two children who need and love me as well. I have so much artistic drive. And I almost ruined our lives for a predator. I just can't believe it. . . ." She covered her face with both hands and let herself go, releasing her pent-up frustrations.

The therapist allowed her to get the current of emotion out of her system before attempting to comfort her. "You made a monumental error. There's no question that you've hurt your family. But try to look at the positive side as well. Because, fortunately, there's a silver lining in all of this. The fact that you left Michael and stayed with your family was not the product of sheer chance. It reflected your deeper love for your family. And if Michael showed his true colors before you moved in with him, it's partly because of your qualms. They spoiled his fantasy of you. So, in a way, your own conscience helped save you," he concluded.

Ana would have liked to believe this nobler account of her actions. But, in point of fact, her lover's behavior had a lot to do with her decision to leave him. "Michael's sudden transformation opened my eyes," she pointed out. "I mean, think about it. On the one hand I had the family who loves me and on the other a heartless psychopath." She laughed out loud, humorlessly. "Gee, let's see... Which one should I pick?"

Dr. Emmert looked at her in disbelief. He was always amazed by how quickly his patients forgot the slowness of healing. The process of emerging from denial was like a litmus paper changing color gradually, over time, to identify the presence of a given substance: in this case, the truth about a dangerous relationship. It seemed as if Ana had already forgotten all the shades of ambivalence, doubt and ambiguity that she went through before arriving at her current conclusion. "Really, Ana?" he asked her. "Was it really that easy for you to see Michael for who he was?"

"No, it wasn't," she quietly admitted.

"Everything that seems obvious to you now wasn't at the time when you were agonizing over these decisions. Because back then, you were still under Michael's spell."

"Well, he broke it," she said with vehemence. "Boy, his behavior yesterday couldn't have opened my eyes more!"

"Alright," Dr. Emmert took that as his cue to return to the facts of the case. "So at what point did your conversation with Michael the other day turn sour?"

"Once I told him the truth."

"Namely?"

"That I saw through his lies and don't love him anymore."

"Did you let him in?" the therapist asked, with a note of alarm.

Ana shook her head. "He kicked in the side glass panel next to the door with his foot," she replied mechanically, like someone recalling events from a state of hypnosis. "He put his hand through and unlocked the door himself. Within a few seconds he was inside and..." Ana touched her left arm with her right hand. "...then he grabbed my arm and twisted it behind my back, which really hurt. He held my hands together with one hand, and then with the other reached around my neck like this," she touched her own neck in the spot Michael had grasped. "That's when they came and saved me. It was so absurd!"

"What was?"

"It was *Dolly Maid Service* of all things! The ladies who clean our house saved my life. Once they showed up at the door, Michael acted as if nothing happened. He greeted them, apologized for the broken glass, said goodbye to me and left."

Dr. Emmert gave her a serious look. "You do realize that this guy's dangerous, don't you?"

Ana adopted the same air of defiance that she had assumed at the beginning of the session. "I'm not scared of him."

"You should be," the psychiatrist countered. "You're provoking him, even though you know by now that such a man knows no limits. If you had asked me before, I'd have counseled you not to communicate with him at all. In my opinion, you made a mistake in engaging him in conversation."

Ana shook her head. "If you only knew how much I hate him..."

"So what? How can your hatred protect you?" Dr. Emmert demanded.

As before, a glimmer of feral emotion was reflected in her dark eyes. "Hatred gives me strength," she replied. "Last night, I dreamt I was given a ballot. The question was: should Michael live or die, and there were these two little squares. I checked the one that said *death*."

"Well, given that you almost threw your life away for a psychopath, it's normal that you should experience a lot of anger," the therapist conceded, not wishing to invalidate Ana's feelings. "But make no mistake about it. Anger can't protect you from anyone. Not even from yourself."

"From myself?" she repeated.

"Sure. Because the hatred you feel now is the obverse of your former passion. What you should be moving towards, in the process of healing, is total indifference. Michael should cease to exist for you." Dr. Emmert folded his hands on his lap, to indicate that he had made his main point, the intended focus of the session.

"But that's exactly the message of my dream!" Ana declared excitedly, glad to point out that her unwieldy unconscious was finally falling into line with the psychiatrist's reasonable advice. "Choosing death on that ballot is the same as him ceasing to exist for me."

"No, it isn't," Dr. Emmert disagreed. "The dream is the symptom of your deep-seated anger. With him and also with yourself for having exercised such poor judgment. It reveals that you're still investing an enormous amount of emotional energy into Michael and into your past relationship with him." He paused for a moment and leaned forward, with concern. "Ana, you've almost gotten this guy out of your heart. It's now time to get him out of your life."

"How do I do that?"

Although ordinarily so matter-of-fact and objective, this time Dr. Emmert spoke with pathos. "I think, in this case, no contact is the only way to go. Any contact with a psychopath will keep you emotionally tied to him, enchained to a fantasy, a life of illusion. Don't encourage or provoke Michael any further. If he shows up again at your house, call the police or Rob. If he calls, hang up. If he writes, ignore him. Give him the chance to forget you, to become distracted by other women. Because he will. Give him that chance," the psychiatrist repeated, with a sense of urgency that she hadn't heard in his calm and soothing voice before.

"It's difficult to ignore him completely," Ana said quietly.

"Why?"

"Because sometimes, though much more rarely now, I still feel torn. Not because I'm in love with the new Michael I discovered. It's because I still miss the old Michael I knew and loved. I miss how he treated me in the beginning. I miss the excitement and the pleasure. I miss his advice, his affection and the constant attention. I miss his jokes and his quirks. I miss the sound of his voice."

"You miss the mask, not the man," Dr. Emmert commented dryly, disappointed to see Ana backpedal to her original stance. Her state of mind was as changeable as mountain climates, shifting constantly between sunshine and clouds, between lucidity and denial. There's only one logical explanation for this, he thought. "You're in mourning," he said. "In fact, you've been in mourning ever since we started therapy together."

Ana looked at him with sadness. "Mourning what? Michael's still very much alive. Even in my own mind."

"You're mourning the death of your own fantasy of the perfect passion. The man you loved never existed. You're grieving the loss of the man you wish he could have been."

Ana nodded in agreement. "I feel that in falling in love with Michael and agreeing to be his partner, I made a pact with the devil. I got everything I ever dreamed of for a few months, but only at the cost of perpetual suffering ever after." She paused before adding, "I want him to feel at least half the pain he caused me and my family."

"Come on! You know full well by now that you're not hurting him through your rejection. He can't feel loss since he doesn't feel love in the first place."

She noticed the psychiatrist's disapproving expression and thought to herself: he understands me intellectually, but from the gut, he still doesn't get it. He doesn't know how intoxicating it can be to be swept away by one of these great seducers; how devastating it is once the curtain goes up to expose the tricks behind it. It makes you want to close your eyes again and pretend that the illusion was real.

"I understand that any intimate encounter with a psychopath is bound to be an alien and devastating experience," Dr. Emmert said more sympathetically, seeing reproach in Ana's gaze. "But you can't control his actions or change him in any way. You can only control your own actions and attitude. Stop playing his game. Disengage completely and for good."

"I have," Ana looked at her therapist with the unblinking gaze of a convert to a new religion, of a true believer. "I just hope that he'll leave me alone."

"I think he will," Dr. Emmert predicted. "Psychopaths view everything as a game, but they're not genuinely competitive. They prefer to take the path of least resistance. If you consistently refuse to engage with them, they delete you from their memory and move on to a new obsession."

"I guess they don't waste their time on a match they don't think they can win," Ana speculated.

"They don't really care," Dr. Emmert commented. "They have nothing to lose, since people are interchangeable to them. You, on the other hand, have a lot to lose. He's dangerous."

I can defend myself, Ana would have liked to respond, moved by the sense of invulnerability which was fueled by the heat of her growing resentment.

It's as if the psychiatrist read her mind. "You've already let go of the love. Why do you want to hold on to the anger?"

Ana was somewhat taken aback by the formulation of his question. She wasn't aware that she had a choice in experiencing a given emotion. "I don't know."

"You think your feelings of anger will protect you from him. But you won't act upon them. Like most human beings, you have internal restraints. Michael doesn't. He made that quite obvious when he showed up at your door the other day. He feels no real hatred or love, yet he's capable of doing anything whatsoever out of momentary frustration or even mild annoyance. Stop playing with fire. Stay away from him," Dr. Emmert cautioned her again.

Chapter 23

"Stop playing with fire. Stay away from him." The therapist's words still rang in Ana's ears as she walked back to the subway station. "The man you loved never existed," Dr. Emmert had told her. But instead of imagining Michael's features, Ana now envisioned those of the man who had been real all along, the man who loved her truly and had the generosity to forgive her now, when she appeared to outsiders unforgivable. She saw Rob's caramel eyes, his smile, a little awkward and shy, his slim body, at an angle, as if not really knowing what to do with himself, a pose expressing both self-confidence and an irreducible timidity. She recalled what her husband had told her one evening, before she had met Michael, when they were sitting next to one another during a reception at a family wedding. "So many people marry and then divorce a few years later. I wonder why that happens," Ana had casually remarked. "Sometimes it's for legitimate reasons," Rob had replied. "But I suspect that a lot of times it's because they never really take themselves off the market. They go into the marriage without making a serious commitment and continue to look around, to see if they can find someone better. I hope that we'll never do that to each other," he looked piercingly into his wife's eyes. Ana didn't avert her gaze, since she had nothing to hide. She told him quite sincerely that she'd never do that herself, not knowing how close she'd come to the brink of divorce in a matter of months.

After waiting outside the building for about an hour, Michael watched Ana exit the therapist's office, where he had followed her. Fuck the restraining order! he decided, tearing it to shreds soon after he got it. He felt like his initial intuition was confirmed. I knew it! She's having an affair with her shrink, he speculated. Dozens of women had washed away every last trace of her. Every kiss, every caress, every ounce of desire, every shred of memory of Ana had been covered over by countless others. Yet he still felt peeved that another man had access to his woman. Because in his mind, no matter what happened, no matter how many other lovers she'd have, Ana would always be his. Lightning doesn't strike twice. The maids won't save her this time, he thought coolly, glancing at his watch. It was 1:05 p.m. Too early for Rob or the kids to be home, which meant that Ana would be all alone. They'd have a nice little chat together, undisturbed. He'd be sure to thank her for filing charges against him.

Ana pressed the key button to unlock her car and stepped inside. She turned on the ignition and checked her watch. It was 1:06 p.m. Before I go pick up the kids from school, I have just enough time to drive to Detroit and retrieve the rest of my paintings from the new gallery, she estimated. She turned on the radio, then turned it off. Every love song left a bad aftertaste, taunting her with embittered feelings and soured memories.

Her thoughts reverted back to the conversation she had had with Rob about fidelity. Having experienced the contrast between the man she almost divorced, who truly loved her, and the man she almost married, who loved no one but himself, Ana grasped much more tangibly that her husband had been right all along. Real love meant regarding one another as unique and irreplaceable: something Rob practiced while Michael only preached. Early into their courtship, her lover had promised her, "I'll be good to you, my sweet Ana. If anything happens to us, it won't be because of me," she recalled. That promise, like all of his loving words, was dust in the wind. Yet sometimes Michael slipped up and spoke the truth, giving her glimpses of who he really was. "How do you reinvest value in a relationship that has pretty much lost its value?" Michael had asked her the second time they met, referring to his fiancée. Since she didn't know then what she knew now, Ana had replied, "By working on it." Michael had countered that to work on a relationship you must have something to work with. And then, she now recalled, he revealed a part of himself that should have instantly set off warning signals, but it didn't. He told her, "If there's anything I've learned from this whole experience with Karen is that if a relationship requires work, it's not worth saving." That much he practiced, not just preached.

I put so much energy into that freaking relationship and this is the thanks I got for it. As my father told me, when I chose her I must have been thinking with my prick. What the hell is she doing now? Michael followed Ana past Myers, to I-94 East. Does she have a lover in Detroit too? He recalled something his maternal grandfather had once told him. I wish I had done away with every damn woman I ever left, so that they wouldn't live on to bother me anymore. He had been referring to Michael's own grandmother, among many others. You're just like your grandfather! his mother once remarked, only half in jest, when he ogled women in her presence. You bet! Michael said to himself. The man knew how to live. Hump them and dump them. Because when you try to love them, they treat you like shit. And to think I trusted her. Fuck you, Ana! But don't you dare walk away from me little bitch, he gritted his teeth. I decide if you stay or if you leave.

"If there's anything I've learned from this whole experience with Karen is that if a relationship requires work, it's not worth saving," Ana recalled, heading towards the RenCen, since her gallery was close to it. That statement rang profoundly true, she mused, but only for people like him, who couldn't form deeper attachments. For Michael, no relationship was worth saving beyond the initial seduction phase. Memories of affection, intimacy and pleasure didn't accumulate for him. He dwelled in the shallowness of a perpetual present. To him, love was just another high whose effect would invariably wear off. It may take only a few hours, as with his innumerable one-night stands, or a few days, as with his countless flings, or nearly a year, as it did with her. But once the conquest was over and the pleasure diminished, Michael would move on to seduce, devalue and discard the next woman whose love and trust he had secured. The hunger for passion, Ana realized, has starved me of love.

Why is she heading towards the RenCen? Michael wondered. He recalled that they had once made out in the glass elevator. Eh, at least she was a pretty good lay, unlike Karen, he told himself. The thought of his fiancée made him smile with contempt. He had a flashback to her last pathetic attempt to show him she learned how to do pole dancing. The poor woman looked like a giraffe rubbing up against a scratching post. If only she had taken lessons from some of his newest girlfriends, he thought, as an image of Tanya, a hot Ukrainian with platinum blond hair, nice tits, a sexy ass and heavenly long legs, popped into his mind. Why the hell am I still wasting my time with Ana? he asked himself, tempted to head back to the Foxy Lady Gentlemen's Club for a quickie.

The irony is that he seemed to be so tender and caring at first, Ana mused, searching for a parking spot next to the RenCen. She recalled how during their second meeting, Michael had bragged about how much Karen's little nephew enjoyed playing with him. He called him "Big Guy," as no doubt he'd have called Allen too precisely because he was so tiny, the same way he called her and probably every other girlfriend he ever had "Baby," at least during the seduction phase, before the restlessness overtook him and he became drawn to someone else. He told her how he liked to toss the "Big Guy" into the air and catch him, turn him upside down and tumble around pretending they were wild animals. That playfulness had impressed Ana at the time. She had interpreted it as evidence of Michael's paternal instincts. But now it occurred to her that she had recently watched a show on *Animal Planet* about how male chimpanzees, some of the most selfish and aggressive primates around, like to rough play with their young to express their dominance instinct. By way of contrast, Ana had a flashback to how lovingly and patiently Rob had taught his son how to ride a bike, despite the boy's initial trepidation. Allen became so proficient at it that he enjoyed riding his bike around the block for an hour a day, right after coming back from school and wolfing down a strawberry pop-tart with a glass of milk.

Her new lover must work in downtown Detroit, Michael speculated, as he found an inconspicuous parking spot close to Ana's. She's still wearing those granny skirts, he gazed disapprovingly at her all-too-familiar pencil skirt, which had made him drool with desire at the beginning of their affair. Even her long, luxurious dark hair that had impressed him so much before now struck him as unmanageable and common. Ana's petite figure, which he had twirled in his arms with such joy, seemed mousy and insignificant. She's reverted to walking like a granny, he observed with scornful detachment, watching her shuffle along, dragging the left foot more than the right. She's nothing but a vicious wasp disguised as a harmless butterfly, Michael muttered to himself. She's not that much hotter than Karen, he decided.

As soon as Tanya says yes to marriage, I'll dump Karen, he consoled himself, once again finding himself in the awkward position of chasing a married woman. Fortunately, her husband, Pavel, who worked as a clerk at a local convenience store, posed no threat whatsoever. The only problem was that they had a kid together, little Sasha, a two year old boy. But that was quite all right. Since Tanya sorely wanted to become naturalized, she'd be awfully tempted by a marriage prospect to an American citizen. And then he'd have his scrumptious private dancer all to himself. Because there ain't no way he'd tolerate his woman showing off her hot little bod to other men. On the other hand, Michael charitably qualified, her female colleagues would always be welcome at his house.

A few weeks earlier, at the end of April, they had had a brief spell of snow in Michigan. This came as no surprise to anyone, since they were used to those disoriented, light flurries of spring that melted almost as soon as they touched the ground. That's how Ana felt about the memories of Michael that currently assailed her, randomly, lightly, popping from all sides into her consciousness, as she made her way through the lunch hour crowd. They were like the scattered traces of a long, tenacious winter that would soon be effaced by the bloom of spring. Some of those memories she must have repressed before. Others she had chosen to interpret in an implausibly generous manner.

Like the time Michael had told her last October that, all of a sudden, his free wi-fi Internet access at home vanished. He had gone on to explain that he filched a free connection from his next-door neighbor and that somehow the connection must have grown weaker or the neighbor discontinued the service. At any rate, he had unfortunately lost it (even though, it now occurred to her, he managed to magically recover it whenever he had something urgent to communicate to her). Ana had not even blinked at his explanation. It rang plausible given Michael's stinginess. Besides, the email exchanges couldn't compare with being together or even to talking on the phone. But now, in retrospect, his explanation rang false. What seemed much more plausible, given what she had found out about Michael, was that he had simply gotten tired of the emails.

Their initially exciting effect wore off once he could see her as often as he pleased. That would have been nothing more than a little white lie coming from a normal person. But then again, a normal person would have told her, Honey, now that we're seeing each other almost every day, let's forget about the emails. Coming from Michael, however, Ana realized, that seemingly harmless lie which she hadn't even noticed at the time was yet another symptom of his malady, of the ceaseless pathological lying, as well as a sign of how easily he'd decrease or discontinue contact with her once their affair became less exciting or inconvenient for him. Ana stepped into the gallery, to discuss with the owner which paintings had sold. She didn't expect much in terms of profits, however. The market in art was still depressed, courtesy of the interminable recession.

Oh, it's just another one of her stupid exhibits, Michael thought, calmly waiting for Ana outside the gallery. What did I ever see her? he wondered, not seeing any of the unique qualities he had attributed to his former idol. He watched her and, he assumed, the owner of the gallery carry like two little ants several large paintings filled with droopy and dark human figures. What shitty work! No wonder nobody wants to buy it. She's back to finger-painting that morbid crap again, he noted with some satisfaction. Must be getting really bored without me around.

As she was placing the paintings in the back seat of her car, Ana recalled how suddenly and inexplicably Michael changed their plans, without consulting with her, but always for a supposedly other-regarding reason that she now realized served solely his interests. During the period when he was wooing her, he promised her that he'd introduce her and the children to his parents. He said that they'd spend vacation as a new family as soon as they moved in together. But once they set into motion the plans for divorce, the process of devaluation began with the same lightning speed with which rigor mortis sets in to destroy the delicate features of a beautiful woman after death. All of a sudden, Ana realized, I wasn't good enough to meet his family anymore. More importantly, given his predatory instinct, she imagined, Michael probably wanted to leave his options open. If I had met his parents and we got along, he might not be as free to discard me whenever he pleased. After all, Michael had learned a valuable lesson from introducing Karen to his folks, she speculated. In his screwed up worldview, once his fiancée complained to them about his behavior and they expressed some half-hearted sympathy for her, that act of carelessness had bitten him in the butt. He'd probably never repeat that error again.

More serious were the lies that Michael had told her by omission, Ana thought, now focusing on the instances of telling silence, not only the empty promises. Following one of their disputes on the issue of divorce, to appease her lover, Ana had walked around her neighborhood picking up flyers that advertised houses for sale. Michael had told her that if she ever agreed to marry him, he'd buy a house next to Rob's so that the kids could walk freely and easily back and forth, from one home to another, from one parent to another. When Ana had handed him the fliers, Michael had barely looked at them. He leafed through like they were some useless coupons he was about to discard. But instead of telling her about his change of plans, he said nothing at all. He only looked at her with the same expression, a flicker of irony in his eyes and a disdainful curve of the lips, that he had had when he told her that Karen's mother, having recently retired and divorced, was talking about buying a bigger house to live with him and Karen in Arizona once the two of them got married. Then too Michael had made no comment. He had smiled with his mouth and even more so with his eyes, allowing Karen's mother to believe that her impossible dream was achievable, all the while secretly planning to leave his fiancée and marry his girlfriend instead. Because in his mind, other people were just "options" and "opportunities": Plan A and Plan B while he was busily working on plans C through Z.

By the time I gave in to his wishes, Ana reflected, Michael's mercurial needs had already changed. In fact, the very act of submission to his will caused them to shift. Identifying Michael's fickle desires followed the same uncertainty principle as pinpointing the exact location of an electron at any given moment. Whenever you shine a beam of light on it, you alter its position, so that it's no longer in the same place. The instant you satisfied any of Michael's wishes, you displaced them, such that he either wanted something more or something else. And then, the deception that really ate the cake, Ana thought with bitterness, that slick move about keeping Karen at his place for a few weeks after having already told her about the affair, ostensibly, "to let her down easy." If you want to let someone down easy you may do it in person, but you don't drag her to every sentimental place you've ever been together to watch her fall to pieces over losing you. He's such a sadist, Ana muttered under her breath, stunned that she could have ever loved or trusted such a man. The self-professed ocean of raging passion turned out to be nothing more than a dirty little puddle.

Why do I even bother with this woman? Michael asked himself again, his anger almost completely evacuated by contempt. She probably made a whole of ten bucks from that junk, he speculated. Karen was right. I was trading a net gain, since at least she earns a decent income, for a net loss, since Ana loves to spend money on herself and all those useless art supplies. What the hell? She's heading back to the subway station. Maybe she's meeting one of her new lovers there after all. Can't wait to see what that loser looks like!

Ana had parked close to the People Mover, the very same subway train that had taken her to the Catholic Church in downtown Detroit where she had first met Michael. She felt like their love story had come around full circle, from being everything to each other to becoming nothing at all; from having all their dreams realized to realizing they were only figments of their imaginations. What bothered Ana most was the intuition, confirmed by the psychology books she had read, that there'd never be any justice for Michael. He'd never experience even an ounce of regret for all the suffering he caused in so many lives. Psychopathy was the only disease without any dis-ease, one of the authors had put it. No matter what happened to him, Michael would merrily move on with his life, from one woman to another, from one conquest to another, from one penultimate moment to the next, substituting lust for affection and ownership for love. How I despise him! she thought.

"Why do you want to hold on to that anger?" Ana recalled her therapist's question at the end of their session. Perhaps Dr. Emmert was right. Perhaps there was a reason why she wanted to continue hating Michael rather than forgiving and forgetting him. I want to hold on to the anger so that I never love him or anyone like him ever again, she told herself. I want to hold on to it so that I will remember that normality and family values—everything that, with all my artistic pretensions and longing for a life of passion and excitement, I had considered too conventional and staid—are the only solid foundations of my existence. I want to remember how it took being almost destroyed by the most abnormal human being I've ever met to appreciate my normal, loving husband. I want to remember that there's nothing more boring than the utter predictability of absolute selfishness, which I saw reflected in Michael and which I almost mirrored myself. Above all, I want to hold on to the anger so I that I'll always remember that I almost threw my life away. I never want to forget how dangerously close I came to being stripped of everything I am and of everything I have. Because without my loving husband, my children, my sense of loyalty and love, my values, my passion for art, my warmth and friendliness, my deeper emotions, my honesty and trust—all of which Michael would have continued to erode, bit by bit and layer by layer, with his possessiveness and mind games—what would be left of me? A Nobody and a Nothing just like him. Only I'd become a Nobody and a Nothing with a broken heart, because unlike him, I do feel pain and I can feel remorse and I would feel regret.

Ana had become so used to her lover by now that she could almost hear his voice in the back of her head: "Don't act like Little Miss Innocent, cause I ain't buying that crap. You knew what you were getting yourself into. You chose to be my lover. You chose me." Yes, I did. My only consolation now, Ana told herself, was that I chose to leave him in the end. I learned the hard way that there are only two options when you become involved with a psychopath: losing a whole lot or losing everything. I chose not to lose everything.

Dang! This is getting downright weird, Michael thought, stealthily following Ana as she approached the People Mover. Some of the trains stopped and left the station while others whizzed by. But she just stood there, frozen, as if she had fallen in a trance. She's acting like she's drugged out. Maybe her new boyfriend's into drugs. I knew she was a nutjob. These artist types are completely out of touch with reality.

I chose to embrace reality and reject the romantic fairytale Michael promised me, which he never delivered, which he never could have delivered since empty words is all he had to give, Ana thought, feeling more confident. She stood still on the platform, watching the movements of the train that had initially brought her to her fate. On that sunny afternoon, without a cloud in sight, Ana had the distinct impression of emerging from a haze. Returning to that spot felt cathartic. For a moment, she had a flashback to the accident scene she had witnessed by the subway, shortly after having met Michael. It filled her with a sense of unease. She recalled that the man who had thrown himself under the train had a wife and children, who probably loved and needed him. She thought back to all those great novels she read as a teenager, including her favorite, *Anna Karenina*. Back then she had been thoroughly impressed by the heroine's noble suicide for the sake of love. But now she wondered how many people sacrificed their lives and families for flimsy fantasies masquerading as great passions.

A sense of resilience permeated her, as it did on that fateful day, a year ago. Ana had the same feeling of roots, of being anchored in love, that she experienced the first time she stood by that train, contemplating the stranger's suicide. I'd never do that to my family, she told herself. Because I love my sweet son. I love my precocious daughter. I love my decent husband. I love my life. Now that this nightmare with Michael's finally over, I'm able to tuck my children into bed at night and look my husband in the eyes again. At that moment, the memories of her lover that had weighed so heavily upon Ana seemed to evaporate into the warm spring air. For the first time in weeks, she felt free. As she took a step closer to the platform, Ana stretched her body upright, allowing herself to expand, to spring back into shape, becoming once again the woman she had been—multidimensional and capable of loyalty and love—until she became lost in a man who, as it turned out, was an illusionist who lived only for his fantasies.

As he saw her there so close to the moving trains, her body upright and tense, leaning slightly forward, Michael spotted his perfect opportunity. He gazed around him. People were entering and exiting the train, moving all around Ana, so the confusion of the crowd would no doubt shelter him. Plus, this could easily be interpreted as a suicide, he thought, recalling that the evening he met his girlfriend, some poor guy had thrown himself under the People Mover. So, he figured, the story would sound pretty credible. In fact, even her own family would believe it, since Ana had already proved to them that she was unstable, ready to up and leave her husband for another man. He walked stealthily behind Ana and just winged it. As easily as he told Karen all those lies on the spot, he now followed the impulse, little more than a whim, of giving in to his underlying drive to eliminate this nagging obsession, this annoying inconvenience, which ached like a rotten tooth right before you pull it out, by extracting his girlfriend forever from his life, as if she never existed.

As she stood there, perfectly still, coming to terms with the dizzying, spiraling circularity of her life, letting go of one lost dream and embracing the promise of a new beginning with her family, Ana felt herself lose her footing. In that instant, it occurred to her that someone had pushed her from behind. It was nothing more than a tap on the back, but enough to make her lose her balance. Ana knew exactly who that person was. She wanted to turn around and grab Michael's hand to drag him along with her, as the heat of hatred rose from deep within, much stronger than her former passion. But she didn't get that chance. Ana's heart raced wildly as she stumbled forward, her hands reaching out desperately to regain her balance, as if begging fate itself for help. But she grasped nothing except for the sting of a fast, unstoppable, massive motion, the ruthless acceleration of steel that mercilessly pulled her under. Time itself stood still as reality became enshrouded by a cloud of darkness.

Chapter 24

She instantly recognized the handwriting on the envelope. She didn't even have to look at the address to know whom it was from. Her hands trembled and her heart beat faster. She knew that she shouldn't even open the envelope. The letter itself, its words, its tone, its calligraphic schoolboy handwriting, its enchanting promises, would be toxic to her. In spite of that, she opened it anyway.

"My Sweet Karen," it began. That opening made her feel nauseous. She imagined to how many other women he must be writing in this way. Yet the tender phrasing still brought her to tears. "I keep thinking about you," it went on. "Not a single day goes by when I don't miss you like hell." 'Like hell' is the operative term here, Karen told herself, no longer believing him. The sugary tone reminded her of a familiar pattern. He must want something from me, she surmised. "I've been on my best behavior and things are looking pretty good here. In a month or so I'll be up for my parole hearing. I was wondering if you'd be kind enough to whip up a letter of support to let these guys know that I have a solid character and that I've never shown any signs of violence towards you. Basically, I've got to prove to them that I'm not going to be a threat to society once I get out of here. That should be easy. The psychologist seems to be on my side and I'm on good terms with the prison staff. I'm asking for your help because you're still the only woman of my life. We belong together, Baby. The sooner I get out of this joint, the quicker we can fulfill our dream of starting a life together. Who knows? Maybe soon we'll have more than just imaginary kids... Love always, Michael."

Karen could almost hear his melodious voice in these phrases, intermingling real requests with imaginary promises. She had fallen for his lines time and time again, even when everyone else turned against him. She recalled how sincere Michael looked on the day he avowed his innocence. "I swear to God, Karen, that I never laid a hand on Ana or on any other woman in my life. Babe, you know that I'm incapable of violence. Hurting a woman physically is the most despicable thing I've ever heard of! Let alone killing her. I may be a jerk and I may have cheated on you, but you know better than anyone else that I'm completely harmless." She remembered how she had nodded in agreement. After all, Michael had never hit her and he seldom raised his voice to her during their nearly three years together. Even when faced with all the evidence that made him appear guilty, Karen took an oath at the trial. She stood by her man, as a character witness for the defense attesting to Michael's gentle disposition. "All they've got is some stupid circumstantial evidence against me. This pack of lies has been fanned by the malicious gossip of the press, which would love to crucify me. I mean, what sells better than some sordid tale about a scorned lover who shoves his girlfriend under the train, in a tragic twist reminiscent of *Anna Karenina*? They're having a field day with me. But they should have read Tolstoy more carefully. Because Anna Karenina committed suicide all on her own and so did Ana Popescu," he had scoffed at the press coverage.

But, in point of fact, the faint echo of Tolstoy's fiction wasn't what drew the press around him like flies to honey. After all, Karen reasoned, there were plenty of scorned lovers who kill their girlfriends in crimes of passion, as they tend to call them. Yet they don't all make it into the evening news. What intrigued the press, and later the jury too, was all the evidence that indicated this was in fact a passionless crime, even if it may not have been demonstrably premeditated. Michael had sown the seeds of his own destruction by having sex with one of his new girlfriends, a blond Ukrainian stripper named Tanya something-eva, right there on Ana's grave, only days after her funeral.

The local news station juxtaposed two clips. The first included footage of Ana's children and husband at the memorial service, the little girl shaking so hard that her thin shoulder blades protruded like the wings of a wounded bird; the boy burying his head into his father's jacket to hide his pain; the husband pale and silent, overcome by genuine grief and real forgiveness, attempting to console his children. The second news clip featured Michael, bending his newest conquest over the cross of Ana's grave. That footage, plus all the people who had witnessed him pushing Ana towards the People Mover, seemed pretty damning evidence against him. Michael's excuse, which he delivered with a cocky smile when the journalists had gathered around him asking for an explanation, was a psychological lesson into the nuances of human suffering: "We all grieve differently," he pontificated. "Some people cry and get all depressed. Others become manic and have sex in public."

This explanation, however insightful, didn't hold water with the jury, no matter how much the defense had tried to depict Ana as an unstable woman with suicidal tendencies. The string of witnesses for the prosecution attesting to the fact that Michael had, indeed, pushed his girlfriend under the train, plus all the coverage of his callous reaction to the death of the woman who was supposedly the love of his life, had proved somewhat more compelling than any speculation about Ana's psychological maladies. After a few days of deliberation, the jury found Michael guilty of second-degree murder, since there was no evidence that he had planned the crime in advance. They sentenced him to eight years in prison with the possibility of parole. Which, Karen knew, was exactly the loophole Michael needed to crawl his way out of that hole. But even when all the evidence pointed to his guilt, she had desperately wanted to believe his explanation. After the trial, she visited him in prison to prove to him, yet again, her unconditional love and loyalty. She took a seat across from Michael, separated from him only by a thin screen of transparent plastic.

Karen felt almost embarrassed to voice some faint, lingering doubts that sometimes troubled her in the middle of the night. "Did you do it?" she asked him very quietly, imploring him with her eyes to deny the charges like he had before. His sad, puppy dog expression faded and all of a sudden Michael looked alive, almost triumphant. His eyes sparkled and his mouth twisted into a familiar expression. She saw the grin he always had whenever she caught him cheating on her. In that mocking smile, Karen recognized the shamelessness of being guilty without feeling any guilt. "Why did you do it?" she asked him, her eyes wide open with a mixture of horror and disbelief. And then, without a trace of regret, Michael laughed out loud and said, "I plead the Fifth."

This time, she told herself as she gazed once again at his letter, he won't be able to reel me back in. But instead of not replying, as the previous two times he wrote her, Karen resolved to let him know exactly how she felt.

Dear Michael, she wrote,

I hope that after reading my letter you'll never contact me again in any way, shape or form. Not only will I not write the parole board anything positive about you, but also I'll mail them a copy of this note, so that they'll know whom they're dealing with. It's true that you never hit me. But for several years, I was emotionally abused by you. I was constantly lied to, cheated on, manipulated and used. And it's true that I can't blame everything on you, since I was partly responsible for allowing the abuse. I bought into your lies. I forgave you each time you cheated on me. I even believed in you when the whole world seemed to turn against you. When they saw your callousness and deceit, I kept my eyes shut. Even after the jury found you guilty of murder, I still chose to believe in your innocence. I didn't want to believe the worst about you. I couldn't accept that the man I loved for so long could sink so low.

But now that I've had the chance to distance myself from you and think about our past, I can no longer go along with your machinations. In fact, I no longer believe that there's anything good or true in you. Each time I took you back, you only hurt me more. We were in an unfair match from the very start. I loved you most and you never loved me at all. Which is why you could do with me as you wished and why I was so defenseless against you. No matter how hurt, or how angry, or how frustrated, or how humiliated you made me feel, you didn't care about my feelings as long as you could bend me to your will. And you're still trying to do that, with all your flattery and promises, conveniently wrapped around the request that I help you again. Well I won't. I know now that you're a human parasite. You're like this strange wasp I once saw on a nature show that latches on to a poor caterpillar. It bores a hole in it, lays its eggs inside and then moves on to some other unsuspecting host. The wasp's larvae eventually eat the caterpillar alive, leaving behind only a frail, empty shell. That's what you did to me. You fed upon my vulnerabilities and hopes. Then, after you had your fill and tired of me, you moved on to Ana. She left you before you could finish her off so you killed her, out of wounded pride and malice.

My worst regret is that I stayed with you in spite of everything. I told myself that each and every sacrifice you demanded of me would be worth it, because it was for you and our relationship. I asked myself: can I live without any faith in my partner's fidelity? Can I live without any kind of trust in him? Can I live apart from him, sequestered somewhere in Arizona, just to save our relationship? Can I live without spending money on myself? Can I live without my family, thousands of miles away from them? Can I live without my job? Can I live with all the humiliations he's making me endure, just to compete with whatever perverse acts the sleazy women he hangs out with are doing with him? Can I accept the assumption that my 'no' means 'yes' to him? To each of these questions I answered "Yes, I can" because I loved you. But each time I made a sacrifice, the rewards got smaller, not bigger as I hoped. Each time I gave in, you were less affectionate, less attentive, less interested and kept demanding more and more out of me, as if I owed it to you. And each time I gave in to you, my strength was cut in half and I became less capable of resisting you the next time you trampled all over me. Our whole relationship became a one-way street. Which makes me wonder why I stayed with you for as long as I did; why I accepted such unfair conditions and kept jumping through all those hoops that never got me anywhere.

I stayed with you at first because I believed the illusion you created for me by using other women for sex while appearing to treat me differently. I was convinced that you lusted after them, but that you loved and respected only me. I thought that I was somehow special in your eyes. But when I found out about Ana, it burst that bubble. Afterwards, I stayed with you mostly because I no longer had the strength to leave. I stayed because I feared ending up all alone, without a man who loved me. I stayed because seeing the truth about our relationship would have meant having to face up to the truth about myself: that I needed you to feel like I was someone worth loving.

But the thing is, Michael, I never really felt safe or happy with you. In the back of my mind, I always felt anxious and insecure. I was suspicious of what you might be doing with other women behind my back. I felt inferior to you and, in some respects, to all those women you seemed to want so much more than you ever wanted me. I felt that, somehow, I deserved the mistreatment or, at any rate, that I didn't deserve anything better. In other words, I stayed with you mostly because I didn't love myself enough rather than because of how much I loved you. But that chapter of my life is finally over. Unlike the poor caterpillar eaten by the wasp, I'm still very much alive and ready to move on. I'm no longer the insecure, incomplete person you once knew. I'm not afraid to be alone and I'm not afraid to love again someone real: someone who promises me nothing but acts in a way that's respectful and honest. I no longer blame only myself for the way you treated me. No one will abuse you unless you allow them to. But, by the same token, no one will abuse you unless they choose to do it. And you did, Michael. You chose to use me.

In moving on from our unloving relationship, I feel like I've survived a war. The toughest battle wasn't the one against you. It was the one against my own insecurities, which bonded me to you in the first place. It's taken me a long time to come to this realization. Now that I finally have, I'm able to let you go in peace, without hating you, without wishing you any harm. I only hope that other women will be wiser and stronger than I was and more fortunate than Ana. I also pray that you won't prey upon others, even though I don't have much hope. Because I don't believe you want to change. You're very happy with who you are. But that's no longer my problem. Being bitter or resentful towards you would prevent me from focusing on myself. Just know that I'll never cover for you again. Don't count on me anymore. You're entirely on your own as, in fact, you've always been. Because, in your heart of hearts, you're a lone wolf. Karen

A few days later, Michael lay on his bed, with one arm folded underneath his head since the pillow was too small and thin, the other holding up Karen's letter. He could hardly believe his eyes. As he was looking over the note, several spasms of anger passed through him. The dark, oblong letters of her careful, feminine handwriting danced upon the yellow page. Once he was done reading, he crumpled up the pieces of paper and threw them diagonally, to the furthest corner of his jail cell. For a few minutes, he couldn't even think straight, he felt so furious. But after a few minutes, he decided to take care of business by eliminating all traces of that hysterical note, so that it wouldn't bug him anymore. He crossed the room with a deliberate gait, picked up the crumpled paper, tore it up into tiny little pieces, then tossed them by the handful like confetti into the latrine, to flush Karen and all of her delusional crap down the toilet, where they belonged. He urinated on those bits of paper before they swirled down into the liquid abyss. I don't need you bitch anyway, he muttered to himself.

Having taken care of this unpleasant business, Michael's disposition instantly improved. Let's see, he calmly reviewed the situation. His parents and some of his former professors and colleagues would write letters attesting to his good character to the parole board. The prison psychologist was absolutely nuts about him. He had her wrapped around his little finger and, he was obliged to admit, he kind of had the hots for her too, a little bit. If everything goes according to plan, within a month or two I'll be out of this dump, he mused, reclining on the bed again.

Michael stretched out his arms above his head and wiggled his body. He enjoyed the cool smoothness of the sheets against his warm back. It made him feel as if he were already back at home, the king of his castle. He could almost see, with his mind's eye, the two large pine trees in his front yard that shielded him from the prying eyes of neighbors. Michael was overcome by the familiar sense that all was well with the world. His bubble had protected him yet again from the malevolent lies of those two-faced women whom he never loved in the first place. Pretty soon, he'd be enjoying life to the fullest again. Michael looked forward to tracking down Tanya and luring her to sunny Arizona. Or maybe even moving to California, to see if he could rekindle the unfinished romance with Amy, his old flame. A wave of glee passed through him as he thought, "Ladies, fasten your seatbelts cause pretty soon it will be SHOW TIME!" in bold capital letters of a flashing neon sign, like at his favorite strip club, *Foxy Lady*.

About the Author

Claudia Moscovici is the author of *Velvet Totalitarianism*, a critically acclaimed novel about a Romanian family's survival in an oppressive communist regime due to the strength of their love. This novel was republished in translation in her native country, Romania, under the title *Intre Doua Lumi* (Curtea Veche Publishing, 2011). In 2002, she co-founded with Mexican sculptor Leonardo Pereznieto the international aesthetic movement called "postromanticism" (see *postromanticism.com*), devoted to celebrating beauty, passion and sensuality in contemporary art. She wrote a book on Romanticism and its postromantic survival called *Romanticism and Postromanticism*, (Lexington Books, 2007) and taught philosophy, literature and arts and ideas at Boston University and at the University of Michigan. Most recently, she published a nonfiction book on psychopathic seduction, called *Dangerous Liaisons* (Hamilton Books, 2011).